THE
LITTLE
BIG HILL

by

ROBB LUCAS

Published by Barbed Wire Publishing
1990 East Lohman Avenue, Suite 225
Las Cruces, NM 88001 USA
www.barbed-wire.net

ISBN 0-9678566-5-5

1 2 3 4 5 6 7 8 9 0

To Ken, who came home.
To Jimmy, who came home shot.
To Mike, who came home too soon.

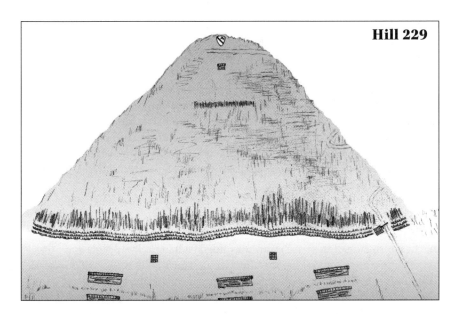

Hill 229

CHAPTER ONE

```
2320Hours 22Dec71
1st Cav Div HQ, Bien Hoa, Republic of South Vietnam
Topographical Hill 229 (Cav Mountain)
```

From the west, Nguyen walked quietly between the rows of barracks toward the floodlights. He came to the road at the bottom of the hill and crossed quickly, then flattened himself against the wall of barracks number 2013, closest to the hill. For just a moment he listened to the soldiers' music inside. Music but no voices. He slipped past the door to the corner and peeked around. In the floodlights' glare were the sandbag bunkers and coils of barbed concertina wire, and in the darkness beyond the wire was the tall black profile of the hill the soldiers called Cav Mountain.

Thirty yards away on Nguyen's right, in the long shadow thrown by the overhead lights, was the square shape of the military police checkpoint with its metal gate across the road. The soldiers had built it to guard the road leading to the top of the hill, but until a week ago, ever since the new general arrived, there had never been a guard in the house at night. Nguyen saw the stripe of light under the closed door. Good luck for soldiers, bad luck for Vietnamese boy-san. Tonight he must sneak through the narrow gap between the wire and the checkpoint, then up through the elephant grass. The rain had left the jungle soaked and steaming with humidity but quiet for walking.

He glanced at his watch. He was early but there was no time to waste, one

1

of the soldiers could come outside to urinate. His eyes were drawn to the lights and guns that guarded 5,000 sleeping soldiers, then back to the checkpoint. There was dark jungle beside the checkpoint where he could hide himself and wait for the new man, Loc.

With a last deep breath he dashed across the open ground and dropped to his knees in the tall brush. There was no shout from the barracks, no shots, no alarm siren. He peeked through the grass. Under the stark floodlights the piled sandbags of the nearest bunker looked like stones. The guard inside was a helmet-less silhouette, and when he lit a cigarette Nguyen watched the smoke rise in phosphorous clouds into the black night. He allowed himself to relax just a little.

For himself, sneaking onto the 1st Cavalry Division base had been easy; a matter of having his sister the whore and her whore friends distract the Sin City gate guards. But he wondered about Tran, coming from his small village on the south side of the base. Tran was older, he had no family left and put all his patient energy into killing the Americans. Nguyen knew he would not see Tran until they were inside the cave because the old man could walk as quietly as a cat. Of the new man, Loc, he knew little, only that he was sixteen years old, two years older than himself, and he'd been living in Saigon.

A faint down-draft brought the sour stink of defoliant to his nose, and he looked up. The soldiers will never turn this hill brown, he thought. A shiver passed through him, not cold but excitement. Tonight he and the others would work in the highest cave on the hill, the one below the abandoned radio building. In the last week Tran and his two old hags had made many trips up to the cave until everything they needed to make the bombs was there: the explosive, the detonators, fusewire, the materials for the satchel bags. Nguyen was excited to learn how it was done. Tran had used this hill before and he had promised to the tell the story.

Movement caught his eye, a soldier's long stride and swinging arms coming up the road toward the checkpoint. Nguyen watched him stop, turn his head, then sprint to the wall of barracks 2013. Loc. Nguyen smiled his admiration. Loc was tall for a Vietnamese, dressed in green and wearing a baseball cap. Instead of using stealth Loc crossed the base boldly in the open. Nguyen watched him look in every direction at once, uncertain what to do next. So, the tall one was just a little nervous. Nguyen stood to his full four-and-a-half-foot height and raised his arm. Loc saw him and ran to cover, and Nguyen heard his hard breathing. With a finger to his lips, he showed Loc the two American guards. The older boy nodded and stared open-mouthed at the steep angle of the hill behind them.

Nguyen pointed to the leather belt around his waist. "Hold on and do not let go, the grass at the bottom is thick. We must hurry or Tran will have the ass."

"What is that?"

Nguyen understood that Loc did not yet know the American language. "The soldiers say it. It means anger."

They crept past the gatehouse guard into the elephant grass where there was no light and no trail to follow. Blind, Nguyen navigated by the slope and pushed his way through quietly, especially in the clumps of bamboo. Once out of the tall, sharp grass it was a hundred meters of easier climbing under a ceiling of tree branches following a switch-backed trail to the road. A bright three-quarter moon appeared in the sky and lit up the base below. Soaked to his skin, Nguyen found a rock to sit on and looked down at the lights of the American base.

"Many targets" Nguyen whispered, pointing down. "But none so far we can't reach them. The soldiers have their name on the hill but it belongs to us."

Nguyen led the way up the soldiers' road a quarter mile then looked for a place to enter the heavy side-hill jungle. Again there was no foot-trail, only his sense of direction and elevation. After a half-hour of steady climbing he dropped to his hands and knees and scrambled up a brushy draw, and at the top of the draw was the narrow trail to the highest cave. Here the trees were over Nguyen's head and thick enough to block the moonlight. He closed his eyes tight and then opened them slowly to let the ghostly path through the black trees show itself. There, along the side of the steep hill. There were branches to hold onto but the trail was a narrow rock ledge and he was glad he couldn't see down. He walked carefully, feeling Loc's tight grip on his belt, until he saw the terraced rock with trees growing out the top. He drew his Zippo lighter, used his body to shield its flash, and allowed himself two seconds of light to identify the rock positively. Holding onto thick roots he fit his tennis shoes in stone toeholds and scaled the rock easily. He bid Loc to do the same. At the top he searched the brush until he felt the narrow crack that was the entrance.

Nguyen's nose twitched. Smiling, he asked, "what do you smell?"

Loc made a face. "Fish!"

"And kerosene."

Nguyen steadied himself with deep breaths, stretched out on his back and covered his face with his hands to keep the limbs from ripping out his eyes. Then he slithered through the crack, until his feet were dangling over the edge that was the cave ceiling. He wormed his way down on hard rock until his legs were inside, making sure his clothes weren't snagged in the stringy brush. He rolled on his stomach and let himself down to the point where he hung by hands in total darkness. The free-fall was as long as he was tall and he was unable to see the cave floor. If he landed wrong he could break a leg. He counted one... two... three and let go, bringing his knees up and holding his arms out for balance. He made a good landing. Seconds later he helped long-legged Loc land on both feet.

Nguyen knew Tran was in the cave ahead of him by the smell of fish and the burning lamp, but there was another smell, just a faint trace of mint. That told him the old women were here as well. But now the cave was black. In a crevice above his head he found the GI flashlight, the kind shaped like the letter L. He swept the cave floor and walls with the light to give Loc an idea where he was and then followed where the tunnel led, around a dark corner into a room as wide and tall as a hooch. In the near corner Tran's dark eyes gleamed black from his squatting position on the rock floor. Across from Tran were the two old women, and piled between Tran and women were the plastic-wrapped rectangles of explosive, labeled M5. Tran had waited for Nguyen and Loc to arrive before beginning his work. He wanted them to observe every step.

"Did I make a noise?" he asked Tran, as the kerosene lamp was re-lit.

"A small one. Your American cigarette lighter will someday betray you. You should use matches. And you are late." Tran had the ass.

Loc looked around the cave in the soft light. The floor was level rock with a covering of hard-packed red dirt, to keep down vibration noise, he thought. The ceiling overhead was mostly smooth, high enough for a tall Vietnamese to stand comfortably, but there were sharp edges to avoid. The kerosene lantern and cooking stove sat on a convenient rock pedestal at the closed end of the cave, and the rock wall above it was stained with the smoke of many fish-and-rice dinners cooked there. There was a metal pot, and assortment of colorful coffee mugs with the names of famous American battles imprinted on them, and a box of Lipton flow-thru tea bags. All the comforts of home. After his strenuous climb, Loc was surprised to see the two old women squatting in the corner.

"The wind comes from Hanoi," Tran said. "We will talk, but quietly."

"It is a fine hill," Loc said, with deference.

Nguyen and Loc squatted down Vietnamese style, with their buttocks touching the floor and knees bent almost to their chins, weight on their heels and feet splayed wide like ducks. It was a comfortable position for working with the hands.

"I am sorry to be late but I am fast to learn," Nguyen told him.

"There is not much time before we go back down. Watch and listen."

Just then Loc noticed the pile of rags behind Tran. "What is that behind you?" he asked.

Tran held up a hand, silence. "Was there a guard in the house that blocks the road?"

The question told Nguyen that Tran and the old women had come from the south side of the hill where the soldiers of the air force worked.

"Yes."

Tran was an experienced fighter with an embittered, distrustful face that made him look much older than his years. He was dressed in army fatigue pants, green t-shirt, and worn canvas tennis shoes. His hair was black like

Nguyen's and his eyes were a darker brown gleaming with intensity. His cheekbones were wide and high, and he had a full nose compared to Nguyen's little button nose. His lips were thin and tightly shut over prominent front teeth. Tran had hard-life lines everywhere on his face, around his eyes, the sides of his mouth, and his wrinkled short forehead. But tonight he seemed almost relaxed.

Tran lit the single burner stove as Nguyen and Loc observed. One of the old women who had accompanied Tran to the cave took up her canvas cloth, steel thimble, and sewing needles. Another poured water from a GI gas can into a pot and began to make tea. As the water heated, Tran turned his attention to the wrapped cubes of explosive. There were many cubes, piled neatly like the little chips in his sister's card game. Without moving from his squatting position, Tran laid the white blocks in four neat rows of three each and counted them forward and backwards. He said something to the old women, too quiet for Nguyen to hear, and they glanced at Loc and nodded. Tran then re-arranged the blocks of explosive into two rows of six each. So there would be two bombs made tonight and many more made later.

"But there are three of us," Loc protested.

"You will carry a rifle," Tran answered without looking up.

"I have already carried a rifle," Nguyen told him seriously.

Even before tea was brewed, Nguyen saw the shape of the satchels the women stitched. As Tran quietly directed, they took the form of a woman's purse six inches wide and ten inches tall, with one large main compartment and a wide shoulder strap attached. This main compartment was then divided into six smaller compartments. Tran passed one 2-inch x 2-inch x10-inch long white block to each old woman to check for size, adjustments were made for a tight fit, and the white blocks were returned to their rows. American C4 plastic explosive, Tran explained to the boys, more destructive than dynamite. When the first satchel was complete and packed with the white blocks Tran told Nguyen to stand. He handed the satchel to Nguyen to drape over his shoulder. The weight was considerable, nearly twenty pounds, but with the wide canvas strap it was quite comfortable for carrying. Tran instructed Nguyen to shake his satchel, to try to make the blocks fall out, and Nguyen feared an explosion. But, even upside down in the satchel, the blocks were a tight fit. Nor, Tran told him, would they be snatched out by brush or grass on the way down the hill. When the second satchel was stitched Tran stood and tried it on but found it too short and the carrying strap had to be lengthened. Then tea was ready.

Tran passed out mugs of steaming tea and kept a black "Iwo Jima" mug for himself. The tea was weak but it was hot. They drank in silence until Tran set his mug down on the rock, dug into his right pants pocket, and brought out a small plastic bag that gleamed in the kerosene light. He unwrapped the bag carefully and laid out the contents with the same care as he had the C4 blocks, three silver-colored cylinders 3 inches long and a half-inch in diameter. Nguyen reached out to pick one up but Tran cautioned him with a raised hand.

"Very dangerous," he said. "Fuse detonators."

They were Chinese, Tran said. They had been manufactured in the 1940's and contained the violent fulminate-of-mercury compound. It didn't take much heat or concussion to set them off.

"Tell me what work you did today on the base," Tran asked Nguyen.

"You were going to tell me how you knew this place," Nguyen replied.

Tran nodded; he had promised. "I have killed soldiers here before. When you were a small boy. It is not important now. Now tell me what work you did."

With a glance at Loc, Nguyen's serious face transformed. Now he was a clown showing all his white teeth. "First, yesterday. Yesterday I burned shit. Shit-burning detail. I was the head honcho of all the head honchos in charge of burning all the shit. I was the best and burned the most shit. Eight times the truck was filled with shit and taken to the dump. Yet, I would rather smell the stinking clouds of burning shit than fill sandbags that protect the soldiers."

Tran nodded approval. "Tomorrow, I will be a worker. Maybe I will burn shit."

Nguyen was astonished, eyes wide. "No! You must not. Never are there papa-sans working on this base. Only the very old."

But Tran's eyes remained stoic. "I must see for myself. I have the picture-card of a white-haired grandfather. You will not know me. Finish your story."

Still concerned, Nguyen's face slowly relaxed. "Today, I am in trouble for burning some shit. I am number 10 Vietnamese boy-san, the worst. My guard is PFC Holloway a stinking, shit-burning jerk; dinky dau. While he talks to his whore I drive the truck and choose the place to burn the shit. The wind is coming from Cambodia, so the big black clouds of shit rise in the air and settle on the base where the colonel lives and everybody is very piss off. The colonel is piss off, then the sergeant is piss off, jerk PFC Holloway is piss off, everybody is piss off at stupid number 10 Vietnamese shit-burner. Tomorrow I am water detail."

Tran's hard face suddenly cracked, his eyes shut tight, and he laughed until he spilled his tea. For a few seconds he was a young man again with tears rolling down his high cheeks.

The moment was broken by the sound of trucks. Far down below they heard the engines whining in low gear out of the motorpool and turning east, toward the perimeter that separated Bien Hoa from the open jungle west of the South China Sea.

"Guard changes," Nguyen whispered.

Tran remained tense, listening. A whistle blew, a door slammed shut.

Men hollered and clanked getting into trucks. Engines revved and the trucks rumbled on their way.

"Toward the villages?" Tran asked.

Nguyen listened, understanding Tran's concern.

"No. To guard the airplanes and runways. Nothing to worry about."

Nguyen was surprised to see Tran glance immediately at his wristwatch. "You know the base well," the old fighter commended.

Nguyen received the compliment instead as a bitter truth, and he scowled at the dirt floor in front of him. He should know the base well, he thought, because he had worked at Bien Hoa all his life, or so it seemed. Six of his fourteen years he had filled the soldiers' sandbags, chopped weeds in their ditches, picked up their cigarette butts, and burned their stinking feces. Unlike Loc, he was not free to move to Saigon and live in the anonymity of the big capitol city: he had two sisters to look after, one with a job like his own, reporting what the soldiers did and said. She was one of their whores. Nor did he yet have Tran's fighting experience and the freedom to move from village to village, killing soldiers at every opportunity. He knew the base because he had been its clown prisoner for six years.

Oh yes, I know the base well. I know the roads and the buildings, the meanings of words on signs, and I know the soldiers. I know the soft-speaking officers who give the commands and the fat sergeants who shout the words and the ignorant sullen soldiers who do the work, and I know the meaning of their insults while pretending to laugh at them. I know when the soldiers work, eat, and sleep. I know which soldiers live here, the clean ones, and which ones come and go, the dirty stupid ones called grunts. The ones who live at Bien Hoa are the worst, and I hate them the most.

He looked up and found Tran watching him. "I would like to put my bomb," he declared, "where stinking jerk PFC Holloway sleeps. If there are grunts to kill I leave them to you."

At this, from a fourteen-year-old, Tran smiled. One of his two old hags snorted laughter and explained the remark to the other.

"I understand," Tran replied, "but you allow the anger show in your face."

Nguyen thought this over. "It is because all soldiers have so much luck."

"They have luck but no patience." Tran explained. "One is meaningless without the other."

"What is a grunt?" Loc asked, looking from one to the other.

Nguyen, the clown again, stood. He dropped his shoulders and tromped around the cave grunting like a water buffalo, until both Loc and Tran had to stifle laughter. When he squatted back down he saw the seriousness return to Tran's dark eyes.

"They are dull as you say, and lucky as well. But they are the ones who killed your father and your father's brother. As for the soldiers here who write words on paper all day, killing them is the same as eating rice without fish: it leaves one still hungry. We will leave them for another time."

Nguyen stared. Tran had just told him their targets would be the barracks closest to the hill. Then he listened until the sounds of the convoy were absorbed by the night. Soon the old women had finished Tran's satchel strap, cut from a piece of camouflage fatigue shirt doubled, and he stood up to try it on. His twenty-pound bag rode on his right hip. He looked down at his two students.

His father, he explained, had shown him how to make the satchels using both dynamite and the new American explosive, C4. For sheer explosive blast he liked the C4, called cyclonite. And it was safer carrying to the target, he said. He had carried satchels of C4 while riding a bicycle in Long Binh and he had carried them under the concertina wire at Khe Sahn. Since the Americans used C4 to wreck villages and shrines, it was quite satisfying to throw it back at them.

Tran put all but one of the fuse detonators back in the plastic bag. He reached into his other pants pocket and brought out what looked like a spool of gray insulated wire. From the same pocket he retrieved an empty .223 M-16 cartridge. Using the brass case to measure length, he carefully cut two pieces of wire and laid them side-by-side on the dirt floor. He handed matches to Nguyen and told him to light one of the fuses while he counted seconds on his watch. The match flared, the fuse wire hissed, an acrid smoke-cloud filled the cave, and a dark worm burn in the dirt was all that remained. Nguyen lit the second fuse and fanned the eye-stinging cloud away from his face.

Each spool of fuse is different, Tran told them. Some burn at two seconds per inch, others take four seconds. This fuse is about three seconds per inch. Tran cut two pieces of fuse to identical three-inch lengths and demonstrated how the cap of the detonator was unscrewed, the fuse wire fed inside, then the armed detonator was forced into the top of the white block. Ready to light.

Nguyen felt a lump of ice in his throat. Nine seconds to get clear? No, not even nine, the last inch of fuse was in the detonator. Six seconds to throw and run away.

"We will arm the charges," Tran said gravely, "at the bottom of the hill."

The shoulder strap, Tran warned, was strong enough to use for hurling the lighted bomb but it was never intended as such. And simply throwing the satchel and running away was imprecise; a lazy man's tactic. If possible, the satchels must be placed exactly. Since the force of the explosion was mostly up, in order to do the most damage the satchel had to be placed low under a building or vehicle, which was hard to do when thrown. Since these satchels would blow up soldiers' barracks they must be placed, or thrown, to the middle of the barracks to kill the most soldiers. At mid-afternoon the soldiers usually played cards or slept prior to their evening meal.

Nguyen glanced at Loc. The sixteen-year-old's enthusiastic smile came from youth and inexperience.

"Now tell us what is under the pile of rags," Loc said.

Tran pretended he hadn't heard. "Because it is the soldiers' sacred time of year they are expecting us. There will be trucks sent to the top of the hill. Soldiers will walk down trying to find us. We will meet again after they are gone, only the men this time. Tomorrow we will sleep here."

Loc spoke again to Tran with his boyish charm. "I would like to keep one detonator."

"Would you show it to your friends like a butterfly?"

"No. I would hide it away and save it."

Tran reached in the bag and then handed the silvery detonator to the boy. "Better to use it than hide it. I have many more detonators. There are more satchels to make."

Loc first showed the detonator to Nguyen, taunting playfully, then tucked it away in his shirt pocket.

"Now the pile," Nguyen asked again. "It is rifles?"

With a glance at the old women, Tran nodded. "Yes. For the day after. There will be more fighters from my village."

"How many?"

"You ask too many questions. It is enough that you know in the next three days at this place, many soldiers will die. The others will lose more of their will to fight. Now it is time to go back down the hill."

Tran was finished talking. He stacked the two satchels neatly in a corner of the cave, while the women put away their sewing needles and nylon thread. Nguyen helped the old women out of the cave and was the last to leave, and when he pulled himself onto the rock he saw a sky full of stars and only Loc waiting for him. The old fighter and his two hags had vanished into the jungle. Loc had his new shiny detonator out and was looking at it again under the moon and stars.

"Put that away."

The sixteen-year old again taunted Nguyen, waving it in front of his face. "I bet you'd like to light this and put it in one of your buckets of shit!"

Nguyen tried not to laugh but gave in. "No. Put in one of the shit houses!"

Nguyen grabbed a strong tree root and half-slid down the rock, making it look easy. Still holding his detonator, Loc tried the same stunt but lost his grip and fell the last five feet, landing on his shoulder and rolling. When Loc stood up his detonator was gone. He and Nguyen looked for it but couldn't find it. It lay at the base of the big rock but there were too many dark crevices.

"Now Tran will really have the ass," Loc whispered.

"We will come early tomorrow and find it. Remember to stay close in the tall grass."

Nguyen took a course straight west to the road. The early morning was damp and cool enough to make him shiver. Once on the road it was only a matter of walking downhill and looking around the next curve for truck headlights. Near the bottom he did see light, but it was the glow of the floodlights. He crept around the last turn and saw the roof of the checkpoint a pebble's throw below; metal gate across the road. He told Loc they must go around as they had going up, and in twenty minutes they'd be on their way to Sin City. He stepped into the elephant grass and felt Loc's hand tight on his belt.

Blind, Nguyen was as quiet as a snake, careful not to snap off stalks with his shoes. In his mind he saw a downhill course that brought him back to the brush where he had waited to meet Loc, a few yards east of the checkpoint. For each ten steps down he counted two steps east. His concentration was so strong that he did not realize he was carrying two buckets of shit on his back, as not only did Loc hold tightly to Nguyen's belt he also leaned on his shoulders to keep from falling. The hill had weakened Loc's inexperienced legs. Blackness, slow progress, the constant drag of grass against his face, and finally the added burden of Loc's weight took a toll on Nguyen's sense of direction, until he was no longer sure where he was. He could not read his watch. With each careful step he expected to see the aura of floodlights, but after a short rest he decided he must turn west. He turned his shoulders and almost fell backwards, as Loc's weight suddenly ceased to be a burden. The sixteen-year-old plummeted face first past Nguyen, making a terrible rushing, cracking noise. The elephant grass curtain parted and Nguyen was caught in a blast of white light.

With all his strength he dived left but the elephant grass held him, a fly caught in a spider web. Instinctively, he covered the back of his head with his arms just before the bunker guard opened fire. The M-16 barked a dozen times from close range. He cringed in a fetal ball until the shooting stopped and the grass curtain closed as suddenly as it opened. Loc was either dead or had recovered and thrown himself back. Getting his legs under him, Nguyen crashed blindly back up the hill. Grass tore at his face and ears and dragged under in his armpits and between his legs. There was another burst of gunfire, and after a few seconds, a third burst that sounded farther away. He heard the GI's shout back and forth. Then the night was quiet.

Alone, Nguyen made it to the bottom of the hill. He hid in the grass imagining soldiers with rifles running everywhere and the base siren calling all the thousands of them out of their beds. But there was no siren and no sign of Loc. He risked a careful peek at the checkpoint on his left. The guard had thrown the door open and stood looking up the road, rifle in hand. Fifty yards away a group of soldiers stood smoking cigarettes in front of barracks 2013. He was trapped between the gatehouse and the soldiers. He had to be inside the gates of Sin City to meet the labor trucks by 5:30 and it was a two-hour walk to get there. He glanced down at his watch, 3:30.

Then, as if by magic, stupid grinning Loc appeared beside him and giggled like a girl. Nguyen was relieved to see him but too angry to smile until

Loc showed him the bottom of his tennis shoe. The heel was blown out as if he'd stepped on a firecracker.

"This time," he whispered. "luck was with you." Fifteen minutes later the MP closed his door and they made a run for the barracks shadows.

0345Hrs 23Dec71
1st Cav Div HQ Bien Hoa
HQ Command Charge of Quarters, Officer of the Day

Sitting at Division Sergeant Major Bierra's wide desk, Lieutenant St John heard the crackle of M-16 fire and looked up from his book, "The Command Vacuum" by retired Major General Enos Chandler. The book presented the case that the loss of the Vietnam War could be attributed to the failure of the junior commanders, non-commissioned officers and young lieutenants and captains, to communicate and carry out orders from colonels and generals.

"Son of a BITCH!" the lieutenant blurted, and slammed the book closed.

Some idiot bunker guard had fired at Cav Mountain. Now he had to write a debriefing report. Now he had to send his runner to wake up Colonel Borg. The colonel did not like being awakened at zero-dark-thirty in the morning, and the colonel would have a case of the ass. Diabolically, St John stared at the brass lever on the desk that tripped the base siren. Wake up the whole damn 1st Cavalry? Better not.

"Private Hagel get over here!"

A sleepy private first-class lifted his head off the nearest desk and dragged himself front-and-center before the lieutenant. "Sir?"

"Watch the CQ desk, listen for the phone, but don't touch anything. I'm going up to Hill 229-er to find out what dipshit fired his weapon! When I get back you're going to wake up the mess sergeants first and Colonel Borg second. Got all that Hagel?"

"Shooting, sir?"

St John hiked a quarter mile to the bunkers on the west side of 1st Cav Division Headquarters. He passed barracks with lights on; others troops had heard M-16 fire. Up ahead, where the in-transit R&R detachment backed up against the floodlighted, barbed-wired zone at the foot of Hill 229, he saw a gathering of GI's in various stages of dress. Not one of them had a weapon. Where the hell was the sergeant of the guard?

"What bunker!" St John demanded.

The half-naked boonyrats stared at him; no salute, no sir, no respect. St John understood these soldiers were all levied for Rest & Relaxation flights out of Vietnam when the Christmas cease-fire was over, to Taipei or Manila or Australia. They could give a damn.

"Down toward the MP checkpoint," one of them told him.

So the culprit was in either 8-Bravo or 7-Bravo bunker. Using the floodlights to read by, he glanced down at his guard roster but found both 8 and 7 Bravo left blank. Routine. God it was bright, he thought, as he started the 200-meter walk to the checkpoint. On his left were ten rolls of rusty concertina wire that kept the Viet Cong from sneaking past the bunkers, a mini-DMZ. A guard in a bunker could look across those rolls of concertina and tell blue eyes from brown, at fifty meters. How anybody could miss even a small man at that range with an M-16, or be mistaken about his target, St John did not understand. He reached 8-Bravo and commanded the guard to clear his weapon. There was no response. 8-Bravo was empty, no guard. He walked west to 7-Bravo.

"Clear your weapon and stand at ease!" the lieutenant commanded, coming along side the bunker. Hearing nothing, he pulled off his glasses and cleaned them looking up at the floodlights.

"Lieutenant St John? Oh my God, sir. I thought I seen two gooks."

"Who thought he seen gooks?" St John sneered.

"Specialist Perkins, motorpool, sir. Oh my God."

"I know where you work, Perkins." St John looked straight ahead from the bunker, but there were no gooks caught in the wire, no body counts laying under it, nothing. "I didn't hear you clear your weapon..." St John listened for the sound of an M-16 action locking and the rasp of a magazine sliding out. "Can I come around in front without you blowing my fucking head off?"

"Yes, sir! My weapon is clear. Oh my God."

He walked around, lifted his right leg over the sandbagged front wall, and sat down on the bench seat beside Sp4 Perkins. He spoke to him as he would a third grader. "Now Perkins, tell me what you saw and how many rounds you fired because I have to write a report. Can you do that?"

"I dig. I mean, yes, sir. It was one gook or maybe two."

"Do you mean by that, a Viet Cong, or maybe two?"

"Roger, sir, a VC. I heard a noise and whoa...!... he came right out at me! Out of the elephant grass. What a rush."

St John turned his head and looked at the elephant grass about thirty-five meters up the hill. With the light hard on it, the grass looked like a textured wall. That VC, he thought, must have had suicidal tendencies.

"Sir, he come right at me. There might have been another one right behind him. It happened pretty quick."

"So this Viet Cong, presumably trying to sneak through our wire, dived head-first out of the elephant grass?"

"That's what it looked like, sir."

"I see. How many rounds did you fire?"

"A full clip, I think."

"Twenty rounds. Are you aware there are gorillas on Hill 229 Specialist? Could it have been gorillas playing grab-ass...?"

"Could'a been... if a gorilla wears pants..."

"Is that supposed to be funny, Perkins?"

"No, sir..."

"Then do you mean pajamas, black pajamas?"

"Fatigue pants, kind of."

"So I'll put in my report to Colonel Borg, 'Sp4 Perkins saw a Viet Cong in fatigue pants dive head first toward the concertina wire... and he shot at him from thirty-five meters but missed with a full clip. You perceive my problem, Perkins."

"Happened so quick... Oh my God."

St John yawned. "This happens once a week. You tell me how to write the debriefing because I don't give a damn, Perkins."

"He rolled around and crawled back in the elephant grass. Man. I think I got him."

"If we walk up there right now and recon... we'll find a dead VC in pants. Alright, let's recon."

At that point Perkins' confidence sagged. When he shook his head the heavy helmet slipped down his forehead.

"It happened so fast... Sir, it probably was a gorilla, like you said."

St John nodded and let ten seconds go by. "Perkins I will put in my report you saw a shadow and you fired at it. And that you may have discouraged the enemy from coming through our wire."

"Thank you, sir."

"You're welcome Perkins. I'll write it, you stop by Division HQ and sign it."

"Thank you, sir."

"Better lock and load," the lieutenant reminded the guard. "Could be a whole gorilla platoon up there."

He walked back to division headquarters and found PFC Hagel sleeping face down on his desk. He shook the private awake and sent him off to wake the battalion mess sergeants and then the division's senior intelligence officer, Colonel Philip Borg. Returning to his reading, St John found that, on page 88 of his book, General Chandler stated that the inevitable difficulty faced by general officers and field grade officers serving in Vietnam was the influx of "ROTC, OCS, and other versions of 90-day wonders, young men rushed to command too soon." Based on that assumption, Chandler went on, junior officers became the weak link "between the planning and the execution" of the ground war in Vietnam. Captains and lieutenants failed to communicate.

"Obviously," St John muttered, "the old fud never met Sp4 Perkins."

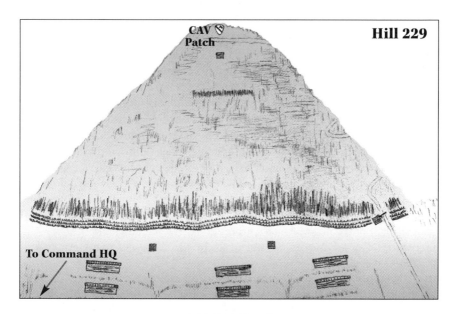

CHAPTER TWO

0615Hours 23Dec71
Headquarters Complex,
Military Assistance Command-Vietnam
Long Binh Province

J. L. Gottlieb squinted into the tangerine sun as her cameraman fussed with light-meter readings and the fine-focus of his CBS video camera. Observing them nearby from the back of a two-and-a-half-ton army truck was the rest of the querulous news crew. Darcy was homesick, Peter was still bummed about Long Binh Jail, Russ had his dysentery back, and Steve was asleep sitting up. She daubed at her short straight brown hair and centered her aviator's sunglasses on her nose.

"Any time, Frank," she said.

"Eat my shorts, Jan."

"C'mon!" Russ hollered from the back of the truck. "Roll that damn thing!"

Jan raised her hand, a signal Russ should understand. Quiet, live camera.

And despite Frank's present ill humor, he had her positioned perfectly to capture the essence of Headquarters MAC-V behind her, huge and bustling. The three-building ellipse-shaped Military Assistance Command - Vietnam complex was in the direct light of the low morning sun. During her narration Frank would zoom back for close-ups of the officers in crisp combat fatigues as they arrived at Building G-1. Then his lens would pan back to convey the

15

height and breadth of this six-story brain center of the American military presence in Vietnam. 'Mack-Vee', as the troops called it, was not lead material for the six o'clock news, but it was a familiar backdrop for Americans who still tracked the slow, torturous deceleration of the war in Vietnam every night on television.

"Go," Jan said, with a last lick of her lips, watching for the little red light.

Through his camera lens, Frank moved Jan just off-center with the American and MAC-V flags hanging dead in the background behind her.

"I'm standing in front of the Military Assistance Command Vietnam, the epi-center of American military activity and intelligence in Vietnam. Quite literally, I'm told, the first call received by the President of the United States every morning comes from the 6th floor of Building G-2, the offices of the army's theatre and corps commanders. The conduct of the Vietnam war, the substance of peace negotiations with the North Vietnamese, and the preparations for an up-coming three-day Christmas cease-fire in Vietnam are the daily business at MAC-V.

"There have been six previous Christmas cease-fires in Vietnam. All six were marred by front-line fighting and rear-area terrorism with counter-attacks. For the officers at MAC-V, Christmas cease-fires have been a microcosm of the frustration of this war: promises made and broken, both sides blaming each other for violations, and nothing changed when they ended. And always, more dead American soldiers to send home.

"The 1971 three-day Christmas cease-fire begins at 1800 hours this evening, 6 p.m. December 23rd, and it stays in effect until 6 p.m. the 26th . Under MAC-V oversight army, air force, and marine field commanders will pull their units back to firebases or rear staging areas. MAC-V has told CBS News that the United States will observe the cease-fire so long as the North Vietnamese do the same. We have heard that before.

"From the buildings behind me the army's four corps commanders will monitor the cease-fire and report to the President through Secretary of State Kissinger. A source here has privately told CBS News that Mr. Kissinger is concerned that while North Vietnamese chief delegate Xuan Thuy seems enthusiastic about the cease-fire some hard-line Viet Cong may seek propaganda victories, particularly around big cities like Saigon, Qui Nhon, and here at Long Binh. Secretary Kissinger will receive briefings on the cease-fire every four hours at his offices in the American Embassy in Paris. If the North Vietnamese do use the American pullback to launch a new offensive, ultimately it will be President Nixon and Secretary Kissinger who must balance a military response against continued diplomatic progress toward the final cease-fire. Everybody at MAC-V, we are told, has his fingers crossed.

"And the war in Vietnam goes on. This is J.L. Gottlieb, CBS News, at the Military Assistance Command Vietnam, Long Binh Province."

Frank shut off the camera and slipped on the lens cover. With the bulky video machine still attached to the tripod, he heaved it on his shoulder and followed Jan to canvas-top truck. Russ Adelman, sitting in the tailgate seat, clapped his hands as they clamored aboard.

"Bravo, hard news from the front!" he quipped. "A cease-fire! Did General Garlett write that one for CBS?"

"Russ, you're an ass."

"No," he corrected, "I have the ass, I believe is the expression."

Frank took his seat beside Darcy, his size-twelve tennis shoes propped on the crew's growing pile of suitcases and duffel bags. Darcy was lost in thought, eyebrows knit in an unattractive scowl and her wide mouth pulled down.

"Just stick to your black-market sleaze pieces, dear," Jan told Russ, "and leave the big stories to the heavy hitters. Where the hell is this tour bus taking us now?"

The engine revved and the driver bumped the truck forward, throwing the passengers backward. The use of the term "tour bus" was a standard bitch both as to the type of transport the army provided and the control the driver exercised. Side-trips were unauthorized. Whether their host was the army, air force, or marines, this group of American reporters traveled in rough-riding trucks to tour sanitized installations and participate in rehearsed press conferences. Except for the color of the uniforms: seen one, seen 'em all.

"The lovely French City of Bien Hoa," Russ told her, "where we will receive a guided tour of Headquarters 1st Cavalry Division Air-Mobile."

Jan consulted her fat, tattered notebook, a daily diary of twenty-four days spent in South Vietnam. "Big base, little base..?"

"Another boring big one, not as big as Long Binh."

Peter Keating, who wrote for the *San Diego Times*, rolled his eyes. "The base commander is Jeffrey Webb, Brigadier."

"How do you know?"

"He lives in San Diego, just my luck."

Jan laughed out loud. "Let me guess Peter; the *Times* trashed him. Great. Darcy girl, cheer up. See if Webb's on your 'Bail Out' letter list. Maybe we can corner him into a little quid pro quo?"

The truck bounced and Peter's head lolled. "Not Webb. He's hardcore. If Bill Westmoreland is war 'hawk' then Jeff Webb's an 'eagle'. Yes, my paper trashed him; no it wasn't me. And the *Times* isn't responsible for anybody's personal problems. Shit, if we'd hit Bien Hoa a week ago I'd have missed Webb."

Darcy glanced at him. "What personal problems?"

"Wife ran off, a draft-dodging son, etc, etc, ...a drag."

Darcy flipped pages in her day-planner. "He's on the list. Brigadier General Jeffrey Webb. He was in-theatre when the letter was written, a division commander. Holy O'Christmas... Webb's been in 'Nam forty-two months. Why does his name ring a bell?"

Jan shook her head.

"I still don't see why you're making that letter such a big deal," Frank griped. "Who gives a damn which generals advised the President to 'Bail Out Now'? For one thing, the President didn't 'bail', for another the army will cover its ass until hell freezes."

She glanced at Frank, then around the inside of the lurching truck. Only Frank seemed interested in her answer. She shrugged. "It's not a big deal, Frank. It's something to write about... called... a news story? Some people who read newspapers, Frank, think that if the army has any heroes left in Vietnam it's those generals. They tried to end the war and paid the price."

"Heroes," Steve Grozik scoffed, opening his eyes.. "The only general linked to the 'Bail Out' letter so far is what's his name from the 3rd Marines. Hickam. When it backfired on him what does this turkey do: he volunteers to help the 7th Fleet bomb the DMZ for six weeks! Some hero. There are no heroes, Darce."

"Maybe. But I asked Four-Star General Creighton Abrams about the letter, I asked Three-Star Lieutenant General Benton Garlett, so I will damn sure ask One-Star General Webb."

Steve sighed. "Well, that's the great thing about this tour: we're free to work independently. Whatever trips your trigger, Darce."

The truck bounced along on the pot-holed highway, kicking up dust that swirled back over the tailgate. Frank patted Darcy's knee and when she looked up at him he was blind Mr. Magoo, one of his many comic faces, trying to cheer her up. The first weeks of the tour she and Frank had been intimate, they had met in South Vietnam and fell in lust. Frank had a great fuzzy brown perm, wore a trim brown mustache, and had sensitive eyes behind his dark-rimmed glasses. He was an attractive man, an artist and a pro in his field, but she found that they were incompatible. He was a regular guy who liked his breakfast on the table at the same time every morning and his sex on Tuesdays and Fridays. He objected to her "showing off her perky tits" at news conferences and when she interviewed the GI's. Their relationship became Woodstock or World War III, nothing in between, and now they were just friends.

"I'm fine," she told him. "I'm just sick of 'Nam. I'm sick of canned news conferences and smirking generals and troops who get a hard-on looking at a naked dog! Sick of it. And I want to be home for Christmas."

"Now, now," Jan taunted, "remember what the State Department told us. We're ambassadors. Your tits help build morale not just hard-ons."

Peter leaned forward. "Yesterday, while you were inside MAC-V falling asleep, my editor sent me inside Long Binh Jail, known affectionately as LBJ. Now that place... is a bummer. A comparison might be TJ, the Tiajuana Jail.

"Your editor is out to lunch," Steve told him. "We've been to Khe Sahn, Da Nang, Pleiku, Qui Nhon, Na Trang... where else... Cam Rahn Bay, and there are no human interest angles about prisoners left to write about. The race issue has been beaten to death. Deserters, resisters and AWOLs are passé, conscientious objectors, protesters, and born-again Christians and Muslims don't raise an eyebrow."

Peter nodded. "Well, I got some Russ Edelman material on the Saigon black market. I met a GI in for pre-trial confinement. He was AWOL four years before they caught him. He lived in Saigon with a mama-san and a kid on $1000 a month selling Cambodian Red to the troops. Now he craps in a bucket."

"Anything you can score in Los Angeles," Russ told him, "you can score in 'Nam. I'm with Darce, I'm sick of the whole place and ready to catch that big silver bird back to the world." He fished out his traveling size bottle of Pepto Bismol and took a slug.

"One more week. We fly out of Tansonnhut on the 30th."

"What's CBS looking for at Bien Hoa," Darcy asked Jan Gottlieb.

She shrugged. "The cease-fire's on the front burner. But I had a heads-up from John Janeski that if Bien Hoa's a bummer we'll move over to Saigon to do the Bob Hope Show. You boys and girls are welcome to tag along."

The truck slowed to pass through a military checkpoint then surged ahead. "By the way, Darce," Peter said, "the reason Webb's name rings a bell is that our Pentagon spies think he's Laird's air war adviser in Laos. He didn't sign any 'Bail Out' letter."

"Right on. But I'm still going to ask."

0630Hours 23Dec71
1st Cavalry Division Air-Mobile,
Headquarters Command, Bien Hoa
East Briefing Room

At any moment, Brigadier General Webb was expected in the briefing room. His place at the circular conference table was marked by a pile of MAC-V mailers, division strength reports, frayed manila envelopes stamped "Div Cmdr Eyes Only" and a stack of mimeographed 1st Cav orders, everything from promotions to pre-trial confinement. In the center of the table were three telephones, a green phone labeled "Cav HQ", a black phone for "MAC-V", and a red phone with the designation "Crypto Clearance", for most-secret communication. Since Webb had reported for duty at Bien Hoa five days earlier this was his second support command briefing, and the first one had lasted five minutes.

Seated around the table waiting for Webb was the 1st Cav support staff, Colonel Phillip Borg S-2 Intelligence, Colonel Charles Shipp S-3 Operations, and Lieutenant Colonel Douglas Geary, S-4 Logistics. The S-1, personnel chief Lieutenant Colonel Raymond Wilcox, had run a last minute errand and was due back before the briefing. Holding his voice down to a whisper, Geary leaned forward.

"Have you seen Sergeant Major Bierra's reception room lately? Sofas gone, lamps and rugs gone... place is starting to look like a bunker."

"Yeah, you'd think there was a damn war on," Colonel Shipp drawled.

Operations officer Shipp was near the end of his career, piling up retirement points and combat pay in his accrual account. He had eight months left to serve in Vietnam and a year after that to bank a thirty-year military career. Shipp's hope of going out wearing a star and the rank of a brigadier general crashed and burned when he learned, four months ago, that his final combat tour was with the black-sheep 1st Cavalry Division Air-Mobile. In Vietnam Shipp had grown a greasy-looking handlebar mustache. Under his mass of forehead wrinkles were a bloodhound's drooping eyes and half-glasses. His chin was scrunched and his speaking voice was pure cornpone cowboy.

Lieutenant Colonel Geary shrugged and sipped coffee. "Bien Hoa was great while it lasted."

S-4 officer Geary was a rarity, a lieutenant colonel without a college education. He'd signed on as an army truckdriver out of high school and had done well in a 25-year career, making the rank of major before ever being assigned a "hardship tour" away from his wife and family. Geary had a pleasant round face, a thinning brown flat-top whitewall haircut, and expressive brown eyes.

"How's Webb seem to you?" Shipp wanted to know. "A little shaky?"

"Tired. Evasive. Going through the motions," Geary answered.

Borg nodded. "His mind's still at Tay Ninh. Forty-two months there is three-and-a-half lifetimes."

The hall door opened and Lieutenant Colonel Wilcox poked his head in. Seeing he wasn't late, he closed the door and hurried to his place at the conference table.

"What's the latest," Borg whispered.

Ray Wilcox exactly resembled a barn owl, myopic eyes heavily corrected by thick round glasses, wide forehead and fleshy cheeks, thin lips and no chin. In his twenty-six years as an officer Wilcox had bounced back and forth between the army's administration and Judge Advocate General branches and he had never served in a forward area. Like Shipp, his career as well as his pay and benefits had plateaued and he was on a downward slide to retirement. Although Lieutenant Colonel Wilcox looked like a wise old owl he was the support staff's most strident anti-war "dove".

"As to the interrogatory," Wilcox replied softly, "is our new base commander one of the courageous minority who signed the 'Bail Out' letter to the Commander-In-Chief and is his reassignment here a shit detail...? MAC-V still has no comment."

"Courageous minority my ass," groused Shipp. "You mean turncoat son of a bitch."

Wilcox gazed back, blinking. "I strenuously disagree, Chuck. But either way, Ben Garlett has the lid on it and that's that." Colonel Wilcox reminded the staff of the recent *Washington Post* piece speculating that in the wake of the 'Bail Out' letter only Jeff Webb's fine combat record had kept him from losing his star.

For months, the rumor swirled that the current 1st Cavalry Division commander was one of the officers who had formally recommended "surrender" in Vietnam to the President. The "Bail Out" letter dogged Jeff Webb wherever he went, speaking at a press briefing in Saigon or training South Vietnamese helicopter pilots at Qui Nhon. At first he flatly denied signing the letter, but in recent public statements Webb's only comment was "no comment." And now, his transfer to Bien Hoa was interpreted as a Nixon pay-back.

The "Bail Out" letter, written by general officers serving in Vietnam and received by the Secretary of the Army in late 1970 for delivery to the President, advised the Commander-In-Chief to order an immediate pull-out of all troops in Southeast Asia on the grounds that the "war of attrition" could not be won without the full support of the Joint Chiefs of Staff and the American people. "Quit, walk away, don't look back," the generals wrote tacitly, "bail out now" on the fighting in Vietnam and on the fledgling South Vietnamese democracy. And, by definition, bail out on the prisoners-of-war in North Vietnam and all the categories of missing-in-action, two groups the letter did not mention. The letter asserted that the President had received poor counsel from his Joint Chiefs of Staff by repudiating the "Domino Theory" of the spread of communism in Southeast Asia, and it downgraded Vietnam to a "civil conflict" in which the United States should have no role, no interest, and no military objective.

But despite an impressive cadre of signatures the "Bail Out" letter failed, and backfired. The Secretary of the Army quietly informed the Joint Chiefs who saw themselves as an offended party, he admonished them to stay the course in Vietnam, and he ordered discreet career terminations for the generals who had conspired against the President. The Secretary regarded the letter so egregious that he kept it secret from the President for almost nine months.

By Christmas 1970, the "Bail Out" letter was a top-echelon rumor, the latest army embarrassment after Me Lai and the Pentagon Papers. By the February 1971 Tet Offensive most senior officers at MAC-V had heard about the letter and denounced it as the worst treason since Benedict Arnold. In August 1971 the text of the letter was paraphrased and leaked to the *New York Times*, and only then did the Secretary of the Army pass the original letter on to Secretary of Defense Laird and President Nixon.

Under unrelenting anti-war pressure and facing an uphill climb to re-election, Nixon was outraged, especially when he learned that the treacherous generals were all still serving him in Vietnam. None had been fired. He reportedly told Laird, "I will personally deal with those bastards," and ordered immediate reprisals including early retirements and transfers to army "shit details." The "Bail Out" letter cast a shadow on all senior officers in the Vietnam theatre, those who had not conspired had covered up.

As to which generals signed the letter, the dust hadn't settled and that was partly because of the timing of Nixon's new re-election strategy called "Vietnamization" of the Vietnam War, wherein the Army of the Republic of Vietnam would incrementally take over the fighting load. In September 1971, a week after learning about the "Bail Out" letter, Nixon ordered most of his senior field commanders out of combat areas back to rear installations where they were accessible to the news media and to train the Army of the Republic of Vietnam. It became impossible for "civilian watchdogs" to determine which transfers were as-scheduled and which were punitive. The juicy rumor floating around about Jeff Webb's transfer held that he was an "acting jack" commander, and that III-Corps Commander Lieutenant General Benton Garlett was pulling the 1st Cav strings from Long Binh.

"I'll tell you this, the man is hardcore," Geary said. "He did PT at oh-four-thirty this morning, by himself. Push-ups, sit-ups, burpies, then he ran from his BOQ to Big Ben Hospital... around the motorpool..."

"You're shittin'!" said Shipp. "Damn. Means we're next."

Geary asked the group. "In fifteen months as this division's commander, has Jeff Webb ever set foot on Bien Hoa?"

Borg shook his head. "Not even for his R&R, six months ago. Webb flew on a C-130 from Firebase Catapult straight to Japan, where he slept for forty-eight hours."

Senior support commander Phil Borg was a tall Swede, blond before going bald. He had penetrating blue eyes, protruding elephant ears, stooped shoulders and a turtle-shell belly. No gentle giant, Borg was soft-spoken but prone to outbursts when his tongue turned sharp as the point of bayonet. Borg had a year of combat infantry on his record, 1966 with the Big Red One, and still had hopes of earning his first star in Vietnam.

"Bien Hoa's always been a combined army-air force facility," he said, "and the base commander has always been a fighter-jockey. So Webb just left support and logistics to his executive officer, our newly-departed Colonel Fish."

"Any word on Webb's new XO?" Wilcox asked.

"I liked old Fish," Shipp whispered, "but the Cav needs a young XO and Bien Hoa needs a hard-ass like Webb. Place has gone to hell."

Lieutenant Colonel Wilcox shook his head. "Webb looks burned out to me. I think Vietnam is over for him. And I'd assume somebody at Bien Hoa will get bumped to executive officer."

All eyes settled on Colonel Borg. While Borg and Shipp were both full-bird colonels Borg was ten years younger and had a year more time-in-grade.

Borg glanced at the closed door to Webb's private offices. "I wouldn't mind the job. But as to the 'Bail Out' letter, Ray, consider this: if Webb did sign it how did he fight off reassignment for three months? How the hell does a brigadier postpone a transfer ordered by the Secretary of Defense?"

"He sure has a case of the ass about his transfer..."

The door opened and General Webb walked in carrying a steaming mug of coffee.

"Ten hut!" Wilcox called out.

"As you were." Webb walked past the conference table to the briefing room's south-facing window. "Good morning gentlemen, and, if it's not too early, Merry Christmas."

"Merry Christmas to you, sir," Wilcox replied. "Getting used to the new quarters?"

The east briefing room was small, sixteen-by-sixteen, with painted block walls and a concrete slab floor maintained spit-shine bright. Of all the rooms in his new quarters at Bien Hoa, Webb decided he liked this one for briefings because it was almost soundproof, it stayed cool all day long, and it had a 3'x5' glass-and-screen window that afforded a south-westerly look at some of 1st Cav Div headquarters, with its rows of metal-roofed barracks, mess halls, battalion command posts and administration buildings.

Webb ignored the question from his S-1. He stood at the window studying the half-moon layout of the 1st Cavalry in-transit detachments, the temporary homes for his infantry and artillery soldiers rotating in and out of Vietnam. A dozen barracks were designated "R&R", rest-and-relaxation, for troops who had earned a week's vacation from the war. Another dozen buildings comprised the "Replacement Detachment", newly-arriving troops with 364 days to serve in the Republic of Vietnam. There were half-a-dozen "Hospital Detachment" barracks for soldiers recovering from light wounds and malaria, and there were barracks designated DEROS, the acronym for "Date of Expected Return from OverSeas." In these happy barracks were enlisted soldiers who had served their 364 days and were out-processing to go home. But Jeff Webb was not happy looking at the DEROS detachment, or R&R, or the others. All his in-transit infantrymen were billeted at the base of the tall cone-shaped hill nicknamed Cav Mountain.

The hill, topographical designation 229, was as steep and thick as any he'd seen in Vietnam, and it was the highest point on the combined army/air force HQ Bien Hoa. At the summit of Hill 229, facing Hanoi, was a 12' black-and-camo 1st Cavalry Division insignia, the same horse-head and diagonal-line patch 1st Cav troops wore on the shoulders of their jungle fatigues.

1st Cavalry Division Air-Mobile Commander Jeffrey Webb was the army's youngest brigadier general, forty-one years old. He earned that distinction by serving three-and-a-half tours in Vietnam during two of the bloodiest years, '68 and '69. Along with many leadership citations Webb had been decorated for personal bravery five times. He stood 6'4" and weighed a trim 185 pounds. His face was tall like his frame, light-brown eyes smudged with purple from lost sleep, small nose, granite chin and long jaw, and jet-black hair cut in a razor-straight military flattop. He wore plain as-issue jungle fatigues, shirttail out and sleeves rolled up like his GI's, but flawlessly pressed. On his collars he wore black stars, over his shirt-pocket a plain black nametag and the crossed-rifle combat infantry badge. His boots were standard GI jungle canvas-and-leather, polished but not spit-shined, cuffs bloused. He did not, so far at Bien Hoa, wear a .45 handgun around his waist.

He turned and looked into the eyes of his intelligence commander. "What was that M-16 fire I heard early this morning?"

S-2 Commander Borg shuffled paperwork. He had only known General Webb a few days but he already knew that the man didn't miss much. Through Borg's former boss, 1st Cav Executive Officer Colonel "Pike" Fish, Borg knew Webb was tireless, humorless, quick-tempered, and "a soldier's commander". Webb would expect a full briefing on any enemy contact at Bien Hoa, and Borg was ready. The officer-of-the-day had wakened him at 0400.

"General, it was one of the bunkers on our side of Hill 229-er. There were three bursts fired, a full magazine. The OD reported that it was probably shadows but the guard was making sure."

"Which bunker?"

Borg consulted the report. "Seven Bravo."

"Which is next to the road checkpoint?"

"Correct. Hill 229 is divided into north and south hemispheres. On the army side the bunkers are numbered clockwise from 1-through12, letter Bravo."

"Do we have two soldiers in every bunker yet?"

"No, sir. We're still building our guard rosters."

"Any other bunkers join fire?"

"No, sir."

"Recon?"

"Affirmative. The officer-of-the-day, 1st Lieutenant St. John, did a recon and reported it was negative."

"What the hell does that mean, 'negative'. Did he look for weapons? Satchel charges? What were the likely targets? If there were no weapons what were Vietnamese doing on our hill? Did the lieutenant try following them?"

Borg glanced at a sardonic Colonel Shipp across the table. "Sir, Lieutenant St. John is an officer in the Judge Advocate General Branch, a lawyer. I'm sure those questions never occurred to him."

After five days at Bien Hoa, Jeff Webb was unimpressed by his support staff. As a group while they did put in the required long duty hours, they seemed uninspired, by-the-numbers, a collection of yes-men and curmudgeons who had been too long in the same jobs. But there were obvious reasons. First and foremost, Vietnam was a lost war, with ten-thousand

24

soldiers a month rotating from Vietnam back to the US, it was hard to keep a good staff. The up-and-coming field grade officers had long since departed Southeast Asia; except for Lieutenant Colonel Geary, the Cav support staff was past their career primes and only Borg had a shot at promotion during Vietnam service. Also, the 1st Cavalry had some serious tarnish on its reputation after its dismal showing in Korea under General MacArthur and then solid defeats during 1967 and 1968 in Vietnam's Central Highlands and A Shau Valley. The Cav was a tough assignment for any bird colonel looking for his first star or any light colonel looking to jump to bird.

Webb walked away from the window, weariness plain on his face. "Gentlemen, I left Tay Ninh Province five days ago. That morning a sergeant in the 7th Brigade stepped on a mine and lost his legs. Echo Company of the 1st of the 9th took a dozen casualties in a village near Landing Zone Buttons. A chopper patrol was fired on leaving LZ Penny. And an eleven-man ambush team walked off LZ Judith and hasn't called in or reported back since. So if I seem a little disconcerted that a lieutenant in my command can't even write a combat debriefing... you'll have to excuse me."

He sat down. "Colonel Borg, how far is Hill 229 from this room?"

"About a quarter-mile southwest, sir."

"How tall is it?"

"Bien Hoa is at 700 feet above sea-level... the summit of 229-er is 1800 feet. So about 1100 feet tall, sir. On it's slope, the 9th Engineers plotted that it averaged 2200 feet from the base to the summit. It's a forty-five-degree hill."

"And what's the average distance between the base of 229-er and my in-transit barracks?"

"That would be... about fifty meters, sir."

"Unacceptable. We're going to have to do something about that." He looked at the four strange faces around the conference table and realized that, for the first time in forty-two months, he considered himself a short-timer in Vietnam.

Colonel Borg smarted. From reading combat debriefings he thought he was familiar with all the Cav's landing zones named for women: Betty, Rita, Penny, Candice... but the name Judith was unfamiliar. Rather than expose his ignorance he stared glumly in front of him and waited for one of the other officers to ask about it. He heard Colonel Shipp clear his throat.

"Sir, I'm not familiar with LZ Judith."

"It's not on any map. It's classified and I shouldn't have mentioned it."

"All the officers in this room, sir," he said, "have crypto clearances."

Webb explained that on the Cambodian side, between the border and the City of Prey, was the largest Viet Cong shantytown anybody had ever seen, code-named "Atlantis" because 90 percent of it was under triple canopy jungle and invisible through air surveillance. Perhaps 100,000 refugee and hardcore Viet Cong were staged there, obviously to strike Saigon from the west. Webb built Landing Zone Judith, a half-dozen klicks southeast and home to 3rd Battalion of the 8th Brigade, as an early-warning on Atlantis. From Judith, Lieutenant Colonel Tom Malloy's job, twenty-four hours a day and seven days a week, was to patrol the border area east and south. His unit order read "reconnaissance"; he was to engage only if fired on. But in the case of this eleven-man squad Malloy had reported a ripe target and Webb had approved a night ambush.

"Night ambush, sir?"

Webb looked at Geary, the Cav's logistics commander. "Affirmative. You've never heard of LZ Judith, Colonel Geary, because we re-log it at night from Firebase Catapult using Hueys instead of Chinooks."

Geary nodded. "And we lost ambush patrol?... five days ago, sir?"

"We think they crossed into Cambodia and got lost. Secretary Laird is on his way to Paris and I can't get an air rescue operation approved. Malloy's keeping me informed. Let's begin the briefing with S-1."

Personnel chief Wilcox opened by reading the 1st Cav Division strength figures, known as "morning reports". He read the numbers aloud as he did each morning prior to Webb's arrival, the current strengths of the 1st Cav infantry brigades, artillery batteries, and support battalions. The figures were twenty-four hours old since they were taken from the previous day's morning reports as compiled at Bien Hoa, but "close enough for government work". Wilcox summed up with the "current change" numbers, including killed-in-action, wounded-in-action, AWOL, in-transit, R&R, hospital, DEROS, and replacement, plus the officers and men assigned to Cav headquarters Bien Hoa. All told the 1st Cav had an operating strength of 16,339 officers and enlisted men as compared to a maximum strength of 19,750. For the second day in a row, Wilcox reported there had been no combat casualties.

Webb sipped coffee but couldn't hold back a yawn. "3rd Infantry and 4th Infantry in about the same shape?"

"Yes, sir. And the Americal Division, and the 101st Airborne. Every division left in Vietnam is about 20 percent under strength. And Cav repo-depo is about empty."

"How do we stand in-theatre?"

Wilcox consulted his reports from MAC-V. "We're under 140,000... and in III Corps... two divisions with under 30,000 total. We're at the point now where we could mobilize every troop in III-Corps and fly him home by the new year. Assuming a permanent truce, sir."

The S-1 droned on and Webb glanced at the calendar window on his watch. December 23, 1971 marked the sad anniversary of an event in Vietnam that every field commander had foreseen, the white flag of defeat. Exactly one-hundred days ago today Secretary Laird ordered all division commanders to the rear, out of combat zones. President Nixon, the MAC-V directive stated, needed all senior commanders near communications centers in order to effect "Vietnamization". Webb recalled that when he arrived in the summer of 1968 there had been 800,000 American soldiers in-theatre.

Wilcox finished reading the senior non-commissioned officer replacement problems, key officer and warrant officer vacancies, and critical job vacancies brought about by the troop reductions.

"Anything else, colonel?"

"No, sir. But I think Colonel Shipp needs your final cease-fire plan."

Shipp nodded. "Sir, as to the cease-fire, we'll need some decisions so I can get word to the unit commanders before morning formations. Such as, quarantining of the Vietnamese nationals, curfews and travel restrictions, guard rosters, perimeter tower duty, etc., etc...."

Webb knew it was coming but had been procrastinating. He'd never run a cease-fire in a rear area. A seventy-two-hour Christmas truce in a forward area around An Khe or Tay Ninh, was a military pullpack to the best-supported perimeter, whether battalion landing zone or brigade firebase. With the exception of 1968, Webb's three Christmases' in Vietnam had been peaceful. Most Viet Cong contact had been in the nuisance category, or "harassing & interdicting": a 122mm rocket here or a 60 mm mortar landing there, shots fired at a guard sitting in a bunker, which meant most troops got three days off to sleep. Once, his division drew the Bob Hope Show. But Bien Hoa in 1971 was a political situation under the watch and control of MAC-V in Long Binh.

"Start with last Christmas," he said.

The Staff looked around the table. Only Colonel Borg had spent the previous Christmas' at Bien Hoa.

"Last year was quiet, general. Officers worked normal duty days with one day off and the NCO's ran things after 1800 hours. E-6's-and-below went to 50 percent duty status, except for guard rosters."

"Some rear areas have a history of taking in-coming at Christmas," Webb commented.

Borg nodded. "This one does. Three bad years in a row, '67 through '69 reading the old morning reports. We've had in-coming rockets and 60 mike-mikes, a fire-fight or two, even a sapper coming down from the Hill 229. We took casualties in '68, I guess everybody did, an R&R barracks was destroyed. But the last two years... nothing at all."

"Sir, " Wilcox added, "50 percent rosters this year would be welcome but they're probably not feasible in all cases."

Wilcox explained that the 3rd, 7th, and 9th Infantry brigade commanders were still sending their in-transit troops in from the field to Bien Hoa. The Christmas cease-fire cut-off date, he complained, was supposed to be 20 December and every field commander had gotten the word both through his office and MAC-V. After 1800 hours today, the 23rd, there were no R&R flights to Hawaii, no DEROS flights from Tansonnhut to Oakland. No flights at all except MAC-V mail, not even a chopper to Saigon until the 27th. So all these arriving in-transits were bottlenecked and made life difficult for Wilcox' people since they had to continue to provide medical checks, records checks, finance vouchers, chow in the mess halls.

"Sir, I'm looking at these growing in-transit numbers and thinking we're going to have to run the administration battalion at full strength just to get the paperwork done. The damn grunts just keep coming."

The air in the briefing room was suddenly thin. Colonel Wilcox had stepped on a mine, and he soon realized it. He used the silence to sort his reports and square away the table in front of him. Colonel Borg watched the young general's face expecting a flash of his famous temper, but there was only mild disapproval.

"I'm sorry", Webb said quietly, "if some of our support troops are inconvenienced because our damn infantrymen keep showing up hoping to leave Vietnam. Or to see their wives in Hawaii."

"Sir, I only meant..."

"I know what you meant, colonel. I've experienced that attitude in the officers and the troops here. Frankly I don't understand it: us against them. Because we know how to use a typewriter and we wear clean fatigues everyday we're elite, but the guys who dig trenches and slop through rice paddies are second rate. A grunt is someone too stupid for anything but carrying an M-16. And I've seen a few of the enlisted barracks here, or should I say condominiums. Their quarters are lot nicer than mine."

"I was referring only to the duty rosters, sir."

Webb let it pass. He started the discussion of the cease-fire around the table with Borg's summary of security at Bien Hoa. Primarily, Borg said, there was no chance Bien Hoa could be "over-run" by an enemy attack. There were pockets of Viet Cong around Bien Hoa but, between the air force's combat wings and the 1st Cav's air support and artillery batteries, there was enough on-base firepower to hold any size force at the perimeter, even a North Vietnamese Army division if one were operating this far south. Secondarily, MAC-V security had forecast "an insignificant increase in harassing activity" during the cease-fire, meaning in-coming mortars and rockets. Finally, Borg reported no Viet Cong activity at Bien Hoa during the previous thirty-nine days, and he had no intelligence to suggest a change from December 23 through December 26.

"Looking at the big picture," Borg added, "it's clear the North Vietnamese are under as much pressure as we are to negotiate the peace in Paris."

Therefore, Colonel Shipp's formal cease-fire recommendations were; 1) starting at 1800 today, go to 50 percent enlisted duty rosters with the exception of perimeter guard duty and staff CQ duty: 2) avoid internal confrontations with all Vietnamese nationals by imposing a three-day moratorium on house-keeping and maintenance labor, with the exception of the those Vietnamese women who worked in the battalion mess halls: fuel and fresh water replenishment would revert to the division motorpool, under Master Sergeant Trumpy: 3) 'live shows' should go on as scheduled: 4) as Colonel Wilcox had suggested, the administration battalion, including records and orders branches, will continue to process in-transits at full strength, Fifty percent rosters only at their commander's discretion: 5) all officers will work half-days and all E-8's and down, from master sergeant to private, will receive one full day off.

Shipp looked around the table. Everybody seemed to agree, except Webb.

"Affirmative," he said "on the live shows, affirmative to a lock-out of Vietnamese nationals, however," and his dark eyes shifted to Borg, "Colonel, your 'big-picture' assessment is absurd. It might be valid if the Cav operated north of Khe Sanh, but we're north of Saigon. Our enemy is not the NVA it's Charles Cong, and he doesn't take Christmas off. So negative on half-strength duty days. We run at full-strength through the cease-fire. Officers and NCO's per SOP, one half-day off for every E-6 and below only at their commander's discretion."

"I'll put out the word," Shipp replied, looking down through his glasses.

Webb held out his palms. "What else?"

"I'd close Sin City too, sir. The troops don't need a piece-of-ass during Christmas."

"Write it down, Colonel. Who schedules the Vietnamese nationals with base clearance?"

"Sir that would be Master Sergeant Janco."

"Police him up for me. I want to meet him."

"Was there some specific concern, sir?" Borg asked defensively.

"More like intuitive concern. Some of the worst terrorism committed against my units has been by Vietnamese considered friendly."

"Today, sir?"

"Early next week is fine."

Next to present, Colonel Geary provided the division commander with what he hoped would be a sobering summary of the division's quartermaster numbers. Forward area infantry and artillery ordnance was Geary's main responsibility but he began his briefing with the 1st Cav's over-supply at Bien Hoa. He described a "ten-year minimum" over-stockpile of small arms and ammo at the current rate of expenditure, a five-year provision of assorted field artillery shells, and triple-digit percent overages in combat-ready-meals, mess hall rations, uniforms, and footgear.

"Point is, sir, the war is winding down and all that hardware is sitting in my area of operation, here. The brigade commanders are hollering 'enough already'. You probably remember being oversupplied yourself, at Catapult. Our commanders don't have enough troops to wear it out, shoot it out, or shit it out fast enough."

Colonel Shipp didn't quite stifle a snort.

"Sir, you inherited this conundrum, which also involves the manpower to secure it. I am now borrowing air force runways to stage logistics. And that's where it stays, staged, under the hot sun where in my opinion it makes great target practice for VC mortarmen. Instead of shipping logistics, I'm rolling out concertina wire and fencing it in. Master Sergeant Trumpy at the division motorpool takes forty percent of Major Andrews' in-transit E4-and-below for quartermaster and motorpool guard posts. Which means that many fewer available for daily perimeter tower duty bunkers, etc, etc."

Webb sipped his cooling coffee and leaned back in his chair. "We don't have enough of our own troops to handle guard duty so we're borrowing from replacement and hospital?"

"Negative, sir. Able-bodied men only, from R&R and DEROS."

Webb stared. "You're telling me you're using my combat troops... sent to Bien Hoa for a week rest-and-relaxation or to rotate home... to sit all night at the perimeter behind an M-60? How long has that been going on?"

"Months, sir. As long as I've been here..."

The division commander was unable to hide the exasperation that swept over his face. "Colonel Shipp, change that ASAP. Combat troops earn their time off and they have a justified damn fear of getting killed when they're short-timers."

Geary looked down at his folded hands, waiting.

Webb sighed. "But Colonel Geary, you are right and I read you 5x5. I was over-logged at Catapult and I saw your runways this morning. It took me twenty minutes to run around them. Open-air warehouses. The reason for your logistical nightmare is your previous commander didn't do his job and your present commander was ignorant, which is no excuse. I should have inspected Bien Hoa months ago. About ninety percent of everything bad that happens to an army in a rear zone has to do with oversupply. So I'll get on the horn to MAC-V. You just make sure when the call comes back that your people know exactly what this division needs to operate and what is surplus."

"Will do, sir. I mentioned Master Sergeant Trumpy? Sir, he's coming up at 1200 to secure his Christmas pass to serve chow to the Vietnamese orphan kids. He does it every year. Maybe you could stop by my office and shake his hand... let him stick out his chest?"

"Christmas chow for Vietnamese orphans? Where?"

"Sin City, sir."

He shook his head in disbelief. "Affirmative, I'll shake his hand."

"Thank you, sir."

The door opened and the highest-ranking non-commissioned officer in the 1st Cavalry Division, Sergeant Major Albert "Bud" Bierra, stuck his head in.

"MAC-V for Colonel Wilcox," he announced.

"Thanks, Top." Wilcox picked up the black telephone and identified himself. He listened hard and then covered the speaker with his hand. "Lieutenant General Benton L. Garlett, sir."

Colonel Borg's long flanking ears seemed to stand out even more. "The III-Corps commander's on the horn?"

A command necessity, The Joint Chiefs of Staff had broken South Vietnam into four corps areas, I-Corps being northern-most and including the Central Highlands, the "Ho Chi Minh Trail" and the Demilitarized Zone below North Vietnam, and IV-Corps being Vietnam's southern boot. III-Corps was the important south-central area that included the major population centers of Saigon, Bien Hoa, and Long Binh, plus the airport at Tansonnut and the seaport at Cam Ranh Bay.

Still covering the phone, Wilcox said "probably just an aide..." but suddenly the owl-faced officer jack-knifed out of his chair and stood at attention. "S-1 Lieutenant Colonel Raymond Wilcox, sir!"

As he realized all eyes were on him, Wilcox' cheeks flushed pink and he sat back down. "Yes, sir, I understand. Sir, General Webb is here in the briefing room, do you prefer to speak with him? Yes, sir. I'll take notes."

Webb about-faced in his swivel chair and wearily pushed himself upright. Coffee in hand, he walked to the window. He knew Benton Garlett quite well. He'd served under then-Major General Garlett as 3rd Army Executive Officer prior to Garlett receiving his third star in 1969 and promotion to the "big show", the Military Assistance Command Vietnam. He remembered Ben Garlett as a politically astute officer with strong career aspirations, likely the next four-Star out of Vietnam and a future Joint Chief of Staff. At all times, Ben Garlett knew which way the wind was blowing. Like General George Patton, Garlett thrived on controversy and publicity and he didn't mind taking a chance, and, as with "old blood and guts", opening his mouth had cost Ben once or twice. But one-hundred days ago today, as most senior commanders bitterly accepted "Vietnamization" as nothing more than a military stand-down preceding an election, Benton Garlett distinguished himself in Secretary Laird's eyes by embracing Vietnamization, buying into it, and making it happen. Garlett was now officially "in Kissinger's camp". For the last few months, with Garlett's influence at MAC-V, Webb had spent as much time shaking hands in Saigon as fighting, and more time training ARVN air-mobile troops than leading his own.

Webb gazed across the long morning shadows. Another new day in the Republic of Vietnam. He watched an M-16 toting soldier escort a flock of old mama-sans in black silk pajamas and straw hats to a jeep-sized pile of sand. There, slowly and without serious complaint, the old women would fill lattice sandbags in the hot sun for seven hours. Behind him the one-way conversation carried on with Colonel Wilcox listening and occasionally mumbling "affirmative" and "yes sir".

Webb crossed the room and stood beside his Lyndon B. Johnson photograph, taken while Johnson was still the President of the United States. It was inscribed "To Colonel Jeff Webb. Good Luck and Good Hunting," dated August 1968. Every time Webb looked at the smiling photo he reminded himself that by August '68 Johnson had made himself a lame-duck President and he had some time on his hands.

Finally Wilcox hung up the phone. He stuck a finger in his ear as if it was ringing. "Sir, General Garlett is trucking up a deuce-and-a-half load of American journalists from Long Binh. They'll be here, possibly, through the end of the truce."

Webb nodded. "Fit's Ben Garlett's command style."

"The one to watch is J.L. Gottlieb from CBS News. She's the big gun and has a cameraman with her. The rest are just newspaper types. Also, sir, the general is most concerned about Cav cease-fire violations."

Webb folded his arms. "I see. He means, now that Webb has reported to Bien Hoa."

"He didn't say that... exactly, sir."

"Operating the Cav from Bien Hoa is his damn plan, not mine. No offense, gentlemen."

"I've seen Gottlieb on the tube," Shipp drawled.

"We're asked to billet the men with the officers, special quarters for the ladies, schedule a news conference, and set up tours of the base."

"News conference?"

"Affirmative, sir. Today or tomorrow, q&a, we're to be ah... 'positive and non-confrontational."

"Positive."

Wilcox glanced around the room. "Positive, sir."

"This has been quite a morning so far. I'm beginning to get the ass."

Webb strolled back to the window. Now the GI guarding the Vietnamese women had called for a smoke break. He sat on a pile of sandbags and lit one up while the old women squatted down in that peculiar Vietnamese social position, buttocks on the ground and weight on their heels, to chatter among themselves.

"What the hell time do those Vietnamese laborers come on base!" he snapped.

Borg looked at Wilcox. "0600, sir."

"Why do we need sandbags filled at six in the morning? This base is ninety percent asleep. Colonel Shipp, effective NOW I want these morning briefings at 0530 instead of 0630, the duty day to begin at 0700, not 0800, and whoever writes those rosters... Sergeant Janco? ...have him change them. I don't want Vietnamese nationals on base until 0800."

"Yes, sir. Except the mess halls, sir?"

"Right, I forgot we have civilian KP's at Bien Hoa! Except the mess halls."

Logistics commander Geary broke the long silence, a twinkle in his eye.

"Any round-eyed women in the news crew?"

Wilcox picked up the green telephone and dialed five numbers. "General Garlett only said they were from the west coast. Los Angeles, Portland."

"I heard of this California crew," Colonel Shipp offered. "Buddy of mine mentioned 'em to me while they were at Cam Ranh, got at least two females. He said one's easy on the eyes but the other one's ugly as mud fence. Ugly one must be Gottlieb."

"Specialist," Wilcox said into the phone, "who's the officer of the day. St. John? Let me speak to him please."

"Billet them where?" Webb asked. "I don't want the press wandering loose all over Bien Hoa."

Waiting on the horn, Wilcox answered "we've got empty barracks over by Big Ben Hospital. Old 11th Mech area, about two miles from here. We'll assign an aide and a full-time driver. We've done it before, sir." Wilcox hung up the phone and scribbled on his legal pad. "Sir, the reporters will be here by 0800. Shall I schedule the conference for 1300?"

"Make it 1100. Get it over with. I detest that part of my job."

"We could introduce Sergeant Trumpy," Geary chimed in smiling. "He's giving those Vietnamese kids a visit from Santa."

Webb glowered. "The senior non-commissioned officer in charge of the division motorpool ...is dressing up as Santa Claus? How on earth do we have time for that foolishness? And don't tell me we're supplying the KP's for Sergeant Trumpy's Christmas dinner..."

"A roster for volunteers is posted, yes sir. Over at admin battalion."

Geary raised his hand but drew only a strained chuckle from Borg.

Writing as he spoke, Wilcox said, "Sir, for your press conference; I thought we might cook up a medal ceremony. The officer of the day is going to wake up CW3 Skelton at records branch. A Bronze Star-Valor might eat up fifteen minutes or so."

"Good diversion. Thank you, colonel." Webb returned to the conference table and sat down. "I don't personally hold the press in contempt," he explained. "They have a job to do. But I don't think military gossip is news, and I don't think combat intelligence belongs on the front-page. And I get tired of the same questions: General Webb, do you know the timetable for all troops leaving Vietnam? General Webb, what will happen to General Donaldson, on trial for war crimes committed by his troops. General Webb, will you be tried for 1st Cav atrocities in the A Shau Valley? General Webb, will you explain the numbers discrepancy between American KIA's and Viet Cong body counts. And my favorite, General Webb, did you sign the 'Bail Out' letter to the President?"

The staff avoided their commander's smoldering dark eyes.

"Even my sons," Webb said tightly, "asked me about that letter, and the other garbage written about me. Isn't it ironic, gentlemen, in 1969 my hometown paper called me a 'war criminal' but after I supposedly signed the 'Bail Out' letter I became a 'folk hero'. I don't know which is worse. My standard answer to the 'Bail Out' question has become 'no comment.'"

Colonel Wilcox hemmed his throat open. "Sir, there's no question about your service record. Subject closed, far as we're concerned," he lied.

Colonel Shipp moved quickly into the general's morning schedule: ops meeting at 0700, General Joyce on the crypto line at 0730, a hearing on a Cav soldier in pre-trial detention at Long Binh who had been found dead in his cell, Red Cross ladies at 0800, Admin Major Warren Andrews at 0830 hours...

"Major Andrews?"

"I slipped him in, sir," Shipp answered, twirling his mustache, "Andrews ain't the sharpest tool in the toolbox, but on this matter he does his homework and you might want to hear him out."

"Say again?"

"Our resident loose cannon, in my opinion, sir," Borg said. "Andrews runs the administration battalion; enlisted records, orders, morning reports, but he has a combat background. Been here since August, a couple other full tours in Vietnam. Been wounded several times including a serious head-wound. He's got an outstanding skin-graft over a metal plate on the right side of his skull."

"What matter are we talking about?"

"Hill 229-er."

"What about it?"

"Because of the cease-fire, Major Andrews will recommend a complete all-out assault on the hill, battalion size. With division artillery batteries and B-52 drops and some napalm for good luck... and if we wipe out a few R&R barracks... well what the hell... Sir, Major Andrews is living in about 1968."

"More like 1868," Borg said. "He wears one of those blue cavalry campaign hats like Custer. I think he thinks he is Custer, trying to even the score."

"Maybe," Webb replied, "I'll invite Major Andrews to speak to the press?" He glanced at Borg's startled expression. "No, it's not funny. A sense of humor, I'm afraid, is something I left behind in '68. Colonel Shipp, you're elected to handle Andrews for me, much as I might enjoy that briefing."

"Sir, if I might interject about Major Andrews?" Borg said. "With our previous commander, Colonel Fish, the decision to sweep Hill 229 fell to me. I have allowed Major Andrews to lead battalion-sized sweeps twice before holiday cease-fires when he insisted the base would be hit. One was... the Birth of Bhudda or some goddamn thing, the other was the day before Thanksgiving. Both were negative, unproductive."

Webb nodded.

"And I did put that S-2 folder on your desk," Borg reminded. "It's a complete military history of Hill 229-er from 1964 through late 1970 when it more or less ceased to be a tactical problem."

"Roger. I will read it."

"Sir, ever since your arrival, Major Andrews has been a real pest. Could you give him just five minutes... two minutes?"

"Two minutes," he agreed. Impatiently, Webb got to his feet, shoved his chair under the table, and stood formally. Briefing over. The officers of the 1st Cav Support Command scrambled to positions of attention.

"Gentlemen, I'll see you at the press conference and we'll meet again here at 1745 to see how the cease-fire gets off the ground. That is all."

Alone in the small room, Webb picked up the crypto security clearance telephone and dialed a Tay Ninh number. He identified himself by his security codes and asked to be transferred to Firebase Catapult, Headquarters 8th Brigade, Commander Art Uhles.

After the usual sixty seconds of relays, static, and vacuum pauses he heard a faint ringing and then Uhles' voice.

"Good morning again, sir. I'm sorry to report nothing new from LZ Judith."

At this point, Webb thought, no news had become bad news. Lieutenant Colonel Malloy's missing squad carried a Prick-25 field radio.

"Malloy break radio silence?"

"Affirmative and on time, sir, oh six hundred. He'll try again at 1200. He has two search platoons ready to break out just about the time of the cease-fire, 1800 hours. Any encouraging news on the air rescue front, sir?"

"Negative," Webb reported. "Ben Garlett's all clanked up about the cease-fire, so no help at MAC-V either."

He hung up and walked around the table with his third mug of black coffee. He paced slowly to the windows and watched the squad of squatting mama-sans filling sandbags under the imposing green vista of Cav Mountain. Day six at Bien Hoa. What the hell do we need with more sandbags? He turned from the window and approached smiling Lyndon Johnson thinking about his most recent press conference in Saigon when he'd been his own worst enemy. Too forthcoming, too frank, too easy to bait. Can't take many more of those. He felt his teeth grinding and his blood pressure rising.

Day six at Bien Hoa. Deliberately, Jeff Webb put down his coffee mug. With burst of pent energy he seized his oak swivel chair, pivoted, and hurled it at the concrete block wall, barely missing the window. The heavy chair hit squarely and smashed apart, wooden legs clattering away like kindling.

The hall door opened a crack and Webb's wide-eyed aide, Sp6 Brian Meredith, peered in. He looked down at the mess on the spit-shined concrete.

Webb inhaled deeply and let it out slowly. "Specialist, I need a new chair. And send in my new housekeeper. Thank you."

Hopefully his S-1 would come up with a grunt for a medal ceremony.

Sp5 Martin Vincent rolled out of his lower bunk naked and crossed the room with eyes half shut. He opened his footlocker and jammed a dry toothbrush in his mouth. On the wall above the locker was his short-timer's calendar. With December '71 all but gone he focused on the miniature-size January '72 in the bottom right corner. He threw both arms in the air, fists balled tight.

"Yes!"

With the handle of the toothbrush, he counted his days remaining in Vietnam for the nine-hundredth time. Including today, nine left in December, eleven in January. He was very short. In ten days he'd be a single-digit midget.

Vinny left the barracks wearing rubber shower shoes and an olive drab towel around his middle, carrying his shaving kit, clean fatigues and shined boots. He crossed the road and angled west toward the admin shower shack, walking with his purposeful small-man's duck-footed stride. He knew the water temperature in the shack would be about seventy degrees but he wanted to get in and get out before the rest of the troops showed up. Fifty meters from the barracks his long Italian nose picked up the asphalt stink of fresh panoprime; the engineers sprayed in on the roads to keep the dust down. His nose detected another odor, the acrid smell of the piss-tube, a four-inch diameter metal pipe sticking up out of the ground some thirty inches. The screen over the pipe was clogged with cigarette butts, and within a hula-hoop circumference around the tube nary a weed survived. He peed carefully around the cigarette butts so that not a drop splashed.

The shower shack was a doorless eight-by-eight building with a round water tank on its metal roof. Inside was a pair of porcelain sinks with shaving mirrors and a shower stall consisting of a single overhead spigot. Standing on the concrete floor-drain Vincent opened the spigot and shivered through a ten-second rinsing blast of cool water. He soaped his tanned body to remove yesterday's sweat, bug juice, and beer smell, then endured another quick rinsing blast before reaching for his towel. He wrapped himself and considered his face in the shaving mirror.

Not too much changed, he thought, from two tours in Vietnam. He was twenty-two years old and still looked nineteen. Teeth still white, no impetigo or other skin crud, no bullet holes in his valuable guinea hide. He saw himself scowling and smiled; "twenty days mother-fuckerrrrrrrrr..."

Vietnam had been good duty for Sp5 Vincent, twenty-three months at Bien Hoa assigned to 1st Cav Administration Battalion. At the end of his first tour he became head honcho of its morning report section, in charge of a dozen clerks who maintained the daily strength reports for the Cav field brigades. By extending for a second Vietnam tour, and because admin battalion was under-strength, Vinny became part-time honcho at records branch, an "acting jack". In that job he processed 1st Cav enlisted soldiers from the infantry, artillery, engineers branches, etc., as they rotated in and out of forward areas for R&R, leave, and reassignment to the US. In twenty-three months he'd met thousands of grunts, and working with them he knew how lucky he was to have served at Bien Hoa.

As an acting jack, Vinny didn't pull charge-of-quarters or kitchen police, and when he drew perimeter guard duty he was the sergeant-of-the-guard who posted the troops and then sat around all night bullshitting and drinking coffee. Otherwise, ten hours a day, his job had been sitting at a desk checking the work of his clerks, making sure the morning report entries were accurate and in the right places on the form. Vinny's MR's were passed up to CW3 Skelton who double-checked them and passed them up to brigade and division headquarters. Anymore, Skelton barely even looked at Vinny's work, it was so good.

There had been casualties at Bien Hoa, one close friend and a couple drinking buddies killed by in-coming. The VC in the villages around Bien Hoa occasionally fired rockets at the base and some of them landed on buildings. A 122mm rocket that landed within fifty meters made the loudest explosion Vinny had heard in his life, bar none. If you heard a rocket "whistle" you'd better find a hole, then pray you can get up and run to a bunker in the aftershock of its shattering, disorienting boom. Usually there were one or two rockets, hit-and-run, rarely a coordinated attack that lasted an hour. But, on a base that was four miles square, after the first rocket landed and set off the in-coming siren, all you had to do was get into a bunker and sit it out until the all-clear. Mortars were a little different, usually some gook sitting on Cav Mountain launching a quick six-pack before running like the hell to beat the gunships, usually at night. If on target, 60 mike-mike rounds landed in a cluster and leveled barracks-sized buildings. It had happened twice on the air force side and two or three times at admin battalion. One cluster of mortars landed so close to his barracks he and Brennan had both been deaf for two days. Sometimes after a mortar attack the NCO's scrambled troops out of their beds and into the trucks to reinforce the perimeter, where two-man fire-teams usually sat taking turns catching some z's. Vinny had never had seen anything in the perimeter wire to shoot at.

And Vietnam had been profitable. Despite being a mile from the greatest post exchange on the planet where there were super-cheap deals on every imaginable appliance, stereo, tape deck, camera, and even cars, Vinny had saved his $60 a month combat pay and most of his base pay. By keeping to a self-imposed $30 a month spending allowance he had saved $5,000 in Vietnam. The only spending exceptions had been his R&R's in Australia and one out-of country leave in Taipei, Taiwan. To board an R&R flight a soldier had to show $200 military pay certificates in his wallet because the army did not want troopies wandering broke in a host city and maybe being tempted to commit a crime on some citizen.

But, he reminded the tanned face in the mirror, two tours of 'Nam was enough. Time to di di, get the fuck out in twenty days. Under three weeks, he reflected, the most dangerous of all his 730 days in 'Nam, as the short-timers jinx kicked in. Getting killed "short" was the worst of the worst but it happened all the time, he'd seen the entries on morning reports. Guys had been shot in the head with two weeks left in-country, with two days left in-country, and why their commanders would leave them in the field so long was one of the great mysteries. Can't predict where a B-40 is going to land, he thought, need a little luck there. But DO NOT fall asleep now. DO NOT go near the perimeter, DO NOT walk within 200 meters of Hill 229, DO NOT volunteer, period. And DO NOT get reclassified KIA on a morning report. And don't think about the hell waiting for you in Camden, New Jersey.

Vinny already knew there would be no hero's welcome. This was 1971, marching bands and parades were as dead as Ho Chi Minh. He'd be lucky to get his anti-war-freak sister to pick him up at the airport. He knew he'd get the cold shoulder in Jersey from talking to all those grunts he processed through records branch heading back to Georgia and Nebraska and Texas, some of whom were treated so rough at home they eventually re-up'd for 'Nam. Like them, he planned to sneak back into his life and forget about both the country and the war. Nobody wants to hear about it.

In clean fatigues and shined boots, Vinny quick-stepped back to his barracks to drop off his stuff and wake up his roommate. Brennan was still in the upper bunk behind the mosquito netting, blanket over his head. Vinny flipped on the light and hollered at the top of his lungs, "Off your ass and on your feet!"

Sp4 Brennan fumbled with the netting and threw his legs over the side of the bunk, eyes open but his chin on his chest.

Vinny looked at him and laughed. Still ripped from last night. Almost a year ago, he remembered, he returned to his barracks after a long day at morning reports to find PFC Brennan sitting on his duffel bag drinking a beer, his new roommate. Among the first of many insights to come from Brennan's college-educated mind was an explanation of the military expression "a case of the ass." Vinny had heard the expression a thousand times but never put together where it came from.

Brennan told him "I got the ass" was actually a medical condition that evolved into an attitude. The soap liberally used in GI mess halls to cut grease gave many troops a virulent case of diarrhea and a painful red asshole to go with it, and it lasted for days. Vinny never forgot.

Gary Brennan was twenty-seven years old, five years older than his roommate. He had blue eyes, a brown flat-top haircut, and a dark beard so heavy that he had to shave twice a day to pass inspection. Drafted at the age of twenty-six after finally flunking out college, Brennan was two-year man with less than a month to serve in Vietnam, already approved for a five-month "early out": when Brennan left Vietnam he also left the army, or, in admin acronyms the "big two", DEROS and ETS on the same day.

For the same reasons Brennan failed as a college student he had succeeded as a soldier. Through three years of college, with the divisive Vietnam War encroaching on every facet of his life, he turned cynical toward secondary education and his effete professors. Education was sanctimonious, Brennan decided, and a professor was someone who couldn't compete in the real world. In basic training Brennan was the oldest draftee in his company and the experience became veritable comic relief. An army drill instructor, he learned, was a soldier who didn't fight. Gary Brennan was unaffected by the army's intimidation tactics with trainees, all of whom feared two things: one, having to recycle basic training, and two, being sent to Vietnam. Brennan already knew he was headed for Vietnam. He was not officer material, not "Regular Army", not an ass-kisser. Brennan struggled through his first eight weeks in the army by standing in a middle squad in a middle platoon, by never calling attention to himself, by typing the company commander's letters, and by maintaining an unshakable attitude toward all army officers and NCO's "what are you guys gonna do, send me to Vietnam?" Brennan was sent to Vietnam as a 74-H, clerk-typist.

At Bien Hoa, Brennan adjusted to a clerk-typist's greatest fear: screwing up and being sent to a forward area as grunt, job description 11-B, infantry. He learned that the officers and NCO's in the admin battalion were even dumber and bigger suck-asses than the ones in his training battalion, therefore, it was possible for him to intimidate them with the right leverage. Given admin's poor junior command levels, Brennan soon found the right leverage: with the war winding down, there was a shortage of replacements for the infantry brigades but an even greater shortage of qualified clerk-typists. So Gary Brennan got by with his sarcasm, irreverence, and his general attitude of "what are you gonna do, send me to LZ Rita?" knowing they never would.

"On with the revolution," Brennan proclaimed, yawning.

"Later."

Outside, Vinny walked east beside the weedy ditch between the barracks and started up the slope toward the H-shaped enlisted records building. Most barracks lights were on and admin troops were headed for the showers or the mess hall. From a squad shagging along toward the mess hall PFC Janssen, 3rd Brigade MR clerk, hollered at Vinny to join them.

"I am too short for breakfast! I am so short you don't even fucking see me!"

"How many days, Vin?"

"Twenty daaayyyssss...!"

He jumped a north-south drainage ditch, angled south a hundred meters following a trail through knee-high weeds, and crossed the open courtyard

39

where the guys played football and frisbie. The double doors of ERB faced the courtyard, and at exactly 0650 hours Vinny threw them open and was surprised to see Chief Warrant Officer Skelton inside ahead of him. Skelton already had the lights on. With an armload of enlisted personnel files, Skelton walked to Vincent's desk and dumped them.

Skelton was 44-years old, a career NCO who made master sergeant before becoming a warrant officer in the administration branch. He had a brown flattop, a simian face, and pinched deep-set brown eyes due in part to a three-pack Pall Mall habit. He looked at Vinny and lit one.

"Specialist Vincent you are records honcho again today."

"Can do, sir. Roger, wilco and all that bullshit, over. Got tons and tons of grunts in our AO, sir. They keep comin'."

"Roger that. How many days do you have left?"

"Nineteen and a wake-up, sir!"

"Got your replacement trained?"

They both knew that was a joke, about the extent of CW3's sense of humor.

"Promote Brennan, sir. He's gung ho for my job, he'd extend for another year in Nam..." Another joke.

Skelton waved a sheet of paper at Vinny. "Colonel Wilcox needs a roster, ASAP, before you do anything else. And don't ask me to explain it because I can't. On my desk by 0800." He turned on his heels and started down the hall leaving a cloud of smoke hanging over Vinny's desk.

"Rounding up those pesky AWOL's again are we? They should know better than to try to sneak by us... no free rides home in this division."

Skelton stopped, turned slowly and eyed Vincent. He puffed on his cigarette.

"There's one more thing. Yesterday, Major Andrews requested a roster of all our troops with 11-Bravo training, infantry. You're name's on it."

Vinny shrugged. "That's a drag. Thanks for the heads-up, sir."

Skelton nodded, smoking fast. "No promises, but if there is a combat mission... you being so short... let me know and I'll advise 1st Sergeant Ree you're exempt. I'll tell him I need you to catch us up in senior NCO records... or some shit. Let me know." Before Vinny could answer, Skelton turned and walked away

The consideration stunned him. In nearly two years working for Skelton their relationship had been all business. Skelton was one of those warrant officers who didn't mix with enlisted men, ever. Vinny realized this warrant officer was saying thanks for covering his ass all those months.

The MR section was long and narrow. It had a center aisle and rows of desks and filing cabinets along the walls. Each desk represented a 1st Cavalry Battalion, each battalion had a clerk assigned to prepare that unit's strength numbers. The language of a morning report clerk was military abbreviations and acronyms, cumbersome at first but easily memorized. Clerks recorded changes through mimeographed orders generated through the EOB, enlisted orders branch. The stacks of orders Vinny passed out to his clerks had heading such as PCS for permanent change of station, R&R, for rest and relaxation, DEROS for date of expected return from overseas, ETS for end termination of service. And sometimes KIA, killed in action.

Vinny's desk intersected the records branch aisle, as the two branches worked in concert. Also organized by battalion and updated through printed EOB orders, the records branch maintained the personnel files of all 1st Cav Enlisted, one section for Senior NCO's E7 and up, another for E6's and below. A records clerk had one thousand manila folders in his file cabinets. He kept promotions up to date, as well as unit assignments, job descriptions, personal histories, R&R eligibility, medals and commendations. When an enlisted soldier processed through Bien Hoa on his way in or out of country, on R&R or leave, one of his processing points was records branch, where he sat down with his battalion clerk and made sure his personnel "201 file" was in military order.

Vinnie sat down and double-slashed December 22, 1971 on the short-timer's calendar his mom had sent, twelve color photographs of the New Jersey coastline. With at least a half an hour of peace and quiet before the troops arrived he read the roster request from Colonel Wilcox.

"What the fuck is this, over. A medal ceremony? Since when."

Quickly it dawned on Vinny that what the colonel needed meant comparing the names on the in-transit detachment rosters to those on today's awards roster. The freshly mimeographed orders on his desk were stapled in batches; promotions, R&R, DEROS, and Awards. He threw aside the first two, browsed through the DEROS orders and felt a tingle pass through his body. The names on these pages were only a couple weeks ahead of him, going home to the world. This time next week, he'd see his own name on a DEROS order. The awards orders batch was small.

There were fifteen pages of military awards, the names of soldiers earning the VSM, Vietnam Service Medal, or the VCM, the Vietnam Campaign Medal, the ARCOM, Army Commendation Medal. There were a few BSM's, the Bronze Star Medal for meritorious service, basically a "clean record" medal for E5's and up and the one he expected CW3 Skelton to recommend for himself. There were only five of the award Colonel Wilcox was looking for, BSVM or Bronze Star for Valor, a combat medal. One was a "cluster", a 2nd BSV to one soldier: Honeyman, Walter E. Staff Sergeant E6, 3rd of the 9th Brigade. Honeyman's name was also on the current R&R roster.

Vinny jumped out of his chair and walked down the records aisle to the 9th Brigade, ripped open the H-K drawer. Honeyman, Walter was an immediate disappointment. His was the fat, much-traveled personnel file of an army lifer. Clipped to the inside left side of the folder was Honeyman's service record in chronological brief from his date of enlistment seventeen years ago to his present duty with the 9th Brigade.

"Bummer," said Sp5 Vincent aloud. Honeyman was a lifer, a grunt, and a fuck-up. It had taken him eight years to make staff sergeant E6 before being busted back to buck sergeant E5, then up to 6 again, back to 5, and he'd just made SSG for the third time in Vietnam.

"Fucking lifer."

Vinny slapped the file closed, dropped it in the drawer, and rolled the drawer shut. He walked back to his desk and skimmed through the rest of the awards. He found a corporal E4 and a buck sergeant E5, both draftee-types, both awarded BSV's. He listed their names on a clean piece of paper and noted that both were in the DEROS Detachment until the 28th. Thinking that was the whole roster, just two names, he almost missed the single 'SSM Cluster' entry at the bottom of the last page.

"Whoa, whatta we got here. Deagle, with a D for delta. William S, Sgt E5." Deagle's service number began with the letters US, another draftee. Deagle William S. was in Brennan's battalion, the 7th. Vinny remembered the name from a hospital detachment entry. Deagle was on base, too.

"Outstanding."

He made a second trip down the records aisle to Brennan's cluttered desk. Deagle's outfit, 2nd Battalion of the 7th Brigade, was the middle four-drawer file cabinet. Vinny found that Deagle, William had a skinny 201 file. He had been drafted July '70, served two months basic training at Fort Benning, three months advanced individual training Fort Polk, five months stateside duty at Ft Dix, then after a three-week leave reported for duty with the 1st Cavalry Division A/M June 71. Unlucky bastard still had six months to go in 'Nam. In-country one month, Deagle had been promoted to buck sergeant. Three months later he had earned his first Silver Star medal for valor. Now, a second SSM, or 'Cluster' on the first, and he was sure to get bumped to E6. Wow. A draftee with two Silver Stars. Must be a hardass.

Vinny slammed the file drawer shut and carried Deagle's 201 back to his desk. He sat down and added 'Deagle, William S.' to his short awards roster, then leaned back in his chair looking at the name. Just like a damn dog. Same age as me, twenty-two. But Deagle's a grunt. After he collects his Silver Star from Colonel Wilcox he can go on Major Andrews' combat mission. I'm too short for that shit.

He hand-carried his roster down the corridor to Skelton's office.

0640Hours 23Dec71
1st Cav Div HQ, Bien Hoa
Admin Battalion Mess Hall

The admin mess hall was empty except for the small roped-off area at the rear where Major Warren Andrews sat alone eating his breakfast and reading morning reports. A large pedestal fan purred behind him. A squad of Vietnamese women buzzed about, preparing the service line and cleaning tables and sweeping the floor, but Andrews was oblivious. He did not notice the two old mama-sans scraping bacon and scrambled eggs from plastic trays into a paper bags and passing them through the screen door to their unseen accomplice.

Wearing half-glasses Major Andrews ate his breakfast eyes-off, reading to the left of his tray heaped with eggs, cold prunes, and a tangle of bacon. The morning report records were dated 1968 and 1969. He knew the numbers and dates cold but he felt he needed every possible fact at his command when he presented his case at 0830 hours for a pre-emptive sweep of Hill 229. This time, he knew, he wasn't begging for troops in Colonel Borg's office; Borg didn't know how to spell the word sweep. This time he would speak directly to the new top gun at Bien Hoa, brother infantryman Brigadier General Jeffrey Webb. He'd served with Webb in '68 but never met him.

Warren Andrews was a large man, with the bulk and barrel-chest more typical of a master sergeant than a major. But he was no slob. Even as he ate he sat absolutely straight with his shoulders squared and his head up. His blond-gray hair was a military whitewall job with a short flattop front. His jungle fatigues were starched, but not tailored, his black leather paratrooper boots were spit-shined to a gleam. He had small blue eyes, pocked cheeks and jowls, a chin that was disappearing into his neck. Apart from the oak leaf collar pin that signified his rank and the round admin insignia for his branch, the only other uniform decoration he wore was the rectangle with two crossed rifles, the combat infantryman's badge. A 1st Cav combat veteran from previous tours in Vietnam, Major Andrews was conspicuous wherever he went because of the vivid purple skin-graft between his right eyebrow and ear and his distinctive blue-and gold cavalry campaign hat. Major Andrews explained his choice of headgear by reminding that the 7th Brigade of the 1st Cavalry Division was same 7th Brigade that Colonel George Custer commanded at the Little Bighorn almost one-hundred years ago. The "purple Cav patch" on his head was in exactly the same spot the Sioux had shot Custer. The scar and hat were part of his uniform.

"DRO!" he shouted without looking up, holding up his empty coffee mug.

Mess Sergeant Arroyo poked his head out from the kitchen. He looked in the officers' dining area and shook his head. He wiped his hands with a towel and walked back, and he spoke to Major Andrews in a kindly voice.

"Sir, we ain't had dining room orderlies in two years. You remember, sir? That senator what' his name, he said we' couldn't have 'em in combat zone. Hey, that says 1968: records branch screw up?"

Andrews glared at his plate, thinking. It was hard to break old habits. He did recall the directive about no DRO's in the Vietnam theatre, a Senate Armed Services Committee decision. The chairman of the Senate Armed Service Committee was named Symington, a son of a bitch and no friend of the military.

Just then the mess hall screen door banged open and four GI's trooped in pulling off their baseball caps. Andrews recognized all four as belonging to him, clerks from EOB and ERB branches. But he could hardly stand to look at them: fatigues rumpled like old pajamas, greasy long hair touching their ears, dusty unpolished combat boots not bloused. There was another new regulation he disagreed with; no matter how hot it was outside troops should always blouse their boots, especially these spoiled brats at admin battalion.

When the four soldiers spotted Arroyo and Andrews in the officers' dining area one of them muttered out loud "shit, look who's sitting back there."

"You slick-sleeves go help yourselves!" Arroyo hollered at them. Then to Andrews he added, "Sir, how 'bout I get you one of my mama-sans?"

Andrews shook his head. "One of those little pigs that just came in can police up my coffee."

"No can do, sir. Tell you what. I got the Christmas spirit today, you know? I'll get your coffee."

Andrews nodded with his chin and returned to his reading. He found the entry date 24Dec68 and turned pages until he saw the heading "HQ, In-transit Detachments". The date of the 24th covered the events and orders cut on the 23rd. He put down his fork and ran his finger to the bottom of the page, "In-transit Present for Duty". On the morning of 24Dec68 there had been a total of 336 troops temporarily assigned at Bien Hoa waiting to catch either R&R flights to cities like Honolulu, Manila, Taiwan, Sidney, and 184 troops waiting for DEROS flights to Oakland Army Air Terminal, California. A Lieutenant Colonel Duckwall had been in command. Feeling the heat of anticipation, Andrews turned one more page, to 25Dec68.

His index finger tracked the entries: "In-transit R&R Detachment", "In-transit DEROS Detachment", and "In-transit Replacement Detachment". There were troop counts shown under each heading, plus smaller numbers for "Temporary Duty" and "Pre-Trial Confinement Long Binh", the infamous Long Binh Jail. The two entries he was looking for were at the bottom of the R&R page, names listed under "Change- In-transit R&R to In-transit Hospital WIA - 9 ", and "Change - In-transit R&R to Oakland Army Air Terminal Graves Registration KIA - 4 total."

Tears filled Major Andrews' eyes.

Graves registration. The GR Point, as they called it in the field.

On Christmas Eve 1968, the Viet Cong came down off Hill 229, crawled through the wire and past the bunkers, and blew R&R barracks 2020 to kingdom come. They killed four soldiers and wounded nine more. On that same day in 1968, while leading a sweep of Hill 686 near the City of Vinh Din, a Viet Cong sniper shot Batallion Commander Warren Andrews in the head. Only the sharp angle of the bullet and his steel pot had saved him from becoming a KIA entry on a 7th Brigade morning report.

In a nineteen-year military career, only three events had ever caused

Warren Andrews to weep like a wife. The memories of two of them still brought tears and the third made his blood boil. One was Christmas Eve 1968, the day that sniper shot him, and 200 miles south VC sappers killed these four fine young infantrymen. The loss of those lives, he came to realize, was a humiliation. They were killed not in combat but in their bunks in a supposedly safe area, on their way to a vacation. A dishonor to the dead, a disgrace for the Cav. The second time Warren Andrews cried was several years later, when after recovering from his head-wound during a short return to civilian life, he drove from California out to Montana to visit the Custer Memorial Battlefield. After reading about Custer all his life and serving in the same 7th Brigade that went down in glorious defeat at the Little Bighorn, he finally got to stand on the spot where the gallant Lieutenant Colonel died, known as The Knoll. The Knoll made Andrews weep.

The Knoll, where Custer and his three hundred troops of the 7th Cavalry retreated from two thousand Sioux warriors to make their "Last Stand", was nothing. It was nothing at all, and Andrews thought at first there must be some mistake. There must be another knoll more like Hill 686. This knoll was not defensible ground. This knoll was barely a mound at the end of long, low ridge. He stared at it, shocked to his foundation. Then, as his eyes scanned along the ridge several miles to the cottonwood trees growing at the banks of Little Bighorn River, he saw the white crosses. One here, two there, all along the ridge from the river to the knoll. Then Andrews understood. The Sioux had chased the 7th Cavalry along this ridge, gaining on the exhausted horsemen and picking off the slowest riders one by one, knowing there was nowhere to run. Custer's deployment here had been desperation, beyond desperation. Beyond hopelessness. Custer, by the fate of the Gods, had been given this place to stand and fight and the indignity of it make Andrews cry.

The only other time in Andrews' life he had physically wept was when the army declared him unfit for duty and temporarily took away his commission. But the medical brass admitted their mistake and gave him a second chance. Now the recollection of that 1970 court martial board-of-inquiry left him with clenched teeth and balled fists.

He closed the MR book and absent-mindedly cut chunks of bacon with his fork. He flipped open a worn leather-wrapped book that resembled a family bible, titled "Battle Diary - 1971." He scribbled a few notes below the date, December 23. He closed the book and folded his glasses and put them in his shirt pocket as Sergeant Arroyo returned with his hot coffee.

"You okay, sir?"

"Fine, thank you, sergeant. Excellent mess."

"Just SOP. Food's good every day at Bien Hoa."

Andrews glanced at his watch and assembled his paperwork while trying to gulp hot coffee. Finished with breakfast, he could have left the mess hall by the officers' entrance but he walked forward in order to pass the table where

45

his troops sat eating. He stopped at their table and all four soldiers abruptly put down their forks and sat up straight. He looked them over one at a time. Of the four, he knew Private First Class Wallace the best. A lazier, more worthless pot-smoking private he had never commanded.

"On your FEET!" he commanded, standing beside Wallace.

Wallace snapped up to attention, knocking his chair back.

Andrews inspected Private Wallace from his scuffed boots to his unshaven face. Then he leaned closer, lips an inch from Wallace's ear and his voice soft as a lover's whisper. "The combination of you and that uniform, Private, makes me sick. The combination of you and that uniform reminds me why my country has lost a war to second rate-terrorists, and that makes me sick. And the reason why I'm whispering, I don't want Senator Symington to hear me. He makes me sick."

Andrews stepped back and retrieved Wallace's chair. "As you were, Private Wallace." He walked the full circle around the table. "Did you troops have to work all night typing? I bet you're exhausted." He shook his head in shame. "You don't know what work is. A Cav officer named Custer marched the Greyhorse Troop fifty miles in three days, mostly on foot and on cold rations. Do you think those men went on a hunger strike or complained to some committee?"

When none of the privates mustered an answer Andrews enjoyed a knowing chuckle; Wallace's name was on his 11-Bravo roster. He laughed again and walked out into the morning heat. The admin jeep was parked where it always was with Sergeant Hooper snoozing at the wheel, helmeted head back and mouth open.

"Morning, Hoop."

Hooper scrambled upright and hung up a salute. "Morning, sir. We ready?"

"Affirmative, we're ready."

"Lieutenant St. John is waitin' at the CP to wish you luck, sir. He seems a little grumpier than usual. Don't forget, sir, I'm standin' in for Sarn't Smith at the 0800 R&R formation." He fired the jeep, scraped it into gear and pulled away.

"We'll get you back here in plenty of time, Hoop."

Staff Sergeant Hooper was a career NCO who had not excelled but did like army life. Hooper was thirty-four years old with twelve years in, never had an Article-15 or been busted, but he had only just made E6 and had another four years before he was eligible for Sergeant First Class E7. On Hooper's plus side, his commanding officers had found him absolutely loyal, eager to please, optimistic and energetic. On the negative side, he had no command presence, being 5'3" and roly-poly shaped with a big belly and fat butt and stumpy legs. Worst of all, he had a broad deep-textured red nose that dwarfed every other feature of his face.

Staff Sergeant Hooper considered himself Major Andrews' most loyal non-com. He considered the major's young friend, JAG 1st Lieutenant St. John, a punk. St. John had become Major Andrew's "askari" at Bien Hoa, because he stood in awe of the major's combat record. But how the major could stand him was a mystery to Hooper. The lieutenant had the most irritating habit of talking to you while looking over the top of your head. Lieutenant St. John thought his shit didn't stink.

Hooper drove the jeep south-by-east as he did every day, seven days a week since the last week of August, taking his commanding officer through his morning reconnaissance routine. The first stop was the highest point in the 1st Cav area of operation, besides Hill 229, the old 9th Infantry field-grade officers' shower tower that Major Andrews referred to as 'the crow's nest'. The tower was situated on a small rise in the center of the officers BOQs, but it was no longer needed because 1st Cav field-grade officers, major through colonel, had showers in their hooches. The tower was twenty-five feet tall with a wooden ladder built into the north-facing wall. Mornings, Andrews climbed to the top of the tower where he got a panoramic view of the 1st Cav AO and the Vietnamese nationals in work details. The 'crow's nest' was the historical name for a similar vantage point Custer had used to study the Sioux Nations camped at beside the Little Bighorn River, in June 1875.

Looking above the barracks rooftops, Major Andrews flipped open his battle diary to 23Dec71 and went through his morning checklist: mama-sans at the sand piles filling bags for the bunkers, boy-sans hosing down the water trucks, getting ready to fill the base reservoirs with fresh water, more mama-sans behind the two mess halls scraping trays. Below, he saw Master Sergeant Janco and Sp5 Dugan marching a squad of hooch-maids toward the officers quarters, right on time. A pair of admin troops with M-16's stood a safe distance away watching boy-sans burn metal latrine half-barrels, six black ribbons of smoke rising above the garbage dump where they blended into one, foul-smelling cloud headed for the South China Sea. And two old papa-sans shoveling out a trench in the R&R detachment...

Andrews lifted his head. "Papa-sans? Hey, Hoop! Bring up my field glasses!"

Sergeant Hooper was overweight and afraid of heights but he jumped out of the jeep and climbed the ladder, muttering to himself. On the top rung he passed up the binoculars and looked back where Major Andrews pointed at two old men in conical hats. They looked very old. Andrews studied the two old men for thirty seconds and then wrote the account in his diary. "Old bastards at R&R. Never saw 'em before."

"Sir? I got that 0800 formation with 1st Sarn't Ree? We're getting short on time."

"I hear you 5x5, Hoop. I want you to check out those two with Sergeant Janco. Ditch-diggers, R&R Detachment, 23 Dec. Got it?"

"Got it, sir."

Climbing down Andrews said, "run me over to the CP and we'll skip the hill recon this morning."

"Roger that, sir," Hooper answered, relieved.

The admin command post, Major Andrews' office, was a 1/4 mile up the street from the mess hall. It was a half a barracks-size building distinguished by its yellow-and black 1st Cav insignia, American flag and 1st Cav flag hanging in the dead morning air, and by its shingle-roofed four-by-eight plywood 1st Cav bulletin board in front. As Hooper gunned the jeep along in third gear a solitary infantryman in faded fatigues and a rumpled boonyhat walked toward them. The 11-Bravo spotted the oak leaf on Andrews wide-brimmed hat and held up a straight salute, and Andrews returned it crisply.

"Good luck son! " Andrews called to the troop.

The jeep pulled to a stop. 1st Lieutenant St. John stepped away from the porch and snapped to the position of attention. He appeared glassy-eyed and unshaven from his long officer-of the-day duty but his tailored jungle fatigues were starched and pressed as always. St. John ignored Sergeant Hooper's salute and walked directly to Major Andrews.

"You're looking very strack, sir. Got your 11-Bravo roster from records branch? I see you have your diary, morning reports, and, of course, the map. Outstanding. I don't see how the commanding general can turn us down."

"Meet you inside Hoop," Andrews waved at his driver, and when the CP door closed he turned to St. John, keeping his voice low. "Lieutenant, are you sure we're on solid ground, uniform code-wise? What we're suggesting is... radical."

St. John winked. "Affirmative. Not even Senator Symington can re-write the UCMJ." He glanced at the CP door. "Sir, can you trust that NCO?"

"Sergeant Hooper? With my life, lieutenant, with my life."

"But, sir, the man is a moron. He resembles a cartoon version of W.C. Fields. If you ever decide to cut him loose, my office has a deserter 201 file that fits him like a glove. I can switch his 201 and have him flown via helicopter out over the South China Sea and dropped from 5,000 feet. Never to be seen again. I could close a case and you can get an NCO worthy of sharing some credit. What do you think?"

Andrews shook his head. "And the troops say I'm nuts. Negative on that idea, lieutenant, negative."

Inside the command post the two officers walked past Hooper's desk and adjourned to Major Andrews' office, leaving the door open. From his desk, Staff Sergeant Stevens lifted his head and snickered. Stevens was younger than Hooper, late twenties, another admin sergeant enjoying a third combat tour at Bien Hoa. Stevens wore tailored fatigue shirts with his sleeves rolled above his elbows, showing off his muscular forearms and biceps. He was a "club hound," a weightlifter, pool-table hustler, card shark, and he liked to bust heads. Especially in-transit 11-Bravo heads.

He glanced at his commanding officer's door, then at Sergeant Hooper. "You and your war games."

Hooper ignored Stevens, who he outranked by six months time-in-grade.

"Andrews is a section eight fruitcake and you know it," he said. "The CG ain't gonna approve no battalion sweep before the cease-fire."

"That's defecation of character of a commanding officer," Hooper retorted. "So why don't you just shut your hole."

"I think you mean defamation, dumbass. Don't fuck with me Hooper. I'll squash you like a bug."

"I got time-in-grade on you, Stevens. You shut your hole or you can explain your problem to the major, right now."

"You two deserve each other. And that groupie 1st Looey too. The Three Stooges. I'm not humpin' down that hill on your pretend combat sweep."

"That's fine, sarn't. I need somebody to pull my CQ shift so I can go."

"Fine by me, too. But it ain't never gonna happen during the cease-fire."

0735Hours 23Dec71
1st Cav Div HQ
Landing Strip Bravo 3 Right

Whipping up a sandstorm, the UH1 helicopter lifted off the pad and the doorgunner threw a half-hearted salute. The airborne taxi dipped its snout and banked right toward the east side of Cav Mountain. Left on the ground holding their boonyhats were two infantrymen in sun-bleached fatigues, one size double-extra-large, the other small. They were still in full combat gear, M-16's in hand, pistol belts with canteens around their waists, tattered rucksacks on their backs, and faded cloth bandoliers filled with 5.56 NATO magazines slung across their shoulders.

It was not the first time a chopper had left this pair on the ground in a strange place. The two had served together for ten months in the same outfit, 2nd Battalion of the 7th Cavalry, same company and platoon. But this time, as their ride whacked the air going away, instead of running for the nearest cover they stood looking around. The small soldier let go with a 7th Brigade yell.

"EeeeeeHahhhhhhh! Goddamn Pomeroy, we made it to R&R!"

But the big man, six feet tall and 280 pounds, was cautious. He watched the chopper fly toward a green mountain that was the highest point in any direction. He turned a slow circle. The door-gunner had said to walk one map klick, 1000 meters, due west to Cav Mountain and look for the R&R detachment at the base. If that hill was Cav Mountain, he thought, there were a hundred army buildings around it to choose from.

"That way," he declared uncertainly.

The small soldier, whose name was so long the letters were crowded on his faded nametag, was PFC James Grossnickel. Jim Grossnickel was the fastest runner and best guitar player in the 2nd Battalion, and he had the quickest grin in Southeast Asia. He had sleepy-lidded blue eyes and shaggy black hair long enough to touch his collar. Jim's GI nick-name had become "Fuck-knuckle", given to him by his platoon sergeant and other best friend, Bill Deagle. Jim was a born fuck-up and his problem, as Deagle explained it to him, was that he couldn't contain his enthusiasm, whether standing in formation, walking point, or getting a briefing from Captain Rule.

"What's wrong?" he asked Pomeroy. "You see VC, GI?"

"Buildings, over. Beau coup buildings. This place does look like Benning. Hope it's not a bummer like everybody says."

Radio telephone operator Corporal Cleveland Pomeroy had a 23-inch neck and wore a size 8 1/2 boonyhat. On the brim of his hat was a plastic bottle of mosquito repellent and the capitol letters BUCKEYES in Cav black. Pomeroy's fatigue shirt was a size 54, pants 44. His huge knees had worn patches in his fatigue pants. His red-stained size 14W combat boots were pooched at the ankles from a thousand miles of walking through jungles and rice paddies. The rucksack on his broad back looked like it was made for a child, the M-16 in his right hand a bb gun. Pomeroy had a broad, flat face under a narrow forehead, pewter gray eyes, and a crocodile jaw. Like his buddy Grossnickel, Pomeroy wore his rank, the double-chevron of a Corporal E4, on his left collar and the blue-and-yellow-ribboned "Garry Owens" insignia of the 7th Cavalry on his right collar. In normal conversation, Cleve Pomeroy's language was as colorful as any other GI in Vietnam, but in his professional communication using the ANPRC-25 field radio he had not uttered a swear word in ten full months. It was, he maintained proudly, part of the sacred code of the radioman.

"Deagle's there somewhere," he said. "He'll show us the ropes, over."

"Hey, mellow out," Jim told him. "Shit, we're at Bien Hoa with a three-day cease-fire so what can happen now? Nothin' but wine, weed, and women for five days in Australia."

"First we gotta get to Australia."

He turned his back to his buddy. "Police up my sling and I'll get yours. We're goin' in there at sling-arms until we figure out where to check these sixteens."

While Grossnickel fished around in his rucksack Pomeroy popped the full clip out of his rifle and jammed it into his bandolier. He drank the last of the warm water in his canteen and then helped Jim find his cruddy rifle sling. Then they walked west between the chopper pads through rolling sandhills overgrown with weeds. They smelled the same chemical defoliant used at LZ Penny. After fifteen minutes of steady humping they spotted traffic on the main roads, jeeps with officers and two-and-a-half-ton trucks filled with troops. The troops wore flakjackets. A perimeter, Pomeroy thought. He hadn't seen gun-towers or concertina wire on the flight into Bien Hoa but he knew there was a perimeter somewhere out there. The closer he got to Cav Mountain the more Bien Hoa looked like a sprawling, sand-bagged version of Ft. Benning, Georgia.

A loose formation of a half-dozen troops in clean green fatigues walked the side of the road toward them.

"R&R?" Jim asked, grinning.

The troops shagged past them to a safe distance and then turned around to stare. One whispered too loud "look at the size of that one."

Puzzled, Jim's jaw sagged. He glanced up at Pomeroy. Something struck him funny and he laughed. "Sick 'em, Pomeroy! Sick 'em boy!"

Playing along, Pomeroy bared his lower teeth and took two long steps toward the troops. They scattered.

"Those bozo's are scared of grunts," Jim said.

"Negative: they think grunts are lower than whaleshit," Pomeroy corrected. "Maybe we shouldn't mess with them. One of 'em might be our R&R clerk."

"Guys who don't like grunts can eat my shorts."

"Jim, with that attitude you're gonna fuck up R&R like you fuck up everything else. You'll spend a week doing KP while I'm in Australia... or wherever."

Jim looked up at him, tongue on his lower teeth. "Whattaya mean 'wherever'? We been talkin' about Sydney for 303 days."

Pomeroy looked west. On both sides of the panoprimed road were well-worn paths. "Think they could be booby-trapped, over?" he asked.

Jim looked around. "Bet your ass Charles works here. Hey man, for the next three days I ain't talkin' to no Vietnamese, I ain't buyin' no Cambodian from no mama-san, I ain't even gettin' my laundry done... Taking no chances, you bic?"

Jim set the pace and Pomeroy took after him. Avoiding the road, Jim humped a shortcut through the sparse hills toward rows of GI barracks, to an open courtyard where shirtless troops tossed a football with their dog tags flashing in the morning sun. He crossed the courtyard and walked between buildings until he hit another road running north-and-south. Now green Cav Mountain was directly on his left so he knew they were getting close. As he stared up, he noticed the yellow-and-black Cav insignia on the top of the hill. The black letters were big enough to read and he pointed it out to Pomeroy.

"1st Cavalry Division Air-Mobile," he read. "Far fucking out." Below the insignia there was fenced-in block building that looked like a radio shack.

They walked west along a drainage ditch between barracks, passing a porch where GI's sat reading and bullshitting. Jim gave a friendly wave but the troops gawked at Pomeroy and then turned their heads. In the next barracks row Jim heard a radio playing "Get Back" clear and loud. He pulled the M-16 off his shoulder and wailed on it like a guitar, singing with Paul McCartney. When the music abruptly stopped Jim pounded on the wall and yelled 'hey man play some Airplane!' but a voice inside the barracks answered "fuck you!" Humorless Pomeroy grabbed Jim like rag doll and tossed him forward. They hit the next road and faced three choices.

To the left, south, it was a quarter-mile walk to the end of the road, an MP Checkpoint, and tall Cav Mountain. Pomeroy figured if nobody else would talk to them at least the MP at the gate would give directions to R&R. Second choice, follow the road the other way where it ended at a big motorpool. He saw the gleaming sun-struck windshields of hundreds of trucks, jeeps, and armored personnel carriers in neat ranks and files behind an eight-foot chain-link fence. Maybe there was a friendly grease monkey down there. Or, third choice, keep going straight ahead between more buildings. It was Jim who squinted up the street and read the distant street sign, "Finance", with an arrow pointing west.

"Captain Rule said we had to draw $200 MPC to get on an R&R bird, remember?"

Up the street Pomeroy saw troops loitering. First just a few, then a dozen, then a platoon or more. He glanced at his watch. 0755, formation time. A stubby NCO in a helmet liner popped out of a building across the street and began corralling the troops into a lazy dress-right-dress company formation. More troops came down the street from the direction of Cav Mountain to join the ranks.

"Move IT move IT move IT!" the NCO yelled. "Got me a bunch of droopy troopies this morning! Move IT Move IT... 1st P'toon, 2nd P'toon 3rd P'toon..."

Jim charged up the hill toward the colorful, rag-tag army. There were sergeants in full dress greens and tiger-stripes, specialists in state-side khakis and jungle fatigues. Jim watched the little round NCO at the head of the formation and was mesmerized by sounds and sights he'd left behind what seemed like a lifetime ago. It was basic training again, with the drill sergeant hollering 'dress-right-dress!' and 'eyes-front!' at his slouched, sluggish troops, none of whom had a rifle or rucksack. R&R, Jim thought, had to be. He pulled his boonyhat down tighter over his unauthorized long hair.

"Hat ease!" Sergeant Hooper hollered. "Smoke 'em if you got 'em!." He looked to his left and saw a grunt no taller than himself approaching. Behind him was another grunt as big as a Japanese wrestler.

"Hey, sarge! Is this R&R?" PFC Grossnickel asked him.

"This here's the Friday R&R orientation. You troops got orders?"

"Nope. We just got here. Company clerk told us we'd get 'em here."

Hooper looked at Grossnickel, who grinned back at him. Then he looked up into Pomeroy's suspicious gray eyes. "Holy sheep-shit son. Sure glad you're on our side."

Pomeroy had heard that one too.

"If you ain't got orders how do I know you ain't AWOLS?" Hopper asked.

"You're past the cut-off. We got us a three-day cease-fire and no birds flying. Lemme see some ID."

The infantrymen pulled their waterproof plastic wallets.

Jim said "Sarge, our company clerk sits in the orderly room all day and reads fuck books and pounds his pud. He's a jerk, you bic?"

Pomeroy added, "he told us to get our R&R orders at a building called echo oscar bravo. You know where that is?"

"EOB is enlisted orders branch. Well maybe they know you're comin'. You troops hop in my formation and soon as it's over you head down the street and check them rifles in the arms room. Then come see me."

As they forged a hole in the front rank a soldier carrying an armload of paperwork approached Hooper. He wore fatigue pants, a white t-shirt, no headgear, and shower thongs instead of combat boots. But he had everybody's attention. R&R orders. Where he walked, the chatter in the ranks stopped. Greedy hands in the front rank reached out to snatch at his paperwork.

"Horton you can't stand in front of my formation looking like that!" Hooper told him.

Horton shoved the stack of orders at Hooper's chest. "Then you fucking do it!" He turned and headed back where he'd come, adding "and that's all I got until the evening formation!"

Hooper shook his head. "That boy works fast but he ain't got no pride in his job." He waddled to the admin CP at the approximate center of the formation and dropped the orders on the porch, with 150 pairs of eyes watching every move. The CP door opened and a stocky 1st Sergeant in a smoky bear hat stepped outside.

SSG Hooper snapped to attention. "P'toons... ten HUT!" Hooper whirled and held up a salute. The raggedy troops brought their heels together.

Master Sergeant Ree ambled off the CP porch and looked them over. He returned Hooper's salute with a karate chop. Sergeant Ree was as tall as Hooper but as muscular and compact as SSG Stevens. Ree was Korean, Major Andrews' 1st Sergeant and the highest-ranking NCO in the admin battalion. Hands clasped behind him, lidless eyes inscrutable under his flat-brim wide hat, Sergeant Ree faced his formation with the unapproachable posture of a drill instructor.

"Hateeee!" he shouted.

Jim leaned closer to Pomeroy and pulled his M-16 off his shoulder.

"Check out this fuckin' guy," he whispered. "Heavy."

Hooper shouted loud enough to be heard on top of Cav Mountain. "1st Sarn't Ree is gonna give us a Friday orientation! You troops lissen up if you wanna go on R&R!"

Jim Grossnickel felt the heat of the asphalt-like street in the soles of his worn boots. The morning air was as dead as platoon Sergeant Harvey. The only thing moving was 1st Sergeant Ree's narrow eyes.

"Genniman..." he said finally, "Igotth'ass."

"What'd he say?" Grossnickel whispered out the side of his mouth.

"Said he's got the ass," Pomeroy whispered. "I had a Korean DI in basic."

"I dig."

Sergeant Ree put his hands on his hips and paced a dozen short steps back and forth in front of his formation, speaking to the ground ahead of his shiny combat boots. It was an orientation speech he'd given on a hundred Mondays and Fridays at Bien Hoa.

"This is... my fo'mashun... my street. You are assine... to me. You wir... wear only authorize... uniform in my street... You wir... sarute officah....You wir... serve on my duty rostah... and at all times act... as a sojer."

"What'd he say?" Jim whispered.

"He's giving the R&R rules. Listen up Jim."

"I am listening."

"On my rii... your leff... is... your assine quata... On your rii... my leff... is arms room and mess hall... mota poo... quatamasta, where you wir receive new uniform, headgear... east of mota poo. ATT shack... where you wir caw home... east of quatamasta... Behind you... large building on hill... records branch were you WIR... hab 201 file checked. Ees of records branch... field medical offices... where you WIR hab... medical check including... yor... pecker check. Finance branch is... top of street where you WIR draw $200 for R&R. All these you muss do before... receiving... ordah. Sergeant Hooper wir... provide visit to rocker where your civilian clothing is... maintain..."

He paused to examine the faces in his front rank. That they were confused meant they were paying attention.

"If you miss... my fo'mashun... not serve my roster... not finish your processing... you are AWOL... wir not go on your R&R. R&R is... privilege... not guarantee... Sergeant Hooper will pass out R&R order... 0800 formashun... and... 1700 formashun...

"Ten HUT!" Hooper screamed in the humid stillness, and the command echoed off the buildings. The troops snapped to attention. The NCO's exchanged salutes and 1st Sergeant Ree spun on his heels and marched back into the admin CP. Hooper shouted "fall out!" and walked to the porch, and called out the names of troops receiving freshly mimeographed R&R orders. The ranks and files of the R&R formation dissolved and reformed around Hooper. All fell out but two.

Unable to check himself, Jim Grossnickel collapsed on the ground. He hugged his M16 and flopped onto his back, convulsed with high-pitched laughter. He laughed until he wheezed, empty belly tight and tears rolling from his eyes. When he finally looked up and saw a disgusted Pomeroy standing guard over him.

"In Jim's family tree," Pomeroy explained, "the branches grow a little close together."

Jim staggered to his feet. "Where the fuck did the army find him. Heavy, man."

"Troop, if you want to go to Australia you better get your military shit

54

together. Me, I think I'll lay around here a week and sleep... catch up with Deagle..."

"Pomeroy would you mellow? What the hell's wrong with you lately? You heard that little red-nosed fucker; first thing we do is check these goddamn guns then we find out where to sign up for Sidney, you bic? Hey, let's go check out R&R. Maybe we'll run into some guys from the 7th."

Pomeroy faced south and eyeballed the shimmering cone-shaped mountain that towered over R&R and all of Bien Hoa. "I wonder where the hospital detachment is? Deagle's been there almost three weeks."

"Shit, you don't think he went to the world in a bag... do you?"

Pomeroy looked at his friend with amazement. "Malaria doesn't kill you it just makes you sweat, over."

0815Hours 23Dec71
1st Cav Div HQ
Casual Hospital Detachment, Barracks 2338

Deagle snuffed out the roach and stepped away from the screen. The breeze from the fans had been just right, outgoing. Wondering if he'd ever get his legs back, he walked to his bunk stretching and flexing. He bent over and tried to touch his toes. Still couldn't do it without dizziness. He wrapped the roach in tinfoil and stashed it with the dregs of his nickel bag in the angle of the metal bunk frame. He flopped on his bed, thinking he'd had enough sleep in the last three weeks for a lifetime but more was all he wanted. Down the aisle, the morning poker-game had started. Those guys knew he hated cards and didn't bother asking him anymore. Deagle's barracks neighbor, PFC Pace from the 1st of the 8th, sat watching the card-players bullshitting about the world and how short he was. Deagle closed his eyes. Sleep.

Off and on during the night he thought he heard the rumble of the New Jersey's 16-inch guns volleying support fire from way out in the South China Sea. They sounded like distant thunder that never got closer, ominous but friendly. The deck guns threw shells that weighed as much as a Volkswagen and sounded like a freight train passing overhead, accurate to within a dozen meters at twenty-five miles. His unit was still too far west for navy support fire, for the past five months the 2nd Battalion of the 7th Brigade operated out of a little garden spot 5000 meters northwest of Tay Ninh City only twelve rolling miles from Cambodia ... named LZ Penny.

Shit, that was nearly three weeks ago, he thought. I wonder if we moved again.

He pulled up his blanket. No pounding deckguns now, only rear-area troops and other in-transits outside, on the move to their duty stations. He heard them hollering to each other and trading cheerful insults with the

Vietnamese boy-sans. He listened to the Vietnamese women in the sandbag details who were as much a part of mornings at Bien Hoa as the rising sun. Nobody, he thought, can describe how six old mama-sans sound having a conversation. It's not talk so much as music, but not music so much as jazz, chaos, with everybody chattering at once with voices rising and falling. He closed his eyes to shut out the world, waiting to see the color images of his thoughts. He felt his breathing slow, heartbeat steady. Body warmth spread outward and he counted pulse beats in his fingers and feet. He felt comfortably stoned. Inwardly he smiled and settled in to watch the familiar kaleidoscope whirl behind his eyes.

But the slideshow in his mind was stuck again, focused on a single frame. He saw Sergeant First Class Harvey sitting against a tree. There were no marvelous bright colors in this chimera, only shades of green. Sergeant Harvey was olive-drab, the tree was green, the sky behind him was green. And Harvey just sat there, expressionless. The cozy warmth in Deagle's body became stifling heat under the army blanket and he threw it off, sweating. He fought the urge to open his eyes, telling himself to wait, the old kaleidoscope will turn yet, and it did. Harvey's image was replaced by dull green Corporal Rinaldi stretched out on his belly, arms flung wide. And Rinaldi just lay there. Deagle's eyes snapped open. The corrugated barracks ceiling was a blur of parallel lines. He stared, knowing if he tried to close his eyes again he'd see PFC Emerson in a trench and Lieutenant Strauss lying on his side like he was climbing stairs. The air whuffed of his lungs as he sat up in the bunk.

The poker-players glanced at him and returned to their game.

Wide awake, Deagle wondered if smoking Cambodian red would ever be good again. The sweat rolling from his armpits made him shiver, and suddenly he was freezing. He stretched out with the blanket up to his dog tags. He felt the rumbling emptiness in his stomach that always turned to nausea. He couldn't help thinking about Rinaldi. Rinaldi had really hurt. Ploughboy and Fuck-knuckle had been tight with him too. For the hundredth time he saw the corporal's agonized face and relived his quick death four weeks ago, only a week before Deagle was medivac'd off LZ Penny with malaria. The three platoons of Company B had moved into the north end of a small hamlet before dawn, with Company C set up to block the south end. Clearing the hamlet hooch-by-hooch Deagle's 3rd platoon unexpectedly flushed a couple of unarmed papa-sans and ten guys took off after them including Rinaldi, and somebody shot him in the back. It happened in a heartbeat, one shot and Rinaldi was down, screaming. Then he was KIA. Deagle carried him half a mile back to the chopper where they put him in a green bag, the first leg of the long ride back to the GR point, and the world. They searched that hamlet for two hours and finally found a Chi-com bolt-action rifle with an empty round in the chamber. But they never found the sniper who got Rinaldi, and Captain Rule concluded it was one of the mama-sans.

Deagle rolled on his side and propped his head on the damp pillow. He thought about Pomeroy and Grossnickel, hoping they made it to R&R. His gaze settled on the wall locker beside his bunk, posted with a copy of his in-transit hospital orders: Deagle, William S. underlined in black. To the left of the locker there were two old bullet holes in the barracks siding. Mornings, the holes let in hard white light and at night the softer greenish light from the floodlights below the hill the troops called 1st Cav Mountain. When the emptiness in his belly turned to nausea he threw his long legs off the bed. He stood up, ten feet tall, and wobbled toward the open doorway.

Outside the sun felt good on his skin. He walked toward the MP checkpoint to the knee-high weeds that the Vietnamese boys kept trying to knock down with scythes. He looked off toward the R&R detachment while his belly gurgled, then he bent over and threw up. The result was only a few dribbles of hot brown liquid. Like the chills earlier, the feeling of nausea ended quickly. A nurse had told Deagle the toxicity in chloroquine was making him throw up.

Ten meters away a small squad of surprised GI's walking a trail witnessed the event. "Man that's gross," one of them complained. "Why don't you guys puke inside."

Deagle glanced at them, taking slow deep breaths. He answer to the complaining soldier was a middle-finger salute. The troops walked on.

"Fini," he said hoarsely, "with chloroquine." Done with malaria.

He took a sweeping look around the base, the rows of barracks, the mama-sans filling sandbags, Vietnamese boys hauling tubs of feces and piss from the latrines. And the strange hill called Cav Mountain. It was time, he thought, to say fini to Bien Hoa too. The reason he couldn't sleep, the reason he was haunted by dead faces, he felt guilty. Dumb as that sounded it was true. Captain Rule had laid a curse on him, calling him a "natural leader" and promoting him to buck sergeant. When he wrote his father about the promotion the old man wrote back about how leadership ran in the family and he laid a curse on him. Now all he thought about 3rd platoon. So, fini, Bien Hoa. If every truck was parked and every chopper was grounded because of the Christmas cease-fire, he'd get back to LZ Penny if he had to hump it.

He walked back inside hospital barracks 2338, his in-transit home after leaving the base hospital known as Big Ben. He opened his wall locker and made a pile of the personal gear he'd carry to the shower shack: boots, fresh socks, clean fatigues, towel, shaving kit, and most important around Bien Hoa, a copy of his orders. He wanted to look clean and shaven when he requested return-to-duty paperwork. The rest of his combat junk, rucksack, pistolbelt, spare uniforms, he threw on the bunk. PFC Pace rolled up his copy of *Car and Driver* magazine and strolled over to observe.

Pace was a small soldier, short and slender like Grossnickel. But unlike Fuck-knuckle this PFC was a cynical little goldbrick. Pace had stolen almost two months of his tour by pretending to have a rough recovery from malaria. Worse, he contracted malaria by refusing to take his "Monday" prevention pills, and he openly bragged about it. Deagle was tired of hearing how short Pace was, down to thirty-five days in 'Nam, and all the great plans he'd made for life in Detroit, Michigan.

"Goin' someplace, Deagle?"

"I don't want to hear about the world today, okay Pace?"

"I'm hip. Where you goin'?"

"Shower, big ben, finance, the PX if I can find it. Then back to LZ Penny."

"Penny is nowhere, man. Why not hang around here a couple months. The war will be over before the monsoons."

Deagle's smile was wry. "I thought you said it would be over by Christmas."

"Fucking diplomats, who can trust 'em. But they're close to a deal. Think how your shitty family would feel if you got blown away after the war was officially over."

"LZ Penny is nowhere but it beats Bien Hoa."

"If you're a lifer. For me Bien Hoa is the last stop before Deeeeetroit. How many days you got?"

Deagle glanced at him. Pace watched Deagle shake out his old faded infantry rucksack.

"Trust me, man, you do not want to wear that rucksack around Bien Hoa. Deagle, you know what's wrong with you, man? You take this 'Nam shit too seriously."

"Is that what's wrong with me?"

"Yeah. In a couple months, or whatever you got left, you'll be back in the world. Working your job, screwing long-haired hippie chicks... you might even vote in an election like a regular citizen. 'Nam will be a bad dream."

Deagle thought about that. "For once Pace, you might be right. I got a letter from a buddy who DEROS-ed in October. He said he was standing on a corner in San Francisco wearing his new greens, his combat infantry badge and campaign ribbons, waiting to catch a bus. A convertible full of kids came along honking the horn and hollering at him, and this chick in the back seat stood up and threw a full can of Coke at his head. Just fuckin' missed him."

Pace shrugged. "Bummer."

"Twenty minutes later he was on a Greyhound bus going to LA. He said he was sitting in the back by himself, minding his own business, when a fight broke out in the front of the bus. He saw these two guys throwing punches and rolling around in the aisle. The bus driver stopped the bus, broke up the fight, and he walked to the back to ask my buddy if he'd mind getting off right there. Another bus would be along in a half hour. Those two guys were fighting about his uniform. One guy said wearing a CIB meant you had killed children, infants, and babies in 'Nam."

"Did he get off?"

Deagle nodded.

"I'd have told that driver to go kiss a big red asshole."

Deagle stood tall, hands on hips. "My buddy's kinda quiet. He got off the bus because he was ashamed of his uniform."

"He fucked up. He shouldn't have traveled in uniform."

Deagle let it go. "Hey, Pace. You got all the S-2 about Bien Hoa, what's the skinny on Cav Mountain? Uniform Sierra or Victor Charlie."

"Uniform Sierra. Some major rounds up a posse of clerks-typists and truck-drivers and sweeps it all the time."

Deagle thought about it and shook his head. "Looks too rough for a sweep. Steep, thick, and lots of rocks. Where there's rocks there's tunnels. An ambush would work better than a sweep."

"Know what?" Pace said breathless, "right on Deagle! I think we should double-time down to the admin CP and volunteer to pull night ambush! Right guys? Let's go! Gung ho!"

The poker-players glanced at Pace. "Dinky dau" one said.

With his gear in hand and a towel around his skinny waist, Deagle headed for the showers.

Buck Sergeant Bill Deagle was a rail, 6'4" and 165 pounds. He was 22 years old, brown-haired and brown-eyed with a scattering of freckles on his cheeks. Looking at him, he seemed to be all bone, wide shoulders, visible ribcage and sharp hipbones, long legs with knobby knees, and long narrow feet. His face was a tight fit on his skull, deep eye-sockets, a broad forehead, and long jaw. Comparing hands with most people, Deagle's were twice as long. But, an ungainly basketball-player, Deagle had been a high school wrestler instead. He was wiry and had unlimited leverage in his long arms and legs. Now, in his sixth month in Vietnam, he was thirty pounds under his wrestling weight because of long duty hours in a steaming jungle climate, a c-ration diet, and a mosquito. Deagle had a tall man's lazy stride and showed the world a cocky, disaffected expression.

The hospital detachment shower for E6's-and-below was fifty meters west of barracks 2338 and was shared with the replacement detachment, which was to say it was almost private. Deagle got there in time to watch a water-tanker pull up and a GI driver jump down from the cab. The driver uncoiled black water hose while a teenage Vietnamese boy climbed the ladder on the back of the shack. A second boy hauled the hose up the ladder to the round tank on the roof. Returning to his truck, the driver spotted Deagle and gave a little salute.

"Burner's on so you still got hot for awhile," he told him.

"Thanks."

The driver opened a valve and the boy-sans shot cool water into the tank. Since the boys were paid a daily rate in piasters they were in no hurry to get the job done and took turns splashing each other. Watching them, Deagle noticed they also took time for a look around the base from their high vantage point. The taller kid pointed here and there off to the east and spoke in rapid Vietnamese.

Deagle didn't like Vietnamese kids much. They seemed to be all hands, always reaching for the Cav wallet from his pocket or the watch on his wrist. A few pocket-picking, disarming children like these had tried to kill him. This pair paid no attention to the truckdriver when he hollered up at them.

"Nguyen that's good enough! Lai dai!"

The boys played, a day at the beach under the hot sun, until the one called Nguyen noticed Deagle watching them. Lowering his voice, Nguyen told the other boy this soldier was a visitor to Bien Hoa, and he pointed out Deagle's faded fatigues and clay-stained combat boots. A grunt, he explained. Nguyen's care-free expression turned mocking. He opened his mouth wide and jumped up and down like an ape, shrieking and scratching his ribs. The boys laughed, the GI driver hollered again. Nguyen stared down and Deagle stared up.

"Nguyen!"

Deagle recognized the defiance in Nguyen's dark eyes; it was the same game the boy-sans in the hamlets played with GI's. Nguyen's eyes said "VC or friendly farmer, you figure it out GI."

"You VC, boy-san," Deagle told him. "You numbah 10."

"Nguyen that's it! Lai dai!"

The driver closed the valve and the boys climbed down. Deagle waited until the truck drove off before stepping inside the shack. He stood under the spray until the hot water was gone, then put on his clean uniform, shaved, brushed his hair and teeth, and walked back to barracks 2338. Everything he owned in the world, except his rifle and sidearm, was on his bunk: pistol belt, empty canteens, fragbags, empty holster, poncho, military compass, P-38 can opener, pocketknife, and a sheaf of in-transit orders, all went into the faded rucksack. He flipped his bottle of mosquito dope into a buttcan half-full of water and cigarette filters.

Taking stock of himself in the hospital mirror, he thought his spare fatigue shirt looked pretty bad by Bien Hoa standards, bleached light green with holes in both pockets. The only places it wasn't faded were on his shoulders and back where his rucksack blocked the hot sun. Without that rucksack on my back, he thought, I look like a fuckin' skunk. But his nametag was legible. On one collar he wore a buck sergeant's 3-chevron pin, on the other collar a 7th Brigade "Garry Owens" insignia. His cuffs were bloused, his red-stained boots were polished. He shouldered into the rucksack.

"Nice-looking target you're wearin', sarge," Pace said, descending on him. "Same same backpack. Your heels will be locked before you make the pisstube."

Deagle turned and looked down at Pace, still in shower shoes and underwear.

"Good luck the rest of your tour, Pace."

"You got orders? Watch out for that deserters' colony they got here?"

"What deserters colony?"

"Barracks down by the motorpool. You haven't heard about it? Permanent party guys with AWOL roommates. Swear to God. The NCO's keep it under observation but they won't go in there. Those dudes got guns and they won't be taken alive."

"So why don't they rush it with MP's, like at 0300?"

"You're all gung ho, you rush it. Some of those guys are killers, man. Meaning our guys. I heard they pay $1000 for DEROS orders back to the world."

Deagle shook his head. He held up his $2 watch, wound it, rapped it, and declared it KIA. It had only lasted a week at LZ Penny, so he dropped it in the butt-can with his bug dope. His plastic Cav wallet was still waterproof, inside it were twelve dry MPC's, his military ID card, a picture of his parents, and a virgin P-38.

"Sarge, the choppers are grounded and the fuzz are on the prowl. But it's your Article 15."

"I can't stay here forever like you, private."

" 'Scuse me. I didn't see your lifer pins."

Deagle's expression should have told the smaller man that he was through bullshitting. "You don't know anything about me, soldier. And you run your mouth too much."

"Want me to drop and give you twenty Sergeant BEAGLE? Fuck you, lifer!"

Pace figured he was quick enough to avoid Deagle's skinny long arms, but he figured wrong. The buck sergeant reached out and caught Pace by the fatigue shirt and slammed him against the metal wall lockers. The impact knocked the wind out of Pace and he stood bellowing like a fish.

At the other end of the barracks, the poker game stopped. "Kick that little fucker's ass, sarge!" one of them told Deagle, "he's got it coming."

Deagle couldn't hit the little guy with his fist. Watching Pace, he re-rolled his shirtsleeves above his knobby elbows.

"What you don't understand, Pace, is that everybody in 'Nam has a case of the ass. I got a case, you have a case, the NCO's and officers got a case, even the gooks have a case of the ass, same same. Everybody hates this place. So what you do... you give everybody some room. Like I tried to give you. You bic?"

Face contorted, Pace nodded.

"Because here's the other thing about that. Next time I give you some room you better take it. You keep pushing... I'll kick your nasty butt all the way to the South China Sea."

Deagle humped southwest around Cav Mountain, taking determined long strides. The sun burned his shoulders through his fatigue shirt, sweat beads popped from his forehead and gushed from his armpits, his boots felt like they were filled with hot sand. After fifty meters he pulled up to drink from his canteen and light a smoke. His head swam and his legs trembled. No damn good, he thought. Can't hump two miles and back today. He scoped the road both ways, looking to hitch-hike a ride in a jeep. He looked back toward the hospital detachment and thought about PFC Pace. Can't go back, either. Not going back to barracks 2338 except in a bag. He moved out again taking smaller steps, and a new hollowness in his belly heartened him, a sensation he barely remembered called hunger. But not for soup or mess hall food. His reward for humping to Big Ben and back this morning would be some stateside snacks from the big PX on this base. A Snickers bar, a bag of Fritos, with an ice-cold glass of juice. He humped beside the beaten trail between hospital and finance and came on a half dozen weathered old mama-sans on a sandbag detail. The private assigned to guard them sat comfortably on a lawn chair in the shade, writing a letter. There was no clip in his M-16.

There were five old ladies in this bunch, squatting on the ground with their backs to him, filling sandbags with spoons and sticks. Four of them wore dirty black pajamas and the fifth had on a mismatched combination of black silk pants and a faded camo fatigue shirt many sizes too big. The way they operated, they stood the bags upright and filled them three-quarters and left them where they stood to be tied and stacked later. They had filled twenty-one bags so far that morning. They were old mama-sans, even for sandbag detail, and painfully slow. Two were so old and sun-shriveled they didn't bother to wear conical hats any more. A third wore a ratty scarf tied over her head to keep the sun off her white hair.

Deagle had learned to pay attention to the old mama-sans too, not just the girl-sans. They were hard to look at with their black teeth and red lips and slitted hateful eyes, and they seemed harmless, frail and always clamoring to get out of your way. But the old ones knew everything there was to know about their village and they had some slick tricks to fool stupid GI's, included kissing ass, selling a nickel bag of Cambodian, recommending where to get a "lob job". Or just yammering so much insane bullshit you thought they were sun-stroked. Anything to distract a soldier from his job, which was finding out where the papa-sans had gone. They knew. He wiped the sweat off his face and watched them work.

They filled one lattice bag at a time, one scoop at a time. The mama-san in the camo shirt was head honcho and did most of the talking, an up-and-down jabber that was both familiar and unintelligible at the same time. Off and on, she put down her spoon and used a stick to scratch a diagram in the sand while the others watched. Curious, Deagle eased up behind her and it was several seconds before she realized he was there. Her drawing was only a series of dots, but, sure enough, when she became aware of him watching she clammed right up. A low warbling came from her throat, a warning to the others. It was a sound cats make before a fight and sent shivers up Deagle's spine.

Furiously, the old woman took her stick and obliterated her diagram. She scratched the sandy ground back and forth until it was featureless. She ran her weathered hands over it making it extra-smooth. Then she turned and squinted up at the intruder, smiling with crimson lips and black teeth.

Deagle smiled down. "Mama-san, let's rap."

The old woman nodded cheerfully. She shifted her gaze from his face to his long arms and fingers, and back again. She was probably seventy years old and as many pounds. Her white straight hair was pulled back against her skull and tied in knot at the base of her neck. Her eyes had long ago lost their delicate almond shape, and she looked up at Deagle through dry slits. Her cheeks were high, lips stained deep red, all her teeth black. White silky hairs grew form her chin and upper lip.

"Mama-san, you VC or friendly farmer?"

She lowered her eyes for a second but kept smiling

"You numbah one," he told her. "You head honcho."

That gave her a laugh. She told the others and they had a good cackle.

"Mama-san, where are all the papa-sans today?"

She picked up her stick and drew in the sand. The finished product was a cigar with two donuts under it.

Deagle played along and grabbed his crotch. "Yeah that's me. How much you want boom-boom short-time?"

She repeated short-time and everybody roared, which disturbed the homesick guard long enough to look up. He saw Deagle and went back to his letter.

"You go Sin City," she told Deagle. "You make lub."

"Sin City. Yeah they got one of those here, too. Maybe I can work a little balling into my schedule. Probably need a pass. Good place to be if the papa-sans start throwing 60 mike-mikes at this base. Which... I'd say is a possibility."

"*Khong biet*," she answered softly.

"Like hell you don't, mama-san."

The old lady shook her head and clucked her tongue, something in his tone put her off. As he shifted his weight from his right to his left foot she hugged herself and ducked, expecting the hard toe of his boot against the side of her head. When the kick didn't come she opened her weathered slits and took up her stick and drew ragged lines in the shape of cone. Then with surprising agility, she stood up and waddled away, and squatted beside another pile of sand. Conversation over.

The guard folded his letter and stuffed it into his fatigue shirt pocket. He looked at his watch and stood up, yawning.

"Hi, Sarge," he said. "Time to di di ladies. Move out. Di di mau!"

Deagle watched them trudge away in front of the guard's empty M-16 rifle. He looked down at the drawing in the sand.

It took a few seconds to realize it was supposed to be a Christmas tree.

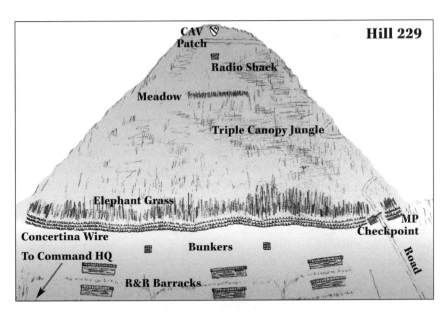

Hill 229

CAV Patch

Radio Shack

Meadow

Triple Canopy Jungle

Elephant Grass

Concertina Wire

To Command HQ

Bunkers

R&R Barracks

MP Checkpoint

Road

CHAPTER THREE

0745Hours 23Dec71
1st Cav Div HQ
Offices, Brig. Gen. Jeffrey Webb

"Fifteen minutes, sir," Colonel Shipp advised, poking his head in the open door. Webb looked up from his desk. "Thank you, colonel."

"Good news from records branch. They found us a Silver Star winner for the press conference. Buck sergeant from 7th Brigade."

"That is good news."

Webb's attention returned to the stack of intelligence reports on Hill 229 that Colonel Borg had assembled. The file was thick enough to allot hours for serious study but, like all army dossiers, it was formatted and easily scanned. There were 9th Infantry Division and 11th Mechanized Infantry field reports, 11th Engineer debriefings, notes from previous HQ commanders, plus photocopies of old morning reports beginning in 1964. 1st Cav documentation of the hill began in July 1968. That date called up a bitter reflection: July '68, Webb had been new in-country and serving with 3rd Army up in the central highlands. Back when the army thought it would win in Vietnam.

In those by-gone days, the enemy in both the north and the south was referred to as "The Communists" or "The Insurgents", before the pajama-clad

65

Viet Cong were separated from the uniformed North Vietnamese Army. Webb hadn't seen the term "insurgents" in a debriefing in years.

According to Company A 1st Battalion 9th Infantry Engineers, Bien Hoa was an open door in June 1964. It was all peaceful countryside and French-influenced white-painted buildings and tree-lined streets. When the engineers moved in with a mission to plan and build a military installation to house an estimated 20,000 soldiers and airmen, the enemy apparently moved out. There were no NVA units this far south. After weeks of studying topographical maps, plotting supply routes, and exploring the city and surrounding villages in jeep-patrols, Lieutenant Colonel Gerald L Hayes selected a base site consisting of four square miles of flat, light foliage gently-rolling hills between the north-east side of Bien Hoa City and the South China Sea. At the geographic center of Hayes' new base was a promontory with the topographic map designation Hill 229. Hayes thought the hill was the perfect spot for a radio shack. He used 250 tons of explosives and spent six weeks to blast two twisting single-lane dirt roads all the way to the top. One road on the north side for the army, one on the south for the future air force.

In the early reports, June through October 1964, the engineers complained in writing about the climate and the temperature in Vietnam. One-hundred to one-hundred-twenty degrees at mid-day, mid-seventies and eighties at night; two or three inches of pounding, straight-down rain every afternoon, and swarms of mosquitoes. They were either hot or wet all the time and they spent considerable time putting up temporary shelters to hide from the sun and the monsoons and the bugs. Factoring in a daily ninety-plus average relative humidity, base construction fell quickly behind schedule.

First things first, the engineers defoliated the perimeter and put up a fence around the new base, a barrier of concertina wire sixteen miles around and 200 meters deep. Then they laid out the ammo dumps, tank parks, supply depots, jet and diesel farms, and the airstrips. As combat infantry and artillery troops were levied and shipped out from the US and the forward firebases were mapped and manned, there came the need for the support troops, the purpose of a large central base at Bien Hoa. These troops would be "permanent party" at Bien Hoa and would serve their full 364-day tours in Vietnam there, providing the infantry with logistical and clerical support. They needed permanent barracks for sleeping quarters, not tents and hooches, and there were just two design guidelines: air circulation and mosquito protection.

GI sleeping quarters were 20'x 60' barracks, ten men to a side with a center aisle. The walls were two-thirds wooden siding and one-third fine metal screening, for ventilation. Roofs were corrugated metal with sandbags every square meter for ballast. Around each barracks was a three-foot high double layer of sandbags, a flak wall against future in-coming rockets and mortars. With so much rain, it was necessary to dig run-off trenches between barracks, east-west and north-south. Local Vietnamese were recruited from the villages to fill sandbags on base between 0500 and 1300 hours, after which time it became so hot it was hard to breathe.

Mess halls, command posts, administration complexes, NCO and officer's clubs, and motor pools quickly followed, all with the same basic open-air construction. Arms rooms, the finance detachment, and the commanding officer's office/bunker complex were constructed with block walls. By mid-July when the rainy season ended, Bien Hoa was eighty percent complete and home to the 9th Infantry Division, the 11th Mechanized, and the Air Force's 3rd and 13th Air Combat Squadrons and 5th Air Support Wing. Daily combat missions were flown and walked, logistic pipelines were filled, rear support became fully operational. On the army side, a 9th Infantry Division commanding general was named and he reported at Bien Hoa to assume his duties and inspect the new installation.

At 0600 hours 20Jul64 a convoy of officers escorted Major General Ames Ludwig around his division headquarters. Barely daylight, Ludwig immediately spotted the tall, steep hill less than fifty meters from his enlisted barracks. He asked to see the reconnaissance reports on the hill; the engineers had not done a recon of the hill. But they had stuck a radio shack on the summit, Ludwig was told, and the hill was "Uniform Sierra". The 9th Infantry XO wrote that his new commanding general "had a case of the ass about that hill".

Reading, Webb shook his head. "Me too, pal. Somebody had his head up his."

Webb read where Ludwig permitted his new troops to live in the barracks at the base of Hill 229 but only after the engineers built a de-militarized zone around it, rings of needle-barbed concertina wire. Then he ordered a month of ground reconnaissance patrols and air surveillance to find what else, besides a radio shack, was up there.

Webb flipped pages in Borg's folder until he found a paper-clipped sheaf of 9th Engineers recon reports, August through October 1964. The reports were impressively formal, each with a stated mission and S-2 summary and the signatures of both the company commander and XO. Starting at the radio shack, eleven-man squads of engineers armed with ANPRC-25 field radios and M-16 rifles, and plenty of water and salt tablets, sortied down into the jungle. They encountered a treacherous 45-degree angle descent, jeep sized rocks, craters, sheer drop-offs, frequent triple-canopy jungle that blocked out the sun, heavy ground brush, and all around the base of the hill a 100-ft deep band of elephant grass mixed with clump bamboo. After a week of patrols, they reported seeing not one living thing, not a human being or gorilla or even an animal trail.

One squad reported an attempt to penetrate the twelve-foot elephant grass from below, finding it sharp enough to cut skin and thick as dog-hair. Two steps into it, at 0800 hours on a bright morning, they reported being blind, visibility one foot. The humidity in there was five-hundred percent. Against the steep angle, they pushed up through the tall grass in a head-to-tail circus animal formation and it took forty minutes for eleven men to get through it. The grass ripped their skin, snatched the steel pots from their head, tangled in the rifle slings and flash suppressors and trigger guards. Above the elephant grass they reported "medium foliage", jungle that was waist high to head high with 10-20 meters visibility. One captain wrote, "it is safe to assume that if we can't see ten meters neither can the communists."

Webb turned pages. Borg had tucked a few old MAC-V reports in the Hill 229 folder. The source, no doubt, of Borg's "big picture" at Bien Hoa. One report suggested that as many as "100,000 male residents of Bien Hoa and surrounding villages may have fled the area ahead of the 9th Infantry Division, between May and July 1964". Half of them were assumed to be communist. Another S-2 report dated September '64 featured the recognizable initials of the III-Corp Commander at the time, Major General Thomas Ottson, signing off at the bottom. "Beginning in September," Ottson wrote "an estimated 50,000 migrating refugees are now stick-building shantytown villages using discarded military trash, in a perimeter around Bien Hoa. This development is a repeat of the tactic used by the communists at Da Nang near the DMZ in I-Corps and it may indicated a longer than expected campaign in III-Corps." Following up, a September MAC-V directive instructed commanders at Bien Hoa and Long Bihn to carefully screen all Vietnamese laborers approved to work on base and to confine them in fenced compounds after 1600 hours.

Sp6 Meredith knocked on Webb's door and walked in carrying a mug of black coffee. "Ten minutes, sir," he advised, and Webb nodded. He read where Ludwig's demilitarized zone around the hill was defoliated again and fortified with bunkers.

But it was on September 2nd 1964 that the engineers discovered Hill 229's biggest secret to date: it had been fought over before, perhaps taken and re-taken at least once. 400 meters above the enlisted barracks, the engineers found a twelve-inch crack in a bolder. At the bottom the crack was a cache of old French-manufactured rifle ammunition. It was useless, virtually soldered into a clump of green verdigris fungus, but it finally sent up the distress flare.

In September 1964 whole companies of infantrymen fanned out to explore Hill 229.

At about center latitude a master sergeant fell into a hollow, later determined to be an artillery shell crater. French artillery fire in the 1950's. At the bottom of the crater was a tunnel entrance, the tunnel led into a cave the size of closet. The engineers blew the tunnel and found the bones of a long-dead Viet Minh fighter. A generation ago the communists were burying their dead rather than let the enemy count them. Taking a closer look at the large rocks on the hill, networks of caves were found.

October 1964, Ludwig made the decision to destroy and defoliate Hill 229.

Troops living in the barracks all around the hill were temporarily evicted. Air force phantoms screamed overhead dropping high explosive bombs that gouged out great hunks of rock. Cobra helicopter gunships sprayed the caves with M-60 rounds and rockets, a virtual practice range. After two weeks of daily raids the hill began to show a patchwork of brown under its emerald green. The air force hit it with phase II, twice-a day chemical defoliating, until the silhouette of Hill 229 was a rust-colored tit against the blue Bien Hoa skyline. The hill stank of herbicide and was declared off limits to all personnel. On October 25th, more coils of sharp concertina wire were added to the no-man's land between the hill and the barracks and the troops were allowed to return to their old homes. A plywood 9th Infantry insignia was placed above the radar detachment on the summit. Hill 229 was formally cleared and declared a US possession.

Webb's office door opened and Colonel Shipp stuck his head in, stroking his cactus-needle waxed mustache. "Time, sir," he drawled.

"Just one more minute."

During TET 1965, communist mortars were launched from the new refugee villages around Bien Hoa and a few of them hit buildings. The next afternoon a mortar landed on a main air force runway a few hundred feet short of a jet-fuel bladder the size of a tennis court. The 60mm round dug a five-foot hole in the runway and sent troops running for the bunkers. The shooter must have had a good view, because he corrected and his next shot hit the three-inch fuel line between the bladder and a tanker truck. The blast lifted a 6x6 MP checkpoint off its pilings and hurled it onto the runway; the fuel truck exploded and killed the driver, and the 150,000-gallon fuel bladder ignited and sent a burning cloud five miles high. The perimeter siren sounded and convoys of reinforcement troops were sent to the towers. Two-man teams armed with M-60 machine guns watched the floodlit sectors of concertina wire, waiting for the invasion of Bien Hoa. The officer-of-the-day recorded that a 9th Infantry enlisted clerk had heard the pop of a mortar being launched right over his head, from somewhere on Hill 229.

In less than four months, while nobody had noticed, Hill 229 had regenerated itself to about fifty percent heavy cover, enough for somebody to sneak up there, shoot a few 60 mike-mikes, and sneak back down.

Next morning before 0800 two companies of clerks, truck drivers, quartermaster specialists, and cooks were trucked up the switch-backed road to the radio detachment. On line, they swept down the north face of 229-er in an attempt to flush the communists into the waiting bunker guns at the bottom on the hill. Troops got lost or ended up on the air force side; others gave up and came down by the road. A few even lost their weapons. There were casualties ranging from scratches and blisters to broken legs. Troops who did make it down to the bottom through the second-growth elephant grass reported they hadn't seen anything because they couldn't see - period. Depressing.

Webb turned pages and read the litany of poor American military performance by both the 9th Infantry and the transplanted 1st Cavalry Division. December 26, '66, during the Christmas cease-fire, a satchel charge blew out the side of barracks 2119. TET '67, a dozen American casualties including a KIA from communist rockets. May '67, 60mm mortars and RPG's launched from Hill 229 landed on an airmen's club, WIA's and KIA's. December '67, 9th Infantry Commander Ludwig and his XO at Bien Hoa, Colonel Hart, rotated to the US and were replaced. The new XO added more concertina wire and more floodlights between the hill and his enlisted sleeping quarters. February '68, during the heaviest yet TET offensive, snipers on Hill 229 killed a 2nd lieutenant standing in front of a guard formation. July 1968, 9th Infantry shipped out and HQ 1st Cav moved to Bien Hoa from An Khe. The Cav XO made the decision to use the barracks at the base of Hill 229 not for his permanent party troops but for his in-transits, his R&R's, DEROS's, casual hospital, and replacement detachment. He built an MP checkpoint with a gate to guard the road leading to the top of Hill 229. August '68, communist sappers, now referred to as Viet Cong, destroyed DEROS barracks 2232, killing two infantrymen who had served their tours of Vietnam and were returning home. Christmas Eve 1968, during the cease-fire again, Viet Cong from Hill 229 slipped past the MP checkpoint, around the bunkers, and left satchels of explosive inside R&R barracks 2020: barracks destroyed, more KIA's.

Webb slammed the file down on his desk and shoved himself out of his chair. He stepped out in the hall and found Colonel Shipp and Sp6 Meredith anxiously waiting.

"A wire within a wire," he said out loud. "Son of a bitch." Then he strode down the hall to meet the Red Cross ladies.

0840 Hours 23Dec71
1st Cav Div HQ
HQ Reception Room, Division Sergeant Major 'Bud' Bierra

Standing in front of Division Sergeant Major Bierra's desk with his blue-and-gold cavalry hat in hand and his .45 semi-auto hanging from its black leather shoulder holster, Major Andrews began to worry. General Webb was ten minutes late. He paced to the wall and back to the desk with his morning reports, 11-Bravo rosters, and his personal map of Hill 229 tucked under his arm. He was inclined to ask the sergeant major if General Webb was in the building but Bierra had no time for him; he was busy with paperwork and phone-calls to MAC-V. Bierra's enlisted clerks banged away on their IBM selectrics and likewise ignored him.

Andrews did not approve the Cav's current division sergeant major. Bierra was cut of the same cloth as Lieutenant St John, the difference being that the lieutenant honestly didn't know he was a prig. Bierra wore his arrogance for the world to see, in his disapproving gaze and simpering little grin. Instead of a military haircut, Bierra wore his brown hair up in a pompadour, like an actor. Instead of clean jungle fatigues, Bierra wore tailored stateside fatigues, which to Andrews looked prissy. But the final proof, as far as Andrews was concerned, was that Bierra kept a dictionary and thesaurus on his desk, possibly the only E-9 in the army concerned about grammar and vocabulary. While Bierra did wear a combat infantryman's badge on his fatigues, Andrews suspected he had never fired a rifle in a firefight. Someday, he thought, he'd have Bierra's 201 file pulled and have a peek inside.

It was widely known that Sergeant Major Bierra was not content serving as the highest ranking non-com in the 1st Cav and had applied to the Department of the Army for a direct commission, a promotion to lieutenant or captain. Bierra's contemporaries reported being interviewed by MAC-V about his personality and job performance. Superior officers in Cav HQ had signed letters of recommendation. Requesting a direct commission from a combat zone was clever timing by Bierra but the organizational wheels turned slowly 15,000 miles from the Pentagon, so he'd been waiting months for a decision. Andrews doubted that the Pentagon was impressed by a big vocabulary.

"Better get out of the habit of calling me Bud," Bierra said quietly into the phone. "But thanks for the heads-up." He hung up and glanced up at Andrews, then brought out a zippered leather notebook and jotted a few lines.

Andrews turned his back to the sergeant major and looked around the 1st Cav reception room. The new commanding general had made some changes. The visitor's couches were gone, replaced by a row of straight back chairs. Table lamps had been replaced with overhead fluorescent lights. Andrews approved of both changes; this was a field headquarters not a doctor's office. Webb's single concession to luxury was allowing the old 9th Infantry swamp-cooler air conditioning system to remain operational, which it was - just barely. Pretty damn quick, Andrews thought, the whole Bien Hoa AO would be shaping up, looking military spare and spotless. Particularly offensive to Andrews were the private suites his enlisted troops had constructed in their barracks. Another time, he thought, after General Webb had come to rely on him, he'd mention knocking down all those interior barracks walls.

The major looked down with approval at the concrete floor, dusted and spit-shine bright. The cement block walls had been painted a pastel shade of Cav yellow but were unadorned except for 1st Cav unit citations and commendations and the 3'x5' portraits of the Cav's two most celebrated commanders, General Douglas MacArthur and Lieutenant Colonel George Custer. Andrews checked his watch, 0842. He glanced down at his gleaming combat boots and cleared his throat, speaking to the Custer portrait.

"I always thought," he said conversationally, "that we ought to display Custer as a general. Maybe an old Civil War tin-type."

Bierra spoke without looking up. "Custer was riffed to lieutenant colonel after the Civil War. Sir."

Andrews knew that - Everybody knew that. And that wasn't his point. There was no point, he thought, in having a casual discussion with Bierra.

"And I always wondered," Bierra added, looking up at the portrait, "why the Cav maintains with such panegyric reverence its most conspicuous failure, an officer who got himself and his whole command slaughtered on the battlefield."

"Pana...?"

Bierra snickered and returned to his paperwork "What was that place called, sir?"

Andrews glowered. Every Cav troop knew where Custer died. It was everyday conversation, called the Little Bighorn. Bierra was rattling his cage. He thought, I'll show the arrogant bastard...

"Greasy Grass Creek," he said, looking up at the portrait.

Bierra's haughty grin slipped.

"All serious Custer buffs," Andrews told him, "know the Sioux spent summers at Greasy Grass. Of course, at Fort Lincoln the 7th Cavalry called it something else: the Valley of the Little Bighorn River."

"Ah. The Little Big Horn," Bierra repeated. "Where three-hundred went up against two-thousand. Custer was a zealot, in today's parlance, a warmonger. And his S-2 was flawed, wouldn't you say, sir?"

Andrews looked beyond Bierra and kept his control. What a horse's rear end.

Behind the sergeant major's desk was the unmarked door leading to the inner HQ offices. Major Andrews had never been back there but knew General Webb's offices were there, plus the S-1 through S-4, some clerical staff, command briefing rooms, and the commanding general's BOQ. At 0845 hours on his watch he was thinking he'd never get behind that door, Webb was in Saigon or some place, when it opened and Colonel Shipp waved him back.

He followed the old colonel down a corridor that intersected a hall with offices left and right. The office doors were painted in Cav black and yellow and were left open to get a little cool air. Colonel Shipp's S-3 office was smaller than his own office at admin, just a metal desk, a pair of four-drawer file cabinets, and two folding chairs. Shipp sat down, smoothed his mustache, and indicated his visitor's chair. Major Andrews preferred to stand at-ease.

A minute later Colonel Borg's big-bellied form appeared in the open doorway, talking to somebody down the hall. He had a mug of coffee in hand and a manila folder under his arm. Andrews acknowledged the senior support officer with a slight incline of his head. Borg stepped in and sat his tired buttocks on Shipp's desk, and his gaze settled on Andrews' bright purple skin-graft.

Hiding monumental disappointment, Andrews stared through the open door. If this was Borg's show, he knew, he was blown away and might as well take his toys and go home. Suddenly his mouth was too dry to swallow.

But this time Borg wasn't lecturing. This time he just sat watching Colonel Shipp reading old 9th Infantry debriefings. Then he mumbled about journalists on base and Lima Zulu Judith, but Shipp shook his head. Major Andrews felt his heart quicken, the colonels were killing time. Then, there he was, closing the door behind him: the tall commanding general of the 1st Cavalry Division Air-Mobile.

"Ten Hut!" Andrews called out. Colonel Shipp got up out of his chair and Borg slid off the desk

"As you were," Webb said quietly, setting the tone for the briefing.

Webb's eyes searched the room and settled on Andrews' fleshy face and the big bruise-colored scar above his right ear. He walked directly to Major Andrews and stood in front of him at inspection distance. It was quiet enough to hear the faint hum of the over-matched air conditioning system.

"Major, excuse my tardiness. I understand you have concerns about Hill 229 during the upcoming cease-fire. So do I."

"Yes, SIR!"

"Stand at ease, major. What is it you are recommending?"

"A full battalion sweep, sir. Truck the men to the top and sweep down to the bottom. Flush any Victor Charlies into the bunker guns."

With that good start, Andrews walked to the near wall and unfurled his personal 3'x3'sized map of Hill 229. He tacked it at eye level where all the officers could see it, then stepped back.

General Webb approached with narrowed eyes. "Where has this been?" he asked.

"In my AO, sir. The admin command post. I've taken it upon myself to keep track of the enemy contact from 229-er, sir."

Webb noted the corps of engineers designation in the bottom right corner, and the date 22May64. Major Andrews had started from a blank elevation map and, hobby or otherwise, had put together the best representation Webb had seen yet of the Hill 229's terrain and density. More impressive, in the map's right-hand margin, in neat upright printing, was a complete combat chronology going back to the year the United States 9th Infantry first took control of Hill 229. For each combat entry in the margin, sapper or sniper or 60 mm mortar, Major Andrews designated a specific point of origin on the hill.

The map was a ground-level view, like a tall photograph showing the north face of Hill 229 where it towered over the 1st Cav's in-transit detachments. The 690-meter 45-degree hill was broken into a patchwork of green colors, from deep British green to a pastel lime, and everything in between. The darker the color, the heavier the foliage. The impenetrable ring of elephant grass and bamboo at the base of the hill was almost black in color. Triple canopy jungle was the same ominous deep green. Ordinary walking jungle, thick brush with spindly trees and vines, was lawn green. Rock formations were brown, trails were red, old VC caves were bright yellow.

There were two features on this map that jumped out at the commanding general. He'd seen daylight surveillance photography of the areas but nothing longitudinal. They were the two white areas, the only white on the map, and indicated open ground. No foliage. The first was about two-thirds the way up the north face, map designation "The Meadow" a rectangular stripe about forty meters deep by two hundred meters wide, east to west. Andrews showed a red VC trail entering The Meadow from above and leaving it below. Webb was not familiar with The Meadow but Andrews' margin references rang a bell: he'd just finished reading about them in Colonel Borg's file. The other white area was a little triangle at the bottom of the hill on the far right, labeled "Garbage Dump".

Webb reached out and tapped his finger. "This dump still in use?"

The question was directed at nobody so Colonel Borg answered. "Yes, sir. We still haul trash out there and bury it."

Webb looked at Andrews. "Significance Major Andrews?"

"Still in use by the VC too, sir. Charles is in there every night stealing chow."

Borg's smile was condescending. "Local Vietnamese, sir. Boys who work on the base and know the kind of garbage we throw out."

"I respectfully dispute the colonel on that point, sir. In the past, hardcore VC have been caught and killed in that dump."

"Operative word - past," Borg responded.

But Webb nodded his appreciation. "This division owes you a debt Major Andrews. I look at your map and I understand why 9th Infantry put wire inside their own wire. What else could they do, that hill was no-man's land. Still is, really. What about this white stripe here, 'The Meadow'? Is it walk-able?"

"Flat as that desk, sir. The French bulldozed it in 1951 to billet a mortar company up there, but they didn't finish the job. It's thirty-five meters deep and two-hundred meters end to end."

"Grass?"

"Yes sir, knee deep. It's Charlie's formation area. He climbs out of the caves, forms up there, then follow the trail down."

Emboldened, Major Andrews stepped up beside the general and tapped the upper center of the hill. "Here is where they'll break the truce, sir. I know damn well they're up there, staging to hit us. You just look at the gooks working on this base, you look in their eyes... they know. They know when and where. Bastards look at you like you're already blown away."

Webb concentrated on the map. 9Nov69, two 60mm mortars landed in the division motorpool: 10Nov69, in a clearing fifty meters below the radio shack, a rusty mortar tube is captured by a recon patrol. It its fullness, Andrews' map told the story he'd just read in Colonel Borg's folder, between the two he could visually condense three years of VC terrorism at Bien Hoa. Half of the 1st Cav casualties attributed to Hill 229 occurred during the two big holidays, TET and Christmas.

"So you think I should order a pre-emptive strike," he said finally.

"I do, sir. We can't hit the hill with air strikes or artillery with troops living so close. We tried mini-guns from cobra's and puff-the-magic-dragon in '66 and again in '68, with no effect. We bombed it with defoliants but the damn jungle just grew back. That leaves just troops, sir."

At this point Borg stepped to the map and with his fingers splayed and traced a line from summit to base. "9th Infantry and 1st Cav have swept this hill dozens of times. While our gunships have killed one or two VC up there, sir, battalion-size missions have never produced a body count or even gained us a piece of intelligence. Which does not show on Major Andrews' map. This hill is too steep and too thick for any size on-line assault."

Andrews nodded, his expression tight. "Affirmative, sir, and I agree with most of what the colonel says but there's a reason. We were using the wrong..."

But Webb had already taken a step back from the map, having made up his mind. "We'll stand by the cease-fire preparations in the a.m. briefing."

Pleased, Borg replied. "Yes, sir."

Webb glanced back at Colonel Shipp. "Comment, colonel?"

"Matter of fact, yes, sir. If it was me... I wouldn't risk troops. But despite what General Garlett says, I'd re-locate R&R and DEROS and bomb the shit outa that hill through the cease-fire. That hill plain gives me the creeps."

Webb turned 90-degrees to face Major Andrews. "The colonel's point is that I can't order a pre-emptive strike without provocation. Every soldier in this man's army works for somebody, and I have a III-Corps Commander to answer to. But I appreciate your concern for the safety of our troops."

Looking in Webb's eyes, Andrews felt an overwhelming closeness to him. "Sir," he croaked, "permission to speak freely to the commanding general!"

"Granted."

"Sir, I am sick of losing this war because of congressional committees and one-way rules of engagement! For this sweep we should let the infantry do the job."

"What infantry?"

"1st Cav Infantry Air-Mobile, sir. There are 236 of them assigned to us right now and more coming!"

It took a moment for the concept to sink in. Seated at his desk, Colonel Shipp's left hand went from his glasses to his mustache. Colonel Borg's long back slowly straightened, eyes on Andrews. And General Webb, who caught onto Andrews' idea immediately, waited for more detail. It was Colonel Borg who finally broke silence.

"You want to use infantrymen from R&R and DEROS to sweep of Hill 229?"

Colonel Shipp's eyes bugged out in disbelief. "What the hell are you talking about? We can't do that."

Andrews gave nothing away by his expression and maintained the position of attention. "I'd like to sweep with 11-Bravos, sir. Not 74-Hotel clerks. I'd like to win, for once, and the hell with Senator Symington."

"Those men were volunteers," Borg reminded.

"With no combat experience. Sir, I'm advised we're on solid ground UCMJ-wise."

Borg shook his head. "Major, it's finally happened. That plate in your head is putting pressure on your brain... You're out of your mind!"

"Just a moment, Colonel." Webb said. "Major Andrews, why don't you fine-tune your thinking for me."

"General," Borg protested, "it's lunacy... he's looney!"

"Colonel, don't make me lock your jaws. Go ahead, major."

Andrews had visualized this moment, a calm and rational appeal, one-on-one, to his commanding general, a fellow combat infantryman. "Sir, it's now zero-nine-hundred hours. We have men of the 1st, 7th, 8th, and 9th Brigades sitting around, doing nothing while there are no R&R flights. In addition, I have a current roster of every admin soldier with 11-Bravo training, and those are the only troops I'd add. By 1200 hours I can have a full battalion in formation and ready to board trucks. On top I can sweep them down through the caves, flush out Charles and blow him away, and be back down long before the 1800 cease-fire deadline. Sir, the Christmas cease-fire is why Charles is on Hill 229."

Webb consulted the map. If Charles is up there, he argued with himself, the infantry would have a better chance of finding him than clerks and cooks. And there are no regulations that say we can't use in-transit infantrymen for a rear-area sweep, but there are moral considerations. Contrarily, even the infantry's chances of finding Charles with a sweep are slim and a night ambush is a better operation. Risking the lives of R&R and DEROS troops in a combat mission is damn desperate... yet they're at risk just sleeping in those barracks...

"Major Andrews, you are well-prepared and I appreciate that in an officer. And I don't like losing either, and I especially don't like my in-transit troops billeted at the foot of that hill like sitting ducks. So tell me about the upcoming cease-fire. Do you have current S-2, a week or a month old? A captured AK-47 assault rifle, a VC collaborator... I'd settle for a cave and a fresh pile of crap! With any of these I'll go to MAC-V and together we'll smoke Charles around the clock. Yes or no, major."

Staring straight into the neck of his commanding general, Andrews answered clearly: "No, sir, not at this time."

The fire in Webb's eyes flared out. "Then my answer has to be negative. But I'm going to pull rank and keep your map. Colonel Shipp, please police up my map and hang it in the briefing room." He about-faced and headed for the open doorway.

"Ten HUT" Borg called out, snapping to attention.

"As you were," Webb called back, and disappeared in the hallway.

Shipp escorted Major Andrews to the door leading to Bierra's reception room and walked back. Borg sat flipping 9th Infantry debriefings on terrorism originating from Hill 229, skim-reading.

"That was close," he said.

"Andrews is a section eight, Phil. That's obvious. What say we send a discreet TWIX to Walter Reed Hospital and find out the extent of his head wound, then maybe call MAC-V and see if we can't get him rotated back to the world. He gives me the creeps like his hill."

Borg held his arms wide. "What have I been saying? I'll send the TWIX myself."

Major Andrews stepped outside and squinted into the overhead sun. He felt good, surprisingly good, despite Colonel Borg's attempt to humiliate him. Plate putting pressure on my head. Webb had seen through that. "I'll show you pressure, colonel," he thought. "that was just the first skirmish... the cease-fire lasts three days and three nights..."

Sergeant Hooper saluted from the jeep as Andrews jumped into the front seat.

"How'd it go, sir. Do we saddle up?"

"Went okay, Hoop. But General Webb is new to Bien Hoa and Colonel Borg still has the upper hand. Borg thinks I'm deranged."

"Sir, meaning no offense to a superior officer, that Colonel Borg is about a smart as a damn duck. Them gooks are up there for sure."

Hooper let out the clutch and the jeep lurched forward.

After a good look around the R&R detachment, PFC Jim Grossnickel
announced his grand plan for a first morning at Bien Hoa: check M-16's at the
arms room and hit the mess hall for a hot breakfast, then go to finance for some
cash, learn where the R&R processing points were, records and medical etc, find
the PX and buy snacks and street clothes, hump to the AT&T shack and make the
call home...

"And if we got time, we'll score some smoke and have a few beers in the EM
Club."

"I think we should find Deagle," Pomeroy said.

"That still blows my mind," Jim said. "Calling my folks in Alexandria, Virginia
from 'Nam... at Christmas!"

"We got three days for all that shit, over. Let's play it cool, get set up in a
barracks, then find our best buddy."

"What the hell is wrong with you? You've been acting goofy since we got off
that chopper. No, before that, since we got on the chopper at Penny."

Pomeroy shrugged it off. "What if all the R&R flights are full. I'm just trying
not to get my hopes up."

"Bullshit. We earned it and we're fuckin' going. But you're right about playing
it cool. We gotta dump our sixteen's. Besides guard duty, we're the only troops on
this base carrying weapons."

The admin arms room was a short hike down toward the motor pool. It was
an all-block building like a stateside arms room, complete with the dutch double-
locking doors facing the street. When Pomeroy and Grossnickel walked up, the
top half of the door was swung open and the armorer sat at his desk with two
fans going. He was hatless and barefoot, wore fatigue pants and a green t-shirt
with his dog-tags hanging out. The plaque on his desk identified him as "Sp6
Karuda, Admin Armorer".

From the doorway, Grossnickel saw that Karuda's arms room was
maintained inspection-ready. It was spit-shine bright and smelled of powder
solvent. Karuda's disassembly bay was a clean as kitchen table. In the darkness
behind the desk and file cabinets Jim saw a thousand M-16 gunbarrels retained
by chains and heavy brass locks in wooden racks, pointed skyward. Karuda pulled
forms and claim-checks from his file cabinet and instructed him and Pomeroy to
lay their weapons on the door's broad surface.

"Well," he said, looking at the rifles before the troops, "I seen worse. Where
you boys comin' from?"

"LZ Penny," Jim said, reading Karuda as a lifer. The Sp6 had dull blue eyes
and thinning curly red hair. In his lower lip was a brown wad of snuff.

"DEROS?"

"R&R, over," Pomeroy answered.

Karuda held Pomeroy's rifle at port arms and looked it over from flash-suppressor to buttstock. "Too bad. Me, I got fourteen days left in this hot son of a bitch." He looked up and saw Corporal Pomeroy for the first time and couldn't help a double-take. "Jesus Christ, boy, chow must be good at LZ Penny."

Pomeroy heard that one too. "Solid muscle. What do we do, collect these before we catch a slick back?"

Karuda nodded.

One rifle at a time he carried out his inspection. He locked bolts to rear, and looked into the actions, check spring tension in the magazine ports, slid the back bolts into battery and worked the fire selectors. "I'll get 'em back as-issue for you troops," he said. "Need some work. Sign them forms and tear the off the bottom half and DON"T fuckin' lose 'em in Bangkok, or wherever you're going"

"Which way to the AT&T shack," Jim asked.

Karuda jerked his thumb west. "Half a mile that way. "You boys can leave your gear here, them bandoliers and rucksacks, if you want. I'll clean 'em up."

The infantrymen were only too glad to be rid of the weight. Business concluded Sp6 Karuda leaned on his counter wearing a conspiratorial grin. "You troops want to see my prisoner? Got him right in back?"

Jim squinted into the darkness behind the armorer. "Government Issue or Victor Charlie?"

"Deserter. Got him chained every which-way. He ain't catching no free ride to the world. He's going to LBJ"

Pomeroy grabbed Jim by the back of the shirt and effortlessly spun him 180 degrees. "That's what happens to guys walking around without orders, over. Thanks anyway specialist."

"You an RTO, ain't ya," Karuda told Pomeroy. "Shit you're big enough to carry a Prick-25 and a M-60 machine gun both!"

"I'm an RTO."

Karuda leaned closer. "They're payin' $500 MPC for one-each ANPRC-25 radio. If you happen to know of one that's gone AWOL."

Pomeroy's eyes bugged. "How would you get it back to the world?"

Karuda held his smile. "How would I know?"

"Not interested," Pomeroy told him, "negative, no fucking way."

Weaponless, they humped up the street to the admin formation area, stopped to read the notices on the admin bulletin board, then entered the command post. Inside they found Sergeant Hooper at his desk talking on the phone. To the right, in a separate office, a major and a lieutenant sat on opposite sides of a desk likewise talking into telephones. The plaque above that door read "Major Warren Andrews, Admin Battalion Commander". On the wall behind Hooper was a blue-and-yellow 7th Cavalry flag.

"Hey check it out," Jim said. "Old Custer's flag. Gary Owens forever!"

Sergeant Hooper put a hand over the phone, "What do you troops need?"

"We're in the 7th , sarge! What R&R barracks are we in?"

Hooper pointed up the street and told them to see Sergeant Boyd when they got there. Then he went back to his phone conversation.

"You think we'll get orders by 1700?" Pomeroy interrupted again. "Sarge, we need those orders, we just heard some troop was chained up in the arms room and we don't want to be in there next to him, you bic?"

Mildly irritated, the red-nosed little NCO said "Sir, I got troops standing at my desk, I'll have to call you back. Spell that name, if you would, sir. D, as in Delta, E as in Echo, Alpha... Golf... Lima... Echo. Deagle. Affirm, sir."

Pomeroy and Grossnickel looked at each other and grinned. "Deagle, as in US-type Sergeant Deagle William S.? " Jim asked.

"You know him?"

"He's our platoon sergeant, sure we know him. He's been here three weeks in your hosp...

But Pomeroy cut him off before he could finish. "What do they want him for, sarge?"

"Beats the hell outa me. That was Colonel Wilcox's adjutant." Hooper rubbed his palms together and cackled like a chicken. "Now ain't this the luck."

He picked up the phone and called Sergeant Boyd at R&R, gave him instructions to set up his two grunt buddies, Pomeroy and Grossnickel, with first class bunks near a front or rear door. Then he called enlisted orders branch and waited while Specialist Mahaffey confirmed both 2nd of the 7th troops were having orders cut "In-transit R&R". Hanging up the phone, he glanced into the other office and saw Major Andrews using the MAC-V telephone line.

"Lissen up men. It'd go real good just now for my major if you could p'lice up this here buck sergeant for me. I'm sure he ain't in no trouble; trouble around here is a MP Lieutenant name of Fredrick, so you steer clear of him 'til you get orders in your empty wallets. Prob'ly some Red Cross donut dolly has a case of the ass at Deagle cause he ain't wrote to his mama. See it all the time. You bring Deagle to my desk, ASAP... I'll get you into the NCO club tonight for the live show."

"Round-eyed show?" Jim asked.

"Taiwan, next best thing. They do all the good songs, Beatles, Stones, Doors, whattaya say?"

Jim started to spill his guts about the hospital detachment but again Pomeroy laid a big hand on his shoulder. With a promise to bring in Deagle, they walked out under the hot sun. Pomeroy pulled out his compass and got his bearings. It was a half a mile straight north to the end of the road and the big motorpool. It was a quarter mile south to the foot Cav Mountain. R&R, finance, and hospital were all south.

"Well," he said, "maybe we should split up. I'll hit finance and find Deagle, you make your call home and hit the PX."

"Where's the PX," Jim asked, having very little sense of direction.

"Back east, past where the chopper set us down. Jim, can I trust you not to fuck up and get stuck on some shit detail?"

"Why don't we both go call home?"

The big man was uncomfortable. "I'll call when I'm ready. I gotta find Deagle because I don't trust that little lifer, Hooper."

"Shit. Deagle can handle himself."

"Rendezvous 1400 at R&R barracks 2022. You bic? No guitar playing, no getting ripped, and no war stories. Not 'til tonight. How do you read, PFC?"

"5 by 5. Don't worry, I ain't gonna fuck up R&R."

As soon as Pomeroy had humped far enough up the street, Jim sneaked back down the street, to the admin mess hall. He banged the screen door open and pulled his headgear off as Sergeant Arroyo's Vietnamese KP's were finishing setting up the lunch serving-line. The only other soldiers eating were a group of three just coming off guard duty. Their steel pots, pistol belts, and flakvests were piled under their table on the shiny concrete floor. There was an empty chair at their table.

"Hey, sarge, can I get chow?"

The easy-going Arroyo took a look at Jim and waved him in. "Come on in, slick-sleeve. You take whatever you want."

Jim snatched a clean tray and piled it high with hot ham slices, steaming scalloped potatoes, green beans, and a big bowl of chicken rice soup. Everything hot, nothing cold. He walked to the table where the admin troops sat and took the open chair.

"What kinda guard duty, guys," he asked cheerfully.

Jim didn't notice that nobody answered him. He ate half his stack of ham and most of his beans before putting down his fork, in heaven.

"Man is this good chow or what. You guys pull guard duty? Shit, I thought all you guys did was type paperwork and drink beer all day."

"We wouldn't pull guard if we had some grunts around here," one of them answered.

Unfazed, Jim picked up his fork and shoveled more food. "Where are you guys from?"

"Records branch," Sp4 Becker finally said.

Confused for just a moment, Jim laughed. "Shit, I mean in the world. I'm from Alexandria Virginia."

"Well shee-it. Matt Edgar, Richmond. Gimme some skin on Virginia."

He reached out, palm up. Jim slapped his hand lightly and rolled his palm up to have it returned. Two Virginia boys.

Sp4 Ritchie eyed Jim with obvious resentment. "You know", he said, "you fuckin' grunts can get new uniforms at quartermaster. You don't need to walk around tryin' to look bad."

Jim showed surprise as Ritchie stood up and carried his tray to another table.

"New fatigues are the wrong shade of green," Jim said. "Too dark stands out like too light, same same." He looked down at his fatigue shirt. "These are just right, you dig?"

Edgar said he never heard that before.

Becker was six weeks in-country with forty-six weeks to go, the new morning report clerk for the 1st Battalion, 9th Brigade. He looked at Jim's sad uniform, tanned face and shaggy hair. They were about the same age. He understood that except for luck and timing they could be reversed, and Becker would be the one getting shot at. He and Jim had had the same basic training, learned to shoot the same rifle at cardboard silhouettes, throw practice grenades into circles, shoot M-79 grenade launchers at distant piles of tires. They'd learned to fire the one-shot disposable LAW bazooka, the .45 pistol, and the M-60 and .50 cal machine guns. The difference was Jim had to use all that training.

Becker saw his "Gary Owens" pin and asked where the 7th was operating.

"Outside Tay Ninh, man. Good old "rocket alley."

Becker asked him if he'd shot any gooks.

Jim's answer was to put down his fork and give serious thought, tongue showing on his lower teeth.

"Yeah. Couple times. In a firefight, man, I shoot whatever's in front of me. Dig? So is the guy next to me. It isn't a big thing who gets what, as long as somebody does. The VC we get are smoked good, you know? Like blown apart from ten hits."

"Is it ever one-against-one? Some gook jumps out in front of you with a gun and it's you or him?"

Jim picked up his fork. "No lie, GI. One time, this gook comes humpin over a hill and I see him when he sees me. Shit, did I hit it quick! I yell at the other guys and four of us chased him into some thick shit. Then the fucker jumps out and hollers 'Choo Hoi!' We didn't know he had rifle until he reached down for it to shoot Pomeroy. You could say that time was him or us."

"What's Choo Hoi?"

"It's like 'I give up.'

"What happened?"

"Somebody got him. Wasn't me. Deagle or Lieutenant Rule, maybe. I know right after that they made Rule a captain. Another time, Deagle got two. They gave him a silver star for it. He seen these two gooks and chased 'em half a mile, shot 'em both and and dragged 'em back to the rendezvous point. Deagle's one E5 they don't want to fuck with."

Jim looked up from his tray and found the two admin troops staring at him. "War ain't over, you bic?"

Thinking about Deagle, Jim laughed out loud. In June, he said, just after Deagle joined 3rd platoon, their senior NCO, Sergeant First Class Harvey, walked Bravo and Charlie companies off LZ Dogpatch at dark to set up a night ambush. Everybody figured it was to blow away this one-shot Charlie who kept sneaking out of a village to shoot at the colonel's helicopter. The plan was to hump around the little village to within about four klicks of the Cambodian border, put out the LP's and set up claymores, and then sit all night and try to stay awake. That was the plan. And that's usually what happened in a night ambush, everybody takes turns falling asleep until about 0500 and then you hump back.

"But this time, man, Charles must've known we were coming and we walked into the shit. Me and Deagle and Pomeroy were right in the middle of it. One minute we're humpin' along the in the dark and the next minute..."

Jim put down his fork in order to use both hands, waving them around his head like fighting off a swarm of wasps.

"...fuckin' bullets are flying and trees are gettin' cut down and guys are hittin' the ground... Jesus Christ was I scared. All I could do was dig a hole with my face. I didn't know where they were or where I was. Then dumbass Deagle, the FNG, crawls up behind me and says we have to find Pomeroy with the Prick-25, and call for help. Yeah, roger that. It was too dark to find Pomeroy, who's like as wide as a jeep, and those gooks had AK's. Deagle tells me to stay down, he'll take care of it. Next thing I hear is a frag going off... Whaaaammmmm!... extra loud, and I hear metal flying... zzzzzzzzz... really close. Then another frag... whaaaaaammmm! ...farther out. Then its quiet. I get up. Here's Deagle standing up... he's a beanpole about eight feet twenty inches tall... just listening. He reaches down and gets another frag and throws it like a baseball... Whaaaammm!... and its quiet again.

"So the whole outfit breaks off at six o'clock, takes off running . It's fuckin pitch black, we're running into trees, running into each other, but we make it. Sergeant Garcia takes a headcount. We're all waiting for Harvey, he's the only guy missing, and nobody else even got a scratch. We wait and we wait. We set up our ambush right there and waited for daylight, and Garcia picked Deagle, me, and Sergeant Johnson to go back."

Jim's eyes lost focus and his thoughts drifted.

After twenty seconds Becker asked. "What's the funny part?"

"Oh yeah. Dumbass Deagle. He said his first frag slipped out of his hand and went almost straight up. It hit the fuckin' trees and came down right next to us. Means Deagle was sweatin' bullets, scared like me, same same. You have to know Deagle. But I was thinking about old Harvey. He was the only one who got hit."

"Good guy?" Edgar asked.

Jim stared past him.

"Harvey was a good guy?"

Finally Jim nodded. "Yeah. We found him propped up against a tree. Charles sat him up like that. From twenty-five meters, you could hardly tell where old Harvey's face was. Me and Deagle and Johnson... we almost walked right into another ambush. We went back and got Bravo company and cleared that whole area again. Charles is a sneaky son of a bitch, you bic?"

After a few seconds Jim pushed away from the table and belched. "Hey, where do you guys score your smoke?"

Edgar looked around the mess hall, grinning. "You want to do some?"

Jim reached into his back pocket and pulled out his cracked Cav wallet. There was only $3 in wrinkled MPCs "Shit, I have to go to finance first."

"Nah," Becker told him. "Save your money for R&R."

Jim thought about Pomeroy and Deagle, wondering if they'd run into each other yet. "You play guitar?" he asked Becker.

"Not very well."

"Me too, any more. My guitar at LZ Penny is a piece-of-shit classical from Brazil."

"I got a Gibson."

Jim's mouth dropped open. "You got a Gibson guitar in Viet-fuckin'-nam!"

"Bought it at the PX, right here. Want to play it?"

"Does a wild bear shit seeds?"

Jim got up and carried his tray to the far end of the serving line, leaving his Cav wallet and military identification card on the table.

1025Hrs 23Dec71
1st Cav HQ Bien Hoa
Armed Forces Vietnam General Hospital

There were jeeps to flag down, but Deagle decided to punish his legs the full two miles to "Big Ben", the combined armed forces hospital at Bien Hoa. He had no appointment to see Major Ross but he had no schedule to keep either. Life for the past three weeks had been un-military, with no commanding officer, no place to be, nothing to do but sleep and eat a little soup or solid food and throw up his guts. Truth was, he missed the regimented days and nights at LZ Penny, and if he had to push a few buttons to get Major Ross to sign his return-to-duty then sin loi, tough shit.

Walking the first mile, the sun burned his shoulders and the rucksack on his back was a bowling ball that rubbed his skin raw. His legs were spaghetti and what little moisture that remained in his body came out in torrents of sweat, until he found something to occupy his military mind. The stroll around to the south side of the base gave Deagle a different perspective of Hill 229. The air force showed it some respect.

There were no air force barracks within three hundred meters of Hill 229, only half-moon rows of concrete slabs where barracks used to be. Like the army, the air force had concertina wire, bunkers, and a road guarded by a checkpoint to the top of the hill, but the AF had some neat defensive stuff besides floodlights and wire. They had M-60 towers, like the ones at the perimeter, and a squad of armored personnel carriers with .50 cal machine guns facing the hill. If Charles decided to try sniping at the south side of the base, air force gunners could hop in those APC's and respond with mobile and overwhelming fire at long range. Of course, they had to make sure not to overshoot or they might hit their own runways to the north.

Mind over matter, Deagle made it to Big Ben Hospital, a four story brick and mortar building that reminded him of the buildings he'd seen at MAC-V in Long Binh. He'd never actually set foot inside MAC-V but he'd seen it from a distance of a quarter mile or so when taking 2nd Battalion prisoners to LBJ. The hospital had a gate and MP checkpoint where he showed ID and orders to pass through. Beyond the checkpoint was an asphalt parking lot full of jeeps, around it some overgrown weeds that had been allowed to grow wild to resemble landscaping.

On the clean concrete sidewalk leading to the glass entry doors, Deagle got in step behind a group of khaki-uniformed officers. Inside, the hospital was air-conditioned and offered a choice of elevator or concrete stairs to reach the upper floors; the officers chose the elevator, Deagle took the stairs. On the third floor, a homely but round-eyed nurse smiled at him and told him to have a seat, Major Ross would examine him in a few minutes. He wiped the sweat off his forehead with his sleeve and shrugged the bowling ball off his back. Now all he had to do was walk back.

"What time is it," he asked the nurse.

"10:35"

He looked at his left wrist, not even a tan line anymore. "My gook watch died on me," he explained, but she didn't respond.

Fifteen minutes later an admin lieutenant in stateside greens came walking in with a Vietnamese girl-san in a white, belted silk pajamas. She had her arm around small boy, maybe 5 years old. The lieutenant and the nurse had a short conversation and Major Ross came down the corridor. Smiling, he waved for the girl-san to bring her boy. This girl-san not only carried a tiny leather purse, she had an ID in it, which Ross looked at before taking the boy into one of his examination rooms. The lieutenant escorted her back to a chair across from Deagle, tipped his hat, and left her. She gave Deagle a polite smile and then half-turned to her right to watch for her son.

She was not the prettiest girl-san Deagle had seen, some of the whores in Saigon were prettier. But she was the cleanest, most manicured, and best-dressed girl-san he'd ever seen. Her black hair was straight and shoulder-length, parted bangs above full eyebrows. Her white top was enticingly sheer and expensive, not at all like the dirty, frayed pajamas worn by the mama-sans filling sandbags. She wore a gold necklace, a gold wristwatch, and two gold rings, one a cats-eye and the other a plain gold wedding band. Her skin was clean and smooth, her eyes were dark-brown almonds. She had perfect teeth white and fingernails varnished to a sheen. He thought, this is not a girl-san you offer $20 MPC short-time. She has friends.

Waiting, Deagle fidgeted. He opened and closed his Cav wallet five times to make sure he'd put his ID back. He walked to the window and looked south-east at the sprawling air force installation, then walked back to his seat, each time glancing at the
girl-san who sometimes showed him a shy smile. Finally, he got up and walked to ask the nurse what time it was.

"It's 10:55."

"Ma'am, I've been here twenty minutes. Is there another doctor who can sign my release?"

"You'll have to wait for Major Ross."

"How come I got bumped by that gook kid?"

"Would you please hush, she'll hear you?"

He glanced back at the girl-san. "She speaks English?"

"She's Colonel Schaeffer's wife."

"Well, that explains it. An officer's wife. She goes to the head of the line. I'm American but only a lousy buck sergeant. I sit around and get the ass."

"I asked you to keep your voice down."

"You think if I offered her $50 all night boom boom she'd take it?"

The nurse glared at him. "Her son has a heart-valve problem. If you don't lower your voice and sit down, Sergeant, I'm going to call an MP."

He walked away from the desk but not back to his chair. He stood by the window peering around the corner to look at Hill 229 under the noon sun, thinking it would be one hot son-of-a-bitch to climb. Today was the 23rd of December and he had 182 days to go in Vietnam. He'd made it to the half-way point. If he survived the next six months at LZ Penny he'd have five months and twelve days left in the army, back in the world. Less than five months qualified for an "early out"; he'd have to pull some strings to get one. He wondered what he'd do after the army. Sometimes, and it surprised him, he liked army life. But right now, hot about taking a back seat for a Vietnamese kid in an American hospital, "early out" sounded just fine. Officers. He walked back to his chair and sat down, and Colonel Schaeffer's young wife glanced at him with dark eyes that had lost their warmth.

He was still hot when a Japanese nurse sat down next to him and drew a syringe of blood from his left arm. Ten minutes later, with the Vietnamese boy still in one of the examining rooms, Ross stepped out in the hall and waved Deagle back. Sitting bare-chested with his long legs hanging off the examination table, he felt the cold stethoscope on his chest and back as he took deep breaths.

"I don't know, Sergeant," Ross said, "if this is a Merry Christmas or not, but you're clear to return to duty. You can catch a C-130 back to Catapult on the morning of the 27th.

"Thank you, sir."

Ross put away his instrument and scowled at his patient. "My nurse tells me you're in a big damn hurry. We don't see many patients so eager to get back into combat. Maybe I should have a shrink check you out?"

Deagle slipped on his faded fatigue shirt. "Nothing wrong with my head. At LZ Penny, Americans go to the front of the line, you bic"

Ross smiled. "Yeah. I understand. Good luck your last six months, Deagle. I don't want to see you again until your R&R physical. You bic? "

"Count on it, sir."

1000 meters northeast Deagle found the 1st Cavalry Division finance branch, where he stood in line under the mid-day 110-degree sun behind half a dozen R&R troops. Finance was a double-wide concrete block building with mesh steel windows and an eight-foot sandbag wall all around. Its 180-degree entrance reminded Deagle of the shower buildings on Laguna Beach, California. Inside, floor fans dried the sweat dripping from his nose and bare forearms. In front of him, finance specialists sat like bank tellers passing military pay certificates through metal cage windows. As he moved forward he noticed the floor was planked, not slab concrete, and it gave underfoot. An underground vault, probably. He wondered what a 122mm rocket would do if one hit here.

"Orders," Sp5 Marin growled. He wore the collar pin of an Sp-5, the same rank as a sergeant, and Deagle passed a copy through the cage.

Marin unfolded the soggy paper, read it, and then dropped it as if it had been pissed on. "You can't go on R&R with these orders," he said.

"I got a long way to go before R&R. I need to score some cash."

Marin copied numbers on a slip of paper and walked away, and returned with a manila file with Deagle's name, service number, and unit on the outside cover. "See what you have in your accrual... $2217.31. You can draw 10 percent on your signature, more on your commanding officer's signature."

Deagle nodded, figuring he could buy a waterproof American watch with $220.

"We don't have change," Marin told him, and began counting out $221 in military pay certificates. Three 50's, three 20's, a 10, and a single. "Sign the bottom and initial the amount, write your reason for withdrawal on the top line." Deagle pocketed the bills in his Cav wallet and scratched his signature and initials. Marin took the form back and showed Deagle a sarcastic squint. "Hardly original."

"Say again?"

"To buy a watch? Right on." Marin pointed at the big wall poster behind Deagle. "On your way out the door read the Uniform Code of Military Justice statutes on the mis-use of the United States Post Office while serving in a foreign military duty zone. You are prohibited from mailing MPC's out of country for any reason. You are subject to loss of pay and allowances, court martial, and imprisonment if found guilty of using the Unites States mail for the purpose of transporting out-of-country any military information, military property, maps, or other materials so described. United States Government property includes confiscated or captured weapons, ordnance, all controlled or contraband substances, precious metals and art objects, and foreign currency. The purchase, possession, or transport of photographs or depictions of American soldiers shown in deceased, disemboweled or degrading states is also expressly prohibited."

Deagle threw him a wristy salute and about-faced. He walked to the UCMJ poster and looked up. The upper half of the poster was red-white-and-blue Uncle Sam, top-hat and steely-eyes, and the bottom half was postal regulations in numerical order, all impossible to read because of graffiti in the form of autographs, slogans, DEROS dates, unit insignias, and poetry that had accumulated over the years. Taking money out of finance at R&R time was a high-water mark in a tour of Vietnam, a goal. And the troops who passed through this door had to let those behind them know they made it. 'Sp4 Andrew Coltrane, 4Jan'66 R&R Hawaii.' Coltrane made it to R&R, and so did thousands more, until there wasn't even a postage-stamp space left to write in.

Deagle stepped closer and grinned. Crowded into the margin he saw 'Cpl-E4 Cleveland Pomeroy, 2nd / 7th, R&R 27Dec71'

"Son of a bitch."

Lieutenant St John, wearing down from his all night desk duty, rubbed his red eyes and put his glasses back on. He spoke looking straight over Major Andrew' flat-topped head: "so Webb liked the sweep but Dumbo Borg advised against."

Andrews sat writing notes in his battle diary. On his desk between himself and the lieutenant were three books about George Armstrong Custer. "My life on the Plains, By G.A.Custer, "Tenting on the Western Frontier," by Custer's wife Libby, and "The Truth about the Little Bighorn Massacre," by historian Oscar White. Andrews finished his entry and put the diary in his top drawer. He took off his reading glasses and looked at the lieutenant.

"Gave it our best shot. Now we wait for Charles. When he hits us at Christmas... and he will... we're on the record, lieutenant."

"Colonel Borg is a pot bellied, ignorant squarehead. He's an embarrassment to every good intelligence officer in the 1st Cavalry. I don't have any deserter's files on full colonel's but if Charles does hit us JAG might be able to make dereliction-of- duty stick."

Andrews shook his head. "Hell with Borg. What our commanding officer needs is proof Charlie's on that hill, and I couldn't show it to him."

"Say again, sir? Did you say proof?"

Andrews nodded. "Proof, lieutenant. The map we prepared was... proof of a pattern... but not the same as a captured AK-47 assault rifle."

St John sat up. His eyes looked crossed and myopic as he took off his glasses and cleaned them. He stood and walked quietly to Andrews' door to check on sergeants Hooper and Stevens in the outer office; he saw Hooper on the phone and Stevens working on one of his duty rosters. He eased the door closed and walked back to Andrews' desk, leaning on it with both hands.

"Proof, such as... what is known in law as... the corpus delicti?"

"Corpus..."

"Victim. Body. Body count, or similar."

"If it came from the hill, roger."

Andrews put on his reading glasses. He selected "The Truth About the Little Bighorn Massacre" and opened the book to the middle. "Listen up, lieutenant. Custer had twelve companies of the 7th Cavalry, 600 men. Each cavalryman carried a single-shot Springfield with 150 rounds, a Colt pistol and 24 rounds, one extra uniform, salt, and ten pounds of oats for his horse. On 22 June Custer marched them fifteen miles to the Rosebud River where they picked up Sitting Bull's trail. On 23 June he marched them thirty miles in high wind and alkali dust, on 24 June thirty more miles. Those men were asleep in their saddles but when Custer ordered them to move out, and they rode willingly. Then the 7th marched eight more miles before daylight on the 25th. It was so dark that night the troops followed one another by listening for equipment shaking in saddlebags. At daylight Custer got to the crow's nest, where he couldn't quite see over the tops of the cottonwood trees to count the Sioux lodges there, still fifteen miles away. Then he marched those final miles and engaged all the Sioux nations, the Uncpapas, the Santees, the Cheyenne, Arapahoes, Minneconjous, San Arcs, and Blackfeet."

"Excuse me, sir, you've read that to me before but right now..."

"Well don't you see, lieutenant? What Custer needed was one lousy Huey! If Custer had had a helicopter he'd have seen over those cottonwoods, and the history of the Little Bighorn would be vastly different. Vastly different."

Lt John sat down, deep in thought. As the idea began to take shape stood up again and paced in front of the desk. He focused above Andrew's head.

"Sir."

"Go ahead."

"Last night, as the officer of the day, I debriefed an enlisted man who might have seen two VC on Hill 229-er. He fired a full magazine at them."

Andrews removed his reading glasses. "Full magazine?"

"Yes, sir, 7-Bravo bunker."

Andrews' small blue eyes danced back and forth before focusing tight on the young lieutenant. "Behind R&R."

"At the time, I did not think it possible that this motorpool greasemonkey had actually seen, let alone shot, a VC in our wire. So I... placated him, and I wrote in my report that a recon was negative. But there was no recon. Are you following?"

Andrews stared, not quite able to catch up with the lieutenant.

"It was zero-dark-thirty in the morning! All I had was a .45 handgun for God's sake! But now, sir, after we use the crypto line, you and I should take a walk up there."

Andrews' confusion was in the relaxation of his jowls, the narrowing of eyes. "Lieutenant I'm not..."

"Sir. That type of contact had to have happened out in the field, Victor Charlie shot at in a firefight. At Firebase Catapult for instance."

"The concertina wire at Catapult is defoliated."

"True, but you're miss the obvious point. There has to be a least one lousy VC body count lying around. From last night, or the night before, or the night before that."

"Most affirmative."

"Sir, stay with me on this. There's the crypto line on your desk, totally secure communication. I know a field grade officer at Catapult, one I can count for discretion. He will wrap us up one dead gook in Christmas paper and ribbons and fly him right here to admin. Can you picture the expression, sir, on that chicken colonel's face when you dump that body smack down on his desk!"

Mesmerized by St John's voice and daring plan, when the lieutenant's fist slammed the desk for emphasis, Andrews jumped back.

"That's unauthorized," he said.

St John sat and crossed his legs smugly. "No, sir, that is the coup de grace. That is your sweep. No way Webb could turn you down."

"The body count was ours... we're saying..."

"You tell Borg I couldn't sleep. I came and got you. We went up there together to do the recon in daylight. We found the body count." Then he had another thought and slammed the desk with his fist again. "As you were, I'll get Perkins! The three of us find the body, right where he says he shot at it. There, you see how easy it comes together?"

Andrews thought about it, intrigued, but shook his head. "No lieutenant. I will not mislead my commanding officer."

St John leaned forward, eyes focused above Andrews' skingraft. "Sir. If this plan abets the discovery of VC on Hill 229-er, then is it not justified?"

His blue eyes were shifty. "Maybe."

"I'll put it another way: sir, do you believe 1st Cav soldiers will die at Bien Hoa during the Christmas cease-fire?"

"I do." Andrews lowered his voice to a whisper. "There are VC on Hill 686."

"Hill 686?"

Andrews looked away. "Of course I mean 229-er. Hill 229."

St John leaned forward. "Then let's give Custer his helicopter... let's subvert the next massacre."

"You're right."

St John put his fingers to his lips. "Sir, I'd advise that just the two of us know the details. I'm a JAG officer and you're a battalion commander... Borg would hang us by our cajones."

"How about Sergeant Hooper?"

"Oh God no. Well, we might use his physical presence. We'll bring him in when we go up to recon. But he knows nothing about this conversation."

Andrews picked up the crypto phone.

In the outer office Staff Sergeant Stevens heard the pistol-shot sound of St John's fist hitting the desk. "Hell was that?" he asked Hooper, standing up. He crept over to Andrews' door and put his ear against it.

"Sarn't, get away from that door," Hooper told him.

But Stevens stood listening through the hollow door for another thirty seconds before sneaking back to his desk, leering.

"Andrews is talking to somebody at Catapult about a dead body. More goddamn war games. Hooper, if you're in it with 'em... I don't even know you."

"The hell you say."

"Wait and see, sergeant."

Hooper's phone rang and he grabbed it. He heard Lieutenant St John's voice, issuing a clear order: "no calls for Major Andrews, he's on the crypto line."

"Yes, sir!"

He hung up and looked across at Stevens. "The major's on the crypto line, so what."

Stevens laughed.

Hooper's phone rang again and this time it was Colonel Wilcox himself, asking for Major Andrews. "Sir, he's on the crypto line just now."

"Sergeant Hooper, send a CQ runner up to in-transit hospital and police up one-each Sergeant William Deagle. Then you personally hand-carry Deagle to Sergeant Major Bierra's desk, ASAP."

"Yes, sir! And I got two men from his p'toon looking for him too."

"Say again?"

"Sir, I told them troops it was only some donut dolly with a case of the ass so they wouldn't be suspicious. You know how them grunts hang together, sir."

"Well, that was quick thinking Sergeant Hooper but unnecessary. All Deagle has done is win a second Silver Star. General Webb wants him to stand up and receive it."

Hooper's jaw dropped open. "Two Silver Stars! We'll find him for you, sir!"

"ASAP, Sergeant Hooper."

"Yes, sir!"

Hooper hung up and, without thinking, marched into Major Andrews' office to pass on the good news. He saw his commanding officer at his desk using the phone and brought himself to the position of attention, but before he could open his mouth St John jumped out of his chair shouted in his face.

"I said we were not to be disturbed, you idiot! Do I have to spell it!"

"No, sir... Beg pardon, sir..."

He backed out and St John slammed the door. Stevens guffawed and Hooper glared at him. He returned to his desk and called a buddy, Staff Sergeant Coyne, up at in-transit hospital.

"Beagle? What the hell is a Beagle... Who'd he shoot?"

"Deagle, D as in delta. Silver Star winner," Hooper added him matter-of-factly.

"They hand them things out like crackerjacks."

"We need him ASAP, sarn't." Coyne replied that Deagle would be standing at Hooper's desk in zero five minutes.

The major's office door opened and he rushed out wearing his .45 and blue cavalry hat. "Hoop, I'm going to meet a chopper but I'll be back before chow."

"Need me to drive, sir?"

"Not this time, Hoop. But you stand by right here."

The outer door slammed behind Lieutenant St John.

"What'd I tell you," Steven said. "War games.

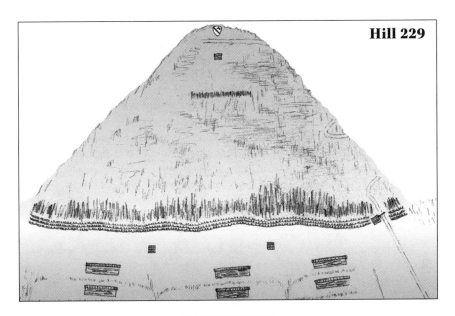

Hill 229

CHAPTER FOUR

1055Hours 23Dec71
1st Cav Div HQ
East Briefing Room

"Showtime," Borg said to himself, getting up from his desk.

He stepped into the hall and, on reconsideration, locked his office; the American press was certainly familiar with the designation S-2, for army intelligence, on the door. The Pentagon Papers had been front-page news, after all. He walked down the corridor and glanced at his wristwatch. A news conference was like a live show, he thought, to the point of being a performance planned and rehearsed. At the end of the hall, guarding the outer door, he saw Colonel's Wilcox and Shipp but no buck sergeant medal winner.

"Find Deagle yet?"

Wilcox shook his head. "Still looking. Last seen at finance."

"We're about out of time, Ray. How many reporters?"

"Six."

"Only six?"

"One television reporter and cameraman, four newspapermen. Two female."

Borg watched a nervous 1st Cav Operations chief twirl his mustache and grinned at him. "You want to warm them up, or should I?"

Shipp grunted. His droopy eyes darted down the corridor. "How'd Webb seem?" he drawled.

"Calm, distracted by Major Andrews. He's still reading that file on 229-er."

"If he gets in trouble with the press," Wilcox quipped, "I'll toss in a hand grenade."

Borg laughed. "Like the one this morning. Those damn grunts just keep coming..."

"Oh, and you were so impressive with your 'big picture' of the cease-fire..."

Shipp kept his voice low. "You guys notice Webb's expression when he heard it was General Garlett on the horn this morning? I did. Pure contempt."

Wilcox nodded. "Garlett didn't care to talk to him, either. The two must have a history... a certain letter to the Commander-In-Chief?"

"Webb has three SSM's for valor, two BSV's, and a chest-full of campaign medals. I'm more curious about Garlett. How come a three-star is running twenty-five percent of MAC-V?"

Shipp glanced at his watch. "Webb'll give a good account of himself with the press. He didn't get them stars on his collars by chargin' Charlie in reverse. It's time, gents."

"Then let them through, colonel."

Wilcox opened the door. He found the American press corps milling, killing time looking at the twin portraits of MacArthur and Custer. He smiled and invited them into support HQ. In no particular hurry, they collected their luggage and struggled in single-file giving Wilcox a fair eyeball assessment. First impression—they'd been traveling awhile. The two women wore baseball caps, green t-shirts, jeans, and GI boots. No make-up. One of them was coarsely pretty, with red hair and green eyes, the other looked more like a GI trainee, and she had to be J.L. Gottlieb. The men looked weary and hadn't shaved in a couple days. They also wore baseball caps and military fatigues. All six carried heavy-looking briefcases and shoulder bags, and a tall young man in granny-glasses carried a camera and tripod on his shoulder. At the intersection of the two corridors Shipp steered them in a column-left toward the east briefing room where Borg waited with the door open.

"Morning," he said, as they walked by. "Morning, ma'am."

The small briefing room had been rearranged. Replacing the circular conference table were six rows of chairs, four across, facing a lectern draped with a black-and yellow 1st Cavalry banner. Conspicuous on the otherwise bare west wall was Webb's autographed Lyndon Johnson photograph, and, on the south wall by the window, Major Andrews' color map of Hill 229. The four men and two women entered the room and spread out, taking two or three chairs each, and began unpacking. Frank Stolle walked to the back wall and set up his camera facing the lectern. In the clamor to prepare questions and record answers given by 1st Cavalry Division Commander Webb, the reporters dragged out portable typewriters, cassette recorders, index card files, notebooks and tattered paperback books, all piled on the empty chairs.

92

Colonel Borg stepped to the podium.

"Again, welcome to Bien Hoa and Headquarters Command, 1st Cavalry Division Air Mobile. As you can see, we didn't know how many of you to expect. Please make yourselves comfortable. I'm Colonel Borg, S-2, to your right are Lieutenant Colonel Wilcox, S-1 Personnel, and Colonel Shipp is our S-3 OIC."

A metal alarm clock hit the concrete floor with a musical clunk. Borg watched the cameraman retrieve it and put it back in a bag full of 35 mm camera lenses.

"What did you say was your job title, colonel?"

"I'm the S-2 at Bien Hoa. I hope your billets are comfortable and if there's anything you need please make your requests to Colonel Shipp or Sergeant Major Bierra."

J. L. Gottlieb leaned on her left arm, writing fast with her right. "Colonel," she said, "we were advised we might be quarantined at Bien Hoa the full seventy two hours of the truce. There are two concerns about that; one, my bureau chief may want me in Saigon tomorrow, and, two, we have video tape to get to Yakoda, Japan this afternoon."

"Ma'am, Colonel Shipp has already procured a C-130 transport for your film, it departs Bien Hoa at 1500. And the Cav will provide a military convoy to move you to Saigon, if and when."

"Trucks?"

"Yes ma'am."

Russ Edelman groaned and waggled his pencil. "Is there a PX on the base where we could score some good scotch?"

"The most complete post exchange in-theatre," Borg replied. Then he went through his standard points of information. The 1st Cav was not anticipating enemy contact at Bien Hoa. RPG's and mortar rounds had been infrequent since late summer, but Colonel Shipp had prepared hand-out maps showing the locations of all in-coming bunkers. Bien Hoa had the same alert siren and all-clear heard at other large installations throughout the theatre: repeated, shrill bleats meant get into a bunker ASAP and one long, steady note indicated that it was safe to return to billets and previous activity.

"If VC activity should become heavy—unlikely—helicopters will fly all civilians out to the New Jersey in the South China Sea. On your hand-outs, please note the shaded areas are off-limits to all civilians but feel free to explore the un-shaded areas of the base and record interviews, take pictures, whatever. The post exchange is on your map and you will receive passes good through the 26th. On Christmas Eve visitors to 1st Cav Bien Hoa are invited to the officers club for dinner and on Christmas Day to an informal buffet in General Webb's quarters."

"Ten hut," Wilcox called softly, as the commanding general opened the hall door and looked around the small room.

"As you were. Colonel Wilcox, am I presenting a Silver Star this morning?"

"Sir, we haven't located him as yet."

Standing at the podium, Webb felt relief at seeing only six civilian faces staring up at him. The American press was both fewer and younger than the last group, but Colonel Borg hadn't warmed them up much. They looked weary, edgy, and serious. Webb had no prepared statement, no jokes, no ice-breaking observations about the freedom of the press. He went straight at them.

"I'm Jeff Webb, Division Commander, 1st Cavalry Division Air-Mobile. I'm sure Colonel Borg has welcomed you so I'll take your questions. Yes, sir."

Steve didn't stand up but he did sit up. Consulting his notes he said "General, Steve Grozik, *Portland Herald-Tribune*. My question has two parts. Would you first comment on the trial of General John Donaldson of the Americal Division, who as you know is accused of the mass murder of Vietnamese civilians in the Quangngai Province. And secondly, sir, are you concerned that as a commanding general you might also be held responsible for similar war crimes committed by 1st Cavalry soldiers in the A Shau Valley?"

"I don't know anything about General Donaldson's situation, and no, I am not concerned about being similarly charged. The 1st Cav has a fine record in Vietnam. Yes ma'am," he said, recognizing J.L. Gottlieb.

"J.L Gottlieb, CBS News. General Webb, a Christmas cease-fire begins today and I'd like your opinion on whether there's any chance it might become a permanent peace, vis-a-vis, have you been advised by MAC-V or Secretary Laird of any progress in the talks, any changes in delegate Xuan Thuy's bargaining positions?"

"My opinion is, yes, there is a chance the cease-fire can become a signed peace. Yes, there have been new concessions in Paris but they came from Secretary Kissinger and not from the North Vietnamese."

"Can you tell us what concessions and if you approve or disapprove of Secretary Kissinger's approach?"

The cameraman at the back of the room closed his left eye and aimed a thick macro-zoom lens at his face.

"As you know, this past May Secretary Kissinger tied any final pull-out of American troops to a complete and total release of American POW's by the communists. That demand has been softened to what is being called a "proportional" release in step with a gradual American stand-down, which has been Hanoi's position since 1968. I believe Secretary Clifford has been involved in that change in our position. I'm a soldier, so I do not judge Mr. Kissinger's approach. He's more informed than I am."

"General Webb, at the Pentagon it's now common to hear Vietnam referred to as a 'civil conflict' off the record of course. This seems a long way from the 'Domino Theory' of communism in South East Asia which got the US in Vietnam the first place. Sir, has Vietnam become a 'civil conflict' because the military lost badly here?"

He looked down at his hands on the podium. "Communism is slavery, Ms. Gottlieb. You fight it where you find it."

The lady reporter on Gottlieb's left had her face buried in her legal pad. Webb watched her yawn without looking up and then rest her chin in her left palm. He pointed at one of the young men.

"General, Russ Adelman, *Los Angeles Times*. Now that the President has been to China this year it appears the Chinese will be seated in the United Nations. Assuming a prominent Chinese world presence, sir, do you now see the Chinese becoming combatants in Vietnam or continuing their role of supplying and training the North Vietnamese Army?"

Webb watched him lower his head to write. "I left Tay Ninh a week ago. I can tell you there has been no change in the fighting because of the President's visit to China. In III-Corps, as you know, we don't see the large units of NVA that operate around I-Corps, up near the DMZ. Down here Viet Cong terrorists carry the fighting load. Yes, sir."

"Peter Keating, General. *San Diego Sun Times*, and greetings from home. General, while it was off the record, I was told yesterday that MAC-V is now concerned about a gigantic Viet Cong shantytown west of Saigon on the Cambodian side, between the border and the city of Prey, code-name 'Atlantis'. My question has two parts: first, is Atlantis a threat to re-escalate the war and derail the peace process, and second, is your division, the 1st Cavalry, the first line of defense should the Viet Cong attack Saigon?"

Webb noticed the redhead in the baseball cap come out of her daze and pull off her reading glasses. Her eyes were green.

Webb acknowledged the question with a nod. "Good question from my home town newspaper. I can't discuss Cambodia or Laos, but yes, my division is based at Tay Ninh and is the first line of defense against a Viet Cong offensive from the west."

Making eye contact with the redhead, he pointed at her. "Yes ma'am."

"General, speaking of Tay Ninh, we were told yesterday at MAC-V the 1st Cav still has troops at Firebase Catapult and at Firebase Enterprise below An Loc. We were also told there are 1st Cav helicopters staged to support Firebase Lolo, which is twenty-one miles inside Laos. General, aren't those strong forward positions an affront to the peace process?"

"An *affront* to the peace process?"

"Sir, there are 10,000 troops going home every month and 46,000 men are dead already."

Webb looked down at his hands on the podium. "The affront, ma'am, is the way you people throw around numbers of American dead, as if the numbers are what matters."

"Sir, I asked you if 1st Cav helicopters are now supporting Firebase Lolo inside Laos."

"I heard the question. On Firebase Lolo or The Parrot's Beak or any operation outside Vietnam, my answer is 'no comment.' I've said at previous news conferences I won't argue the strategic part of my job with the American press. We have helicopters in forward areas, Miss..."

"Sorry. It's Ms. Devlin, *San Francisco Examiner.*"

"...Ms. Devlin, because that's what we do. The 1st Cav is air-mobile. I haven't pulled back from Tay Ninh because, for one, III-Corps Commander Garlett, has not ordered me to do so. Second, pulling the 1st Cav back at this time would jeopardize American lives. Those who assume this war is over... are misinformed."

But Darcy Devlin stood up, consulting her notes, one combat boot on the ground the other on her chair.

"General, we have somewhat more detailed maps than the ones Colonel Shipp has provided us with. Looking at them, it's obvious that the 3rd Marine Division has pulled back from Firebase Sarge and the 4th Infantry is in the process of consolidating around Chu Lai, going home. We were at Cam Ranh last week we found it deserted except for the navy port and off-shore operations. With rear areas like Cam Ranh empty, and with two full divisions of Arvin infantry west of Saigon, isn't the upcoming Christmas cease-fire the perfect time to pull the 1st Cavalry back from Tay Ninh?"

On his left, Webb caught Colonel Borg's warning under raised eyebrows. In-coming. The young lady's question was challenging enough, and as she spoke she added that flavor to her posture, in the straightening of her back and the slight incline of her head. Webb understood she'd asked this question of other commanders.

"My unit order reads, 'Saigon Security'. Between Saigon and Tay Ninh are approximately 100 miles, and about the same between Tay Ninh and Phnom Penh in Cambodia where there are several hundred thousand North Vietnamese troops staging their next offensive. The 1st Cavalry is part of the secure cordon around the capitol city."

"You're saying your division is being held in a forward area so that it could operate inside the Cambodian border, if called upon?"

Irritated, he answered, "No ma'am, you are. Ms. Devlin, I'd like to ask you a question: has anyone from your newspaper asked Secretary Laird about Cambodia?"

Darcy put on her glasses and riffled through note-pages. "General do you mean... after his Feb 18th 1971 statement... quote 'there will be NO combat troops in Laos or Cambodia again,' did my newspaper ask Laird about... B-52 raids near Veng in March '71... more raids in May '71... the July '71 offensive in the Parrot's Beak... B-52's and F4's again in July... US Helicopters shot down by the Pathet Lao 17 miles inside Laos in August '71... On and on. Oh yes, we asked the Secretary. We asked why he continues to lie to the American people and we got the same 'no comment' you just gave me."

"So you asked the Secretary of Defense about troops in Cambodia and you determined that his answer was a lie."

She looked down at her notebook. "Since the Feb 18 statement, quote 'no troops outside Vietnam', there have been eleven incursions into Cambodia resulting in the death of thirty-one Americans and the loss of six helicopters. Explaining that on September 20, 1971 in the White House briefing room Laird said... quote 'the six-week Cambodian incursion... bought time... for the continued 12,000 man per-month withdrawal of American troops'... First the Secretary lies, then he evades."

"If, in your opinion, Ms. Devlin," Webb said, "the Secretary of Defense lies and evades regarding Cambodia, what kind of statement are you expecting from me and what credibility would it have?"

From the back of the briefing room Frank Stolle's bark of laughter echoed in the small room. Colonel Borg snickered but waved at Webb not to pursue the remonstration. As J.L Gottlieb stood up, Devlin sat down, green eyes smoking.

"General, my question has two parts, with this preface. After eight years of failed American involvement in Vietnam, the pressures mounting at home to end it seem irresistible. Right now we have, as you say, Secretary Clifford softening our POW stance, 'end-the-war' hearings in the Senate, and Senator Symington has begun a hearing on the B-52 strikes over Laos. You may have heard of the 'Dump Nixon' effort by some Republican senators, and there are now constitutional challenges in the House to the so-called 'Nixon Doctrine' that promises material and air support to the South Vietnamese. General, the 1st Cav has a mission; but against this avalanche of anti-war sentiment how in the world can you carry it out?"

"1st Cavalry troop morale remains high, a matter of doing more with less. Less operational freedom and fewer replacements mean shared combat responsibilities. That's how I see morale."

"You've touched on my follow-up question, general. In 1965 President Johnson consigned the 180,000 American troops to Vietnam. That number escalated, as we all know, but now there are less than 150,000 American troops left in Vietnam, only two divisions in III-Corps. If you have 10,000 infantrymen between here and the Cambodian Border, that works out to something like two per square mile. Even if Cav morale is high isn't this a token presence?"

"Asked and answered, ma'am."

Unrecognized, Darcy Devlin stood up holding a sheet of white paper under her glasses. "General, Congressman Ron Dellums said this week that if we were to take seriously the army's enemy body count figures, it means in the past seven years every South Vietnamese male citizen has been killed twice. To believe the army's figures means we believe the NVA and Viet Cong have buried half a million of their own. Congressman Dellums is concerned that while American casualties have dropped dramatically, we still see large Viet Cong and NVA body count numbers being reported by the 1st Cavalry, the 3rd Marines, 1st Infantry, and so on. My question is, how does the army arrive at its enemy body count figures and isn't all this a huge embarrassment to the army?"

He nodded, looking down at his podium. "A perennial question. I answer it only for the 1st Cavalry Division, this way: combat debriefings are written by career field grade officers who know they will be reviewed here, by Colonel Borg among others. Falsified numbers of enemy body counts, captured weapons, and so on subject the writer to every punishment the IG or the JAG can throw at him."

"General," she said, "excuse my throwing numbers around, but somebody is lying to somebody. We've lost less than 50,000 and the Viet Cong alone have lost four times as many? There's no credibility in those numbers."

Webb glanced at Borg, the corners of his mouth turned slightly up. The green-eyed reporter had an Irish temper. "Asked and answered, Ms. Devlin."

"Was there something funny in that question, General Webb?"

Ignoring her, he pointed at the balding fat young man with his hand in the air. "Yes, sir."

"General, Peter Keating again, and no, I won't ask you if you're running for the California senate. Sir, MAC-V told us that the Ho Chi Minh Trail is handling two thousand trucks a day from the north, mostly through Laos. Whether that does or does not justify the American air campaign in Laos, it's a hell of a lot of troops and supplies. Is that number accurate, and, if so, how can just 75,000 Arvin soldiers save their country's democracy?"

"Two thousand trucks a day through the Central highlands challenges my imagination. But if it's accurate, it's a shame. I was in the Highlands in 1968 when President Johnson had B-52's bombing that trail around the clock. And that's what it was, a foot-trail. Now it's the Ho Chi Minh highway."

"And the Arvins? Is there any chance at all they can win?"

Poker-faced Webb answered, "My only comment about Vietnamization is that it has been partially successful."

Ms. Darcy Devlin got his attention again and sat up in her chair, and as if a signal between them had been passed Frank Stolle clicked on his video camera. "General Webb were you signatory to the 'Bail Out' letter to the President and is your presence here at Bien Hoa punishment by Secretary Laird for your opinion to end the war now?"

The briefing room was quiet enough to hear sweat drop on the polished floor.

"No comment, except that my present duty at Bien Hoa is strategic, not punitive."

"Signing the letter," she said, "is viewed by many Americans as an act of extreme patriotism."

"Sorry, Ms. Devlin, I have no comment."

Darcy sprang out of her chair to fire her follow-up. "Did you refuse to sign because you feel the Vietnam war can still be won or because signing the letter is a violation of Article 88 of the Uniform Code of Military Justice, a criticism of the Commander-In- Chief?"

"Asked and answered, Ms. Devlin. Yes, sir."

"General Webb," Steve Grozik followed immediately, "you have no doubt read Vice President Agnew's public assessment of the political left. Do you think characterizing Congressmen Parren Mitchell, Ron Dellums, Bella Abzug and Senators Gene McCarthey, George McGovern, and Marc Hatfield as 'effete snobs' will help end this conflict or merely raise the level of the rhetoric?"

As the camera whirred softly Webb looked straight into the lens. "The Vice President, in my opinion, did not characterize Congressmen Mitchell, Dellums and Abzug or Senators McCarthey, McGovern, and Hatfield as effete snobs. The Vice President characterized Jane Fonda, Donald Sutherland, Mike Nichols, Elliot Gould, Dick Gregory, Jules Feiffer, Peter Boyle, and Barbara Dane, among others, as effete snobs. In my opinion."

As Russ Adelman stood, barely choking back laughter, Jan Gottlieb clucked and Darcy slammed her notebook on the empty chair beside her.

"General, Russ Adelman again, but you know the Vice President was looking toward the election with those labels," he said.

"There have been many labels, Mr. Adelman, including 'war criminal.' As I recall it was Mr. Keating's newspaper that ran a piece about the five worst war criminals since the two Adolphs, Hitler and Eichmann. They were General William Westmoreland, Admiral Elmo Zumwalt, General Creighton Abrams, Lieutenant William Calley, and... General Jeffrey Webb."

Russ waggled a finger again.

"General, you've just arrived here from Tay Ninh. Do you have a sense yet whether or not the Viet Cong in the villages around Bien Hoa are going to violate the cease-fire and what counter-measures you might take?"

He paused to glance left at his support staff. "Let me answer that this way: in the short time I've been at Bien Hoa I've learned that changes in combat readiness are necessary, and are forth-coming. Any Cav response to Viet Cong cease-fire violations will be measured and swift."

"With MAC-V oversight?" Gottlieb asked.

"Of course."

Peter got to his feet and asked Webb to explain so many cease-fire's on the calendar, the Lunar New Year cease-fire, the TET cease-fire, the birth of Bhudda cease-fire, the Monsoon cease-fire...

The jeep pulled to a stop and threw up a cloud of red dust, and Sergeant Hooper bailed out the driver's side. He and Sp4 Perkins pried the awkward package off the rear seat and over the side of the jeep. It hit the ground with a dull canvas thump. Major Andrews and Lieutenant St. John affected final adjustments to their uniforms and combat gear. Andrews checked his gigline for the tenth time and adjusted his sidearm, now cocked-and-locked in a standard flap holster. Instead of his campaign hat, a steel pot was pulled down hard on his white-walled head.

"Ready?" he called to St. John.

St. John, in tailored fatigues and wire-rimmed glasses, looked strange wearing a flak jacket and helmet.

"Affirmative."

Hooper staggered under the weight of the duffel on his shoulder but he got it to the front door. St. John flung the door open and Hooper lurched into 1st Cav Division Headquarters, straight toward Sergeant Major Bierra's desk. The lieutenant felt a shiver of anticipation as Bierra lifted his head and saw the four of them approaching.

He ran interference for Hooper to the desk and pointed down at it. "Right there, sergeant!" he commanded. "Sergeant major, please stand back."

Bierra, too stunned to respond to the young lieutenant, pushed his chair back just in time to avoid getting hit in the head and shoulders by the green duffel bag as it thumped down on his desk, scattering paperwork and knocking the phone out of its cradle. Major Andrews stood beside his desk looking down at him with pig-angry eyes.

"Sergeant major, I want you to get Colonel Borg out here."

"Colonel Borg is in a press briefing."

Lieutenant St. John's eyes opened wide. "American press? Maybe we should go find him?"

Andrews' lower lip jutted. "He wanted proof, I got him proof. I guess I'll go find the good colonel myself. Hoop?"

Bierra blocked his way. "Major, you can't go back there!" he said, firmly.

"What do these two warmongers' have in the bag?" he muttered to himself, stalling. He reached simultaneously for the phone and the duffel's drawstring. He pulled the cord and leaned down, and he got a whiff of something dead about the time he realized he was looking at blood and bare skin. He had inadvertently touched the dead thing and it disgusted him.

"What the hell are you up to..."

"Calling the MP's, sergeant major?" Andrews asked politely.

"You bet I am."

But on Andrews' signal Sergeant Hooper was on the spot and had the duffel shouldered again, and St. John ran ahead again to the staff door.

"You can't go back there!... major!... that's a secure area... major!"

Hand on the knob, it was only at the last second that Andrews changed his mind. He turned and squared his shoulders to the division sergeant major. He aimed a finger: "I will broach no more of your misconduct! You get Borg out here now! That is an order! Or I will bring charges and have you court-martialed. Do you read!"

Bierra picked up the phone and called Colonel Borg's extension in the briefing room.

With the press conference almost over, Borg had all but given up on presenting Silver Star winner William Deagle to the reporters today. His dim hopes were renewed when the phone rang, then dashed hearing Bierra's strained voice.

"Sir? Could you come out here immediately? It's Major Andrews and he brought a dead body in here..."

Borg glanced at the members of the press watching him and felt heat climbing from his collar. "He what?" he said too loud.

"A dead Vietnamese in a duffel bag, sir."

From the podium, Webb threw him a glance but kept talking about the birth of Bhudda.

Panic gripped the full colonel as he put down the phone, and his long legs seemed rooted to the ground. Wearing a too-casual smile he moved in slow motion to the podium and whispered in Webb's ear.

"General, is there a problem?" Russ Adelman asked.

"In your office," Webb told Borg.

"Something we need to know, General?" J.L. Gottlieb asked, standing up.

"No ma'am. A matter that needs the colonel's attention."

Borg nodded to the group and left the room. At the end of the corridor he opened the outer door and saw Major Andrews and, one step behind, diminutive Sergeant Hooper with a military duffel draped on his shoulder. The third and fourth soldiers were a blur. Coming to the position of attention, Hooper dumped his burden on the floor.

"You wanted proof," Andrews said. "Show him, Hoop."

Colonel Borg watched as the sergeant yanked the duffel's drawstring and upended most of its contents, the bloody, dark-haired head, left arm, and shoulder of a human being.

"Bring it to my office. All four of you... in my office!" He looked up at Bierra. "Call Colonel Wilcox in the briefing room. Tell him what you saw, tell him I want him to entertain the reporters for a few minutes in General Webb's absence."

"Reporters," St. John giggled. "American journalists!"

Borg held the door and Hooper dragged the dead Vietnamese through the hall and into the small S-2 office. Borg considered locking the two officers and two enlisted men inside but realized there was a telephone on his desk. Andrews might do anything. With the door closed, thinking fast, he picked up the phone and dialed Sergeant Janco's number.

"Get over here, sergeant. I need you to ID a body count."

Andrews glanced at St. John, who said matter-of-factly. "Shantytown-type refugee, sir. Hardcore."

Borg walked around his desk to stand by the door, waiting for Webb. "Thank you, lieutenant."

The door opened and Commanding General Webb squeezed into the small office. Sergeant Hooper saw him and froze. Sp4 Perkins forgot himself and hung up a salute indoors. Major Andrews had not expected General Webb and his fleshy face drained ghost white as he flattened against the near wall at a rigid position of attention, his chin buried in thick neck. Lieutenant St. John turned to stone with his eyes bulged and staring dead ahead.

"Ten Hut," St. John said weakly.

For five seconds Webb stared down at the mortified bloody body.

It was male, more papa-san than boy-san, bare-chested but wearing Arvin-sized fatigue pants. From being crammed in the duffel bag he was stiff and twisted and balanced like a dead spider, turned on his left side with his left arm up and his right arm out almost straight. His thin legs were bent at the knees and curled back to his buttocks.

"Major, I assume this VC was shot by our bunker guard last night?"

"Yes, sir!"

"Very sorry about this, sir," Borg said. "Ah, how did you leave it with... in the other room?"

"Colonel Wilcox has the podium."

There was a double rap on the door and Webb opened it to find Colonel Shipp standing there. He saw the body on the floor and edged in sideways, closing the door behind him. The S-2 office was overcrowded. Major Andrews leaned down and pointed out the large gore-dried hole where a bullet had caught the VC and blown out a portion of his spine.

"Going away, sir. Back up the hill."

"Did you recover a satchel charge or weapons?"

"My men are doing a recon right now, sir. We thought the colonel should see this as soon as possible..."

Webb glanced at his watch again. 1129 hours. "Colonel Borg, as discreetly as possible, would you go back in the east briefing room and capture the major's map of Hill 229?" He sat on the edge of Borg's desk and rubbed his tired eyes. "Lieutenant St. John, go to the admin CP and start putting together a roster of senior NCO's. Not a word to anybody."

"Yes, sir! St. John jammed on his helmet liner and marched stiffly to the door.

Major Andrews started for the door but Webb stopped him with an outstretched right arm. "Just a moment, major."

"Sir, I thought I'd finish the recon above 7-Bravo."

"You told me this morning you needed two hours to put together a 300-man battalion of infantry to sweep down Hill 229."

Andrews straightened. "Yes, sir. In two hours I can have my infantrymen on the hill, and in three more I'll have 'em back down with more body counts."

Webb checked his watch again. "Sergeant Hooper, same orders. Return to the CP and not one word about this body count."

"Yes, sir!" Hooper bolted into the hallway.

Colonel Borg returned with the map dangling in his hand. "They sense something's up." He posted the map of Hill 229 on the back of the door and General Webb aimed an index finger at the bottom. "You found him in this area, Major Andrews?"

"7-Bravo, Sir. Next to the checkpoint, above R&R."

Unable to contain himself any longer, Borg threw his arms wide. "General, we're not falling for this, are we? That body count is bogus..."

Webb calmly put a finger to his lips. "It occurred to me. Major, how did your troops find this VC?"

Now it was Andrews who turned red. "Sir, this is Sp4 Perkins, the man who shot him last night!"

Eyes bulging and still holding his wooden salute, Perkins waited.

"At ease, specialist," Webb told him. "Tell me about it."

"SirIseenthegookandshotathim! Himananotherone!"

"From bunker 7-Bravo, son?"

"Yes, sir! Last night, me and the lieutenant thought it was a gorilla but this morning he come and pulled me off the maintenance line and we went up there and seen him layin' there, sir!"

"There were two?"

"I think so, sir. One for sure."

Webb opened the door and peered down the empty corridor. "Specialist Perkins, I want you to return to your duty station. You can't talk about this yet, you understand? Good job, son."

When the door closed again there were only officers in the room. "This Vietnamese had been dead longer than twelve hours," Borg said softly

Webb looked to Andrews. "Tell me again how you found him"

"Recon, sir. Lieutenant St. John brought my attention to his OD debriefing, prepared for Colonel Borg." He advanced a step toward the tall colonel. "And may I say, sir, as to what the colonel is implying... .he can go straight to hell!"

Webb stepped between them. "Be very careful, major, and keep your voice down."

Andrews took a step back and came to the position of attention. Then he spread his boots shoulder-width and put his hands behind his back.

"So you and the lieutenant and Specialist Perkins went back up on Hill 229 and found this VC?"

"We did, sir. The lieutenant said he couldn't sleep. He said a guard may have shot a VC in our wire. We took a walk and he was there, sir."

Borg's arms were folded against his chest. "You went looking for this VC after our briefing this morning? After we agreed there would be no battalion sweep"

"We had to double-check."

Shipp reached for a green handkerchief to cover his nose and mouth. "Getting ripe in here. Major Andrews, I been trying to reach your office since 0900 but Sergeant Hooper said you were on the crypto line. Why?"

"Trying to see if there were other coordinated attacks before the truce, sir."

"Crap," Borg said. "You used the crypto line to call Firebase Catapult and you ordered that VC like ordering a hamburger!"

"We don't have much time," Webb said, turning his attention to Major Andrews map.

Despite his reservations Borg dropped to one knee and examined the dead Vietnamese. "I called Sergeant Janco to ID him. If he is local we'll know soon. I say he's imported and he's been dead for days. I say battalion sweeps on 229-er are worthless under any circumstance."

"You gave me clerks and truck drivers!" Andrews fired back. "I am sick and tired of losing this war, colonel, and fighting with one hand tied behind my back! I want our best!"

Borg wagged his lop-eared head. "Sir, if I may offer an opinion, Major Andrews is single-minded but he isn't diabolical enough to have dreamed this up by himself. Let's get Lieutenant St. John back in this office and I'll take him apart like a cheap watch. The... plot... is one thing, but the idea of using R&R troops on a rear combat sweep is particularly appalling, in my opinion."

Andrews pointed down. "Sir, permission to speak freely!"

"Go ahead, Major."

"You're new to Bien Hoa, sir. I've been keeping track of that hill and the Vietnamese nationals on this base for four months. I am certain that a substantial force of Viet Cong is living like permanent party up there, caching stolen munitions, and they will hit this base during the cease-fire! Let's put the infantry up there first and kill the bastards!"

Webb looked down at the bloody VC, then at the map of Hill 229. Once again, if true, the enemy contact had come from the north side above the vulnerable R&R and DEROS barracks. His eyes trailed down from the radio detachment, past the old caves, through 'the meadow' straight down to bunker 7-Bravo. He turned to the group and looked hard into Major Andrew's eyes.

"I'll co-ordinate with the air force. They can sweep down the south and south-east sides of the hill. Major, you sweep the map areas, the north and north-west side and you complete it before 1800 hours."

"Yes, sir! All I need is the infantry, sir."

"Yes, I know you do."

While Webb studied the map, Borg watched Major Andrews with a skin-tingling foreboding. He couldn't prove it but knew that VC came from somewhere else.

"Put it together, Major Andrews," Webb told him. "Take your men from R&R and repel but not DEROS or hospital. Draw admin soldiers with secondary 11-Bravo MOS's first, but if you come up short of battalion you'll have to fill in with truck drivers and clerks, volunteers only. Arm your people with M-16 rifles and fragmentation grenades, no M-60 machine guns or M-79's or LAW's. And tell your troops not to fire at the skyline. Is that clear?"

"Yes, SIR!"

Borg stepped forward. "General, Major Andrews can report me to, if you like."

"Fine. But you and the Major will have to set aside your differences."

Borg looked across at him. "Can do, sir."

Andrews held the Colonel's gaze. "Agreed, sir."

"Bring those men down off the hill before 1800, gentlemen. Colonel Shipp, notify the AF side, have Wing Commander Cottelier call me on his crypto line. And make sure the bunkers below have a gunner and an A-gunner, no exceptions."

Andrews stood his straightest and held up a salute to his commanding general. "Sir, thank you for the opportunity. We're gonna surprise those sappers, sir."

When the door was closed again, Borg opened his side drawer and brought a bottle of Jim Beam and three short glasses.

"Sappers," Borg repeated, disgusted.

"I wonder if he's going to wear that damn Custer hat..." Shipp mumbled aloud.

Borg felt a rattle up his long spine. He looked down at the dead Vietnamese. "Please don't bring up Custer at a time like this."

Webb sipped the warm bourbon and looked at the chilling figure on the floor. Touring the forward areas around the Tay Ninh, he was always proud when his troops showed him dead VC. But at Bien Hoa, the feeling was different.

"Gentlemen, between the three of us, wherever papa-san here came from doesn't really matter. Nor does it matter that a sweep is the wrong mission. The fact is, I've been looking for an excuse to put troops on that hill since I got here, and reading those old 9th Infantry reports confirms my suspicion: Hill 229 has more tunnels than an ant-farm. Maybe Major Andrews can get us a small victory, the Cav could certainly use one, but the objective of our sweep is to learn if those tunnels are active going into a cease-fire."

Borg and Shipp exchanged glances. "Which would be classified a cease-fire violation?" Borg said, finishing the thought.

"Whereupon we'd be authorized to smoke that hill," Shipp added, "if MAC-V will let us?"

Webb's expression was thoughtful. "Afterwards, I'll need to see the debriefings from the officers and NCO's. The next step would be night ambush missions. As we know, they're damn dangerous."

"Any word on LZ Judith yet?"

"Negative."

Borg knocked back his drink and opened the door. "Well, sir, if it comes to that we've got troops at Bien Hoa for ambush duty, the special forces. Come on, Ray. Should we tell the press you're coming right back, sir?"

"Roger. I'll finish my Bhudda lecture then we'll put the reporters in staff jeeps and haul them to the PX. Colonel Shipp, could you make sure they're out of this AO during the entire operation?"

"No problem."

Alone with Andrews' body count, Webb poured himself a second short one. Sipping, he put his right hand on the MAC-V phone to call the offices of Lieutenant General Benton Garlett, III-Corps commanding officer. He thought about how he should explain a rear-area combat sweep four hours from the start of the cease-fire, using R&R troops. The door opened a sliver and owl-faced Wilcox peeked in. He saw the dead Vietnamese on the floor and quickly pulled the door closed behind him.

"Dear God," he said. "Sir, Colonel Shipp gave me a quick heads-up. I just wanted to recommend that we be very circumspect in any matter concerning 1st Lieutenant St. John. He's what the anti-war kids call a trot."

"Say again?"

"A follower of Leon Trotsky. A sort of establishment super-Nazi."

Webb stood, fighting back a yawn. "Colonel, stay with papa-san until Sergeant Janco has a look at him, then have him removed the way he came."

"Can do, sir."

"Hell with MAC-V oversight."

"Beg pardon, sir?"

"Nothing." He closed the door and walked back to the press conference.

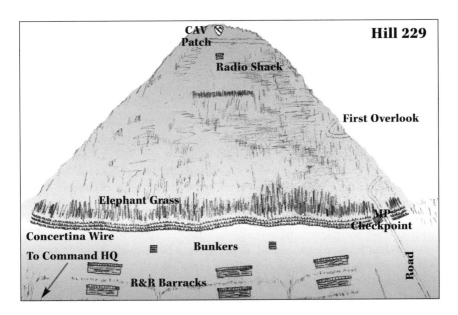

Hill 229

CAV Patch

Radio Shack

First Overlook

Elephant Grass

Concertina Wire

MP Checkpoint

To Command HQ

Bunkers

R&R Barracks

Road

CHAPTER FIVE

```
1205Hours 23Dec71
1st Cav Div HQ
Checkpoint, Hill 229
```

The MP inside the checkpoint shack came to the window and saluted the idling jeep.

"We missed you this morning, sir. Going up?"

Major Andrews snapped a salute under the brim of his steel helmet. "Most affirm. Going up to the first overlook."

The young MP turned and retrieved his clipboard. "Weapons in your vehicle, sir?"

"Just my sidearm," he said, showing the .45 semi-automatic Colt.

"And the purpose of your trip?"

Andrews glanced at Hooper and grinned. If he answered the question truthfully the news would be all over admin in zero five minutes. And then, considering the nature of today's enlisted soldier, by1400 hours there wouldn't be an R&R troop within one thousand meters of Hill 229. He looked at the smiling military policeman, a rare replacement troop as young and green as they came. The kid was barely shaving and had a face-full of pimples.

"Put on your report that Sergeant Hooper and I are following up last night's M-16 fire from 7-Bravo," he said. "What have you heard about that, corporal?"

107

The MP's smile broadened, one hand on his gate counter-weight. "Sir, I heard Sp4 Perkins blew away a damn gorilla. Major, you don't think the gooks are gonna screw up Christmas, do you?" He leaned on the counterweight and the gate tipped up, and he held up a smart salute.

Andrews laughed and snapped one off. "If they do, we've got a ho-ho-ho for them! As you were, corporal, as you were."

Hooper gunned the motor and started up the steep grade in first gear, making an immediate sweeping left-hand turn. In second gear he pushed the under-powered vehicle through the switchbacks, slowly gaining elevation, until they reached the west-facing overlook, one-third the way to the top. He nosed the jeep to the edge of the drop-off and killed the engine. The sun was straight over-head and there was not a breath of wind.

Andrews wiped dripping sweat away from his eyes and studied the finance detachment through his binoculars. He saw 11-Bravo troops moving through their R&R processing and, to the north, a handful of admin permanent party soldiers standing around in t-shirts outside their barracks. They either had the afternoon off or had spent the night at the perimeter. Other troops were stretched out on beach blankets, catching the last hours of the sun before the afternoon rain. He swept the area all the way to the motorpool: no Vietnamese nationals. It was a half-day for them because of the cease-fire. Altogether, 23Dec71 looked like any normal duty day at Bien Hoa, but that was about to change. He stood in the jeep and focused his glasses on the blind-ended, single-lane road going in and out of the dump. No trucks on that road today.

He turned 180 degrees and stared at Hill 229. "Go ahead and try again, you gook bastards."

A stone's throw from the jeep, the foliage was six feet high and as dense as any jungle. The Viet Cong could be five meters away, right now, and invisible. Andrews looked up the 45-degree angle; fifty meters beyond the road edge he saw 30-foot tall treetops intertwined with vines and thick ferns. It was a good place to be at mid-day, not quite as cool as a cave, but out of the burning sun. He drew his sidearm, racked the action, and slipped the safety up. He aimed at the trees.

"Right in there, Hoop," he said, keeping his voice low.

"Yes, sir."

"Now listen up. I brought you here to remind you about the road. It's your west boundary. The troops will be sweeping down through there and you gotta keep 'em off the road. They're gonna want to walk the road because it's easy. Not my infantry sweepers, they'll do their jobs, our lazy admin troops like the ones I saw this morning at breakfast. Any troop walking this road... is a coward. Any coward you find on the road, you jeep 'em back to the top and start 'em over. Otherwise... shoot 'em. You hear me, Hoop? You shoot any coward that won't get off this road."

"Sir, ain't that... "

"Most affirm. It is a heavy punishment, the ultimate. But keep in mind two things; one, it is axiomatic with cowards that one always incites others. He's a coward, after all, and he can't run from his enemies alone. Consider the scum that run to Canada rather than serve their country, it is my understanding there are colonies of them hiding in Montreal."

Hooper looked up.

"And the other thing to remember, sergeant, there are Viet Cong living on this hill. Living here with impunity, under out noses." He took in a deep breath and let it out slowly through his nostrils. "I am more sure of that fact than any other in my life. There are VC on Hill 686."

"Hill 686, sir?"

"Hill 229, of course. But it reminds me of 686. Steep, thick... " He tapped the side of his head. "That's where I got this."

"Yes, sir."

"Hoop, you ever been in a gook tunnel?"

"No, sir, an' I'm too fat now to start."

"I have. Lots of 'em before they put this plate in my head. You can tell a hardcore tunnel by the smell of ammonia. Like an old pisstube. Charles is so close to his target he sleeps in his hole, takes chow in his hole... sometimes for weeks before he attacks. This hill is one big tunnel, Hoop. I smell it every time we come up here. After the sweep, I'm gonna fill Charlie's tunnels with blister gas."

"That's some nasty stuff."

"I always wanted," he said quietly, "to come face to face with Charles in a dark cave, with just my .45 sidearm. Him or me, close enough so I could see his eyes when I put a bullet right through his buck teeth."

"Sir, you're givin' me the willies."

Andrews looked east. "Big cliff up there. Half a dozen 105 rounds hit all in the same spot and a whole hillside cracked off. Make sure none of my infantrymen walk off the edge."

"Roger that, sir. You want me to run us up to the second over-look where we can see R&R?"

Andrews shook his head. "Too close to the caves. I don't want Charles to know I'm one step ahead this time."

Looking west, he shielded his eyes and saw the dark horizon rolling toward him, right on time. His troops would be sweeping during the afternoon rain. He dropped his gaze to the garbage dump and counted the bald, reddish holes in the earth where garbage was piled and buried. Five of them now. The Cav had been at Bien Hoa too long. He visualized where he'd set his ambush team, on the high ground between the hospital barracks and the north side of the dump. A squad of seasoned men there would see Charles skulking off the hill and catch him on open ground. It would be close-range fighting.

He pointed at the spot. "That little tit down there, Hoop. That's where the one squad will set up."

"I volunteer to lead that squad, sir."

Andrews smiled. "No, sergeant. That's for my grunts. Drive me back down."

Hooper wrestled the jeep around and guided it back down the twisting road with his foot on the brake. Beyond the checkpoint, Andrews saw a solitary troop in helmet and flak vest walking toward the admin CP, and when the jeep pulled in front he saw that it was admin SSG McFadden. The staff sergeant snapped to attention and threw up a salute.

"Congratulations, sir!"

"Thank you, sergeant. But not a word to anybody just yet."

"Roger that, sir." Then, with Hooper in hearing range, McFadden whispered, "Lieutenant St. John gave me a full briefing, sir."

Andrews scowled. He herded his two NCO's into the admin CP before the troops spotted them. The command post was crowded. Cynical Sergeant Stevens sat at his desk trying to work duty rosters while a half a dozen officers and senior NCO's crowded around Hooper's desk. The officers had drawn sidearms and the NCO's were in full combat gear. Andrews recognized Captain Olivette and Lieutenant Yost, and, at the center of attention, 1st Lieutenant St. John. St. John saw the major in the doorway and straightened respectfully.

"Ten hut!" he called.

"As you were, gentlemen."

Captain Olivette shoved out his hand. "Congratulations, Warren. By God, with a dead VC on his desk Borg finally pulled his head out and gave us the infantry!"

Andrews shook his hand, then checked his watch.

"Gentlemen, we have the enemy in sight, but we don't have a lot of time before we attack. We have two hours to get our troops in formation, truck 'em up to the top of the hill, and start 'em down. We've done it before so we all know what we're looking for. The difference is... this is an 11-Bravo sweep, combat infantry. It is therefore understood that our mission is not merely to recon Hill 229 but to 'seek and destroy' the enemy living on it. Any Vietnamese national on that hill is the enemy. You instruct your troops shoot first and collect ID cards second! How do you read?"

A dozen pairs of eyes looked back at him. "5x5, sir."

"Good. We're to take grunts from R&R and repel only, we don't touch DEROS or hospital. We have a roster of admin permanent party with 11-Bravo training. Lieutenant St. John will command R&R and repel, where Sergeants Timmerman and Hooper will round up R&R troops: Timmerman, you get 'em in formation, Hoop you march 'em a platoon at a time down to the arms room, then bring 'em up here and leave 'em with Sergeant Dornhaus, combat-ready. Captain Olivette will command at admin, with Lieutenant Fredrick second in command. Keep in mind, the more grunts the better."

"Sir, the admin branches are on afternoon duty, we'll pull them right off their desks."

"Fine. Colonel Geary has committed trucks to roll out of the motorpool at 1345 hours, pick up three hundred sweepers, and convoy them up. On top, you NCOs set up an assault line with a five-meter spacing, start 'em down at 1400. M-16's on single-fire, all NCO's carry M-67 grenades. No M-79's or M-60 machine guns. Do not fire at the skyline. Another concern is the cease-fire deadline, 1800 hours. By 1800 we want our troops back in formation and our body counts on the street like ducks in a row. Any questions?"

"Sir, is it true we all report to Colonel Borg?"

Andrews nodded. "Borg will be in the street, observing. I doubt he'll be shooting off his mouth. It absolutely kills our S-2 OIC to think 'the major with the plate in his head' was right all along."

The phone on Hooper's desk rang and Sergeant Dornhaus grabbed it. "Sir, Master Sergeant Feagins is our convoy leader. Trumpy has duty tomorrow."

Hearing that name, Sergeant Hooper's eyes popped.

"Don't forget," he told Stevens, "to post a new volunteer roster on the bulletin board for Sarn't Trumpy. Second notice, Christmas dinner for the Vietnamese orphans."

Andrews started toward his office. "Should be a few more Vietnamese orphans by tomorrow morning."

Stevens leered. "You go play commando, I'll post your stupid notice. And you owe me, Hooper."

"You just get the job done, Sarn't."

"I'll will, don't you worry about it."

"I ain't worried!" he huffed, and marched out the door to collect his TO&E.

1215Hours 23Dec71
1st Cav Div HQ
Enlisted Barrack 2632

Eyes half closed, Jim ran his sore finger pads lovingly up and down the Gibson's flawless neck before carefully leaning it against the wall. He took a sip of Black Label, the last warm dregs. Beside him was an empty Crackerjacks box and a torn potato-chip tin. Across the room, sitting with his back against the bottom bunk, Becker lazily reached over and opened the small refrigerator door and pulled out two fresh ones, opened them with the magnetic churchkey on the side of the fridge.

He passed Jim a cold one. "Give my left nut to play like that."

Jim let out a contented sign. "What time is it, man?"

PFC Edgar reached out his hand. "Gimme some skin on that playing, man."

He and Jim exchanged palm taps. "Wow. Some heavy weed. I'm trippin', man. Didn't mean to hog the guitar."

"Shit, I always thought there were two or three guitars in classical gas. That was great."

Jim's eyes rolled shut. "I still have trouble with the French horn part."

All three of them rocked with laughter and Edgar rolled another Marlboro between his palms, sprinkling tobacco into a buttcan. He held the empty paper tube vertical and deftly crumbled fine Cambodian marijuana into it, and packed it down by tapping on the filter. He twirled the open end closed, reversed it and tapped again, twisted off the filter, and passed it to the guitar picker.

"What time is, man?"

"Twelve fifteen. Seems like you been playin' a week."

Jim shook his head. "Seems like zero five to me. This is one far-out guitar. Oh well. I'm gonna buy a cheap guitar in Australia just to get me by until February. February 12, 1972, guys. The best day of my life, can you dig? DEROS."

"You're getting' short man. I can't even imagine being that short. I still got more than 300 days... "

Jim buried his head in his hands, protesting "No don't say it... don't say it. That's my worst nightmare, man. I dream there's been a mistake and I have to start 'Nam all over again. Pomeroy and Deagle go back to the world I'm stuck in this hole another 364 days. Now that's a nightmare. Unless, I could score a hooch like you guys got."

The 10'x10' room had a camouflage poncho-liner ceiling, a rug on the floor, and both inside and outside locks on a wooden door. It was an apartment. The double-decker bunks had mattresses and full mosquito netting.

Becker said he inherited his half of the hooch as is, and all he'd done to it was buy a few things at the PX to decorate the walls. Seven months before Becker arrived in country, Edgar inherited the room, now at least 4th generation. The whole admin AO, Edgar said, was an apartment complex, private and comfortable, and nothing like what he'd expected in Vietnam.

The transformation to apartments from single-room sleeping barracks began in 1968 when the Cav replaced the home-bound 9th Infantry. The Cav XO required an NCO in every enlisted barracks, an E6 or E7. Naturally, if a guy had responsibility over twenty other guys, he needed some status, you know, privacy. So he put up a wall. Then he got a door with a lock on it. Then a ceiling overhead, pictures of his mom on the wall, a shelf for his steel pot, a rug for the concrete floor, that way he could come back to his room and get out of his combat boots and into shower shoes. Unscrew the light bulb, put in a triple-tap outlet, got power for a stereo and an electric shaver. Then, another E6 moves into the barracks before the first one DEROS's back to the states. Since he's E6, he wants a private room. Then all the sixes want rooms. Then E5s become barracks NCOs, and all the E's want private rooms.

"When the officers don't say shit, the walls go up everywhere. All they make us do now is put our name on the door so they can find us to pull detail. Some guys who get short don't even do that."

In the corner beside the double bunk was a small white refrigerator, big enough to store two soldiers' monthly ration of beer, about two cases, plus other canned food, crackers, and snacks. At eye-level across one wall were playboy centerfolds arranged by month, April to December 1971. Below the centerfolds were Becker's family pictures and Edgar's wife, plus snapshots of each playing football and sitting with the guys drinking beer in jungle fatigues. There was a barstool, convenient for guitar playing, a big Akai tapedeck with a collection of reels of music taped from the AFVN radio. Below the photographs were two army footlockers, more sitting space. On a high shelf was their TO&E field gear, helmets, canteens, pistol belts, flakvests, all looking neat and new. Using every available space, more goodies were stashed under the bottom bunk; folding chairs, a small cooler, a Magnavox turntable, and an amplifier with two speakers.

"The stuff just stays with the room," Becker deadpanned. "Matt owns the fridge. I bought the stereo and speakers for $50 from his old roommate. Shit, he didn't want to drag that stuff back to the world."

"What if you didn't want to buy it?'

"No sweat, GI. Tack up an ad on the admin billboard. 'Stereo for Sale. $50. Sell it or trade it for a gook souvenir, same same'."

Edgar adjusted the small pedestal fan, aiming it at the narrow strip of ventilation screen above the top bunk.

"Not bad, huh?"

Jim looked around. "I could get used to it."

"Hey, you said if I let you play the Gibson you'd tell me what it's like on Penny."

"What time did you say it was?"

"Sneaking up on 12:30."

"What time do they shut down records branch. I promised Pomeroy I wouldn't fuck up my R&R... And here I sit, wrecked, playing guitar, telling war stories."

"Vinny's there 'til 1700, usually. He's a short-timer so he acts real cocky but he's okay. Everybody at admin gets a half-day off but records branch, too many grunts on base during the cease-fire. 'Cease-fire', that's a joke. It's always a cease-fire around Bien Hoa. I been here six weeks and we've taken one in-coming mortar round. It hit somewhere out near the air strips. This place used to get hit with mortars day and night. But it's nothing like what you've been through, huh?"

Jim yawned and sat up against the wall. Reluctantly, he handed the Gibson back to Becker who lovingly put it back in it s hard case.

"Whattaya wanna know?"

"What's it like, man? Are you surrounded by jungle? Is there a line where you cross and say 'this is ours and that's Charlie's?' What do you do all day? How far is it from here?"

Jim laughed. "What do I do all day? In the morning we get chow. On Catapult we had a battalion field kitchen and the companies took turns with hot meals. But on LZ Penny it's all C-rations, so far. Sometimes we build a fire and heat 'em up, but not for breakfast, just dinner. 'Supper,' Pomeroy calls it because he's a ploughboy from Iowa. Then, every other day or so, if we're not pulling guard duty on the LZ we climb into Hueys and slick out to some clearing in the jungle. Then we hump, man. We walk around in the fuckin' jungle and hope we don't get in the shit. Hump, that's what's I do all day."

"How many guys?"

"A company," he said, "sometimes the whole battalion if there's a village to check out. Pull a sweep or hump up and down a hill. Hump all day. Up the hill and back down the hill. Around the village, across the rice paddy, into Mrs. Thieu's rubber plantation. Chase Charlie in there because he knows we can't use gunships and artillery in Mrs. Thieu's fucking plantations. Then we fly out or get re-logged in place."

"What's re-log?"

"Re-log? Re-log is more food, more fuckin '16 and '60 ammo to carry, more fuckin frags... we get re-logged with so much shit we can't carry it all. Man, we get so many frags we have contests to see who can throw one the farthest. Pomeroy always wins. Throwing frags into a river is pretty cool. You hear this muffled 'vvoooommm' and water heaves up.... fuckin' fish floatin' everywhere... "

"Logistics."

"Roger."

"Then what. You get in the shit and then what."

Jim's eyes drooped from half closed to quarter-mast, then he laughed again. "Hump some, get in the shit with Charles, hump some more after that. Then they bring us back to the firebase to get some hot chow and fatigues... see a movie. Walking all the time, always hot, always sweating, always tired enough to sleep standing up. Then it rains, everyday it rains. Fuckin' rain, looking for a dry place to throw a poncho down. Straight down rain. When it stops raining hide at least your face from the mosquitoes. Fuckin mosquitoes. One of 'em got Deagle good. But no VC ever will, not Deagle. That's about it."

"When you spend the night out there do you dig trenches like the marines?"

"Roger that. Dig and move and dig again. Dig in and set up our claymores and LP's and figure out who gets to sleep and who's stuck with the '60 on guard duty. Then wake up and have chow and start humping to some coordinate. Hump back to base a different way. That shit's up to Deagle. He figures out the compass stuff. Each time its called an 'operation', when you hump somewhere. They all got dumb names. Operation 'Sleigh Ride.' Hump 'til you're hot and sweating, take chow and a salt tablet and drink a warm quart. Then it rains. Fall asleep after chow. Fall asleep on smoke breaks. Fall asleep in formation... "

"But sometimes you get in the shit."

"Sometimes we get in the shit," Jim answered. "Not too much since Deagle got acting platoon sergeant, he's pretty smart. Twice a week, different stuff. Get ambushed by some one-shot Charlie, one shot and done. We get him sometimes. Or somebody flushes one, chase him down. Anybody in the jungle carrying a rifle ain't no friendly farmer, man. Sometimes we pull ambush duty. S-2 says Charles will pass north of "Phuck Yu" Village at 0200, a dozen of 'em comin' east from the border. Hump out a couple klicks and get some half-assed sleep. Nothing."

"I had to give up getting stoned all night when Deagle took over. Good NCO for a draftee. But he doesn't like looies much. Nobody likes a looie until he makes captain."

"How come?"

"They come on like they know it all after a week in-country. Some of 'em last about a week, too. We had six platoon commanders before we got Lieutenant Triggs. Triggs goes by what Deagle tells him. Pomeroy's RTO for 3rd Platoon, the best one in the whole brigade. In ten months old Pomeroy has never violated the sacred code of the radioman; he never once used a swear word on the radio."

"Aw come on! Not once? Not even damn?"

"Not even darn. And he never will."

"Want another beer?"

Jim yawned. "Negative, troop. I gotta go get my records check, my pecker check, finance... all that shit. If I don't get R&R squared away, Pomeroy will kick my ass. That is if he's still going on R&R. He's been acting like an FNG since we left Penny. I gotta di di."

"Watch out for the fuzz, man," Edgar said seriously, reaching to shake Jim's hand. "Later."

The barracks hallway was a dark tunnel with bright light at the both ends. Jim stood outside Becker's door, wondering which way to go. He heard the inside door latch slide closed. On my own now, he thought. He headed toward the near door and stepped outside, waiting for his eyes to adjust to sunlight, and his lungs to the blazing heat. He looked up and saw clouds building. In two hours it would be pouring rain, like Pomeroy always said, pitchforks and hammer-handles. As always, that made him laugh, the thought of all those pitchforks hitting these buildings. He reminded himself he was pretty stoned and not to talk to anybody.

He stepped away from the barracks and looked around. Buildings, everywhere. He forgot to ask which way to go. He forgot where the road was. The ground had a pitch to it so he decided to try downhill. He saw green uniforms in a column-of-two, more green uniforms standing formation. Green guys were VC, man. He walked until he came to a four-inch pipe sticking up out of the ground, its rusty screen piled with cigarette butts. He walked around it a couple times before his nose told him what it was, and realizing that, he laughed and hung a leak as the cigarette butts flew. Beyond the piss-tube he jumped a drainage ditch and met a pair of grunts in faded fatigues, walking fast. He flagged them down.

"Hey guys, which way's ERB?" He noticed the black bars on their collars. "Oh shit."

The officers waited for a salute that came about five seconds late. "You're going the wrong way, private. Orient yourself by Cav mountain and go east five hundred meters."

The officers were cool and gave him a pass. He watched them walk away and then turned a slow circle, like Pomeroy, until he found the green Cav mountain above the barracks roofs. He read the sign on top. The dark clouds rolling toward Cav mountain came from the west, toward LZ Penny. He faced east and picked an empty lane between barracks, looking as far as he could see—all clear. Making a game of it, he did some of his best sneaking until he crossed a road and snuck up on three Vietnamese women sitting on a barracks porch. He looked up the road and saw four more mama-sans sitting on another porch.

The two older mama-sans urged the young one to stand. She wore a dirty white au dai, sandals, and a straw hat. Holding out both hands in front of her she approached, smiling. She had something she wanted him to see. Jim stared slack-jawed, and she came close enough to look up into his eyes. She had nice white teeth, almond eyes, and lips a little too big for her mouth.

"You buy watch?" she asked, with a glance back at the old women.

Jim acted as if he didn't hear. She came a step closer and opened her hands, showing him one gold and one silver wristwatch. "You buy watch," she said with sweet encouragement.

Jim backed up. "*Dung lai*! Halt," he said. He reminded himself to keep an eye on the old women on the porch. The girl-san came close, showing him that her five-dollar watches were fine indeed. Panic was a dry mouth and a ringing in his ears. "*Di di mau*," he commanded. The ringing in his ear became an approaching truck engine.

"Buy the damn watch, you cheap bastard!" somebody said.

The tip of Jim's tongue stuck out. He looked up and saw troops in the front seat of an army deuce-and-a-half staring down at him. In the back of the open-bed truck were two-dozen more mama-sans. Hoochmaids, being trucked back to their village.

"You cheap Charlie!" a mama-san yelled from the truck.

The engine revved and the truck rolled down the street. One of the departing hoochmaids showed him her middle finger. Jim stared. *Dinky dau.*

He walked to the porch and sat down, laughing at his own paranoia. Sometimes when he smoked too much Cambodia red in the field he got paranoid, and Deagle made him take a nap instead of go out with the platoon. That was what he needed, a long nap. Where the hell was Deagle, anyway.

"Stand up, soldier," said a voice above him. "Let me see that nametag."

Jim looked up. Under the helmet liner was an officer with a recruit's whitewall haircut. Fuzz. This one had dark starched fatigues, cuffs perfectly bloused in MP style leather boots. He wore a flakvest and carried a .45 in a flapped holder. Looking up into his scowling face, Jim stood up and dusted the seat of his pants. He looked at the nametag. Fredrick.

"Full name, unit, and service number," Lieutenant Fredrick said.

Jim grinned. "No pushups today, sir. Grossnickel, James C. PFC, 3rd Platoon Bravo Company, 2nd Battalion 7th Brigade. US 53653775."

Lieutenant Fredrick took a step closer and looked hard into Jim's heavy-lidded eyes. Going down from there, he inspected Jim's uniform and boots, until he shook his head. "Have you forgotten how to stand at attention, private?" he asked

Jim pulled his shoulders back. "Am I going the right way to get to ERB?"

"ERB? Yes, I think that's where we're going next. At Bien Hoa, enlisted men addressing officers end with the word 'sir'."

Jim nodded. "Right. See, in the field, smart officers don't want you to say 'sir' too loud because Charles might hear and take a potshot at his helmet. That's how come we don't say 'sir'. Sir." Jim chuckled at his cleverness.

Fredrick stared. "Show me some in-transit orders, Private Grossnickel."

"We're supposed to get' em tonight, from Sergeant Hooper. NCO with the record nose?"

"I know Hooper. Then show me your military ID card."

"You bet." Jim reached back for his Cav wallet but slapped an empty pants pocket. He checked all his pockets. "Shit. I lost it. You see? I couldn't have bought that cheap gook watch even if I... "

"SHUT YOUR HOLE! No orders, no ID. See, smart privates like you show up AWOL at Bien Hoa all the time, and we know what to do with them. We're going to ERB." He turned Jim by the shoulder and shoved him. "You're under arrest."

"This is bullshit... "

"I said shut your hole! Now move it. This is not your day, private. If you are AWOL, you're going to Long Binh Jail."

Fredrick steered Jim across the courtyard to the largest building in the admin area. There was a long line of grunts at the front door, above which a wooden sign read "Enlisted Records Branch", and Fredrick had to wave his arms to clear a path. "Stand aside, stand aside there!" Inside the noisy building more in-transit troops were lined up, orders in hand, and the commotion

117

turned every head. Fredrick marched Grossnickel to the front of the line that ended at Sp5 Vincent's desk. Vincent rocked back in his chair and looked up. Fredrick had captured another grunt, a little one.

"This is bullshit," the grunt told him.

Jim looked right and left at ERB, one very noisy building. A platoon of records clerks sat pounding on typewriters. A dozen old pedestal fans hummed. There were fifty conversations going on at as many desks. The combined racket bounced off the open corrugated-metal ceiling and bare concrete floors. Cigarette smoke was a gray haze that hung between the fluorescent fixtures and the open rafters.

Jim read the sign on Sp5 Vincent's metal desk: "Have One Copy of Orders Ready: Have your Military ID Card Ready." On the wall behind the desk was a red-white-and-blue re-enlistment poster, in Spanish and English. Another poster advised "Extend Your Tour for Early ETS." The division chaplain had a poster, "God is Non-Denominational." The only place behind Vincent's desk that wasn't an army advertisement was a small area blocked-off by a tall, folding room divider. It was solid black with big silver dragons and birds and snow-covered Japanese mountains. Under the divider, Jim saw two pairs of gleaming spit-shined boots.

Vincent looked from the lieutenant to the private. Fredrick's prisoner wasn't intimidated by the harassment. Grossnickel; big name - little troopie. Then Vinny caught the PFC's glazed eyes and disoriented expression and had to keep from cracking a smile.

"Sir, we're kind a busy around here. The cease-fire?"

The MP lieutenant carefully placed his helmet on Vinny's desk then turned to PFC Grossnickel. He grabbed Jim by the shoulders and snatched him out of his slouch. He kicked Jim's heels together and twisted his chin to force his wandering eyes straight ahead.

"I understand all that, Specialist Vincent! Now you ask him the usual questions!"

"Sir, it's Christmas? I'd like to get out of here by oh dark thirty? Okay fine. Orders!"

Jim looked down at the young Italian face, broad mouth, large nose, and lively dark eyes. "This is bullshit," he said.

"Okay it's bullshit, but gimme your wallet anyway."

"I lost the fucker."

Vinny held out his hand. "Then gimme your ID."

Jim's eyebrows shot up and down. "In the wallet. In the mess hall, maybe."

Fredrick spoke over Jim's shoulder, "Satisfied?"

Vinny leaned back in his chair, knowing what Fredrick would do next. From behind the Japanese room divider, a pair of burly MP's emerged. Their helmet liners gleamed black and white and their boots creaked. They got Private Grossnickel by the arms and pulled his boots back from the desk. One

MP held him face down on the desk while the other body-searched him.

Jim tried to protest but a strong hand on the base of his neck had him pinned, and it was all he could do to breathe. He felt rough hands going up his right calf, behind his knee. A hand snaked up the back of his thigh and into the crack of his ass, and he bucked like horse until a nightstick whacked him in the ribs and took away his wind. He sagged, but fought hard again when the rude hand checked his left side, ankle to ass. The MPs stretched him, spread-eagle. With a hundred soldiers watching, they searched Jim's armpits, crotch, uniform pockets, and even his hair. When they stepped back and let Jim go he was red-faced and ruffled.

"This is bullshit!" he shouted "You guys try chaining me on no floor... I'll sick Pomeroy on your ass!"

Vinny picked up the phone, dialed, asked to speak to Mess Sergeant Arroyo. The MP's looked at Fredrick and shook their heads. The PFC was clean, no contraband.

"Arroyo's got his ID, if anybody's interested," Vinny said, hanging up. "Thanks, fellas," he called to the departing MP's. "Great work as always! Merry Christmas to you Haldeman! Merry Christmas to you too Ehrlichman! Pigs. Lieutenant, I think ERB can take it from here. PFC Grossnickel, what's your unit?"

"Garry Owens. 2nd battalion 7th Brigade."

Vinny turned his head aside and hollered. "Specialist Brennan! Front and center!"

Brennan, who had watched the show from his desk, hopped out of his chair and double-timed down the hall. In front of Lieutenant Fredrick he snapped himself to a chesty position of attention.

"SPECIALIST BRENNAN PRESENT AND ACCOUNTED FOR... SIR!"

Fredrick was not amused. He sat on Vinny's desk, arms folded. "Knock it off, Brennan," he said.

"YES... SIR!"

"I said, knock it off!"

Vinny said, "Specialist Brennan, take PFC Grossnickel here and go through his 201 per SOP. Call EOB and see about his R&R orders."

"Roger! Affirmative! Willco, SIR!" Brennan shouted.

"Brennan unless you want an Article 15 you better get the fuck out of my sight!"

Obeying the lieutenant's order, Brennan whirled, a stiff over-rotated about-face that ended up facing Fredrick again. He saluted twice and then marched off to his desk with his neck bowed and his elbows out like Popeye.

Lieutenant Fredrick watched Brennan's back. "One of these days... somebody's going to get that guy... "

"Well somebody better hurry up, sir," Vinny told him. "Brennan's got twenty-six days left in-country." Vinny's phone rang and he answered it quickly, listened, and hung up. "Message for you, lieutenant. 'Tell him to haul his ass to the admin CP and report to Captain Olivette, ASAP'. Sir." Vinny grinned up at him. Fredrick retrieved his helmet and left.

Brennan's desk was chaos, files piled, two half-full coffee mugs, an ashtray heaped with butts and gum wrappers. A small blue-and-yellow plague read "Sp4 Gary H Brennan, 7th Brigade Records". Sitting down, Brennan rolled open his 2nd Battalion A-G file drawer and began to sing, sounding something like Dean Martin: "everybody... loves zzzombody... zzzometime..." He found Jim's Grossnickel's 201 file.

"Nice job with those pigs," he said. "Helps being totally wrecked, I'd imagine." Jim grinned, feeling better.

"Now listen up, troop. Your R&R processing WILL be complete before you climb on that airplane and it WILL consist of one-each finance check, weapons check, records check, security debriefing, medical check, pecker check, locker check, and pre-flight shakedown. This portion of your R&R processing is a records check, is that clear sol...JER? Did you meet 1st Ree yet? What a trip."

Jim laughed. He liked Brennan right away. He glanced back at Vinny's desk and found the little Italian Sp5 watching him, smirking. He shot a thumbs-up and Vinny shot one back.

"I thought all you guys would be assholes," Jim said cheerfully.

Brennan held the 201 file open where Jim could read it. "I am an asshole. I am also your records specialist, Brennan, Gary C., twenty-six days left in-country. I ask the questions and you WILL answer with the word, no. ...Do you require immediate medical attention... no. Do you require emergency dental work... no. You see how this goes? Since you arrived in-country has there been a death in your family that would classify you as a sole survivor... hmmm? No? Since you arrived in country have you been classified AWOL, POW, MIA, or KIA... hmmm? I especially enjoy meeting guys the army says are dead... and they don't know they're dead... "

Jim choked up, unable to catch up with Brennan's rapid-fire drill.

"At ease, troop. No laughing in ERB, this is serious shit. Now you will answer YES to all questions. IS your current rank, unit number, duty station correct as it appears... YES. IS your designated insurance beneficiary CURRENT AND CORRECT as it appears... YES. ARE your army commendations and awards up to date... FUCKING-A-SKIPPY! Okay, so much for that, end of record check. Now let's see about some orders." He slapped the folder closed.

Jim caught his breath while Brennan picked up the phone and made the call to EOB. He recited Grossnickel's serial number, rank and unit from memory and had an answer in thirty seconds. "In-transit R&R orders were cut, here's the number," and he wrote it on the outside of the 201 file. "Where you going?"

"Australia."

"Ah, down under. Good choice, mate. But Australia flights fill up fast so you better move it." He leaned closer, keeping his voice down. "That's where I went. Round-eyed women. Never could bring myself to fuck any of these Vietnamese, you dig?"

Jim's smile was conspiratorial. "I got a buddy who had a whore that put ground glass in her vagina."

"Sounds gruesome."

"Another buddy of mine has a buddy who's stuck on some island in the Quang Tri Province with incurable VD. They won't let him go home."

"You don't believe that shit, do you? Incurable VD? Nah, all it takes is a million units in each cheek... kills the drips in a week or so. Penicillin Numbah One, GI."

Jim felt himself coming down. "Wow. Hey specialist, would you check a Deagle, William, also 2nd of the 7th."

"Name's Gary. Never specialist. Or Brennan, or fuck-up. Deagle's in Bien Hoa? All you grunts are always trying to find each other. You're not supposed to have tight buddies in a combat zone. Buddies are unauthorized. Me, I have no friends. I got Vinny instead."

Jim laughed. "Deagle calls me Fuck-knuckle, same same. He's in the hospital detachment."

Brennan's expression was pained. "And I got another question: why are we carrying so many of you grunts MIA on the morning reports?"

Jim shrugged.

"Every one of my companies has at least one MIA. Gotta be old AWOL's not re-classified, right? What's the skinny on this."

"Yeah, we got AWOL's. We also got a couple LBSOL's in 7th Brigade. Left Behind and Shit Out of Luck. They should be KIA's, prob'ly," he added, matter-of-factly.

Brennan stared. Recovering, he whistled as he rummaged in the 2nd Battalion file drawers. Deagle's 201 file came up missing.

"Specialist Vincent!" he hollered over the typewriter clatter. "You got my Deagle, William at your desk?"

Vinny looked up and hollered back. "That is affirmative! Who wants to know?"

"Buddy of his! You WILL hand-carry it back to this desk ASAP."

Vinny pulled the 201 from his top drawer and walked down the aisle. "Your buddy's getting a Silver Star cluster."

Jim had no idea and his jaw dropped open. "Another one?"

Vinny opened the 201 and showed him the freshly-cut order. "I'd like to meet him. Is he pretty mellow or a hardass?"

"Deagle's... like both. You'll meet him if I can find him."

"Me and Brennan can take care of that. Stick around. Then we'll di di and grab some cold beers."

As Vinny turned and walked back to his desk there was another commotion at the front door, and he wondered if Lieutenant Fredrick was back. He saw two EOB troops in the middle of a mob of records clerks. Whatever they were talking about attracted the attention of the grunts in line, too. A squad of them jammed on their boonyhats and headed for the exit. Somebody hollered "Hey, Vin!"

"Something's up." Brennan told Grossnickel. He lifted his nose and sniffed like a dog. "I smell... a shit detail... "

Vinny walked to the door and most of enlisted records branch followed. The EOB clerk with the breaking news was a Sp5 with six months left in his second tour in Vietnam.

"Andrews is pulling another sweep of the hill, man," he said. "This time they're taking grunts from R&R and all 11-Bravo secondaries from admin."

"Can they do that?"

"I don't know. He sent Hooper and Timmerman up there to get volunteers."

"Volunteers, my ass," Vinny told him. "A grunt with ten months on a firebase is gonna volunteer to pull a sweep here?"

"They're grunts, Vin."

"Hey, I'm 11-Bravo secondary and I work here and I'm not fuckin' volunteering. I'm too short for that shit."

"I think I'll go. What the hell."

Vinny read the faces of the ERB troops around him and shrugged. "Any of you guys want to hump that hill? Go right ahead. Me, I'm gonna get stoned and get a good seat at the show. Dismissed, get outa here!"

There were a dozen grunts still in line from the front door waiting for records processing. Vinny pulled on a baseball cap and called them to his desk.

"Listen up, men. We got this major with a plate in his head. He's rounding up grunts to sweep that big hill behind your barracks. As you can see, there ain't gonna be any records processing the rest of the afternoon. But, because of the cease-fire, me and my troops are workin' Christmas Eve so you can get it done tomorrow. My advice to you guys is 'get the fuck outa Dodge'."

With all the typewriters quiet and the fans shut down, Vinny's boots echoed in the aisle as he walked back to Brennan's desk.

"Battalion sweep of Hill 229," he told Brennan. "A drag."

Brennan put his stuff away and stood up. He drew the invisible sword from his invisible scabbard and slashed the air. "Jim, you come with us while Major Andrews, a.k.a. "The Scarlet Pimpernel" is saving admin. On with the revolution!"

At LZ Penny, any time day or night, Pomeroy could fall asleep. He could lean against a tree and fall asleep, standing. But inside stifling R&R Barracks 2022, lying on a soft bunk, sleep was impossible. R&R 2022 was full up, eighteen out of twenty bunks taken, counting the one saved for Grossnickel. He lay with eyes stuck open, listening to the chatter about Hawaii and Australia and Kuala Lumpur, wondering where the hell Deagle was, maybe gone back to LZ Penny. Or, as Jim had worried, he was really sick with jungle fever.

Then Pomeroy admitted it to himself. The reason he couldn't sleep, he was just plain chickenshit.

"Where's Godzilla?" somebody hollered.

Pomeroy recognized the voice of a 1st of the 9th troops he'd met in the R&R detachment. He closed his eyes, pretending to be asleep.

"Hey, big guy! We're going to the PX to blow some money. You're payroll guard."

Pomeroy had $250 in his wallet and a new set of fatigues from the quartermaster, part of his plan to keep a low profile. The troop shook him until he opened his eyes.

"Negative," he answered, "I'm crashed right here, over. Got to wait for my buddy."

Ten minutes later he was staring at the barracks ceiling when the barefoot kid from the morning formation, Private Horton, showed up with in-transit R&R orders. The kid was still barefoot and the cuffs of his fatigue pants scuffed on the concrete as he walked.

"Souvenir from Sergeant Hooper."

The orders, ten copies each for himself and Grossnickel, didn't specify an R&R city, only assignment to the R&R detachment for a five-day out-of-country vacation. Pomeroy's name was underlined on each of his personal copies. Jim's name was on the same page, the very last entry, one of only two PFC's going on R&R. Only good friends, Pomeroy thought, and the Good Lord had made it possible for Jim Grossnickel to survive ten months in Vietnam and make it to R&R. But at least Jim was out there going through his processing and not laying on his back too scared to move.

Sweat rolled down Pomeroy's elbow to his fingertips and onto the corner of his orders. He ripped off one copy, folded it and put it in his Cav wallet, stowed the rest in his wall locker. When he lay back down the sheet felt damp. He sat up again. Everything in this damn country was either wet or hot. Finally he threw on his shirt and boonyhat and walked outside. Barracks 2022 backed up against the concertina wire and bunkers at the bottom of Hill 229.

He looked across the rolls of wire at the tall elephant grass fifty meters away and felt an urge to stay behind cover. He was a big target. Stranger things had happened, he knew, than a one-shot Charley sticking an SKS out of tall grass and blowing away an un-suspecting GI on R&R. What a way to die. He hung close to the corner of the barracks wondering if Deagle had seen this mini-DMZ. Way too close, he thought. No room to maneuver in a firefight here. And barracks walls don't stop bullets.

He took a defiant step into the open. The DMZ was quiet. The sky above was clouding up and he smelled the afternoon rain approaching. There was a bunker twenty meters to his right, another thirty meters to his left. He walked right, looking past the bunker to the MP checkpoint, and the road going up the hill. He thought he heard a jeep chugging up the road earlier. He stood beside the bunker and looked at the defoliated, wired dead zone straight ahead. Beyond the wire, the tops of the elephant grass swayed in furnace-hot gusts of wind. He saw bamboo clumps intermingled with the sharp grass. Tough walking, he decided, grass and bamboo, a bad angle... tough even for the gooks.

The bunker was about 4'x 4'x 6' high. From the outside all Pomeroy saw was sandbags, three rows deep in the walls and two bags high on the roof. The shooting port was about two feet tall, set up for sitting. The only way in was to crawl in through the front. Back to the wire, he leaned his head in for a look around and was surprised to see a plywood interior to go with the dirt floor and rusty metal folding chair. It reminded him of the deer-blinds his dad had built for him in the alfalfa-field corners of their Iowa farm. On the back wall his eyes were drawn to a familiar name carved into the plywood, "Elvis Rules," and he felt a pang of homesickness.

The inside of the bunker was a graffiti mural. All the troops over all the years, sitting in the dark, scared or bored, scrawling their initials as proof that they'd been there. Or just homesick and posting the name of a personal hero, a DEROS date, or a heartfelt social commentary as to what the army could do with Vietnam. The history of the war in Vietnam, he thought, is written on these walls. Someday when the gooks have it back they'll tear it down and not realize what any of it meant, if anything. Birthdays, ETS dates, hearts with initials, "Hawaii Jun'66", "Janice", "Jimmy", "Airplane", "The Dirt Band", "The Doors", and "Tet sucks". He didn't recognize any names from the 7th Brigade, so he reached in and scrawled "Cleve" with his folding knife. His dad always referred to him as "son number four" but his mom still called him Cleve. A single tarnished .223 case caught his eye on the dirt floor.

"No daytime guard," he wondered aloud.

He stood back and had a better look at the bunker. There were cigarette butts on the bare ground in front of it. The sandbags around the shooting port in direct sunlight were faded and frayed and a few leaked from old bullet holes. On the roof, a few sandbags had grass sticking out. He turned, the brim of his boonyhat pulled down under the high sun, and followed the rows of spiraled wire to where they curved out of sight around the hill. Then he noticed the banks of floodlights on the corners of each barracks.

So they manned the bunkers at night. It would be easier for Charles to hit this base in the daytime, Pomeroy decided.

Feeling miserable and lonesome. Pomeroy shagged back toward barracks 2022. There was no getting around it and he knew it, he was scared to death to make that AT&T phone call to his parents. The thought of speaking to his father for the first time in fifteen months had ruined R&R for him. When the cease-fire was over, he might just as well go back to Penny and spend the week sleeping.

He heard a truck engine whining closer. He reached the front of the building as a covered deuce-and- half pulled up. He saw Sergeant Hooper jump down wearing a steel pot and flakvest. Hooper stumped into barracks 2019 and came out pushing a dozen troops toward the truck. When he saw Pomeroy his face broke into a smile, red nose like Santa Claus.

"Hey big fella, where's your little buddy?"

"Processing, I guess."

"C'mon with us. We're gonna push Charles down off that hill this afternoon."

A combat sweep. Pomeroy felt almost grateful.

1250Hours 23Dec71
1st Cav Div HQ
Bien Hoa Military Post Exchange

Walking east to the PX with his M-16 slung on his shoulder, Deagle thought about meeting Sp6 Karuda, the admin armorer. He was one for the book, a reminder that there was indeed a lot going on in a US Army rear area. At Bien Hoa, a soldier had to pay to get back what belonged to him.

"Goin' home or goin' on our little picnic this afternoon?" the armorer had asked him, passing his orders back over the dutch double door.

"What picnic?"

"Battalion sweep of that hill up the street. Gonna bring some pee on Charles."

Deagle looked up at Hill 229 over his right shoulder. "Waste of time," he said.

"Says who?"

"Says me, specialist."

"How come?"

"I've humped some other hills like it. Do I have to sign something?"

Sp6 Karuda found Deagle's M-16 in back and ripped the hang-tag from the triggerguard. "Sign here, sarge. You get hit or what?"

"Malaria."

"Well, that's nothin'."

Deagle checked his rifle's serial number. He worked the action, snapped the trigger. and switched the fire selector back and forth. He looked the weapon over from end to end. The plastic stock was scratched and the parkerized metal finish was rubbed away in places but Karuda returned it to him looking clean and deadly, if over-oiled. He borrowed a patch and wiped it down, then slung it on his right shoulder.

"Magazines?"

Karuda leaned his elbows on the split-door and spat brown tobacco juice out into the nearest weeds. Then he pushed across a dozen full clips at Deagle, watching his eyes. Deagle picked one up and checked the round on the follower. It was red-tipped. Deagle shoved all twelve magazines right back at the armorer.

"I'll take the clips I checked in with. Where I'm going tracers are numbah ten, GI."

"Yours got confiscated and you'll take what I give you, sarge. Trade 'em in when you get home."

"Confiscated? Plain GI ball ammo?"

"Everything has a price," he shrugged.

Deagle looked him over and Karuda's gaze collapsed. Thinking it over, Deagle reached down for his wallet. "I got kumshaw if you got my clips."

The E6's eyes narrowed. "What kinda kumshaw?"

Deagle pulled a blue-and-brown paper bill from his Cav wallet and held it up to the light. "Piaster. Vietnamese currency."

Karuda laughed. "That shit's worthless! Even the gooks won't take 'em."

Deagle grinned. "Better take another look. You see that writing in the top right? Says North Vietnam. Not South."

Suspicious, Karuda held the bill at arms length. "How'd you come by it?"

"Took it off a captured North Vietnamese major. Trade you even for my magazines."

Karuda disappeared behind his file cabinets and returned with a waded t-shirt. Inside the shirt were Deagle's full magazines and the trade was consummated. Deagle picked out one magazine and thumbed eighteen rounds onto the counter-top, and there were no tracers. Satisfied, he poked the clips into his bandolier and tied it around his waist.

"You're another one," Karuda said, "loads eighteen rounds in a twenty-round clip. Sarge, lemme tell you what: when I work on a rifle there ain't no reason to load short. That rifle won't never double-feed the first round, I guarantee it."

Deagle nodded. "I guarantee it too, specialist. I load eighteen rounds. I'll take my sidearm, too, unless it's confiscated. Which if it is... I'm comin' over this door and takin' my pick... you bic?"

"Thought you might have forgot about it," Karuda grinned.

126

The .45 was in the top drawer of a gray filing cabinet. It was clean and slick and gleamed from too much gun oil. The clip was gone.

"How about some .45 ammo?"

"Sorry, sarge, you didn't have none."

"Had an empty clip."

"How come a buck sergeant's issued a sidearm anyway?" he said, opening a drawer and scooping up a handful of tarnished GI hardball rounds and a single clip.

Deagle locked the slide and looked into the chamber. "I pull prisoner escort duty to Long Binh, sometimes. Good duty, because I get to spend the night at Hotel Saigon."

"I'll give you one full clip, no charge. But you gotta see my prisoner. Got him right in back."

Deagle squinted into the darkness beyond the racks of M-16's. "What'd he do?"

"Deserter."

"Let's see him."

Karuda opened the bottom half of the door and Deagle followed him down a narrow aisle between rifle racks. The prisoner sat on the concrete floor with his back against the wall. He had no hat, no boots, and no dog-tags around his neck. His hands were cuffed in his lap and his leg irons were chained to a u-shaped rail in the floor slab. Deagle dropped to squatting position, eye level with the prisoner, and looked him over. He didn't recognize him.

"What unit?"

The young man rolled his head. He looked at Deagle's nametag and three-chevron collar pin. "Don't much matter."

"Well lookee here," Karuda said, "he's got a voice after all."

"I'm with 2nd of the 7th. LZ Penny."

After ten seconds the prisoner said. "2nd of the 8th . LZ Rita... 6 months ago... "

Deagle nodded. "They're still there. You guys are op-conning with the Arvins now. Pulling sweeps. Not too bad. You need anything?"

With a glance at Karuda he said. "What'd it cost you for a ticket to see a deserter?"

"I could write your folks, tell 'em I saw you and you were okay, something like that."

"You gotta be trippin', man."

Deagle nodded. He straightened up and walked toward the sunlight.

"Hey buck sergeant," the prisoner called. "take a good look at the magazines this fucker gives you... "

Deagle nodded. "Roger that. Thanks."

Now, a mile east of the arms room, he walked through the open sand hills criss-crossed with GI foot-trails. It was easy going and his long legs stretched out in the afternoon heat. The rifle on his shoulder, the slightly heavy rucksack in the middle of his back, and the confining pistol belt and bandolier around his waist were all familiar burdens. The sun was behind the clouds but the temperature was still 100 degrees, and he wondered if he'd make it to the PX and back to admin before the rain. Sweat popped from every pore and he took another salt tablet. On his left, he watched a convoy of canvas-top deuce-and-a-halfs lumber out the back motorpool gate onto the main road. Half the trucks turned east, the other half went west and then up toward the hill. A little picnic, Karuda had said. He'd escaped admin just in time.

A half mile further east he saw the Bien Hoa Post Exchange, a white flat-roofed building with an eight-foot fence around sitting in an open field. There was a blacktop road in and out and two MP checkpoints, one at the gate and the other in the middle of a parking lot filled with army and air force jeeps. From a distance of 500 meters the PX looked a like a sugar cube.

He humped across the open field to the gate checkpoint and showed his ID to an MP in creased khakis.

"No weapons in the PX, sarge. Check 'em at Bravo shack, okay?"

It was another 100-meter hike to the Bravo Checkpoint, and he fell in step with a dozen admin troops on a Christmas-shopping mission. Getting closer, he saw that the white sugar cube had attracted ants, a swarm of Vietnamese boy-sans on the front sidewalk. After checking his rifle and handgun with the MP he stared in amazement. The PX at Bien Hoa had so many black-market scroungers that a GI had to do hand-to-hand to get in. It looked like a Saigon fish market

"All those Vietnamese got passes?" he asked the MP.

The MP looked up to see who asked the question. "They work here, man."

It was expressly illegal, not to say immoral, for an American soldier to purchase American goods for any Vietnamese but here it was on a grand scale, with a pair of MP's standing at the front door observing. The Vietnamese boys formed a blockade and intercepted GI's shouting "hey Joe! hey Joe!". They waved MPC's, Deagle noted, not their own worthless Piasters, and they had Christmas lists of what they wanted to buy.

Deagle stepped up on the sidewalk and emptied his pockets, wallet, knife, compass, and P-38, and wrapped them in his boonyhat. Hat high overhead, he plowed toward the glass doors using his knees and hips to push the boys aside. Almost there, a boy-san got hold of his fatigue shirt and hung on as of his life depended on it. He tried to climb up Deagle's back until one of the MP's called his name sharply.

"Din! *Di di mau!*"

Deagle turned and confronted the twelve-year old. Under the bill of his baseball cap, Din's dark eyes were huge. "Joe! You buy radio! I show you. I gib you MPC two times!"

Deagle looked to the MP's. "You guys just let this shit go on?"

"Hey, cut some slack, sarge. Just tell him to di di."

"Joe, I want battery radio, you bic? Battery radio. I gib you MPC."

"I'm not buyin' you shit. Di di!"

"You buy me battery radio, I gib you MPC!" and the boy showed him three American $20 Military Pay Certificates in his tight little fist. With his other hand the kid managed to get a good grip on Deagle's pistolbelt.

Deagle pried the small fingers loose and backed toward the door. "I not buy you radio... I buy you Ex-lax, you little cockroach. Now get the fuck away from me."

The kid's face swelled with defiance. "You boshit! You fuck you... you fuck you!"

"Yeah, yeah... learn to speak English."

The PX doors closed behind him. His first sensation was cool air on his skin. Air conditioning? Second impression, with 200-foot long aisles the place looked bigger inside than outside. Third, there were no Christmas decorations, not even a picture of Santa, only a mob of Christmas shoppers. On the front wall was the same Uncle Sam poster he'd seen at finance, a reminder of the U.S. Postal Service regulations on the shipping of goods home from of a combat zone.

He stowed his possessions in his pockets, flattened his hat and tucked it in his belt. On his left, an air force policeman in dress blues, paratrooper boots, and an AP helmet liner beckoned him over. Behind the AP was a rack of helmets and a rucksack or two.

Without the rucksack, sweat dried on Deagle's back and a cold shiver wracked him. He pulled his shoulders together and walked between the merchandise aisles on his right and the cash registers on his left. At each register station was an attractive, longhaired Vietnamese girl-san dressed in a clean white *ao dai* and a long line of GI's with armloads of goodies. Fifty suspicious pairs of eyes watched him like a shoplifter.

He ducked into the aisle on his right under a wide overhead sign, "United States Army Issue." The aisle was green from front to back with full-length mirrors at every pillar, and each mirror had a crowd of GI's in front of it trying on fatigue shirts and field jackets. He walked past shelves piled with folded green jungle fatigues, stateside jungle and stateside green socks, green t-shirts and shorts, towels, belts, bootlaces, blankets, and poncho liners. Why would anybody buy this stuff, he wondered, when the government issued it for free? He stopped at a full-length mirror and studied the reflection of a tall, gaunt-faced buck sergeant in lime-green fatigues and clay-stained scuffed boots. *Sin loi*, Mr. Inspector General.

The color in the next aisle was black: shelf upon shelf of jungle boots, garrison boots, paratrooper boots, and low quarters. Boots were not what he was looking for, either. At the center of the PX he found the packaged foods, shelves stacked with canned Vienna sausage and tuna and Spam and ham spread, and little jars packed with corn-wrapped tamales. There were tins of potato sticks and Fritos, bottles of peanuts and cashews, candy bars, and plastic bags of jelly beans, licorice, and Pomeroy's favorite, salted sunflower seeds in the shell.

Deagle scooped two cans of Hormel Vienna Sausage, one bag of red licorice, a plastic bottle of apple juice, and headed up to the cash registers. When his turn came, he smiled down at the pretty Vietnamese girl, nametag "Mia", but Mia was all business. He spent $1.63 MPC and received a voucher for the thirty-seven cents coin change. He walked back to the AP stand and sat with his back against the outer wall, cracked open the Vienna sausage with the slotted key on the bottom of the can. He devoured the miniature hot dogs while the stoic AP watched. He drank the whole quart of apple juice and finished half a bag of licorice as desert. He stood by a buttcan and had a smoke.

"Still hungry," he told the air policeman.

Using his boonyhat for a shopping bag, he returned to the food aisles for powdered donuts, two little bottles of pre-cooked Libby's tamales, deviled ham, and a medium bag of Fritos corn chips, more Vienna sausage, and sunflower seeds for Pomeroy. He cruised through the electronics, the stereo players and turntables, tape decks, recorders, radios, speakers, televisions, electric shaves, can openers, blenders, and coffee pots. The brands were American and Japanese, Akai, Magnavox, Philco, Amana. There were three sizes of refrigerators for sale. At the end of the electronics aisle was a busy U.S. postal booth with Vietnamese girls wrapping packages and labeling boxes for shipment to the states.

He found the PX jewelry section at the back wall, a glass-topped counter the length of a swimming pool. It was two-troops deep and elbow-to-elbow, officers and GI's alike competing for the attention of a squad of Vietnamese salesgirls. Wrist-watches were in the middle between insignia rings and Asian cat-eye opals. He squeezed himself up to the counter and claimed a space by setting down his over-stuffed boonyhat. The watch assortment was fifteen feet of American, Swiss, Japanese, Korean, and the ubiquitous two-dollar Fugi watches. It took only a few seconds of looking at price tags to find the small selection of Rolex and Omega watches, and he stopped right there. He caught the eye of a girl-san and pointed down through the glass.

"GMT Master."

"Officah watch," she replied after glancing at his three-chevron Sergeant's collar pin.

The Sp4 beside Deagle asked her to police up a less expensive watch and she obliged, bringing it out carefully and setting it on the glass. Deagle waited to catch her eye again and pointed at the Rolex. "That one, please girl-san."

"Officah watch" and ignored him.

Deagle looked to the admin troop beside him. "She got a case of the ass about something?"

He shrugged. "They just do what they're told, man."

On Deagle's right a JAG captain and admin 1st lieutenant had a half-dozen engraved 1st Cavalry gold-and-blue engraved Zippo's on the glass. Deagle tapped the captain on the shoulder.

"What is it, sergeant?" His nametag said Ridell.

"A little help, sir?" He called the girl-san over again and pointed at the $185 Rolex diver's watch. She looked at Ridell, who looked Deagle over from his shabby boots to his mop of brown hair. Finally Ridell nodded and she put the colorful Rolex on the counter in front him.

"Expensive toy," Ridell commented.

Deagle liked the big red-and blue-fringed black face, the phosphorous tipped hour and minute hands, and the metal heavy metal bracelet.

"Maybe you should spend a few MPC's for a new uniform, instead."

Deagle smiled. "Yeah, I look a little rough, sir." Then he shook his head, and set the watch on the glass. "It's okay, but I bet you can't read it easy at night." He pushed it toward the girl-san and pointed to the Omega displayed beside it. Eyes on Ridell, she replaced the GMT and brought out another large-faced watch, an Omega Seamaster 300. Black face, silver bezel, huge phosphorous hands and numerals, heavy chain bracelet with a safety bar fastener. It had a price tag of $140, almost three-fourths of an E5's monthly base pay.

"Rotating home, sergeant?" Captain Ridell asked him.

"Got six months left, sir." He picked up the Omega and hefted it in his hand. It was even heavier than the GMT. Slipping it over his left wrist he snapped the clasp and found the band needed a one-link shortening for a perfect fit but he wasn't about to ask this grim-faced girl-san to fix it. He counted out his three $50 MPC's on the counter. "I'll take it."

She stared at the money.

"Girl-san, do I have to get an air policeman over here to buy a watch?"

"No need for that, sergeant," Ridell said. "And you don't speak to her like some village prostitute, she goes to college. It's alright, Nuang."

The watch was one of the new ball-bearing perpetual automatics. To start it ticking Deagle had only to roll his wrist a few times. He watched the sweep of the second hand and then pulled out the thick stem to the time for 1:39. Nuang pushed the empty Omega box and his $10 MPC across the counter. As he stepped back from the counter with his boonyhat Lieutenant Berkowitz moved to block him.

"Paul, would you take an expensive watch like that into the field? I wouldn't. Maybe we'd better see some orders, sergeant."

Ridell folded his arms across his chest to observe.

Deagle looked from one officer to the other. "Whatever you guys want." He fished the folded copy of his hospital orders from his shirt pocket.

Berkowitz read them carefully, glanced at Ridell, and handed them back.

"Tell me something, sergeant. You've been in a rear area with a fully stocked quartermaster and PX for three weeks. Why are you so dirty?"

"Lieutenant, if you'd ever served in a forward area you'd know."

Berkowitz stepped closer, looking up. "I don't think that answers my question."

Deagle moved a half step closer. "Sometimes, new green uniforms make you a target. So do shiny bars on collars."

"Is that so."

"Most affirm. Sir."

"Well this shiny bar entitles me to some respect from E5 types. This is an officer talking to you, and I want your heels locked and your eyes straight ahead."

Deagle looked left, then right. "We're inside a PX. I'm not going to stand at attention for you like a goddamn recruit. That's bullshit."

Captain Ridell uncrossed his arms and moved in. "You better shut your hole before you've got more trouble than you can handle."

"Shut my hole? He's the one who started it, tell him to shut his hole."

"It's okay, Paul. I know how to handle garbage like this." Berkowitz looked straight up in Deagle's face. "He thinks because he's 11-Bravo the UCMJ no longer applies to him. We're going to get that straight right now. Position of attention, sergeant, that's an order."

Behind Berkowitz, a stocky major cruised the jewelry counter. Deagle couldn't see what branch he wore on his collar but his uniform was almost as faded as his own. Taking a chance, he stepped around the 1st lieutenant and caught the major's eye.

"Excuse me, sir, could you help me with a problem?"

The major's name was Zorn, artillery branch.

"What problem," he asked.

"This yoyo," he said, indicating Berkowitz.

Zorn pulled in his chin.

"There's no problem at all, sir," Berkowitz said. "As you can tell, Buck Sergeant Deagle here has a mouth on him."

Deagle offered Zorn a copy of his orders and major checked them. "What's the problem?" he asked Deagle.

"This lieutenant says grunts are garbage."

"I told you to shut your hole," Ridell reminded Deagle. "You're going to learn military manners."

"Garbage," Zorn repeated, jaw hardening.

1st Lieutenant Berkowitz stood a little taller. "Not quite true, sir. My point to the Sergeant..."

"I know your point, lieutenant. I read you 5x5. You think you're better than everybody else. I get that same crap all the time myself. Did you know that some of us who work for our pay don't like brand new fatigues because in some jungle light, dark green shows up as solid black? Did you?"

"No, sir, I didn't"

"Well now you do! So, unless there's a colonel around, you officers go back to your shopping and leave the sergeant to me."

"Yes, sir."

Deagle smiled. "How are my military manners now?"

Captain Ridell glared at him but walked away toward the front of the PX. Deagle quickly checked to see if there was another way out but there was only the front door.

"Better watch it around JAG types," Zorn told him "They take notes."

Deagle nodded. "I could have walked away, sir, but I got a big mouth."

"Yeah, me too," he said grinning. "And sometimes I'm deaf from all those 105 rounds... know what I mean? What outfit?"

"2nd Battalion 7th Brigade, sir. Bravo Company."

Zorn checked Deagle's nametag again. "I know your battalion commander. They just medivac'd him in from LZ Penny this morning. We went to school together, he was a senior when I was a junior. Son-of-a-bitch is always one step ahead. I make major and he makes light colonel. He even beat me to Sydney."

"Colonel Hutton, sir?"

"Affirm." Again, Zorn checked Deagle's nametag. "He's okay. Not enough mortar metal in his leg to even send him home early. But he was telling me about a buck sergeant he'd just recommended for a second Silver Star. I thought he said Beagle, like a dog." Major Zorn stuck out his hand.

The buck sergeant's shoulders came up a little as they shook hands. "Thank you, sir. Anybody else hit?"

"Yeah. A corporal... Grover... ?"

"Glover?"

"That's it. He's okay too. A couple stray rounds before the cease-fire."

Glover was Pomeroy's replacement as 3rd Platoon RTO. Well that only lasted a day or so, and Ploughboy had used up another life.

"Going home, sir?"

Zorn grinned. "Australia. But I'm down to sixteen days, sergeant Deagle. Taking no chances. When I get back from R&R I'm riding a desk for my last nine days. This old gunner's not getting killed short."

Deagle nodded. "That's how I'll do R&R too, sir, when I'm a single-digit midget, right before my 'early out'."

Zorn looked up at him. "From what Hutton tells me, maybe you should think about staying in the army? It's not a bad life and Vietnam can't last much longer."

Deagle shook his head. "I'll take the 'early out' and another run at college."

"Flunked out, huh."

"Yes, I did, sir. And the army nailed me."

"Well every man should do what he does best, I always say. Good luck the rest of your tour."

"You, too, sir."

He strolled around the PX watching for Ridell and Berkowitz but didn't see them. At the liquor section he found a crowd of GI's surrounding a half dozen American civilians escorted by a squad of strack-looking MPs. Two of the civilians were women, one had red hair and pert tits under her t-shirt. He watched her smile as she talked to the GI's, taking notes on a yellow legal pad. When she looked his way he saw green eyes. He tried to get close to her but two of the MPs shoved their chests at him. He walked around the crowd and tried to find green eyes again but she couldn't see him. He paid for his second load of snacks, collected his gear from the AP, and walked out into the afternoon heat.

The black-market action was over for the day, all cockroaches back in the ground. The front sidewalk was empty. Overhead, the sky had closed up as the rain clouds moved closer. He humped through the parking lot and claimed his weapons at Bravo shack and started up the road to the gate. Beyond the gate he saw a pair of canvas-top troop trucks. Then he spotted Captain Ridell talking with Admin Sergeant Olson.

"Here he is now," Ridell said. "Well, Sergeant Deagle, I see you've already drawn your M-16 and you're going to need it. Major Andrews has something for you to do this afternoon. Get in the truck!"

A jeep pulled up behind him with Lieutenant Berkowitz behind the wheel, barely recognizable in aviators' sunglasses and a square-cornered Marine-style baseball cap.

"I believe it's going to rain," Berkowitz said. "I hope that new watch is waterproof."

The tailgate dropped down and Deagle glanced into the crowded truck. He looked over his shoulder at Captain Ridell. "A sweep on Cav Mountain is the dumbest idea I ever heard," he told him.

Ridell smiled, then pointed at the air policeman. "Airman, arrest that man, please."

Deagle threw up his arms. "Okay! I'll hump it. If I'm with him, Major Andrews will have at least one good NCO."

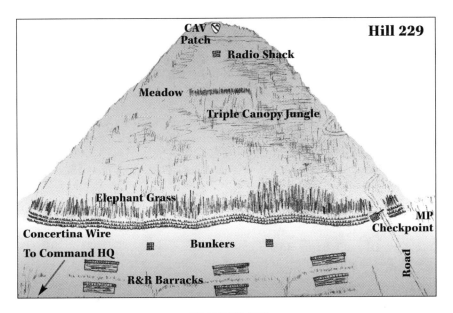

Hill 229

CAV Patch
Radio Shack
Meadow
Triple Canopy Jungle
Elephant Grass
Concertina Wire
To Command HQ
Bunkers
R&R Barracks
MP Checkpoint
Road

CHAPTER SIX

1345Hours 23Dec71
1st Cav Div HQ Bien Hoa
Enlisted Records Barracks 2616

Hearing boots in the hallway Vinny doused the joint. He looked at Jim and lifted his finger to his lips. Fuzz. Very quiet.

The slack-jawed PFC sat Indian-style on the floor and looked across at Brennan's smug expression; if Brennan so much as glanced at him he broke out laughing, so he counted *Playboy* centerfolds on the wall above Brennan's head. Twenty-three. These guys had it dicked, he'd decided, stereo, refrigerator... good supply of munchies... He caught Vinny's signal and clamped his teeth shut. No laughing.

"Fall out!" said the voice in the hall.

No doors opened and nobody answered.

"I said fall out, goddamn it! I need Sp4s Brennan!... Elliot!... Haffler!... and Simpson!... fall out! And I need Sp5s Gates and Vincent! Fall out!"

Vincent mouthed the name to Brennan. Wismer. Lifer. Flaming red asshole. Jim rubbed his hands together, ready to play too, as Wismer began to pound on closed doors. He called out the names again but nobody answered up.

"Elliot, fall out you little pussy! I know you can hear me. I got a truck waiting for you troop. If you're AWOL this time you belong to me!"

Wismer's voice echoed louder and closer in the hall, his fist pounding on

135

the door of Vinny's neighbor sounded like a battering ram. Then the sergeant was right outside, two yards away on the other side of the plywood door, and his fist was a hand grenade. "Vincent! Brennan! Fall out!" Jim's eyes opened wide as he heard Wismer's boots scuff the concrete. Vinny held up a hand; steady, troop. The next sound they heard was Wismer speaking softly, cajoling through the door. "Vinneeeeee... I know you're in there... I can smell you... fall out!" he added, with another reverberating bash on the door. Vinny gagged himself with both hands to keep from busting out. Sergeant Wismer beat on one more door and stepped into the street.

Vinny opened the refrigerator door and passed out three cold CBL's. "Fucking lifer."

1345Hours 23Dec71
1st Cav Div HQ Bien Hoa
Admin Battalion Formation Area

In the street in front of the admin command post, combat-ready troops shuffled urgently into platoon formations. The admin NCO's posed in their steel pots and flakjackets while the officers, including Major Andrews in his colorful campaign hat and a flock of captains and lieutenants, huddled aloof on the porch smoking last cigarettes. Standing at "parade rest" in a middle rank in a middle platoon, Sergeant William Deagle observed and graded the major's report-card. In six months at LZ Penny, Deagle had become more comfortable facing the other way, giving platoon orders rather than taking them.

He looked up at the threatening sky and shook his head; first mistake. He didn't need the new Omega on his wrist to know it was time for the afternoon monsoon. Andrews had missed the best part of the day and now his sweep would coincide with two hours of blinding rain. Andrews' second mistake was thinking he had to beat the 1800 cease-fire deadline; if Hill 229 was classified "Uniform Sierra" and if there were VC on it going into a cease-fire that's a NATO violation and justification for an offensive mission. So Andrews should slow down and run it right; he should saturate the target areas with HE and gunships while his troops wait in trucks inside the motorpool, already briefed and out of sight of every Vietnamese national remaining on base. But most obvious to Deagle, Cav mountain itself was too thick and too steep for an on-line operation, too many ways for Charles to hide and evade. A night ambush would be a better operation. Three strikes, major, you're out.

He empathized with the other bewildered grunts in the mob-scene. Field formations, like Captain Rule's LZ Penny, were often informal, more like a football huddle. No whistles, no screaming, no dress-right-dress. Rule relied on eye-contact, individual assignments where possible, lots of q&a to make sure everybody got it right. Standing in this formation with the admin NCO's shouting at them "count off!" and "dress it out!" and "sling arms!" the groundpounders hung their heads like they'd been drafted to police up cigarette butts, not Victor Charlie.

By contrast, the strak-uniformed 74-Hotel clerks were on a combat adventure, adjusting their gear and futzing with their rifles. Watching them, Deagle was reminded of another mob-scene when the urgency had been false and the execution poor, one special night at Fort Benning, Georgia, eleven months ago. His senior drill instructor blew the formation whistle at one in the morning.

On that unforgettable night, because he was the trainee platoon sergeant, a panic-stricken barracks fireguard shook him awake saying he thought he just heard the formation whistle. The formation whistle at 0100? Yup Deagle recalled how he'd stumbled to the second-floor window and looked out, and there, under the bright Georgia moon, was the solitary and unmistakable shape of Sergeant First Class Pellican in his slanted smoky bear hat. Even now, after six months in the Republic of Vietnam, he felt the icy fear in his stomach.

Everybody fell out, his platoon first and then the whole training company. With their fatigue shirts hanging out, boots unlaced, and baseball caps missing, his troops sleep-walked through the dress-right-dress and the "all present and accounted for" routines. They stood in formation dazed and grumbling about the unfairness of the formation whistle blowing at one in the morning. They soon found out they had fallen out a little too slowly, not in the requisite thirty seconds. And SFC Pellican had the ass. He didn't say he had the ass, you could just see he had the ass. His face was invisible, only the smoky bear hat moved as he looked the company over. Then the great hat moved side-to-side, and Sergeant Pellican spoke. He was very disappointed. "Too slow, trainees", he said in a quiet voice. "We're gonna try dis again. But dis time you trainees bring dem foot-lockers with you when you hear dat whistle. Fall out, trainees!"

And so, racing back to the barracks in the dead of morning to retrieve his inspection-perfect footlocker, Deagle understood it was going to be a night of character building, a false sense of urgency.

When the whistle blew the second time the troops crashed back to the formation area carrying their wooden foot lockers full of socks, shaving gear and underwear all neatly folded edge-to-edge from the night before. Four platoons waited in the dark night for SFC Pellican to let them go back to bed. But he just stood shaking his head again. "Too slow, trainee." Unbelievably, he instructed the troops to return to their barracks and try again, "dis time with dem wall-lockers. Fall out!" Five minutes later the formation whistle blew a third time and one-hundred and sixty trainees dragged their wall-lockers full of their neatly-hung uniforms from the barracks down to the formation area. Now, with footlockers and wall-lockers in formation, there was almost nowhere to stand, and platoon ranks and files roller-coastered. Breathless, everybody looked up the hill at Sergeant Pellican hoping the nightmare was over. Slowly, torturously, the smoky bear hat wagged side-to-side. Still to slow. Pellican told the trainees to fall out and return their mattresses.

Nobody could believe it was happening. Back in the barracks, tearing their double bunks apart in frustrated disbelief, fights broke out. After they dragged, kicked, and flip-flopped their mattresses into the formation area, Sergeant Pellican sent them all back one last time for their bed frames.

Thinking about it now, Deagle well remembered Sergeant Pellican's final words, as he stood in that chaotic formation in the middle of the night, exhausted and angry, with everything he owned strewn about in the damp Georgia sand, "Trainee, get this shit out of my formation area. Fall out." And with that he walked away. It was a memory that made Deagle smile now, one that cheered him in dark times. It was a memory that made him swear to himself someday he'd be the one handing out the harassment.

"Daylight men, we're wasting daylight!" Sergeant Timmerman hollered as he marched past Deagle's platoon.

Deagle looked up. Any second now, that solid cloud would let go. What a joke.

The troop on Deagle's right nudged him. "You ever walk that hill?"

"Negative."

"Me neither. Can they really do this? Make us pull a sweep when we're on R&R?"

"They're doing it. And we're going to get wet."

At 1350 hours, canvas-covered trucks began to rumble up the street from the motorpool and line up across from the formation. The officers field-stripped their cigarettes and headed for their jeeps. Deagle took his own head count of troops and trucks and it added up to three-hundred men, half admin and half grunt, for twenty-five vehicles. They'd be packed in tighter than Vienna sausage. He watched the NCO's take their final headcounts and recognized a few of them under their steel pots; Timmerman, Olsen, Wismer, Dornhaus, Hooper, McFadden... And some of the officers were familiar: 1st Lieutenant St. John and Captain Olivette... and Andrews. He didn't recognize the pot-bellied bird colonel.

Squat Staff Sergeant Hooper was assigned to Deagle's platoon. Waiting for the command to "fall out" Hooper jitterbugged back and forth picking out grunts in faded uniforms from his front rank. "You, you, you, and you sergeant," he whispered loudly, "step to my right... your left... you're my squad leaders." Deagle remained in the middle of the twelve-man second squad.

Deagle watched 1st Lieutenant St. John approach, marching stiff-assed and carrying his JAG briefcase in his right hand. He stopped in front of Sergeant Hooper and waggled a finger in his face; Hooper nodded. Then St. John marched stiff-assed to the next platoon and repeated the warning to Sergeant Dornhaus.

"Who the fuck is he?"

"JAG looie," Deagle answered.

"So that's where the name jagoff comes from."

Hooper hollered as quietly as he could: "2nd p'toon fall out!" The ranks dissolved and forty-eight men headed for the trucks. Deagle took his time, determined to get an eyeballing seat by the tailgate. He looked back over his left shoulder and saw Lieutenant St. John with his arm around Sergeant McFadden; the lieutenant opened his briefcase and handed the sergeant two yellow smoke grenades.

1400Hours 23Dec71
1st Cav Div HQ
Offices, Brig. Gen. Jeffrey Webb

Webb studied Hill 229 with field glasses through his briefing-room window. From a distance of 400 meters his 8x binoculars brought the congested jungle terrain close enough to feel the humidity.

"Look at that damn thing", he said aloud.

Seven hundred meters tall, 45-degree incline, with triple canopy jungle and elephant grass above caves, tunnels and craters. The 9th Engineers had shelled it with HE, defoliated it with agent orange, burned it with napalm. But Hill 229 was regenerated and formidable. He swung the glasses to the road and watched the front of the convoy pass through the checkpoint.

It was an upside-down assault, in Webb's experience. His brigade commanders ran sweeps of enemy-occupied hills from the bottom up, with his troops well apart and moving closer together as they flushed the VC ahead of them into a narrowing net. But this enemy hill belonged to us, supposedly, and it had a road all the way to the top. Major Andrews had to maintain on-line troop spacing coming down the hill in order to push the VC into the waiting guns. Not easy at a forty-five degree angle. Also, the major had responsibility for only half the pie, and there would be seams for Charles to slip through.

Webb knew he would not see his troops sweeping down but with Major Andrews' map relocated to the wall beside him he could visualize their battleground: the caves high up, the grassy clearing called "the meadow", the lighter grassy jungle mixed with a twenty-foot tall triple layer of vines and branches, the rain-eroded rock formations and boulders, shell-craters and cliffs in the hill's center. They were all on Andrews' map. He wondered if his desk-bound legs could make it from the top of Hill 229 to the bottom.

As he turned from the window he checked his watch, just on 1400. The troops should hit the ring of bamboo and elephant grass above the bunkers in two or three hours, well ahead of the 1800 cease-fire, and there was nothing for him to do but wait and listen on the horn.

"Trucks rolling, sir?" Colonel Shipp asked.

"Affirmative. On time, at least."

Colonel Wilcox ran his hand over his sweaty face. "How many troops, sir?"

"The air force is sending up 600 men on their side, Major Andrews reports just over 300. Colonel Shipp, do you think you could scratch up one-each Prick-25 radio so I could monitor Andrews' frequency? And could you set this room up a little better... some desks where we could spread out... maps... that sort of thing?"

"I'll do both, sir. In fact, I'll build us an 'Eisenhower Bunker'."

"I'm not sure we need... "

"No trouble at all, sir. Be something to do. And sir, if you don't mind my sayin' so, you oughta go lay down 'fore you fall down. Me an' Ray can run things from here while you take a snooze. I'll call you if there's word on Lima Zulu Judith."

Shipp and Wilcox waited while Webb panned the hill again with his binoculars. "Our troops will be coming down in a monsoon rain," he said finally. "Colonel Wilcox, I need a volunteer to break the news to General Garlett." He turned to look at his sweating S-1, whose stupefied owl's eyes blinked once. "At ease, colonel. I'm kidding. As I said, my sense of humor isn't what it used to be. I'll call Garlett myself. After those men start down the hill. Then I will grab a nap."

"AF side going to keep in contact with us, sir?" Shipp asked.

"Roger, every thirty minutes. The air force has as an oversupply situation like the Cav. It wouldn't be a total shock if Charles tried to hit them during the cease-fire. When you get that Prick-25 I'll call Major Andrews and wish him good hunting."

1400Hours 23Dec71
1st Cav Div HQ
Hill 229

Deagle took a last look around, hoping to catch a glimpse of Pomeroy or Grossnickel, then he threw himself up into the truck and wedged onto the bench seat between the last soldier and the tailgate. A truck in the middle of a convoy was never a bad thing, he thought, in case the road was mined. He'd rather eat dust than sit close to the truck's front wheels. Sergeant Hooper came chugging along and slammed the tailgate shut.

Deagle looked at the troop sitting across from him, a sullen Italian or Spanish buck sergeant named Palmyra.

"Not exactly a secret operation," he said matter-of-factly.

Palmyra was 11-Bravo but he was not inclined to conversation. But the soldier beside Palmyra, an admin Sp5 named Benke, looked out the back of the jeep and nodded his head. "Yup. Most of the gooks that work here have been off-base an hour now. They've had time to tell Chuck we're coming."

The engine revved and the truck slipped backwards as the driver eased out his clutch. The transmission caught and the truck surged, the passengers snapped back toward the tailgate. Deagle hung onto his rifle with both hands as he felt the weight of ten bodies pinching him against the gate before the truck jerked into second gear. Deagle watched Sp5 Benke drop his M-16 magazine in his hand to check it. The top round was a tracer. Well, he thought, in the afternoon rain tracers should burn out pretty fast.

He glanced down at his new wristwatch. In the dim light under the canvas top the dial and hands glowed bright green. It was exactly 1400 hours. Through the metal floor, he felt the drive-shaft disengage and the engine rev, and he braced himself as the heavy truck lurched to a stop. The MP checkpoint.

Sp5 Benke said "hang onto your weapons and your guns, boys, we're going up."

"Done this before?" Deagle asked

"Couple times. Like... after some officer goes out to take a leak and gets shot at. This is the first time since I been here somebody got a VC up there."

"What kind of walking is it?"

Benke glanced at Deagle's nametag. "Unbelievable, even for you slim. Head-high shit at the very top, then some trees and canopy, a couple bad-ass cliffs. My advice, don't worry about your five-meter spacing. Find yourself some buddies and stick together down to the elephant grass."

As the truck rolled forward Sergeant Palmyra came out of his funk and glared at Benke. "You work here, man?"

"That's a rog."

"Can that major do this? I DEROS in four days, man! I'm not supposed to pull a combat sweep!"

"Mellow out, man. Nothing ever happens. We truck to the top, we walk down, nobody can see shit because it's too thick."

Palmyra was steaming. "What about that body count? Huh? That don't sound like fun an' games. I'm turnin' that clown in to Symington! My tour is supposed to be over, man."

Through the checkpoint, the truck bounced and shimmied as it started up the winding road and the troops slid back like a load of plywood. Around a steep right-hand curve the driver hit a pothole with both right wheels and everybody on the left side was dumped on the floor in a pile. Deagle kept his M-16 pointed skyward and scrambled to get back on the wooden bench. The nose of the truck climbed higher in a sweeping turn, and the left rear wheels under him seemed to drop off the edge, a stomach-turning eye-bulging dip that threatened to roll everything, until the wheels hit bottom and Deagle's teeth clashed and his steel pot flew off his head. He felt like he was going to upchuck his licorice and sausage. He stuck his bare head out the back of the truck and sucked in dust along with fresh air. He saw some of the high canopy on Hill 229, intertwined branches and ferns twenty feet above the ground, like around LZ Penny. At Penny, the colors under the canopy were fantastic shades of pastel green, aqua, and the waxy pale greens in an aquarium. The air under the canopy was about as humid as a fishtank too, with a chlorophyll heaviness. And, through the dust spirals, Deagle saw huge faceted rocks taller than the truck. That meant VC spiderholes, caves and tunnels. The truck swung through a hard tilting right turn, transmission grinding in a low gear, he pinched his M-16 between his knees and hung onto the tailgate with both hands, stomach ready to blow. But the front wheels leveled and the driver gunned it, a final 30-mile-an hour surge on flat ground before the truck whistled to a stop. Deagle was glad to be humping back down.

Sergeant Hooper appeared from nowhere and let the tailgate down softly, finger to his lips, waving his arms and whispering his relentless cheerful "move IT, move IT, move IT, troopies... move IT, move IT, move IT..."

Deagle jumped down, grabbed a deep breath, and walked toward Sergeant McFadden's platoon, already herded into an assault line facing down the hill. He let himself be pulled along by the rush of bodies until he ended up on line, facing north. The jungle ten meters in front of him was shoulder high. Looking both ways, east and west, he saw the full battalion assault line stretched out of sight on both ends. Overhead, the sky had taken on its gloomy, blue-gray denseness, and rain was imminent. As the last trucks of the convoy hit flat ground and the troops jumped down, Hooper scurried back and forth looking at his watch and taking a head count. Deagle craned his neck and saw that one of McFadden's 11-Bravo's had a familiar gargantuan shape.

"Smoke 'em quick if you got 'em!" Hooper whispered. "Zero five minutes, men. Zero five 'til we move out."

Deagle took a step forward to have a word with Hooper. Hooper's helmet was as high off the ground as Deagle's armpit. He kept his voice low. "Hey, sarge, this hill *tu dai?*"

"Say, again?"

"Is it booby-trapped?"

"Negative, there sarn't," Hooper answered jovially.

"I got time to sneak over and speak to a buddy of mine from the 2nd of the 7th?"

That unit rang a bell with Hooper. Deagle's nametag rang two bells. "Sarn't Deagle!"

"How about it?"

"You take five but I need to talk to you, ASAP."

"Affirm. Hey, sarge, don't forget to give 'em an azimuth. Looks pretty thick down there."

Hooper grinned. "Roger that. 'Preciate it."

Deagle walked down the assault line and sneaked up behind Pomeroy. He smacked the back of his helmet, "hey, Ploughboy."

The big man whipped around, gray eyes exuberant. Deagle suffered through one of his suffocating bear hugs and they shook hands mightily, testing each-others' grip strength, and Pomeroy won again.

"Man, am I glad to see you! Bien Hoa is numbah ten thousand, GI!"

Deagle grinned and checked out the corporal's new fatigues. "Nice uniform, soldier."

With Deagle's sleeves rolled to his knobby elbows, Pomeroy saw the silver and black watch. "Nice new watch. Can you believe this shit, Bill? I'm on R&R and you're casual duty, and we're pulling this dumb detail, over."

Deagle nodded. "No shit. You and Fuck-knuckle both here for R&R?"

Pomeroy looked down at his boots. "After the cease-fire, over."

"You still going to Australia?"

"Going on R&R is like getting drafted. You have to get shots, get your pecker checked, get your 201 checked, talk to the chaplain, call your parents back in the world... it's all army bullshit. I shoulda known."

"Where is Fuck-knuckle?"

"Don't know. We split up and I was supposed to find you. How come a field-grade officer's looking for you?"

Deagle lit a smoke. "Something about my 201 file. You call your dad?"

The big man looked down, an embarrassed 10-year old. "Negative, over."

"You got to get that done, troop."

"I know it. Just couldn't pull the trigger today."

"When you get back to the world," Deagle reminded him, "everybody but your family is going to be fucking ashamed of you, calling you 'baby-killer' and 'lifer'... There's no point in making it through this crap if you can't live on that farm, you dig?"

The steel pot wobbled. "Yeah."

"Maybe this will give you some incentive. I ran into an artillery major in the PX. Guess who got medivac'd in here this morning: Colonel Hutton and Corporal Glover, your RTO replacement. Both hit, both okay."

Pomeroy's jaw fell like Grossnickel's.

"You used up another life, troop. So don't make me get in your face again, you're calling your dad tomorrow."

"Think we could rap tonight? They got a big Taiwan live show, over."

Deagle inhaled deeply and blew a stream skyward. A raindrop splashed on the top of his helmet. "Yeah. In my rucksack, fish out my sidearm and poncho and a bag of seeds for you."

"Here it comes," Pomeroy said, looking at the sky. He spun Deagle around and opened the top of the rucksack. He unpacked the .45 and handed it to him. Holding both rifles, Pomeroy watched Deagle attach the holster to his pistol belt. "What's up? You see VC, GI, over?"

Deagle pointed down the hill and held up his watch. "Meet me below in half an hour and we'll hump the rest of the way together. Call it a hundred meters for shits and giggles.

"Roger"

"Cleve, listen up. This sweep is all fucked up, but there's a cease-fire in four hours and there could be VC on this hill." Deagle never called him Cleve unless he was dead serious.

"I won't walk through any gates, GI. See you in three-zero, out."

Deagle walked back and took his place in line in front of Sergeant Hooper as more fat drops spattered. The curtain of rain was only minutes away now, and when it fell visibility would close down to a few meters. Hooper had better hurry, he thought, watching the little NCO hustle back and forth urging his troops to put out smokes, check chinstraps, and take very small steps on the steep slope below. Hooper didn't have much military bearing but he did have energy.

"Hey, sarge," Sergeant Palmyra whispered loud. "Are those baby steps or midget steps? We gonna play 'Simon Says'?"

"Military steps, buck sergeant!" he shot back. Hooper's Sp4 RTO called in ready to assault Hill 229. Major Andrews' call-sign for this operation was "Claymore."

The rain began to tap steadily on Deagle's steel pot. He pulled it off and slipped his poncho over his head and shoulders.

"Lissen up!" Hooper half-whispered. "You men get into them ponchos. We're goin down. It's 690 meters to the bottom. You stay five meters apart to start, no more than ten after that, stay on zero degrees heading, if you hit the road you're too far west. Any of you swingin' dicks finds a cave... don't do nothing. Send word down the line an' I'll frag it. There's a two-story drop-off west of us, watch for tree-tops and steer east. When you get to the elephant grass halt right there: because them troops on the other side of the wire will have itchy trigger fingers! We'll form up an' go around through the MP gate."

Looking to his right, Hooper saw Timmerman's platoon start down.

"Fire selectors on single, men. Move out!" He grabbed Deagle by the rucksack. "Sarge, you gotta report to Colonel Wilcox. He's got a Silver Star he wants to pin on you. Meet you down below."

Deagle started down in chest-high grass, feeling for solid ground with the heel of his boot. On both sides of him, the troops were up to their steel pots with their first steps. His height allowed him to see about fifty meters below, and he looked for the trees Hooper mentioned. Trees, as in canopy and shelter from the rain. He stopped to rip a papery stalk of grass from his rifle's flash suppressor. A dozen steps away an unseen soldier grumbled, "who's fuckin' plan was this."

He hitched down sideways in a north-south descent and used his rifle to fend off the sharp grass. Impossible, he thought, to hunt Charles and move at the same time, too thick and too steep. Better to stop, listen, and look for cracks in the ground. He heard troops whispering on his right, boots breaking brush on his left. The slope was a bitch for his weakened legs. He resorted to tacking and counting steps, ten to the west, ten back to the east. He rested against a tree with a spider-web of connecting ground-vines, no longer hearing voices. Then, like a dam bursting, the afternoon rain hit.

His poncho-covered steel pot crackled and he felt the weight of the heavy drops on his shoulders, and visibility dropped to ten gray meters. The only sound was a torrential rush, drowning out even the metallic popping above his ears. He slugged downhill in virtual fog until a green-gray wall loomed in front of him. Still up to his neck in grass, he waited for sweepers left and right but none showed. He edged closer but the wall of trees seemed to move away from him. He strained his eyes down and discovered he'd been suckered by an optical illusion. Those were tall trees, all right, thirty feet high or more, but they were at the bottom of that cliff Hooper said was to the west. He looked down; he'd walked to the edge of a sheer drop-off.

He climbed back from the cliff and leaned against a tree to wait for the sweep to catch up. No sign of troops. Which way had Hooper said to turn? East, toward the New Jersey. He switched his M-16 to his right hand to use its butt like a walking stick and counted two hundred steps to the east before starting down again. When he checked his watch he was surprised to see it was 1430, half an hour since he'd seen or heard another soldier. Knowing grunts as he did, he figured the rain and terrain had them bunched up on both sides, they were probably in nice single-file patrols. Around him, the brush was over his head and the pitch of the hill was even steeper. He edged down using stalks for footholds and hanging onto branches until the foliage underfoot became too slippery for his treadless jungle boots, and he sat down. He fumbled a smoke from his shirt pocket, got it lit, and managed a couple of drags before the rain killed it. Either this was the roughest hill he'd ever humped or his legs were gone. Hell with it, he decided. Can't hunt Charles... and it ain't my hill... slide over to the road and get off the son-of-a-bitch.

Blind, legs cramping, he climbed fifty meters and pulled himself along perpendicular to the slope on a compass heading of 270 degrees, due west. On a vine as slick as monkey shit his right foot slipped and he landed hard on his left hip. He pulled his poncho over his knees and took steadying deep breaths. He wasn't lost or alone, he told himself, and all he had to do was stand up and yell like hell. There were three hundred guys on this hill and somebody would hear him. Or maybe shoot him. He stood on shaky legs and managed to get his M-16 slung on his right shoulder before he slipped on his back, and started to slide down. Grass tore at his face and eyes as he dug in with the heels of boots but couldn't get a grip on the wet ground. He hurtled down like a bobsled out and over the edge of the drop-off.

Airborne, Deagle had a quick glimpse of gray sky above and green landscape below. He fell ten feet in free-flight and slammed into the upper branches of the triple canopy. He clung to a wrist-sized limb in a life-or-death hug until it snapped, and came down with him. He landed on his back in light brush on top of his M-16 with the rain smashing his face and no air in his lungs. He opened his eyes but the rain closed them.

Deagle was unable to see the Vietnamese standing beside the granite cliff twenty-five meters away.

1435Hours 23Dec71
1st Cav Div HQ
Military Checkpoint, Hill 229

Rain hit the metal roof of the checkpoint like nails pouring from a keg. Inside, using a sketch of Hill 229 drawn from memory, Major Andrews tracked the sweep by talking to his NCO's on the radio. As the platoon sergeants called in, he plotted how far they'd come on the map. One by one, his NCO's reported breaking out of the grass at the top and into the heavy jungle. From there, Hill 229 was Victor Charlie all the way down. Old Caves, a foot-trail network, and, confirmed through aerial photography in '68-69, tunnels from the upper-middle of the hill down to the elephant grass. Andrews kept a close eye on the platoons' latitude on the hill because he knew the NCO's were guessing about their longitude. When Sergeant Timmerman called in and reported moving his men through the same boulders and craters as Sergeant Hooper minutes before, he slammed his fist against the wall. Timmerman was fifty meters off his azimuth already.

"He's too far west!" he told Sp4 Knox. "Tell him I want him to work his platoon back up the hill, then fifty meters east, and start down again! Tell him!"

Knox keyed the mike and shouted. "Romeo Mike, this is Claymore, Romeo Mike this is Claymore, over."

After twenty seconds of static Andrews finally heard McFadden's faint voice come crackling back. "Claymore, this is Romeo Mike, over."

"This is Claymore, advise you are too far west! You are too far west! You are to go up the hill and move fifty meters east. Move fifty meters east, over!"

Andrews threw up his hands. Sp4 Knox had a loud voice but he was no RTO. Waiting, he heard Timmerman's reply, ten seconds of low-volume static.

"What'd he say?"

"Said he was in un-godly thick shit but, roger, he's moving."

Andrews nodded. "That's better." On the map he moved Timmerman back where he belonged, on Hooper's right flank.

While Andrews stayed dry inside the checkpoint, Lieutenant St. John donned his poncho and his steel pot and stood vigil on the hood of the command jeep, watching for the sweepers with binoculars. Major Andrews was well impressed with the lieutenant's sense of duty but he could not imagine what St. John could see through 300 meters of the driving rain. Such staunch behavior, however, was appreciated, usually the lieutenant complained about such irritations as mosquitoes, heat, and monsoon rain.

"Sir!" he shouted suddenly. "Major, there it is! Yellow smoke!"

Major Andrew's pulled on his campaign hat and charged outside. He fought the rain to look where St. John pointed but he saw nothing but shades of green and gray. The scar on his head throbbed purple as blood rushed to his face.

"They've found a tunnel, sir! Must be on top of it otherwise he'd call it in."

"Could be Sergeant Olson!" Andrews shouted back.

St. John didn't disagree.

"I'm gonna give him permission to blow the son-of-a-bitch!" he said. He turned and issued the command to RTO Knox through the open checkpoint door. But after the transmission Sergeant Olson called back saying he had not popped yellow smoke, nor did he see any.

Andrews banged the hood of the jeep with his fist. "Then he's too far west, too, goddammit! Tell him to back up and move fifty meters east! Who's that leave, not Olson or Wismer, not Timmerman, ...maybe McFadden. If it's not McFadden it's got to be Hoop. Old Hoop will come through for me, wait and see."

On the road below the checkpoint shack, the single black star on the front-end of General Webb's jeep came into view through the downpour, in the passenger seat the huddled, poncho-wrapped figure of S-2 Colonel Borg. As it pulled to a stop, Andrews was surprised to see Sergeant Major Bierra behind the wheel. The S-2 commander and the division sergeant major jumped out and marched in lockstep toward the shack.

"Ten hut!" St. John called, still on the hood of the jeep. He brought up a sweeping salute.

"As you were."

"Sir, Sergeant McFadden has a VC tunnel just below him! That is, we assume it's sergeant McFadden."

"I wish I had my goddamn map," Andrews grumbled

The colonel and sergeant major moved into the shack and flanked the Andrews' RTO. Major Andrews squeezed inside and showed McFadden's map position.

"Right about here, sir."

Knox put down his mike and tried adjusting the radio controls again.

"Sir, I think it is McFadden but I can't hear him very well."

"Have him pop another yellow."

Knox called it in. Lieutenant St. John joined them in the shack and Borg took the field glasses, and stepped outside for a look. Borg saw the brief yellow smudge against gray-green background.

"Right there!" he hollered. "I'll be damned."

147

The radio crackled and Knox listened hard. "Sir, Sergeant Dornhaus has a man with a broken leg. He's requesting medivac."

"The first casualty is ours, again," Borg said.

Major Andrews had only to look at the colonel's blue eyes and elephant ears to feel the old defiance. "Specialist Knox, tell Sergeant McFadden he has clearance to blow that tunnel."

"Are you sure, major?" Borg asked him.

"Yes, sir, I'm sure. You saw the smoke? McFadden is a hundred meters east of the craters where we found caves in '68. This is a new area. Specialist Knox, call all platoon leaders and have them hold their positions. Then advise McFadden I want him to blow that tunnel and run a recon. Tell him I want his body counts hand-carried off the hill to Colonel Borg at S-2! When you get his affirmative, call in a medevac request for Sergeant Dornhaus."

1435Hours 23Dec71
1st Cav Div HQ
Hill 229

When the jungle ceiling opened above him, Tran instinctively flattened himself against the rock wall. He didn't actually see what came crashing down on his left but he heard it hit the ground. Moving only his eyes, Tran scanned the brush until he saw the soldier on the ground, either dead or knocked out. He slowly lowered himself on his belly.

Tran considered himself very lucky. He had no weapon but his sheath knife. The cliff was only one hundred feet wide, the soldier could have landed closer or even on top of him. Or, if the soldier had fallen a few minutes ago, he would have been walking on the trail just below and caught in the clearing. Rain dimmed his vision but he saw that the soldier was not moving.

Tran was in the elephant grass when he first heard the trucks, an hour ago. That there were so many soldiers surprised him, also that they had waited for the rain. As he moved up the soldiers moved down. Three times after the rain came he had had to change course to let them pass. The first time he almost walked into a group of them, smoking cigarettes under the canopy. The second time he heard their talking and the crackle of radios, a whole long line of them following each other like ants. The third time he eased into a rock cave and let a dozen of them walk directly over his head. With so many, he decided, it was safer to get to the cliffs and just let them all walk past.

And now this one.

The soldier lay face up under the open sky with only his upper body and one leg visible. Tran tried watching his chest for movement but the rain beyond the canopy was too heavy and he was too far away. Hiding, he felt the pressure of time wasting. He had a long climb to the cave and the rain would

148

last only another hour. So there were only two choices, avoid the soldier or make sure he was dead. If he was not dead, kill him and hide his body. He must get closer.

He raised himself to a crouch and slid inch by inch along the cliff toward the closest heavy cover. Reaching it, he dropped to one knee and stayed there watching the soldier now only fifteen yards away. He felt his heart pounding and knew that time moved slowly. What seemed like an hour was only one minute or two minutes since the soldier fell from the cliff. He drew his four-inch knife from its sheath and took careful steps in the brush. He used his hand as he would to shield his eyes from the sun, to block the rain. He advanced to within ten meters and saw the soldier's chest moving up and down. He was alive.

Now there was no time to waste. He took two swift steps. Above his head, the sound of the rain hitting the trees was that of Chinese firecrackers popping and it covered his approach. His knife was wet in his hand but his grip was good. Then he was startled by a single explosion of ten thousand firecrackers, a blast that ripped the jungle behind him and sent rocks clattering. He dove to the ground and covered the back of his head with his arms.

1440Hours 23Dec71
1st Cav Div HQ
East Briefing Room, Brig. Gen. Jeffrey Webb

Webb lifted his eyes to the window and listened to the muted echo of McFadden's fragmentation grenade. He was angry at himself for not over-riding the major's command to blow the tunnel. What Andrews should have done was post a squad to hold it until the sweep was over and then recon with a full platoon.

He leaned back in his chair to stretch his long legs. Colonel Shipp was out of the office again, which was good. Trying to put together his "war room" Shipp hovered like an old hen. Shipp had scrounged a new Prick-25 radio and set it up on the Claymore frequency but as yet he hadn't found an RTO. Colonel Wilcox, the only other officer present, stared at the radio that filled the small room with soft static.

Impatiently, Webb picked up the MAC-V phone again and tried General Benton Garlett, III-Corps commander, and after identifying himself four times in various offices he heard Garlett's silky, deep voice.

"Webb, my answer is still negative. There will no air operation inside Cambodia, end of discussion."

"Sir, this is another matter, an advisory."

"What now."

"Are you familiar with topographical Hill 229-er sir, here at Bien Hoa?"

"I've seen it from the air."

"It's two miles inside the base perimeter. Last night, we believe, one of our bunker guards shot a Vietnamese on Hill 229. At the present time, I have a battalion sweep of the hill in progress which I expect will be complete before 1800 hours."

"What do you mean 'we believe'? Do you or don't you have a body count?"

Webb looked toward the window. "Affirmative, we do." He waited, hoping Garlett had more pressing things on his mind, to see if that explanation would fly.

"General, where are those American reporters right now?"

"At the PX, sir. They were not informed."

"Well, thank God for that. Within this corps area, general, I do not want to hear about or read about ANY cease-fire violations which may become a factor in the peace negotiations. Is that clear? You keep those reporters away from that hill until you get those men down."

"Affirmative, sir."

"Call me tonight in my quarters. I'll see if I can have the reporters transported to Saigon. Good afternoon."

Webb hung up and yawned. "Same, same," he said to Colonel Shipp. "Call me in my quarters if there's contact with Charles."

1440Hours 23Dec71
1st Cav Div HQ
Hill 229

Something stirred him. Maybe a sound, maybe the hard rain in his face. He lifted his head and realized he'd lost his steel pot.

He lay on his back with his rucksack between his shoulder blades, one blunt-shaped rock under his back and another under his left kidney. He tried to sit up but the ground held him down. He was in low brush at the edge of the canopy he'd fallen through. If he could move another few feet he'd be out of the rain. Below him the angle of the hill looked walkable, almost flat. Another optical illusion? The rain gushed down, blurring his vision and forcing him to think. As he tried to sit up again something tugged his right shoulder. His rifle sling. He wasn't lying on rocks, he was on top of his M-16 and canteen belt. With a right arm that still seemed to work, he managed to yank the sling, pull the rifle free, and sit up.

Bad news. The muzzle of his weapon was packed with mud and its flash suppressor had long jungle beards festooned in its blades. Maybe the action was busted, too. Move to the canopy, he told himself, stay there until the rain quits in another hour or so. He flexed his right knee, then his left, no broken bones there. He crabbed two meters down the slope where the rain through the trees was only a trickle. Rain or no rain, he had to get out of the poncho to find out what was broken or bleeding. He performed the amazing feat of first pulling his poncho over his head and then shrugging out of his rucksack. Back okay, no broken ribs. He saw his steel pot at the base of a tree, an up-ended turtle full of water. His .45 pistol was still dry in the flap holster.

What the hell had happened and where were the other guys on the sweep? He wiped his sopped hair away from his forehead and eyes. He sat like a skinny buddha, thinking. He dumped the water from his steel pot, pulled the leafy junk out of its chinstrap, and stuck it back on his wet head. He worked open his rucksack and located a half dozen sticks of red licorice. He ate them like spaghetti with his gaze fixed down the slope below him. And, as it sometimes happened when his eyes were locked unseeing, he saw something that snapped him out of it. The jungle below him zoomed into sharp focus: a clearing; some kind of opening. Off to the right a VC trail disappeared into tall elephant grass: a wide trail.

Ten steps west, Tran dared to lift his head. He saw the soldier sitting up, facing down the slope. He froze, not even blinking, until he knew the soldier hadn't seen him. He was out of the soldier's peripheral vision, hidden from his view by two things: he lay in a shallow rocky depression, and the soldier was sitting not standing. Should the soldier stand up, he would be plainly visible. A millimeter at a time, he lowered his head. By being tentative he had lost his chance to kill the soldier and now he had one choice—to escape. Heavier jungle was just below him. There was brush thick enough to re-direct a bullet, if he could get there. It was two body-lengths away.

Tran looked under his eyebrows. The soldier was chewing. Carefully, feet first, he reached down with his left leg, then his right. He wormed down half a body-length, his luck holding. He gathered himself again and slid down half of his own length, belly dragging on the hard rock. His lace-less left shoe touched the brush. He must not to kick the branches. He wriggled backwards into the brush and spent agonizing slow minutes getting into a squatting position. His legs felt strong and ready to spring. By gently moving one leafy branch he could just see the American through the jungle. Carefully he turned his head to his right and looked for a good place to run. The jungle was thickest just below and high enough to hide most of his body. Once there, he could walk quietly around the cliff's edge where he would be safe from bullets. One last time he pushed the springy branch to check for the American, and pulling his hand back the fabric of his shirt caught on it.

Deagle saw the movement, and his eyes zoomed in like a camera lens. The branch had moved horizontally, not vertically. It shook because something touched it, and it wasn't raindrops. Fear gave his legs new life, and he stood up in a crouch. Another GI from the sweep? He left his useless rifle on the ground and slipped his holster flap, and felt for the .45. The wooden grips of the well-worn Colt felt good as he closed his wet fingers. He pulled the gun free and racked a round into the chamber with his left hand. The metallic sound of the slide overwhelmed the sound of the rain. Now, he thought, let's see what we got. Keeping the gun close to his body, he stood up to his full height.

Tran cursed his luck. It was bad luck to alert the soldier, worse luck the man was a giant and an officer with a hand pistol. A few more steps and he would see Tran in his hiding place. Through the brush, he saw the soldier looking straight at him, perhaps a little to the left. He gathered his legs and made his dash, showing only his head above the brush. He ran hard diagonally up the slope toward the rock wall. His legs were short but powerful and in only seconds he doubled the distance between himself and the soldier. As he dropped into a shallow crater his strides lengthened, running full speed, but then more bad luck, his legs out-ran his eyes. He tore through an opening in the brush and for a heartbeat he was exposed and an easy target.

Deagle saw the blur of a dark head and short body, the zig-zag of legs running hard to his left, as quick as a spooked rabbit. He pointed the .45 and swung with his target until it disappeared, reappeared, and disappeared again. Looking above his sights for those short seconds, he had no doubt he was seeing Charles Cong twenty meters away and gaining ground. He held on the spot where he last saw him, waited, and when the dark head reappeared five meters left he swung the barrel in front and fired. The gun bucked in his hand but the VC kept breaking brush. The report of the shot bounced off the cliff and came back at him, then it was quiet under the canopy. He stood listening to the rain.

Tran heard the soldier's shot and the bullet snapped past his left eye. His legs carried him swiftly through the jungle around the rock wall. He stopped, fighting the sound of his heart in his chest, and listened. There was no crashing in the brush, the soldier was not following. He knew this part of the hill and looked for the brush-covered drainage that would take him almost to the caves at the top. He dropped on his hands and knees and crawled. Concentrating his thoughts inward, he crawled quietly and forced his heart to slow, slow. He became aware of heat coming from his face. He reached to scratch his left cheek and felt the warmth of blood. His bloody fingertips told him the bottom half of his left ear was gone.

Deagle ducked down and listened to the rushing rain, steady as a hard wind. Son-of-a-bitch! Pull your head out, Deagle! How many more like him were hiding within rock-throwing range! Deciding fast, he grabbed his rifle and helmet, threw on his rucksack, and broke contact in the direction of nine o'clock.

He ran east, opposite the VC, out from under the canopy and into thick jungle where the slope of the hill returned to its treacherous 45-degree angle. He ran through face-stinging rain feeling a cold target zone in the small of his back. The shots that could have blown him away didn't come. Through the trees below he saw the strange clearing and the trail that ran through it: no place to be either. He crashed chest-first into a heavy clump of brush, crouched, and turned to watch his back-trail. Still no shots fired at him. With wet fingers he tried the magazine release on his M-16. It resisted but worked, and the clip dropped into his hand. He thumbed the top round off the follower and used the bullet tip to pry the mud out of the muzzle and flash suppressor. There were still crumbs in the barrel but a bullet should get through. He flung the cartridge away and heeled the magazine home. The bolt closed with a rasp. He wondered if he was carrying a single-shot rifle.

The threshing sound of an approaching helicopter distracted him. A gunship? It was climbing the hill and would pass close overhead. Instinctively he looked for heavier cover and saw more triple canopy to the east. A Huey, he decided, not a Cobra. A medevac bird maybe? The egg-beater blades suddenly swung east and made him wonder if a field grade officer, maybe the S-2, was monitoring the sweep from the air. He wondered where Pomeroy was. He watched his back-trail for two more minutes before slipping into the triple canopy, a pale green ghost in the gray downpour.

1450Hours 23Dec71
1st Cav Div HQ
Military Police Checkpoint

Major Andrews felt pressure building against his right temple, a headache coming on. He stared at the ceiling of the checkpoint, listening, but the only sound was continuous rain. It was at least ten minutes since Sergeant McFadden began his reconnaissance using two R&R grunts from the 8th Brigade. Volunteers. He was both worried and hopeful, they'd been in that tunnel a long time. Even Borg was moody, standing slouched against the wall smoking one Marlboro after another and staring at the Prick-25. It had killed him to do it, but Borg was the one who cleared the grunts to go into the tunnel.

Borg lifted his head. "You just hear a shot?"

St. John nodded. "Yes, sir. On this side."

Sergeant Major Bierra stopped pacing. "Didn't sound like a M-16. Maybe it was an M-16 inside a tunnel...?"

"We have to get up there," St. John announced. "Sir, I'm going up. I can't sit around with my thumb up my ass doing nothing."

Borg looked at Andrews and shrugged his shoulders. "It's your command post. But I'll stay by the horn."

The rain was at its heaviest, the ride to the top of Hill 229 in the open jeep promised to be miserable. Andrews shouldered into his poncho and St. John, saying he couldn't see to drive because of his glasses, jumped into the passenger side. Andrews fired up the engine and pulled through the gate. As he wrenched the vehicle through the first curve Lieutenant St. John suddenly shouted for him to pull over.

"Sir, I just needed a word in private! There is no tunnel!"

Andrews glared at him and kept driving. The jeep's wipers slashed at the sheeting rain on the windshield. Steering clear of the edge, he drove beyond the first lookout to the mid-point of the hill. In front of him a helmeted form materialized through the rain, a soldier walking on the road. The soldier froze in his tracks. Behind him was a squad of three more walking single file, M-16 muzzles sticking up under their streaming ponchos. Andrews knew the only way they could have gotten this far, this fast, was by walking the road. He gunned the jeep toward them and swung the wheel left, blocking the road. He jumped out of the jeep and splashed up to the startled troops, and he felt the pressure on the right side of his head ratchet up a notch. He looked under their helmets and saw records branch troops. Private Wallace.

"You men were told to stay off this road!"

"Sir, we got lost!" Wallace shouted back.

"But you found the road, didn't you. Get in the vehicle. Get in the goddamn vehicle!"

The four 74-Hotels piled in back and Andrews pushed the jeep up the winding road, engine screaming in second gear. On top, he rammed the transmission into third gear and raced to the sweep staging area below the radio building, and braked hard. He climbed out of the driver's seat with his cocked .45 pistol was in his right hand. "Out!" He formed the four deserters into a rank facing down the hill.

Andrews waggled his pistol in their frightened faces, down the line. "Do you have one of these, private? How about you, do you have one of these?" He stopped in front of Private Wallace. "You carrying a .45, Wallace? Answer me you little coward!"

"No, sir!"

Unable to stop himself, Andrews knocked the helmet off Wallace's head. With his left hand he reached out and grabbed the hood of his poncho and pulled hard. Wallace went down but Andrews stayed with him, yanking on the poncho and kicking Wallace with the toe of his boot, until the poncho came free over the muzzle of the M-16 slung on his right shoulder. He lifted the private by his fatigue shirt to the position of attention, snatched his rifle, and shoved it into his chest. Hair streaming in his eyes, Wallace rocked backward but managed to hold onto the rifle.

"Then how do you plan to fight Charles? Hand-to-hand! You men get out of those ponchos. Get 'em off!"

He holstered his sidearm and waited for his troops to throw off their ponchos and come to "port arms", heels locked, heads up, eyes front, M-16's diagonal in both hands. Rain water-falled from their steel pots, all but helmet-less Private Wallace. Andrews stood in front of him watching his eyes, daring him to even blink. He bent down and retrieved Wallace's helmet and stuffed it back on his head. He pointed at the edge of the jungle.

"The enemy is down there. With your weapons in your hands, not on your shoulders, you find the enemy, you engage him, and blow him away! That's your mission! If I see you men on the road again I'll have you court-martialed or I'll shoot you myself. Move out!"

The four admin soldiers dived into the brush.

Andrews wiped his streaming face with his soaked shirtsleeve. He sat in the jeep and pressed his hand against the right side of his pounding head.

"It'll be 2100 before those drowned rats make it off the hill," said the lieutenant.

Andrews brought up his field-glasses and tried to focus straight across the hill. "Sweepers should be a third the way down. Still can't see McFadden. We should have stayed in the checkpoint."

"Sir," said the lieutenant, "I needed to speak to you away from Colonel Borg. There is no tunnel. I arranged with Sergeant McFadden to pop a yellow smoke canister and throw a grenade into a shell crater."

"Crater?"

"Affirmative. I thought it a necessary charade in case the sweep produced nothing. Our credibility is at stake here, sir."

Andrews' temple throbbed. He wiped the rain from the rearview mirror and saw his own angry face. A small blood vessel in the corner of his right eye had broken. He pulled off his helmet and let the rain cool his head before turning the jeep around.

1545Hours 23Dec71
1st Cav Div HQ
Hill 229

Deagle moved from cover to cover figuring he was at least a half an hour behind the sweep, which was an ideal time for Charles to move up He found the whole north side of Cav mountain a disorienting tangle, consistently steep but unpredictable; one minute he was in high brush being pounded by the rain, visibility two meters, and the next he was under a green tree canopy with dead air and a 30-meter field of fire in every direction. Under the canopy, just like LZ Penny, it was like walking in a fish tank.

After hacking his way west through the rain and head-high scrub he ran into a band of short grass. It was almost flat ground, as deep as a four-lane highway running east and west. He'd been here before and realized he was really lost. On the far side was the tallest elephant grass he had ever seen. He patrolled the edge of it to another familiar terrain feature, the rock cliff where he'd almost broken his neck. He lowered himself to the ground and studied the cliff over his rifle sights. Back in Charlie country. For the second time this hill had led him in a big loop. A shiver of fear gave way to anger; stupid son-of-a-bitch! The only way off this hill is down! He back-tracked, then low-crawled through the meadow to the elephant grass. He slipped down through the elephant grass into lighter brush where he had a quick cigarette. The rain began to let up. There was still no sign of a 300-man battalion sweep ahead of him.

Legs, he said to himself, we're going down. Even if we come out at the South China Sea.

The rain quit at 1600. The sky broke up and there was a pink hue of sundown in the west. Humping down, he chewed the last of his licorice and drank warm water from his canteen. At 1615 on the Omega he heard voices below. He sneaked close to a squad of GI's taking a smoke break. He recognized Sergeant Palmyra and admin Specialist Benke. The wide-bodied one, stretched out on his back and spitting sunflower shells, was Corporal E4 Cleveland Pomeroy. He smelled Cambodian and walked in.

"You guys are nuts," he warned.

Palmyra was dry, relaxed and glass-eyed. Seeing sopping-wet Deagle gave him a good laugh. He offered a hit but Deagle waved no thanks. Pomeroy sat up and scowled at him. He glanced at the .45 hanging on his belt.

"Was that you, over?" Pomeroy wasn't ripped like the others.

"Most affirm."

"Some hill, eh, sarge?" Benke said. "I told you it was a bitch."

"Say that again, man," Palmyra agreed. "You couldn't cover this hill with a division sweep." He lay on his back taking the sun and stretching his legs. "Fuckin' lifer games. No more for me. Until I catch that bird for the world... I'm makin' myself scarce around here."

Pomeroy pointed to his shirt pocket and then up the hill. He'd found something up there. Deagle nodded.

"Hey, sarge," Benke asked Deagle, "you know where we are?"

"Hell, no".

"We're above DEROS, and the MP shack is about due west," Palmyra told him. We're off course maybe... a quarter mile."

"Right on. Man, I hope we don't have to deal with that bamboo and high grass; too tired, GI. You think its thick up top... you haven't seen thick. Hooper said we're..."

"I'll take a pass on the elephant grass," Deagle said. "I'm getting off hill ASAP. I'm humpin' to the road."

Palmyra yawned. "Mellow out, man. We got it made in the shade. The plan is to take a little snooze and kill another half hour or so 'til dark, then chogie on down for some hot chow."

"Most of the battalion ended up on the other side of the road," Pomeroy told Deagle. "What's over there?"

"Garbage dump," Benke said, sucking smoking deep into his lungs and holding it.

"You see Hooper or his RTO?"

"Our little bowling ball E6? He's down below, man. He probably rolled down the hill."

Pomeroy sat up. "Well, let's us roll on down and get a beer."

Deagle stood up. "Yeah, but keep an eye over your shoulder. We got VC above us."

Palmyra sat up and looked at him. "What VC, man?"

"You see one?" Benke asked.

"Saw one-each Victor Charlie by that rock cliff. At least I think it was one."

Pomeroy reached into his pocket and brought out something silver. "One of the troopies found this at the top, over."

Palmyra jumped to his feet and gathered his rifle rucksack and poncho. "That's it for me, man! I'm too short to fuck with any VC! You guys comin'?"

Palmyra and Benke took off down the hill. Pomeroy handed Deagle the detonator and he unscrewed the cap where the fuse wire went.

"No rust," he said.

"What do we do now? If we show this to that Major Andrews... me an' Fuck-knuckle will spend our R&R on this damn hill, over."

Deagle nodded. "Roger. Besides me, there's one other good NCO at Bien Hoa. He looks like a turkey but he's a good man."

They humped down another fifty slippery meters following a drainage and found Sergeant Hooper at the edge of the elephant grass. Under a picnic-blue sky Hooper had rounded up his platoon and part of somebody else's. His RTO had un-slung his heavy Prick-25 and lay flat on his back trying to call in to Major Andrews.

"This here is Alpha Hotel calling Claymore over... Alpha Hotel calling Claymore come in..."

Deagle grinned at Pomeroy. "How's that for radio manners."

Pomeroy shook his head.

The admin RTO called in again but the major wasn't home.

"You better show him how it's done," Deagle said.

Pomeroy walked over and relieved him of the mike. "Claymore, this Alpha Hotel. Claymore, this is Alpha Hotel, over."

Specialist Knox came back immediately. "Alpha Hotel, this is Claymore over."

"What do you want me to tell him, Sarge?"

Hooper frowned at his RTO. "Tell him I got my p'toon down in good shape, plus some of Timmerman's. No casualties except this here heat-stroked RTO, he calls hisself. Ask him if he wants us to come in."

"Claymore, this is Alpha Hotel. We are at our objective, I say again, we are at our objective. Request permission to return to base, over."

"Alpha Hotel, that is affirmative. Return to base."

"Alpha Hotel, affirmative and out."

"We flush any VC into those bunker guns?" Deagle asked Hooper.

"Why heck no. Sweep had holes in it a convoy of VC coulda drove through. P'toons... off your ass an' on your feet! Let's move IT, move IT, move IT..."

Hooper's tired army patrolled single-file to the road. On drying hard-packed

157

dirt he formed his troops in two columns and paraded them through the checkpoint gate, singing a cheerful cadence... "yo LEFF!... yo LEFF!... yo LEFT right LEFT!... "...all the way to the formation area where the trucks had picked them up. Two-thirds of the battalion was there ahead of them, sitting on porches and stretched out on the ground, and greeted them with jeers. After Hooper released the platoon Deagle looked for Major Andrews but didn't see him.

"Looks like a GR point," Pomeroy quipped, looking at the bodies.

"Just in time," Hooper said, checking his watch. "Cease-fire starts in twenty minutes."

Deagle lit a smoke. "Not for Charles."

Hooper stopped to check the 1st Cav bulletin board for Sergeant Trumpy's Christmas KP roster. In the only corner of the bulletin board where there were no 3"x5" cards advertising refrigerators and stereos, he found the neatly-typed sheet of paper:

"2nd Notice! - Volunteers Needed for 24 December
Christmas Dinner for Vietnamese Orphan Children
See Sgt Trumpy, Motorpool, before 0800 24Dec71"

NAME & RANK	COMPANY
1) PFC Dick Hurtz	EOB
2) Sgt Ben Dover	ERB
3)	
4)	
5)	

"Well would you look at that," he said, disgusted.

Pomeroy laughed. "Those guys show up on every duty roster, don't they sarge."

"They shore do. And old Trumpy will have the ass." He looked up at Deagle. "Well, guess I better hand-carry you up to the colonel's hooch so you can get that cluster."

Pomeroy looked at his friend. "Cluster?"

Deagle scratched his light chin whiskers. "Let's move where nobody can hear us and you can show him what you got, Ploughboy."

Away from the CP, Pomeroy held the gleaming detonator up to the sun. "You guys got trouble, sarge. Numbah ten, GI."

Hooper's nose, Deagle decided, wasn't really red it was more the purple color of a canned beet. Pomeroy passed him the detonator but he didn't know what he was holding, at first. He turned it over on his palm, unscrewed the fuse end with his chubby fingers, and then held it up to the sun. "Detonator?"

Pomeroy nodded. "Brand new, sarge, enough explosive to blow your hand off. Means you guys got sappers on that hill, over."

Hooper's voice was hushed. "Holy hanna. The major said they was up there."

Deagle moved a step closer. "Sarge, did you hear a pistol shot about 1500 hours?"

Hooper thought about it and nodded. "Thought I did."

"You did. I took a shot at one-each Victor Charlie but I missed. He went up."

"Lord. We got us a big problem."

"That is affirmative. But look around. Your troops are heat-stroked, your officers are green, the other NCO's are idiots... this sweep was worse than an Arvin sweep. So it's up to you to get Andrews to pull his head out."

"And you know what that means, over," Pomeroy told him.

Hooper looked up from one to the other.

"You guys gotta be up there," Deagle told him, "when Charles steps into an opening,"

Hooper nodded. "Ambush."

"Keep all this shit to yourself until the area clears. Then take the detonator to the major and write a debriefing recommending day and night ambush duty, tonight, tomorrow, and tomorrow night. That's what I'd do."

"Right as rain, sarn't."

Deagle looked up the street as more soldiers straggled down to the formation area. Above the checkpoint, the base of Hill 229 was in shadow but its summit sparkled with all the shades of green, from pastel to dark emerald. He looked down at the Omega, 1745 hours.

"One more thing, sarge. Pomeroy is the best friend I've got and he's going on R&R on the 27th. I don't want him on that hill, you bic? Me either, I'm going to slick back to LZ Penny tomorrow if I can bum a ride. We did our part, now it's up to you guys."

Hooper stuck out his hand. "Major Andrews can get some of them green berets for his ambush squads. Hey, why don't we all meet at the NCO club later for the live show."

Deagle shook hands. "Maybe if I drink beer I'll get my legs back... "

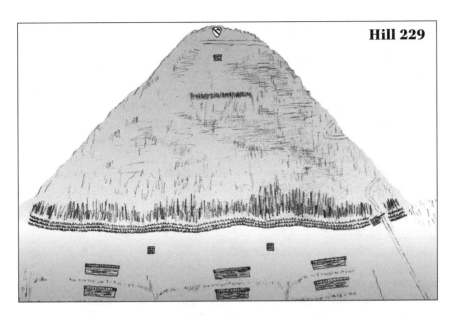

Hill 229

CHAPTER SEVEN

In wet fatigues and steel helmet, Colonel Borg closed the door behind him. His grin broadened into a smile seeing how Colonel Shipp had converted the small briefing room into a WWII-era command bunker; army blankets over the windows, emergency lanterns, flashlights, watercans, C-ration cases, and folding tables lined up along the wall below President Johnson's smiling face. On another table a squad of telephones was aligned in a neat row. There was a working table for old 9th Infantry debriefings, topo maps, surveillance photography, another for 1st Cav intelligence. Major Andrews' map was at the center of the conference tables, where General Webb had monitored the sweep.

"Very impressive, Chuck." At that moment, Shipp was busy setting up a mission-log for the sweep, and possible follow-up.

Colonel Geary winked.

Colonel Wilcox rolled his eyeballs as he fiddled with the new ANPRC-25 Radio. Borg heard the purr of static and realized the commanding general had audited the radio communication between Andrews and his NCO's on the sweep.

Borg walked to the window and peeked at Hill 229 under the corner of the blanket. The north face was almost dark and the floodlights at the base were on.

161

"Sorry I'm late, sir. A couple of our troops needed a private word."

Webb nodded.

Wilcox noted the soggy fatigues. "We don't mind waiting a few more minutes, Phil."

"Sadly, this report will take about zero five."

Shipp looked up from his log. "Ain't been our finest hour, I presume."

"It was quite a show," Borg told the support staff. "No, not at all the Cav's finest hour. Is there any other cease-fire activity? Violations? Did the air force turn up anything on their side?"

Wilcox sat down and shook his head. "Negative. Quiet on all fronts."

"Where are the reporters?"

"Watching an F-111 bombing run. Colonel Shipp arranged an air support demonstration a mile from the South China Sea," Webb answered. "They should be back soon."

Borg grinned. "For the 20th time?"

"I'm sure."

"Sir, you called General Garlett?"

"After the troops were up there, yes. What did we learn, colonel?"

"Sir, it depends on your expectations. Speaking for myself, about what I expected from Major Warren Andrews; as for Hill 229, I think it will be obvious. I've got the debriefings from all the NCO's except Sergeant Hooper. I have all officers' but Major Andrews'." Borg knew which one Webb wanted to see first and handed him SSG McFadden's.

Webb scanned it quickly. The sergeant's handwriting was poor and his grammar was basic, the bare bones of his debriefing being that he'd swept down no more than one hundred meters when one of his squad leaders stepped into a tunnel opening. He wrote that he smelled stale cigarettes in the tunnel, called it in to Major Andrews, and received permission to blow it. He did that: one one-each M-67 fragmentation grenade. A tunnel reconnaissance was negative.

Webb looked up. "Here it is again—what the hell does he mean 'negative'! Can we find the tunnel again? Did he just stick his nose in it?..."

Borg fought a cynical smile. "Sir, what you're reading is baloney. McFadden threw a frag, all right, I talked to a troop who saw him do it. But not into a tunnel, into an old 105mm crater."

Webb's eyes narrowed.

"I suspected something between McFadden and Lieutenant St. John. The yellow smoke was a side-show and they pre-arranged it."

"Why would they do that?"

"Andrews wanted to impress you, Lieutenant St. John wanted to impress the major... something on that order. Sir, I'm sorry and ashamed to tell you there was no tunnel, and when I confronted St. John he spilled his guts. He's in my office writing an encyclopedia on the whole misadventure. Essentially it was

Major Andrews' plan. St. John claims he only recently realized that Andrews is mentally unstable, his head has some missing parts... and so on. The body count was a ringer; Andrews had it flown in from Firebase Catapult. My God, what you must think of the lunatic officers running around Bien Hoa..."

Webb flipped the debriefing on the desk.

"Sir, I know of one or two other serious charges against the major in regard to this sweep, and I'm going to be fairly hard on him, career-wise."

"All right," he answered, disinterested.

"He should go to jail for what he's done. But I'll recommend a court-martial and reduction back to E6, return to state-side duty to serve out his twenty years."

Colonel Shipp stroked his mustache. Wilcox sat writing notes with stars and underlines.

"Let the army shrinks find out what's left in the major's head," Webb told him. "Meanwhile, the Cav moves on. I need a replacement commander for admin and I still have that hill in my back yard. Are there Viet Cong on Hill 229, colonel?"

"General, you should know he threatened to kill four enlisted men. I have their statements..."

"I asked if there are VC on the hill," he repeated tartly. "Do I need to carry out night-ambush missions during the Christmas cease-fire?"

Borg piled the rest of the hand-written debriefings on the table. "We found no active caves, no caches of weapons or supplies, and no Victor Charlie. We learned, I believe, the enemy is in compliance with the cease-fire."

"What about Sergeant Hooper's report?"

"I'll have it soon, sir. Hooper's platoon was in the middle of the sweep area, one of his troops might have fired the shot we heard."

Colonel Wilcox asked, "Sir, if you're allowed to share the information, can you tell us what General Garlett said?"

Webb stuck out his chin. "General Garlett was, of course, concerned about the timing of the sweep." He policed up his briefings and walked to his office door. "Confine both Andrews and St. John in their quarters, and I'll be in mine with these. Bring me the other debriefings as soon as they come in."

When the door closed Borg stuffed his head inside his steel pot. "I'm getting used to this damn hat."

"Well, I, for one, am relieved," Wilcox said quietly. "We should not have had put troops on that hill today. Jeff Webb's already in Garlett's doghouse about the 'Bail Out' letter. We don't need a uniform-code issue during a cease-fire."

Shipp glanced over and studied the owl-like expression. "What the hell are you talking about! Webb didn't sign any 'Bail Out' letter."

Wilcox blinked. "It's obvious that he did, Chuck. That *Washington Post* story... his transfer here... his relationship with Garlett..."

Shipp picked up an empty manila folder and whacked the desk. "I'm saying 'read the man', Ray. Webb don't act like a man who recommended a theatre-wide stand-down."

"Shadowboxing. Throwing punches at Viet Cong who aren't there. As a parallel, our psychotic major tries to ingratiate himself with Webb, Webb does likewise with Garlett to save his career..."

"That's ridiculous."

"It's not a criticism of Webb; on the contrary, signing that letter was more valorous than any combat award. He had to know the cost if it failed. But Webb is exhausted and he's making poor decisions. Using R&R troops for a combat sweep is reprehensible. I'm glad we didn't get caught."

Colonel Shipp stood, blood-hound's eyes dog tired. "Your opinions." He looked around at the briefing room, remembering the work it had taken turn it into a command center. "Well," he said wearily, "s'pose I gotta take all this shit down now."

Borg smiled. "Leave it until tomorrow, Chuck. It looks strak, and we like it. Now, I think I'll clean up before I arrest Andrews."

1900Hours 23Dec71
1st Cav Div HQ
Admin Command Post

Sergeant Timmerman opened the door and asked the major if he wanted the battalion in platoon formation, adding that it was getting dark on Hill 229. Andrews sat at his desk trying to compose his thoughts to write his debriefing, but it was really too soon, he hadn't talked to Lieutenant St. John or Sergeant Hooper yet. Old Hoop had never let him down.

"Not necessary, sergeant." he said.

The major opened a side desk drawer and found a three-quarter full bottle of Johnny Walker Red and poured himself two fingers. The smoky heat going down his throat was soothing, and he hoped the scotch would do something for his headache, soon. From the collection of George Armstrong Custer books on his desk, he selected "My Life on the Plains," and opened it to the pages describing some of the lieutenant colonel's happier times at Fort Lincoln, in 1874, eight months before his death. He looked up and found Sergeant Timmerman still standing in the open door.

"Two hundred and thirty-one troops are down, sir," Timmerman reported.

"Have you seen Sergeant Hooper?"

"I seen him, but I ain't spoke to him. Want me to police him up?"

"Let him grab a smoke break. Tell him I'm going to return the admin jeep and to meet me back here at the CP."

"Roger, will do, sir."

There were seventy-three admin and R&R soldiers either still on the hill or over on the air force side, lost. But he didn't much give a damn right now. He turned the pages of "My Life on the Plains" until he realized Timmerman was still watching him.

"Release the battalion, sir?"

"Oh. Affirmative. And tell them they did a fine job."

"Thank you, sir. We by God sent those gooks a message today!"

"Don't forget a written debriefing, soon's you can."

"Already wrote one, sir. Colonel Borg has it."

"Oh. Then that's all, sergeant." The office door closed.

Tell them they did a fine job. He choked on the thought. In I-Corps he had pulled dozens of battalion sweeps. Some of those had been up-and-over hill's like 229-er and others went through miles of rice paddies, hour after hour of running in hip-deep muck... trading shots with Charles behind some treeline. But afterwards in formation at the objective, in spite of being bug-bitten, heat-stroked, cramping, dry-heaving... and too exhausted to take chow... those soldiers stood on their feet like men. And when he gave the order to move out, they took their spacing and humped two or three more klicks to the next compass point on the triangle, then two or three more klicks back to the base where some of them had to immediately stand in guard duty formation. On their feet like men.

He took a pull on the scotch. How times had changed. After just two hours of walking downhill, these troops, even the grunts, lay sprawled in the middle of the street, flopped on the flak walls, or sat dazed on barracks steps. Barely a man vertical. Already the troops were calling the sweep "Andrews Last Stand."

Unable to think for the hammering in his head, he left the CP and walked to the mess hall, where his jeep was parked. He drove it to the motorpool and found the front gate rolled shut. He sat in the jeep with the engine idling, too dispirited to get out and open the gate. He wondered how the air force had done on their side of Hill 229-er. Thinking again about his debriefing to General Webb, he brought out his notepad and checked the first page; one frag thrown by McFadden, one shot fired, source as yet unconfirmed. It hadn't been a rifle, and that was interesting. None of his NCO's had carried sidearms. But then he had a sinking thought; maybe St. John faked that too. Check with the armorer and see who had been issued a sidearm. He was glad that nonsense with McFadden hadn't been his idea, but if he put it in a debriefing as fact then he was as guilty as St. John.

Master Sergeant Trumpy appeared at the gate and shoved it open. Andrews shot past him and drove around behind the offices and garages, and parked the admin jeep in its slot. Because of the cease-fire the motorpool was almost deserted—a few walking guards but no maintenance work. As he walked back to the gate he spotted a newly washed deuce-and-a-half and the components of a field kitchen, and he remembered Sergeant Trumpy's

Christmas Eve dinner for Vietnamese orphans. It was a gesture he approved of even if his troops did not.

"Keys on the desk, sarge," he called, "about half a tank."

"Good 'nuf , sir," the master sergeant called back. Trumpy was as big as Andrews, with a mighty chest and a fat-man's rolling laugh that carried all the way to the R&R detachment. "Is it safe for me to go into Sin City tomorrow, sir?" he laughed. "Or are them whores gonna be shootin' at me!"

Andrews glowered. Trumpy meant no disrespect but he couldn't think of an answer. He dragged himself back up the street. Troops in wet fatigues milled in the street, and like skunks in their holes, they scurried away as he walked by. Far to his right, the admin shower shack had a long line. Big show tonight at the NCO Club. The mess hall was crowded with troops from the sweep, but he wasn't hungry. He walked on. He saw 1st Sergeant Ree close the admin CP door. Ree whipped up one of his karate salutes and he snapped one back. "Evening Top," he said.

The admin CP was lights-out, deserted like the motorpool. Sergeant Stevens had abandoned the CQ's desk, probably gone to the live show. His office was empty, his desk chair inviting, and "My Life on the Plains" was open at the page where he left it.

He sat and looked down at the black-and-white portrait of Custer under a cavalry campaign hat. Custer looked up with benevolent, understanding eyes. G.A. Custer had been busted once, sort of. From brevet general to lieutenant colonel after the war between the states. But he'd made the best of it.

"Didn't lose any men today, sir," Andrews told the face.

He poured two fingers of amber Johnny Walker Red into a metal canteen cup and drank half of it. He swung his boots up on the desk and leaned back in the chair, right hand resting on his Cav form 36, Commanders Field Debriefing. Before settling in to write his report he reached down and drew out his .45 and laid it beside the Johnny Walker. He took his pen and underlined the word "Mission" at the top of the form. The army provided three blank lines to describe it.

"To Search and Destroy... To Search and Clear..."

Head throbbing, he placed both palms on his temples and tried to massage away the ache, but it persisted. "Skip that for now." Below it were the words "Co-ordinates / Topo Map Number" he wrote "Topographical Series 1964 C.E. Hill 229 III-Corps." He leaned back and sipped scotch.

How many debriefing reports had he written in a career that included four combat tours? Five hundred? He was not a college-educated officer, not the master of language like 1st Lieutenant St. John. But he was experienced, he had written and reviewed hundreds of official debriefings over the years. Army terminology, the absence of civilian slang and double-talk, was one of the things he liked best about the military. Military meanings never changed, once you understood something it remained true for an entire career. One of his old commanders, a bird colonel whose name he'd forgotten, used to call written debriefing reports "de-griefings" because the news always seemed to be bad, KIA's, WIA's, MIA's... but except for cuts and scrapes and the one broken leg there were no casualties in this report. Hell with the broken leg, medics can write that one. No enemy casualties, either. In fact, no enemy contact unless Hooper came through. The bad news in this debriefing was failure.

He picked up his pen and stared at the blank report. That same bird colonel had taught him, always "take a partner" when describing defeat.

"With full agreement from and" ...but he scratched that out and tore up the page. He ripped off a new form and wrote, "In support of, as directed by, the Commanding General, 1st Cavalry Division A.M., took two infantry companies and swept Hill 229-er with the objective to destroy, drive out, or disrupt the Viet Cong and their activities."

He glanced at Custer and winked. "Got me a partner. I bet you never had trouble with this crap. I wish St. John was around. I need to work off of his report..."

The outer door opened and closed. Thinking it was Hooper, he looked up and saw the unmistakable form of Colonel Borg filling his doorway. Borg flipped on the overhead light.

"Working in the dark, major?" He sauntered closer and looked down at the desk. He saw the square scotch bottle and the .45 Colt, hammer back, pointed toward his groin.

"Debriefing report, sir." Andrews swung his boots off the desk and sat up.

The S-2 colonel had changed into fresh fatigues since Andrews had last seen him. He'd shaved and showered and his long face was pale-pink. As he pulled off his baseball cap Andrews' eyes were drawn to the huge long-lobed ears.

"You should know General Webb is expecting that debriefing ASAP. I won't tie you up too long."

"I appreciate that, sir."

"What's wrong with your right eye?" Borg asked him

Andrews struck a proud pose. "Nothing, sir."

"I've assigned a squad of MP's," Borg told him, "to look for the nine enlisted men still missing from our... pre-emptive strike... starting on the air force side. I've visited the half-dozen GI's in the infirmary, one broken leg, one torn ankle ligament, a couple cases of convulsions from heat exhaustion. And we left a truck up there off the road, broken axle. In your report, please don't blame these accidents on... what did you call them... 'inexperienced clerks and truckdrivers?' Not this time, major."

He walked a full circle around the desk and glanced at the picture of Custer in the open book. "That's a little ironic. Some of the troops are calling the sweep 'Andrews' Last Stand'."

"Yes, I heard that, sir."

"Oh you heard that?"

"Yes, I heard that."

Back in front of the desk, Borg pulled on his baseball cap. "Consider it true, and your final combat mission. You had nineteen years in the army, major, and you'll probably see twenty. That depends on JAG. I've recommended to General Webb that you be court-martialed here in Bien Hoa and returned to duty in the states as a staff sergeant E6. That way you can retire, at least. The worst of it for you is the VC body count. Thanks to Lieutenant St. John, I know all about your use of the crytpo line, how you had it flown in from Catapult. I have statements from two admin staff sergeants in your command supporting the lieutenant. The grenade incident is regrettable but not important, but you'd better put it in your debriefing because General Webb will read about it in the other reports. And I have the statements from the four soldiers you threatened personally to shoot. Those charges will also be quite serious."

"Colonel, those cowardly draftees were on..."

"Major, don't even bother to explain. It's disgusting and embarrassing to this division. You betrayed a fine officer who trusted you. Now he's accountable to MAC-V. I'm not interested in any defense, any explanation, any apology from you. I only want you off this installation. Leave your debriefing on Sergeant Major Bierra's desk, along with and Sergeant Hooper's. Afterwards, consider yourself confined to quarters pending charges and pre-trial disposition. Is all of that perfectly clear, major?"

"It is, sir. And may I say, you've waited months for this."

The corners of Colonel Borg's mouth twitched. He looked down at the handgun on the desk still pointed his way.

"Affirmative. I'd ask you to surrender your sidearm but then you couldn't kill yourself with it, if that were your intension. Leave it on Bierra's desk with your debriefing."

He snapped off the light and closed the door behind him. The outer door closed.

Andrews stared at the door until his lips trembled. He reached past his .45 for the Johnny Walker bottle and poured three inches into the canteen cup, and drank all of it down. But the liquor didn't stop the incessant throbbing in his head. He closed his eyes against the pain and when his lids rolled open he found Custer looking up at him, a commander who had also suffered humiliation and defeat. Ultimate defeat. He swiveled away from Custer's gaze and for the fourth time in his life tears welled in his eyes.

He wrapped his fist around his .45, holding the muzzle to the ceiling.

"An attribute of the Gods," he said. "To point the finger... and smite..."

Tears squeezed from Andrews eyes and rolled down his cheeks. Staff Sergeant E6? Serve in the same capacity as Hooper and Stevens? Pistol tight in his right hand he counted with the fingers of his left: O1, O2, O3,... E9, E8, E7, E6... a seven grade reduction? George Armstrong Custer had fared better. He felt his eyeballs bulging from the pressure inside his skull, his ear-drums ready to blow. Of its own will, his right hand brought the muzzle of the gun to the purple scar above his right ear. He sat straight, back arched and chin out. His thumb found the safety and flicked it down and his finger settled on the trigger...

The outer door opened and slammed shut. There was a knock before his office door swung wide open, and Sergeant Hooper switched on the light. Wearing dry fatigues and his usual cheery grin the staff sergeant burst into the room and dropped his one-page debriefing on Andrews' desk.

"They tole me you was here, sir," he chirped. "There you go."

Major Andrews quickly shoved the gun into the top desk drawer and wiped the tears off his cheeks. "Hoop, how you doin'. Got your debriefing, huh?"

Hooper pulled off his baseball cap and dragged a chair over. "Takes me forever to fill out one of them dang forms." He saw the bottle and grinned, waiting to be invited. But Andrews swiveled in his chair and stared at his Custer portrait. "Mind if I take a pull, sir? After that walk this afternoon I'm one thirsty staff sergeant."

The fog lifted in front of Andrews' eyes. He looked at Hooper and heard Borg saying, "I have the statements of two of your staff sergeants..."

"You get a bug in your right eye, sir?"

"Loyalty" Andrews said to himself, " is an asset in a man. Help yourself to a drink, sergeant, then please leave and turn out the light."

Hooper took the bottle, upended it. "Damn good. You feeling alright, sir? You look a little punk just now. Is your head bothering you again?"

"What did Colonel Borg tell you about my head?" He picked up the bottle and upended it himself.

"Colonel Borg? I ain't talked to him since this morning. If I did talk to him, I might get right up in his chops and say 'we told you so.'"

"Say again?"

Hooper took the Johnny Walker bottle and helped himself once more. "Hooeee that's good stuff."

"You say you haven't talked to Colonel Borg?"

"Roger. Oh, I seen dumbo-the-elephant just now, leaving, and I threw him a salute." He pointed at his debriefing on the desk. "But I kept my trap shut 'cause I wanted you to see this first so we could plan our ambush. Sarn't Deagle says you'll want to set day and night ambush missions for sure. He and Pomeroy don't want to climb up there again an' I don't blame em for that..."

"Deagle?"

"Yes, sir. He was in my p'toon this afternoon. Took a shot at a gook with a .45 but he missed. It's all in there, sir."

Andrews held his palms against his head to hold the pressure in. He saw the hand-written words on the debriefing but he couldn't focus. "Hoop, I'm real tired and my head's killing me so start over... who is Deagle... what gook... what ambush..."

"Sir, Deagle's the Silver Star winner Colonel Wilcox was looking for. He was with me on the sweep. He got lost comin' down the hill but when he done that he found one Victor Charles and fired at him. Everybody heard the shot."

Andrews lowered his hands to the desk and looked up. "I heard a shot. I thought it was... Say it once more Hoop, slow."

"Sarn't Deagle come eyeball-to-eyeball with that VC, sir. Just like you said, they're up there."

Andrews' expression changed as he stood up. He balled his fist and slammed it down on the metal desk. "God DAMN!"

It was a roller-coaster ride, from the frustration of "Andrews' Last Stand" to the despair of Borg putting him under arrest, now the exhilaration of vindication. He ran his hand over his flat-topped head. "Took a shot... but missed... so that VC is still up there... in the caves..."

"Yes, sir. An' that's only half of it. This here is for you from Corporal Pomeroy."

Andrews strained his eyes trying to see through a migraine headache and an alcohol haze. He reached out and Hooper carefully placed the shiny detonator in his hand, as in bestowing the bread of communion. Andrews held it, rolled it over, and when he spoke his voice was a hoarse whisper.

"Where'd this come from."

"Pomeroy said up at the very top."

Andrews laid the detonator on the desk. "Have a seat Hoop. Take another pull on that bottle while I read."

His vision cleared, his headache vanished, and blood sang in his veins. He read the complete report, folded twice and stashed it in his shirt pocket, along with the detonator and his own unfinished debriefing. He opened the drawer and grabbed his .45, stuffed it hard into his holster.

"You know what this means, Hoop?"

"Sappers, major."

"That is affirmative. They're back on Hill 686. They're gonna blow a barracks... maybe an airstrip..." He looked up at his good and loyal friend. "You son of a gun. You... son of a GUN! You came through for me again."

"Hill 686 Sir? You mean 229-er. We got lucky, sir. An' I'm ready to pull on my gear and go back up."

Andrews showed him both palms. "Negative. We have to think first. Listen up. They all think we failed; the gooks, our troops, Colonel Borg... everybody. Everybody but you and me."

"An' Deagle and Pomeroy. We're gonna brief the general ain't we... I mean, he wanted proof and we sure as heck got it now..."

"You don't understand, Hoop. They won't believe us now... Colonel Borg thinks... never mind what he thinks... we have to keep this detonator and the VC to ourselves for now. Some of our brave men must sacrifice their lives to save the brigade."

"Beg pardon, sir?"

" 'Fraid so, Hoop."

Confused, Hooper helped himself to another swallow of scotch. "Talkin' about night ambush duty, sir? I know it's dangerous work, but I volunteer."

Andrews smiled benevolently at his NCO. "You're a fine NCO. I'm going to see you make E7 out of this. But for tonight... not a word to anybody."

"If you say so, sir. Can I go to the NCO Club and catch part of the show? Deagle and my buddy Pomeroy will be there..."

"Negative, Hoop. Grab your headgear."

Andrews closed up the CP and steered his best NCO outside. They stood on the porch listening to the amplifiers blaring from the NCO club, the Tai band was warming up for the live show. The empty admin street was illuminated by the rising moon and a dozen barracks lights.

Andrews' voice was a whisper. "You're not going on an ambush tonight, but you will tomorrow night. Tomorrow we'll both hump up that hill. Do you have any buddies on the air force side?

"Shore do, sir. You don't need me here?"

"Listen up: tonight and tomorrow I don't want you anywhere near this AO, Hoop, especially not R&R and DEROS. You go see your air force buddies. Stay with 'em. Have some Christmas cheer. Got that?"

"How come..."

"That's an order, sergeant."

"Yes, sir."

"I'll meet you here tomorrow at 1900. We'll get our TO&E, pick our squads for night ambush duty, and we'll catch those sappers on their way down the hill. I know where Charlie holds formation."

Andrews watched Hooper walk up the dark street and turn into his barracks. The major headed down the street to the motorpool, with new life in his legs. The sliding gate was locked but the side entry door was open. Inside there was no sign of Master Sergeant Trumpy, only his truck loaded and ready to roll. The offices, the yard, and all the garages were dark.

He left the office lights off as he prowled Colonel Geary's unlocked office for the keys to 1st Cav vehicle 0774, the admin jeep. They were not on the desk, not in the drawers, but in the padlocked wall locker behind the desk. He had no intention of bothering the S-4 for his keys. Instead, he went into Sergeant Trumpy's alpha garage, located a pair of bolt-cutters, and snapped the lock like a pretzel. Keys and bolt-cutter in hand, he started the jeep and drove it to the main gate where he cut the padlock.

He swung the nose of the jeep south. He followed the road around Hill 229 to the two-lane panoprimed highway that connected Bien Hoa to South Vietnam's capitol city. He had the road to himself all the way to the shantytown outskirts of Saigon.

"Thank you for coming."

"How could I refuse a chance to get even," she said.

"Are your quarters comfortable?"

"You put us in a fenced compound, like prisoners."

He closed the door. "Let's get our sparing done before dinner."

"You took me to the woodshed this morning, general."

"But it's Bien Hoa not the White House briefing room."

Darcy allowed Webb to walk her from the door into his small living room. One drab gray couch, one old comfortable chair, a reading lamp on a small glass-top table, one military writing desk and two military footlockers, all in a 12' x 12' main room. She picked the reading chair and sat with her eyebrows knit, hands in her lap. She was still miffed at herself for accepting his invitation.

Webb watched her sit down. A half hour's notice had given Ms. Devlin time to shower and change. She wore loose-fitting Levi's and an orange, collared golf shirt with no bra, tennis shoes with no socks. Her red-brown hair was brushed to a full-body sheen and her face was scrubbed ruddy clean. Apart from light liner around her wide green eyes and a thin layer of orange lipstick, she wore no make-up.

"Glass of wine? Beer?"

"Beer if it's cold. You know, I don't write for your home-town paper. Peter does."

In a kitchenette not much bigger than a closet he opened his mini-refrigerator and brought out two cold cans of Falstaff, two glasses. He cracked the cans with a churchkey and poured for them both."

"Name's Jeff, and I'm still not looking for votes."

"And I'm still Ms. Devlin. Boy, anything cold in a can tastes good in 'Nam. What shall we spar about? How about effete snobs and body count numbers?"

He nodded. "Why not. First tell me, are you related to the activist?"

"Bernadette? As far as I know we're both Irish."

"How long have you been a newspaperman?"

"I've been a newspaper woman for eight years."

"Like it?"

"So far, except for South East Asia. Too much prepared material."

"And you're going back soon?"

"The whole bunch of us, on the 30th. General, in the PX, which was a great end-run by the way, we heard rumblings about a combat mission before the cease-fire deadline. Know anything about it?"

"Sure. I provided the artillery support. The air force has a lot of supplies sitting out on runways and they've been concerned about in-coming during Christmas. It's precautionary and very routine."

"That's funny. At their little air-power demonstration, another clever ruse, the air force told us they were supplying support for a 1st Cav operation."

"A co-operation, call it."

She sipped cold beer and looked around his quarters. "Is this... what's the military expression... SOP... for a brigadier general. It's pretty basic."

Webb leaned back on the sofa and crossed his ankles. "First time you've seen a commanding general's quarters, Ms. Devlin?"

Her expression went from pleasantly pissed to icy cold. "That question reminds me of today's press conference, and I don't think I care for more of that. This wasn't a good idea and I should go." She put down the unfinished beer and stood. "Peace now, general."

"I'd like to talk about the good old USA. I miss the place. Dinner is rare roast beef, whole white potatoes in butter sauce, and green beans. Salad first, pecan pie with ice cream for desert. I hope you'll stay and join me."

She stared at him. He sat with his ankles still crossed, the bastard.

"Ms. Devlin, they tell me I get roast beef once a month at Bien Hoa. I'm using a two-month ration."

She let her breath out and sat down. "I don't want to talk about the good old USA. I want to talk about the war. I want to hear the truth, for a change, and I don't care to be condescended to by another smirking general officer!" She reached into her purse for a cigarette and lit it. "Do you mind if I smoke!"

"Not at all."

"Thank you! I do like roast beef."

"Off the record, what do you want to know about the sweep?"

"Has the air force or the 1st Cav violated the Christmas cease-fire, and if so, why? Simple."

He sipped his beer and nodded. "Yes, it seems simple. I've been at Bien Hoa less than a week, not by choice. This afternoon, two officers in my command brought me a dead Viet Cong shot in our wire last night, on a hill about a quarter mile from where we're sitting. As a precaution, with the air force assistance, I decided to sweep the hill. Not all the debriefing reports are in, but they appear negative and 90 percent of my troops were down before 1800 hours. No cease-fire violation."

"So why run us to hell-and-gone like it was a big secret?"

"You were at MAC-V yesterday. Did you feel any tension because of an up-coming cease-fire?"

"So thick you could cut it."

He shrugged. "American violations are a legitimate concern. The officers at MAC-V want the peace talks to move forward."

"But you were concerned about security at Bien Hoa? Did you have to notify MAC-V first?"

"The answer to your first question is yes; I focus on my mission, and on a division full of good men and valuable hardware still in III-Corps. I'd like to get all those men and that property back to the US without further loss. And, yes, I advised my superior." His thoughts drifted, and after a few seconds he recovered. "I have probably authorized the Cav's last offensive mission. Now I'm on defense and it's a learning process. Another beer?"

"You mean today's mission?"

He stood. "I'm sorry, I was thinking about Firebase Catapult. Today's sweep was defensive."

She looked at her empty glass just as he picked it up and carried it to the kitchenette. "You said that those who think the war in Vietnam is over are misinformed. Now you're saying... the way you come across... it is over and you're just trying to back out. So like I asked this morning, why not pull the whole division back. Aren't Laos and Cambodia are just running up the score on both sides?"

Webb returned with beer and sat down. "I get a little defensive at press conferences."

"Just a wee bit, general."

"I won't pull the Cav back from Tay Ninh and leave the door to Saigon open from the west until ordered to do so. Look at your map. It's a big job and I'm understaffed. Believe me or don't believe me, my division isn't sitting around in the jungle waiting to support the next incursion into Laos.

"Then answer this," she countered. "At the Pentagon, when press conferences get a little noisy about Laos and the generals skulk away to hold their little ad-hoc huddles and figure out how to explain another helicopter getting shot down fifty miles outside Vietnam, why do members of the press think they hear the name 'Webb' used as a reference? As an example 'send a TWIX to Webb'".

Webb's expression was blank.

She knew she'd scored a direct hit. Looking in his eyes, she had an inspiration and tried her best disarming smile. "Did the Pentagon turn you into a spook because of the 'Bail Out' letter?" She saw a whimsical spark in his dark eyes.

"You have a lurid imagination. Are we still off the record?"

"No way. But let's see how dinner goes, maybe I'll change my mind."

"Fair enough. If you want a quote, here's a quote. In my opinion, we lost the Vietnam War in the summer of 1968 when my friend and Commander-in-Chief Lyndon Johnson grounded the B-52's bombing the Ho Chi Minh Trail in order to put Humphrey in the White House. Up to that point, while hardly anybody remembers, we were getting better at jungle fighting. We finally figured out the difference between the NVA and VC. Maybe you should write a book about that someday."

She shook her head. "Nobody gives a damn, general, whether we could have won in Vietnam. The reality in 1971 is that Vietnam was a mistake and we lost. If the American people can accept a military defeat, why can't the military?"

"It isn't just pride, Ms. Devlin. It's lives and property."

"Darcy," she told him. "Look. Laird's tired speech about 'buying time for troop reductions' is a joke, and 'Vietnamization' is oxy-moronic. How do you Vietnam-ize Vietnam for God's sake! What's that if not phony military pride."

"The hell with that broken record. Listen to what I'm saying. The North Vietnamese Army, Darcy, the communists, might play Kissinger's game but the Viet Cong, who are terrorist guerilas, never will. They're one reason why your pull-back idea won't work."

"The Viet Cong are citizen patriots. When the fighting ends, they'll go back to their rice paddies."

He nodded, uncrossed his ankles and leaned forward. "Try this. We're both from California. Suppose an invading army flanked the west coast from San Diego to San Francisco and occupied everything in between for six or sever years. Your 'citizen patriots' were forced up into the high Sierras to become guerila fighters. Hit and run, terrorize, disrupt, demoralize the invaders. Suppose the invaders flattened most of Los Angeles and made it into their headquarters, same for San Francisco. The officers moved into the Bel Air Hilton, their men moved into all those nice houses in the suburbs. Total control. Meanwhile, they bombed and burned what they didn't control, they made laborers of the citizens to build bases and fill sandbags, and they committed every unspeakable atrocity imaginable against neighbors, friends, and relatives. So the time comes when you finally you have them on the run, retreating to the coast to board ships and leave the way they came. As they're leaving, are you going to lay down your weapons and wave goodbye? Or are you going to come down out of the Sierras and kill every one you see. I know what I'd do."

"The analogy is effective but I'm not sure it's accurate. The Viet Cong used to be the Viet Minh. They've been fighting invaders a hell of a lot longer than six or seven years. More like sixty or seventy. They're tired and there aren't many left. The VC I've seen were all kids."

"Point for you. But there are hardcore types out there, and they're on automatic pilot."

She settled back in the chair and crossed her legs. "Isn't dialog more fun than diatribe? Did you say Jeff or Jeffrey?"

"Jeff. Does that mean I'm not a smirking general officer anymore?" he asked dryly.

"When was the last time you smiled?"

"I don't know. Probably about a hundred days..."

"Did you sign the 'Bail Out' letter...Jeff?"

He shook his head. "No comment."

"If you didn't sign, do you know who did?"

"Matter of fact, I know a couple names. Including the author."

"Can you give me the names? No wait... can you just nod or shake your head if I give you the names?"

"Sorry."

She lit another cigarette, watching him. Despite her suspicions, she liked his defiant jaw and the way he smiled only with his eyes. "I won't give up. I'm going to hit you with it again after dinner."

"I'm glad you're staying. Is the 'Bail Out' letter an important news story for the American people?"

"Important? To historians and biographers and the political left, definitely. Is it news? To most Americans, yes, but their interest would be prurient."

"More army officers disgraced?"

"Or glorified. Like I said, the anti-war crowd thinks those generals are martyrs."

"Including you?" he asked.

She looked across into inquisitive dark eyes. "I've seen the war from both sides. History will show those generals did the right thing. What do you think?"

He shook his head. "I think, on the one hand, the 'Bail Out' letter was a sort of passionate frustration, and good men gave in to it. On the other hand, it was pure political opportunism."

"So you know what the letter says, which means you saw it."

"I'm going to be more careful around you."

"You understand your credibility problem: why has such a great field commander, which everybody concedes you are, been relegated to Bien Hoa... the military expression is, 'shit detail'? Is it Vietnamization or the 'Bail Out' letter?"

"No comment, Darcy."

"Then tell me about the youngest brigadier general in the army."

After a long pull of his beer he relaxed deep into the couch. "The youngest BG in the army, 41 years old, is an example of the cookie-cutter formula for success and happiness. Grandfather was a bird colonel, father made major general, and I went to West Point. Good student, good athlete, fearsome debate-team adversary, trustworthy all-around guy, and then lots of service in a combat zone. That's about it and you've heard it all before. I'm assigned at Bien Hoa to train Arvins."

She laughed. "Right on. Here's a guy who is verbose as hell and pisses me off royally by dancing around the important questions... showing me modesty." She wagged a finger at him. "You forget, general, I know a reporter from your home town. I can get the dirt on you from Peter Keating."

There was a tap on the door and Specialist Brian Meredith brought in a tray of steaming covered dishes. Darcy stood up, surprised that she felt high on two beers.

176

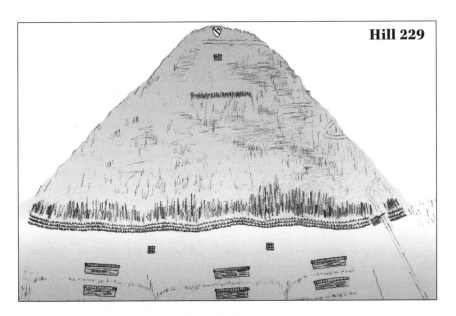

Hill 229

CHAPTER EIGHT

2140Hours 23Dec71
1st Cav Div HQ
Admin Battalion NCO Club

Deagle showed his ID card at the door and entered the smoke-filled NCO club. The Tai band was already into "Hey Jude" so the show was two-thirds over, their version of the Beatle song a heavy lead guitar, electric organ instead of a piano, and a faintly audible solo vocal. Jimmy Fuck-knuckle would approve. He squeezed through the crowd at the long bar on his right, and, waiting to trade MPC's for his first cold beer in a month, he turned and looked the place over. The band played from a stage set up at the far end of the club. In front of the stage was a GI cheering section in folding-chairs, singing, and stomping their boots and reveling in the eye contact with the sexy girl singer. Like all the live shows in Vietnam, it wasn't so much about the music as the memory.

The NCO Club looked like two barracks stuck end-to-end, long and narrow. Between the bar and the bandstand was a cloud of cigarette smoke above crowded tables piled high with empty beer cans. The show was a sell-out; the club was wall-to-wall E5's-and-up. A GI bartender hustled past and Deagle slapped down a five-dollar MPC among the accumulated plastic cups. A sign read, "Minimum 2 Beers" so he asked for two Carling Black Labels. The bartender cracked both open with his churchkey and gave him back four wet

177

one-dollar MPC's. No Vietnamese bartenders here, he thought, only GI's scratching for some extra bucks. He drank half a beer with his first swallow. It was almost cold.

Man, they had it all here, he thought. The place was a combination orderly room, dayroom, club, and concert hall all in one. Pool table, pinball machines, folded ping-pong tables against one wall. As "Hey Jude" wound down, a mighty rebel yell erupted from the cheering section, followed by an earthquake of clapping and screaming that shook the bar. Deagle put down his beer and cheered with the others, then pulled his pack of Marlboros and lit one. Somewhere in that mass of green uniforms Pomeroy and Grossnickel were supposed to be holding a chair for him. How they got in here, an E4 and an E3, was another rear-area mystery. But nothing seemed impossible at Bien Hoa. Cigarette smoke teared his eyes and sweat dripped from his freshly-soaped armpits—this was great.

He squinted through the haze, looking for his two best buddies. The last live show they saw together was Korean, at LZ Penny right after they got it set up as a forward base. That was in October, a million months ago. Those Korean singers couldn't pronounce the American lyrics as well as these Taiwanese. That had been an open-air concert downwind of the mechanized infantry's slit trenches; through the whole thing he and Ploughboy and Fuck-knuckle had smelled shit and ammonia and dope. The band's electric guitars had been powered by a five-horse generator that surged every couple minutes, trying to break his eardrums. The temperature that afternoon was 110 degrees; the Chinook pilot who flew in their beer, hanging in his net-like belly cargo sling, hovered above LZ Penny in that heat for thirty minutes before landing. That CBL was so hot when you stuck one with a churchkey foam exploded in your face, losing half the can. But, as far as Deagle remembered, nobody complained about anything.

This band was pretty much SOP, he thought: one-each lead guitar, one girl singer/piano player in a tight dress, a drummer, rhythm and base guitars, all seventeen or eighteen years old. The boys had George Harrison haircuts, Neru jackets, jeans, and pointy black boots. The girl wore a skin-tight satin blue dress with tall slits up both thighs and matching blue high-heel spikes that made her petite legs look long and strong. Tonight she wore her hair in a long black ponytail, and when Deagle closed his eyes she even sounded like Linda Ronstadt: "You and I... travel to the beat of a different drum..."

Deagle watched the band take its bows while the GI's screamed and stomped. He spotted the band's manager, a middle-aged man, just off stage, and he blacked out to the joyful noise around him. Time stood still, no sound but his shallow breathing. He saw the band in slow-motion, standing, staring into the luminous smoke in front of the stage. Somebody, he thought, had pulled their plugs. Seconds ago they were rocking; now they waited out the storm of GI applause oblivious, unappreciative. Without the music they were heavy-lidded, stoic, oriental teenagers working a job. The manager jabbed a finger at the lead guitarist, calling the next tune, and current flowed from his fingertip. The lead guitar player suddenly leaped to the front of the stage, a spotlight on his pained expression. He struck the first resonant, rising notes of "The House of the Rising Sun". The audience reacted with a spontaneous roar. The spotlight found the girl singer, pretty face now contorted, as she added her haunting electric organ to the melody.

Deagle crushed his beer can and picked up his second. He wondered if these Tai children understood the despair in the English lyrics. He wondered how much money they made, how much their manager kept. And he wondered why any of it mattered and why he couldn't just enjoy the show. When "House of the Rising Sun" ended, the manager signaled and the band fired up the Beatles version of "Twist and Shout"—"Well shake it up bay...be...ee now... dwis and chowwww..." The rhythm guitar player struck a bow-legged pose astonishingly close to John Lennon.

Deagle glanced at his new watch, 9:29 exactly, 2129 hours. The show would be over by 2230, in time for everybody to be in the sack by 2300. The Omega had survived a rough first day without scratches. He remembered how well the big green numerals and hands showed up in the elephant grass. At least one piece of his equipment would survive 'Nam. Pondering the combination of alcohol and chloroquine, he looked around for Pomeroy's distinctive shape and noticed the Christmas tree for the first time. It sat on a little table to the right of the stage, a green aluminum tree decorated with red and yellow and gold ornaments topped by, what else, a Cav patch. It looked like Hill 229.

When he spotted Pomeroy sitting at a table with two admin guys he ordered ten more CBL's. The bartender shouted that he had to crack all ten, the rules, but he offered a wet cardboard beer case to carry them in. Holding his beer high, Deagle maneuvered between the troops to Pomeroy's table. Judging by the number of butts and beer cans, and Jim Grossnickel's air-guitar playing, these troops had caught most of the show.

"It's about goddamn time!" Pomeroy hollered, standing. "Here, lemme make some room." He pulled a half-full garbage can to the table's edge and swept most of the cans into it with his thigh-sized forearm. One of the admin guys hauled a folding chair from under the table and popped it open. "Have a seat. Gary Brennan, US 53598973, twenty-six days left."

Deagle set the beer down and shook his hand. "Bill Deagle. Hey Fuck-knuckle, how you doin'?"

Jim's eyes popped open and he staggered out of his chair, and came around for a bear hug. "Where you been, turkey! Guys, this is the BEST... fuckin' buck sergeant in the fuckin' army... for a draftee... my best friend... along with Pomeroy."

Deagle looked closer at Jim's eyes. "Oh, oh."

Vinny stood tall and shook hands. "He's on vacation. I'm Vincent, twenty days left in country, nice to meet you."

At first glance, Vinny was disappointed in Sergeant William Deagle, the double Silver Star winner. He expected a hero. But the buck sergeant being described all day in such worshipful tones was a kid like himself. Deagle was as broad-shouldered as Pomeroy but skin and bones, and more cocky than handsome.

Deagle spotted Sp5 pins on both Pomeroy's and Grossnickel's collars. "Let me guess where those came from."

"Everybody's a fuckin' five tonight," Vinny shouted him. "Even Brennan. You look thin. How's the malaria?"

"Fini." He held up a full can of beer and drained most of it. "Feel pretty good."

"What was it like?"

"Well, you get hot and you sweat, get thirsty then sweat, then you get cold and you sweat, you get the shivers and you puke. Then you get hot again. That's about it."

"Sounds like menopause," Brennan said, and Deagle laughed.

The lead guitar player stepped forward and hit the first notes of "Satisfaction"—"dot daaa... der der derrr... der derer dererrr," and every GI in the joint jumped to his feet, beer cans hoisted. They stayed on their feet, singing, dancing, and with each chorus they reveled in deafening unison..."I CAN'T GET NOOOO... I CAN'T GET NOOOO... NO NO NO!" Vinny watched Sergeant Bill Deagle singing, dark eyes studying the corrugated ceiling instead of the band, as if he was listening for in-coming rockets.

In the calm following the ovation, Brennan tapped the side of his head to unclog his right ear. "Shit, buddy, we still got 'Proud Mary' yet! Not to mention 'THE Green, Grass of Home'. I, for one, will probably cry when that girl-san does Tom Jones."

Jim leaned over and hollered at Deagle. "These guys kept me out of that sweep! It was cool, hiding from those NCO's. You gotta see their hooch. Psychedelic, man."

Brennan leaned closer with one eyebrow cocked. "So, Deagle William, serious question. Ah, do you smoke canabis?"

"Affirmative."

"Very cool. After the show, we'll adjourn to the commune and share one of Vinny's cigars with some S&G. That's Simon and Garfunkel to you groundpounders."

Taking advantage of the situation, two admin branch troopies at his table, Deagle pulled a copy of his orders and passed it to Brennan. "Translation, please?"

"Certainly... whatta we got here... Comma, comma, down, doobie doo, down, dowwwnnnn... comma, comma, down... Deagle, William... in-transit hospital... blah blah... morning report status is... casual hospital... 1st Cav hospital detachment... yeah, yeah... medical release needed... no shit, Sherlock... return to duty... ah, to be avoided... by the 30th they have to cut new hospital orders or cut you loose. Stay right here and fuck off with us. We'll teach you how to steal grunt care packages from their moms."

Deagle laughed. Like Grossnickel, he liked Brennan right away. "I got my release this morning, but no orders."

Pomeroy leaned closer. "You thinking of going back to Penny?"

Deagle nodded. "Might as well." He looked around the table, everybody watching him but Jim, who was playing air guitar with his eyes closed. He looked at Pomeroy. "You tell these guys anything?"

Pomeroy shook his head. "Negative."

"Tell us what," Vinny asked, leaning in and looking from one to the other. "C'mon guys, what's the skinny."

Brennan joined in. "Yeah, tell Vinny the skinny."

"You guys got room on your floor tonight for three more?"

Vinny nodded. "You three? Yeah, and the reason is..."

Pomeroy shook his head. "No need to bother these guys. By now there's a platoon of troops pulling night ambush details. Nothing to worry about, over."

"Ambush?" Brennan said. "Jeezus, for a second I thought you said ambush!"

"He did, asshole. And he's serious, so would you listen up for once in your life? Go ahead, Deagle. What's up?"

Vinny watched Deagle and saw something remarkable, a kid transform into a commander. All eyes on him, he squared his shoulders and looked at the four faces around the table. In Deagle's deep-set eyes Vinny found casual but irresistible self-assurance.

Deagle studied the admin clerks, measuring them.

"Okay. But it stays right here."

"We're cool."

"You got sappers on the hill you call Cav Mountain. If I was a sapper I'd hit the barracks closest to hill, R&R or DEROS, maybe hospital. So I don't want these two guys anywhere near R&R."

"Sappers," Vinny whispered. "Brennan, you remember the MR reports a couple years back? Sappers did hit R&R!"

Brennan's blue eyes were focused on the buck sergeant. "The, ah, village idiot, Major Warren Andrews, a.k.a., 'THE Scarlet Pimpernel', thinks there are gooks up on the hill. You think so, too?"

"That's Hooper's CO with the skin-graft, right?" Pomeroy asked.

"Andrews is goofy about that hill," Vinny told Deagle. "You think there's VC up there right now. Right this minute?"

Deagle nodded. "I don't think so, troop. I know so. I took a shot at one this afternoon."

Vinny sat up straight and gaped. "You saw him and he saw you?"

"Close as from me to the bar. He didn't have a weapon so he used the back door, all asshole and elbows."

"Holy shit. Holeeeeey Shit! So what are doing about this..."

"Cleve told you. I'm sure the colonel with the big ears has Hooper's debriefing and one-each Chinese-made detonator found during the sweep. So he's got troops either humping up right now or saddling up for night ambushes." He glanced around the crowded NCO club. "If too many troops find out, maybe it'll get fucked up. But you guys'll hear if one blows, close as that hill is. Anyway, Pomeroy and Grossnickel stay in your hooch until their R&R flight."

"What about you?"

"Just tonight. Tomorrow I'm gonna catch a chopper going to Catapult, from there back to Penny."

Brennan looked across at Pomeroy, grinning. "Cleve? That's your first name. Like Clever? Anybody call you Clever the Beaver..."

Embarrassed, Pomeroy shook his head. "Not and live to do it twice."

Vinny was still trying to control his breathing. "Brennan for God's sake! Would you get serious one time?" He glanced at Grossnickel, who was back to playing a wailing air-guitar. "Didn't you hear what he said? We're talking about satchel charges, here. Bags of explosive the gooks like to throw into buildings. Right here, right now."

"I heard the man, I heard him. So, Deagle buddy, what do we do? Get forged passes and ride the cease-fire out in Saigon?"

Pomeroy grabbed his beer, and Deagle lit a Marlboro.

"Ignore him, he's fuckin' hopeless," Vinny told them. "You think it's being handled? 'Night ambush.' I'd love to go on just one night ambush with you guys, but I'm short. I'm so short I got to stand on my helmet to piss on Brennan's boots."

"Nobody's going on any ambush," Brennan said. "That job is for... you'll excuse my French... the fucking grunts."

"No, I'm serious," Vinny insisted. "If I could go with these guys, I'd go. Why don't we all volunteer? What a trip, got your M-16, sitting there in the dark..."

"Choking your chicken...", Brennan finished for him.

"...you can't see shit... don't know if Charles is out there... if he can see you... Pomeroy, c'mon, what its like on night ambush?"

"Mostly sitting around until you fall asleep."

"No bullshit?"

"Been my experience. I've only blown two ambushes in ten months. Deagle was with us the 2nd time. Remember, Bill?"

Deagle nodded.

Up on stage the song ended with a drumroll and smothered cymbals and the cheering erupted again. Jim Grossnickel popped out of his trance and sucked down a half a beer. "Hey, we're going to Sydney, Australia! Not any

182

fucking night ambush. That's bo-shit, GI. Ain't that right, Pomeroy."

When big Cleve just stared down at his beer Deagle knew he was thinking about Thomasville, Iowa. Pomeroy was a farm-boy, uncomplicated, hardworking, ferociously proud, unafraid of anything that walked or crawled not wearing a uniform. But it had taken getting drafted and ten months of Vietnam for him to find out he was still a hayseed ploughboy. Trouble was, now he knew and he couldn't go back. Pomeroy's character showed in the fact that he had never touched a Vietnamese girl, but, unlike guys who railed loudly that Vietnamese women were diseased and dirty, his abstinence was moral and no big deal. His reason was a girl back home named Fran. With orders for Vietnam in hand, Cleve said goodbye to his girl by taking back his engagement ring, telling her she shouldn't wait for a dead man. Cleve just figured he was still engaged, because he wanted to be.

Pomeroy looked up and caught Deagle watching him. "I'm not fired up about R&R yet. Shit, I just left LZ Penny this morning. I'm thinking... a couple hours after me and Fuck-knuckle catch a chopper to Bien Hoa what happens: my replacement gets hit. Another life used up. I don't know how many more I got left, you bic?"

Deagle nodded. "Think about this: if you talk to that girl of yours, she could meet you in Hawaii. The Honolulu Hilton isn't just for military wives."

Pomeroy sadly agreed, eyes down on the table. "The only girlfriend I ever had. I was really a dope when I was a kid. Well, I did have this one other girlfriend, but so did some others guys. She was sort of the 'widest cut in the valley', if you know what I mean."

Vinny aimed a finger at his roommate. "Another life used up. Brennan you hear that? See how close Pomeroy came today... to being one of your graves registration entries? Getting short is so fuckin' dangerous, man. He's got what, sixty days left? Hey Pomeroy, you can sleep on my floor until hell freezes!"

Pomeroy laughed half-heartedly.

"How many lives did you start with?" Brennan asked him.

"A feline gets nine, you get seven in the 7th." Pomeroy recited.

"That stuff is bullshit!" Grossnickel informed the table.

While Deagle laughed, Pomeroy counted on his fingers. "I think that was it. *Sin loi*, GI."

"The trick," Deagle told him, leaning over the table, "is not getting the army involved. Pay for her ticket to Hawaii yourself? I told you, I got money in accrual."

Pomeroy nodded. "When I was in high school a buddy of my older brother was in 'Nam. He wanted to meet his girlfriend in Hawaii for R&R. He applied for an army flight for her out of Oakland, California. They both lived in Thomasville and everybody knew she was waiting for him to DEROS. Listen up: the army took his request and informed both parents they'd be staying together at the King Kamaymaya Hotel. Not married. So what happened; the

183

whole town found out. They held a town meeting, for Christ sake! Should they or shouldn't they? Her parents wouldn't let her go. And she didn't."

"That's bullshit!" Jim cried.

"Ancient history, buddy," Brennan told him. "This is 1971 and unofficial shacking up happens all the time. Hey Deagle, how much time you got?"

"One hundred and seventy nine days."

Brennan's blue eyes went wide. He made a gagging noise and grabbed his throat. As the whole table laughed, Brennan shook and shivered and let his head fall on the table, dead. Then he snapped his head up. "If I ever ask that question again buddy, please don't answer me. However, there is one ray of hope. My girlfriend works in Washington DC. She says the Paris peace talks started again because Nixon is clearing the mines out of Haiphong Harbor. You could be back in the world in sixty days."

"I keep hearing the war's over," Deagle said. "But today I shot at a VC sapper."

Pomeroy nodded. "Tet is February 17th. Me and Jim just have to make it through Tet, then we're home free."

"Night ambush," Vinny said, eyes wide. "I love the sound of it. Night... ambush... sappers..."

Brennan looked at his roommate and rolled his eyes. "There's the proof. We can now conclude smoking Cambodia red does permanent damage to brain cells. Vinny, you better drop and give me twenty, and pull your head out."

Vinny waved him off. "I know an E7 who's a drinking buddy of the Sergeant Major Bierra. Bierra runs the CG's personal staff. He says this morning Bierra overheard Webb say it was over in Vietnam. We're down to 140,000 guys in Vietnam."

Deagle stared at him. "You mean in III-Corps."

"In-theatre. In all of Vietnam. You guys are out there practically alone."

Deagle' chewed on the inside of his cheek. "Roger that."

"There's no cherries in repo-depo. The well's dry. They're sending 10,000 guys home a month, replacing a third."

"Better enjoy R&R now," Deagle told Pomeroy. "By the time mine rolls around my choices will a three-day weekend in-country at Vung Tau Beach, take it or leave it."

The band was into a foot-stomping, heavy-drum Dave Clark Five oldie, with the girl singer wailing out "...crine' all ovah... yes I'm ah... crine all ovah... so glad you're my...yi...eye...yi...eye...yine..." Deagle sipped his beer and tried to catch up with the tempo. It was Pomeroy's turn to buy beer and the temperature in the NCO club climbed to the boiling point. The faster Deagle drank the faster it leaked right back out through his skin.

He turned in his chair and watched the guys scatter as big Cleve made his way to the bar, and in his wake they all stared after him in disbelief. Nobody in a uniform could be that big. Deagle knew it had to be hard for him sometimes, being gawked at like a freak because he was physically twice the size of anybody else, and none of it fat. Another statement of character, Deagle reflected, Pomeroy had never used his size to intimidate or bully, and he had to be pushed pretty hard before using all that power to retaliate. Deagle remembered a lazy afternoon at the newly created LZ Penny. Captain Rule had found some old boxing gloves and the men took turns sparing in an improvised ring. One soldier, PFC Whitehead, had been a golden gloves boxer in Chicago.

Whitehead was built like Deagle, tall and long-armed, and he had a taunting fighting style like Cassius Clay. After Whitehead whipped four or five less experienced troopies, Captain Rule ran out of volunteers, and PFC Whitehead asked for a piece of Cleve Pomeroy. At first, Pomeroy smiled and said no thanks, but the whole company saw the possibility of a great battle and started taunting. Long-armed, lightning-quick, stylish-boxing Whitehead against plodding, powerful Pomeroy. Deagle wasn't surprised by the outcome, he'd seen Pomeroy almost casually throw a hand grenade half a football field. But boy, did the rest of those guys get an eyeful.

Pomeroy stripped off his shirt, laced on the gloves and banged them together. He stretched his massive arms above his head a few times to loosen up and bounced on his toes. Then he lowered his chin, brought the gloves up and focused on PFC Whitehead, pewter eyes under a massive shelf of forehead bone. "Let's go," he said, and moved in. Whitehead saw Pomeroy coming at him and started backing, confident and loose. And backing. And circling. He threw one of his long-range deadly left hooks at Pomeroy's head. On his toes, and moving forward in his Marciano crouch, Pomeroy merely flicked his right glove to divert the punch wide. He saw the opening to the right side of his opponent's face and threw a straight left jab that landed with a stinging solid "pok", the only punch landed on Whitehead all afternoon. All three platoons heard it, saw it. Stunned, Whitehead tried to stand his ground and throw flurries of quick combinations at Cleve's massive head. Every punch glanced off Cleve's forearms, parried. Whitehead threw a round-house right at Cleve's belly that grazed his elbow; Cleve threw only his second punch of the fight, another straight left that landed with another solid "whopp" on Whitehead's right cheekbone. For about ten more seconds Whitehead danced around, backing and circling and trying to figure a way to sneak a punch in between Pomeroy's gloves and steely eyes, and then he just stopped, quit. He dropped both arms and walked out of the ring. "No man," he said, "I ain't fighting him." And neither did anybody else.

"Where the heck is Bob Hope when you need him!" Pomeroy yelled, returning with the beer.

"Bob Hope's in Saigon!" Grossnickel shouted back, snatching a full one.

Vinny shook his head. "He's in Vientienne. I just read it."

Grossnickel shook his head. "Nope, Saigon."

"Same same," Brennan offered. "He's not here. You ready to blow this joint. How's that for double entendre, eh, guys"

"Double what?"

"Finish these and let's go," Deagle said.

The live show took its final dramatic turn, the predictable, emotional, drunken and drawn-out grand finale triple-killer, consisting of "Yesterday", "The Green, Green Grass of Home," and a rousing "Dixie/Glory Hallelujah." This package always brought down the house, always left the troops feeling drained. With just the McCartney guitar and solo coming through the speakers, the soldiers who didn't sing along sat quietly, some maudlin staring into their beer, others gazing lustfully at the now-irresistible girl singer as she lightly shook her gourds. "The Green Green Grass of Home" began before the audience could cheer its approval, and it was impossible for anyone to leave the NCO Club. Poor Tom Jones. Instead of "…four gray walls…"—the girl singer clearly sang "…fa gay wah…" making ol' Tom's green, green grass, growing six feet above his coffin, that much more ironic. Then the beat changed, and all the southern boys leaped to their feet and waved paper napkins like confederate flags, for "Dixie." Deagle stood up and drained the dregs of his beer and headed for the exit.

Vinny poked full beer cans carefully into each of his four pants pockets, hidden under the tail of his fatigue shirt, and Brennan and Pomeroy cleaned up the rest. Two streets away, enlisted records branch barracks was lit up and rowdy. It was the night before Christmas Eve and the cease-fire was officially on. Half an hour to lights-out, the clerk-typists sat outside in the warm night wearing GI shorts and shower thongs, sipping beer and talking about the world. As Vinny approached, leading a pack of five that included three grunts, somebody hollered "twenty Daaaaays" over a chorus of boos and catcalls.

"At ease, at ease, or Pomeroy will have you clowns for breakfast…"

Inside the barracks, beer-drinking rooms were those with open doors, anybody welcome, smoking rooms were those with doors closed and locked from the inside. Brennan unlocked his door and they all filed in except Deagle and Pomeroy. Deagle lit a smoke.

"What time does that AT&T shack open in the morning," he asked.

"0600," Pomeroy answered too quickly. "What time is that in the world?"

"I don't know. What are we, fourteen hours ahead? Who gives a shit. You think they won't take your call no matter what time of day. Our idiot company clerk mailed them a heads-up a month ago. They're waiting for the call."

"That's what I'm afraid of."

"0600. You get it done."

"I know dad's still sore. He probably won't even talk to me. He had four sons; the first three bailed out on the farm and then it was just me and him. Then I left, fucked up, and got drafted."

Deagle blew a smoke ring. "You think you know your dad? You don't. I told you my old man was a marine corps colonel? On one of his reserve weekends he came to visit me in basic, at Benning. Here I am, a private E1, lower than whaleshit, the lowest form of life on earth who thinks a sergeant is a king and a looie is God. And here's my old man, a bird colonel. The base commander at Benning was also bird colonel, but my old man had time-in-grade on him. If the two colonels met on the sidewalk the BC would have had to salute my old man. Can you believe that shit? So give your old man a chance."

"Dad's gone through four hired guys this year. It's a tie down, milking sixty cows twice a day, every day of your life. Nobody wants to be tied down like that anymore. But here's dad, still trying to run a class-A milk operation..."

"Class A milk and class-B cheese... you told me a thousand times. Who gives a shit as long as you're on that farm?"

Pomeroy nodded, gazing off down the hall. "Couple years ago... the thought of pulling tits the rest of my life... my worst nightmare. But now, I'd run that farm for him and it'd be the cleanest class-A operation in Iowa. And if Fran would take me back I'd have a perfect life."

Deagle whacked his broad back soundly. "Find out tomorrow. Call your old man: ask your girl to meet you in Hawaii, that's an order."

"If Fran... if she isn't married... if I have the guts... I'll ask her to meet me in Hawaii. But don't tell Fuck-knuckle, over."

2255Hours 23Dec71
1st Cav Div HQ
Quarters, Brig. Gen. Jeffrey Webb

She closed the bathroom door and walked back to the bed wearing one of his fatigue shirts, unbuttoned. She saw his long body stretched out under the sheet, hands folded behind his head and feet hanging over. She curled up close beside him, left knee on his hard stomach.

"Just when I think you're falling asleep," she whispered, "you come to attention."

They shared another beer and he let her beat him again about the 'Bail Out' letter before talking about herself. She was married but separated almost a year, using her maiden name again. She had no children and wasn't sure if she'd ever wanted them, a factor in her dissolved marriage. She was schooled at conservative Martha Weil University in Redlands, California but became a McGovern democrat. When she closed her eyes and drifted off, he slipped out of the bed and padded barefoot to the phone in the kitchenette. He dialed the headquarters number and the officer of the day got it on the second ring.

"1st Cavalry Division Air-Mobile, Lieutenant Ross speaking."

"Lieutenant, this is General Webb. I'm expecting a call on the crypto line and I'm in my quarters."

"Yes, sir! I have that information."

"Good." He started to hang up but had another thought. "Lieutenant, does the sergeant of the guard responsible for Hill 229-er report to you?"

"Sir, that is affirmative."

"Check on him every hour. Make sure he has two men in those bunkers and that they're wide awake. If there's contact tonight I'll probably hear it, but call me in my quarters anyway. You read, lieutenant?"

"Yes, sir!"

He hung up and glanced back at the bedroom. Through the open doorway he saw the sleeping figure in his bed had not moved. Ms. Darcy Devlin enjoyed lovemaking with the light on, as did he. He dialed Colonel Geary's quarters and asked his S-4 about the guard situation at air force runways 3 and 7-Bravo-right where 1st Cav supplies and munitions were stacked behind concertina wire.

"Sir, with the moon it's like daylight out there. You can see five hundred meters in every direction."

"Walking posts and a CQ assigned?"

"Yes, sir. Per your request, doubled through the cease-fire."

"If there is in-coming tonight, your people are exempt from perimeter duty. You stand your ground around those air-strips."

"Yes, sir. But I'm sure it will be quiet."

Webb glanced behind him again at the bedroom and lowered his voice. "Colonel, I need Major Andrews' debriefings from the sweep, but I can't find Andrews. He's been confined to quarters, but he's gone. He's not at the officers club and nobody has seen him since about 1900. Sergeant Hooper seems to be AWOL, too. I know it's late but could you make a few discreet phone calls?"

"Can do. They both have buddies on the air force side. I'll check around and call you right back."

He hung up and called Borg, just climbing into his rack, and told him about Andrews.

"That nutcase will get what he deserves. In the morning I'll check his BOQ and the admin CP for his debriefing, whatever it's worth."

"Is Lieutenant St. John secure in his quarters?"

"He was an hour ago. He gave us everything we need for a court-martial." He paused to yawn. "St. John would rat his mother to stay out of Long Binh Jail, where he's sent his share of AWOLs. General, you're not still worried about Hill 229-er are you?"

"Habit. I don't like my troops sleeping under hills designated Victor Charlie."

Borg chuckled. "Don't worry, this one's Uniform Sierra. I remind the general, despite a dubious premise and a mentally unstable commander, we did put a thousand men on that hill and turned up nothing. Get some sleep, sir."

Webb hung up and walked back to the bedroom, dropping his robe on the chair. Naked, he slipped in beside Darcy and lay on his back, staring at the ceiling and listening to her even breathing. Thinking about Hill 229, he suddenly remembered how hungry Ms. Devlin had been. She wiped out everything on her plates, salad, roast beef, potatoes, the whole nine yards. Then, dabbing her lips delicately with her napkin she had said, "I'll just eat the tablecloth while we wait for desert." He turned his head and looked at her.

She slept on her back, tousled red-haired head toward him. He reached down under the sheet, parted the two halves of the fatigue shirt, and ran his palm across the smoothness of her belly above her silky, red-haired little mound. He remembered where her delicate folds came together her hair looked like a vertical curly capitol I.

"Animal," she whispered.

He looked down at her. "Want the fan?"

She opened her eyes and shook her head, enjoying what he was doing. She reached up and put a hand behind his neck. "Negative."

As he kissed her yielding mouth the phone rang and he walked naked into the other room. It was Geary.

"Regarding Major Andrews, nothing yet on the air force side. But I've had a few beers with him now and again, sir. I know he's got a full-time girl in Saigon."

"If he's in Saigon his career is over, no question. Advise me of any contact on those runways."

"Will do, sir. It was a strange day. See you in the briefing room at oh-five-thirty."

"Good night, colonel."

Back in bed he stared at the ceiling. "Who was that?" Darcy asked.

"The officer in charge of 1st Cav hardware."

"Are you still worried about that hill?"

"It's in the middle of my AO, and I think it's Victor Charlie."

"Why do think it's Victor Charlie?"

He turned his head and looked into green eyes. "It's perfect for him. It's steep and thick and as the hair on your... head, and it's close to my in-transit barracks. We know it has tunnels and a combat history. There's red blood under all that green, Darcy."

She put her hand on his chest, fingers spread wide.

"Hill 229-er reminds me of some others my troops have fought for. I know this: you can fight for and win a hill like 229-er, but you won't own it for long. The minute you turn your back... The hell of it is, if I'm right, I don't know what to do about it."

"What are your options. You can't move the base."

"What I'd like to do is knock it flat."

She shook her head, smiling. "Little boy with his pick and shovel."

"Yeah."

"I know. Call the Arvins. Tell them to bring picks and shovels."

"What do you know about the Arvins?"

"Miniature American soldiers with oriental faces, in miniature American uniforms and helmets carrying American rifles. The Arvin soldiers I've seen all looked sort of confused and polite."

"Did you know there are no red-haired Vietnamese?"

"Blarney."

"There are no Vietnamese with red-hair. Or green eyes. Not if both parents are Vietnamese."

She looked in his eyes, unable to tell if he was sincere or silly. "No sale. I'm the journalist, I'll find out for myself if there are red-haired Vietnamese."

"You do that."

"Tell me, off the record, can the Arvins win?"

"Of course not."

"Off the record, tell me about Laos, the Pentagon, and Jeff Webb."

"Off the record, not much to tell. Laird specified an air campaign, I'm an air-mobile commander. He asked me to draw it up for him; maximum destruction, minimum time, zero casualties. They came pretty close. I convinced Laird to let me hang around for the finish, which is what kept me out of Bien Hoa until last week."

She rolled on her back. "Wow. Not much to tell? I need my legal pad. One, they came pretty close means you weren't inside Laos. Two, your transfer to Bien Hoa isn't Nixon pay-back. Three, you're not a Pentagon spy... four, maybe you didn't sign the 'Bail Out' letter... Have I got all that right?"

"No comment, Ms. Devlin."

"Tell me about your wife."

"What about her."

"Peter says she split. Personal, politics...?"

"My wife is in Washington DC, living in an apartment on 14th Street. She makes her living writing leaflets for the People's Mobilization Movement, whatever that is."

"The Mobe. Anti-war heavy-hitters. But three years is a long time to be away from home. People change."

"So I'm told. In forty-two months in Vietnam I've had three R&R's and two out-of-country leaves. I spent them all with my wife and boys."

"You can bet your bippy she didn't just wake up one morning and decided her husband was a war criminal and she was actually a democrat..."

"No. But she did fall for the women's lib thing. After two children and never working a day in her life... she decided to start making fifty percent of a bed, cooking twenty-five percent of a dinner... paying herself a monthly salary from my check... that was the beginning of the end. The end came when I wouldn't quit the army to become... a college teacher."

"What do you mean 'that women's lib thing?' It's not a trend you know.

190

It's women seeking equal treatment under the law, equal job opportunity, equal recognition..."

"Are you one of them?"

"Damn right I am. Maybe not to the point of making half a bed..." Looking at his expression she laughed.

"What."

"College teachers are called professors. And there's graffiti on the back of your little bathroom door. Can you imagine a major general, like some poor lonesome PFC, sitting on the can scratching his initials and DEROS date? I added one little peace sign."

"The hell you say."

"Go look. There's a peace sign on your bathroom door, General Webb. How will you explain that to the III-Corp commander."

He thought about it. "You ask too damn many questions."

She laughed until he rolled her toward him and kissed her. His hand found her left breast.

She propped her head under her elbow and studied his tanned face. "Sometimes you smile with your eyes."

"You smile with your whole face."

"I'm not holding back."

He thought about it. "I had a sense of humor before Vietnam. Right now my job satisfaction is equivocal; this war is never clear victory or clear defeat, it's always both. Hopefully for only six more months."

"Then back to the world or off to some other jungle?"

"Definitely the world." He watched her eyelids flutter and the slight flare of her nostrils as she breathed out. In the amber light of the lampshade her green eyes turned indigo. "Would it be an affront to ask if I could see you, back in the world?"

She smiled at the thought of it and then buried her face in his shoulder, laughing soundlessly. He ran his hand through her tangled hair and waited, and finally she looked at him.

"In San Francisco, sir, I couldn't be seen dead with a man in uniform! Let alone an infantry general."

"You don't agree opposites attract?"

"As you said, this is 'Nam not the world." She looked into his steady eyes. "Okay, name three things you like about me."

His fingertip made a slow circle on her rubbery nipple.

"I'm serious," she smiled.

"Help me get back my sense of humor..."

She closed her eyes, feeling the blunt prodding between her thighs. Her nostrils flared and her sudden deep breath had a catch in it. When he moved above her she opened her mouth wide to accept his.

Just before 0100 hours Christmas Eve morning Webb was awakened, but not by gunfire. It took him a moment to realize where he was and what the jangling noise was, the telephone in the living room. He rolled out of bed without waking Darcy and answered it. The officer of the day told him there was a call from Firebase Catapult on the crypto line but the caller, a Colonel Malloy, asked that Webb return his call because the entire AO was on red-alert. Webb hung up and padded quietly to his kitchenette. He placed the call and waited several minutes before hearing Malloy's distant and distressed voice.

"Sir, we found them. They're all dead."

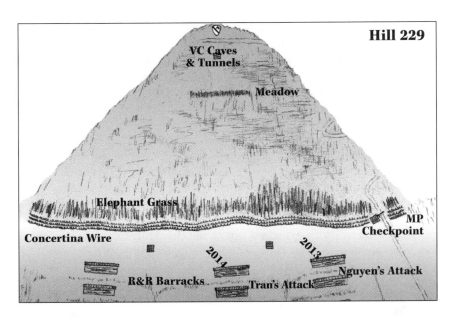

CHAPTER NINE

0550Hours 24Dec71
1st Cav Div HQ
Hill 229

Tran heard a distant shout and opened his eyes, as he had a hundred times during the night. One soldier calling to another, far below. He waited to hear an answer but it never came. A truck engine coughed and fired, idling at a high pitch. Breaking up the sound of the engine was the slapping noise of a helicopter going in the direction of Cambodia. At the bottom of the hill it was light enough to see and soon there would be a swarm of sounds. A deep breath eased his tension but his eyes refused to close.

He thought of the boys again, Nguyen and Loc. They would soon be here if they were alive. He had heard the shooting as they left the cave the night before. With children, things could go wrong. With children, one must always have alternative ways to bring an attack, such as carrying two satchels instead of one. He turned his head and felt a stab of pain on the left side of his face. He tried concentrating on the day ahead, not allowing himself to think the reason for sleeplessness was the throbbing where the soldier's bullet had taken off the a lower half of his ear and cut his cheek to the bone.

He sat up, fighting the pain in his head and stiffness in his back from sleeping on the rock floor. He touched his cheek and found it bleeding again. That must be stopped. He struck a match on the rock and lit his kerosene lamp, watched ripples of dark smoke climb to the cave ceiling. There was a small danger of smoke leaving the cave so today he would take no chances. He used the lamp only to start a pot of tea over a sterno can and to locate all his flashlights and arrange them to throw light on the cave walls. After the second attack, the 25th, he would abandon the hill for a time, so if he used all his flashlight batteries and all his cans of sterno in the next two days, just as well, there would be less to carry.

He examined every stitch of his two satchel bombs. He pulled the straps, shook the pockets, held the satchels upside down. The white blocks of C4 explosive remained tight in their pockets. He set the satchels by the cave entrance and unpiled the old rags that covered the rifles. He selected one rifle and held it up to the light.

The American battle rifle was not his first choice. He held the Russian made AK-47 assault rifle in highest regard. But this American M-16 was very fast when pointed and fired like a shotgun, and it could empty its twenty-round magazine in less than two seconds. This rifle, like the others he had stolen, was brand new and still had grease in the barrel. It had been stolen from an unguarded depot at Cam Ranh Bay. Using strips of cotton t-shirt, he wiped the oil from the barrel and receiver. He fashioned a cleaning rod from a piece of string tied to a cotton patch and pulled the patch through the barrel until the grease was gone and the rifling gleamed when held to the flashlight. He ran the bolt back and forth, testing the strong spring that helped it cycle so fast. He pushed a loaded magazine into the port and felt how it changed the balance of the weapon in his hands. When the boys arrived they would be given the task of cleaning all the rifles and that would keep them occupied until it was time to leave the cave.

He took the rifle and his steaming tea and made a comfortable place to sit watching the cave entrance. If the boys did not come, he decided, he would destroy one barracks, the one closest to the guard shack, but with two bombs. He opened a metal ammo can and brought out two rice balls mixed with smoked fish, but each time he bit down he felt a jolt of pain under his left eye. Waiting for Nguyen and Loc, he visualized the day ahead of them, the timing of the attack, the targets, the retreat, and possible consequences. Voices overhead brought him out of his deep thought and he glanced at his watch. The boys were late by ten minutes. He heard them whispering, but if they thought they were being clever or playing a game with him he was in no mood and he'd make them clean all the rifles twice. Another ten minutes passed before Nguyen's skinny legs inched through the crevice, hung in mid-air, and he dropped to a good landing.

"We are here," Nguyen announced, seeing the rifle pointed at his head.

"What were you doing?" Tran demanded.

The boys looked at each other.

"I heard the shooting. I thought the soldiers had killed my foolish children."

Nguyen stuck out his chin. "Nevah happen, GI." He and Loc sat down on the rock, and Tran poured them hot tea while Nguyen told the story of how Loc had fallen in the elephant grass and the soldier shot him in the shoe. When Tran turned his head Nguyen saw the crusted blood on his ear and the oozing cut across his cheek, but the old fighter just smiled.

"It is a sign of changing luck."

"A sign?"

Tran nodded. "What seemed like bad luck becomes good luck. One soldier's bullet hit a shoe. Another soldier's bullet hits an ear. They had their chances."

"I lost the detonator," Loc told him. "It was my fault."

Tran put down his rice ball and sipped tea, thinking. So that was why they were late. "You will learn to be more careful. What is being said in the city," he asked Nguyen.

"That others are coming. It is said, one of them is my mother's brother."

"Did you sleep?"

"I could not close my eyes. All night I saw the soldiers' faces who will die from my bomb."

"I have seen the buildings, now show me the map where all the soldiers sleep."

Nguyen brought the folded drawing from his pocket and held it to the light. The hill was not shown, only the rows of concertina wire, squares for barracks 2013 and 2014, dots for the bunkers, and a small 'x' for MP checkpoint.

"The soldiers going home sleep here," Nguyen told him. "None can leave for two more days. They eat first, before seven o'clock. Then they walk around and meet with the soldiers who work here, until the next meal. Then they have nothing to do and sleep with their bellies full until late in the afternoon."

Tran pointed at the MP shack. "Will there be a guard here?"

"Yes. Ever since the new American general arrived, there is always a guard."

Tran nodded, satisfied. "He will die quietly. For now, you can satisfy your curiosity as to the number of rifles while you clean them. Then in seven hours we will walk down. Today we will place our bombs during the rain, and tomorrow before the sun rises."

0530Hours 24Dec71
1st Cav Div HQ
East Briefing Room, Offices Brig. Gen. Webb

Wandering, Colonel Shipp idly snapped on the Prick-25 and ran the volume up until it squawked at him, then shut it down. "Anybody remember what's the range on this baby?" he asked.

Nobody answered.

Shipp looked around his bunker briefing room. Without the comfortable chairs and conference table, the support staff sat in metal folding chairs at map tables that divided the room in half, facing Webb's desk. Shipp saw Lyndon Johnson's smiling face and read the inscription to Webb again. Lately, Webb hadn't had much good luck or hunting. Restless, he carried a full pot of coffee to the table and poured for the group.

"Well," he drawled, "can't blame the old man if he's got a serious case of the ass this morning. Yesterday was an all-time worst."

"We should not have put troops on that Hill," Wilcox insisted. "Let alone R&R troops where we invite a uniform code issue."

Shipp scoffed. "Been thinkin' about that. We borrow R&R troops for guard duty all the time, Ray. What the heck's the difference?"

Colonel Geary grinned. "Maybe yesterday was bad, but not last night. Specialist Meredith tells me the red-headed news lady spent the night in his quarters."

"The old man at III-Corps will be the one with the ass," Wilcox replied, deep in thought. "We probably wrecked Garlett's chances for Joint Chiefs Chairman."

"I wouldn't be too sure," Geary answered. "It was 0645 yesterday when I asked our new BC for some help getting rid of my over-supply. Before 0900, Garlett's S-4 calls me, says he's looking into it. And in the MAC-V package this morning here's a note from "Bill" saying on the 28th a whole goddamn flock of C-130's will fly in and haul it all away. I think I'm going to like working for Webb."

Colonel Shipp fixed him with one of his hang-dog looks. "You're shittin'. You know how times Fish called about that stuff?"

Geary laughed. "No, I'm not, Chuck. Poof, it's gone. Magic!"

"Wasn't Webb one of Garlett's brigade commanders up in I-Corps?"

Finally Borg shook his head and joined the conversation. "Negative. He was 3rd Army XO."

Shipp grinned. "I wonder if Ms. Devlin whispered in his ear about the 'Bail Out' letter Bet she damn sure found out Webb was hardcore! 'Bail Out' letter, my ass."

Wilcox leaned closer. "All infantry generals are hardcore, Chuck. That's what makes the 'Bail Out' letter significant."

"God, I wonder what he's going to do about Andrews. When was the last time anybody had an AWOL major 04. We get that TWIX back from Walter Reed?"

"Negative."

After sixty seconds of thoughtful silence Wilcox whispered. "At the press briefing he said 'personnel changes' are coming to Bien Hoa. Speaking for myself, I am too old to get shot at. If Webb reassigns me to a forward area I'll write to Senator Symington."

The door from Webb's private offices opened but it was Sp6 Brian Meredith carrying more paperwork for General Webb.

Shipp pointed at the window. "On the window sill Brian, that's where he'll go first."

Meredith glanced around the "command bunker" and smiled at Shipp. "Room looks pretty strack, sir", he said. "Maybe we should leave it this way."

Shipp's smile was sardonic. "It ain't done yet. I still have to find window turrets for the .50 Cal machine guns..."

As Meredith was leaving Webb carried his coffee mug into the briefing room. "Ten Hut!"

"As you were."

"OD Report on the window sill, sir," Meredith said.

"Thank you, Brian."

Colonel Borg studied Webb's chiseled jaw and intense eyes. If Geary's information was correct, that he had spent the night with the red-headed reporter, then Webb should be at least somewhat relaxed. But the tall brigadier looked tight as coiled steel, ready to spring.

Sipping from his mug, Webb looked out the window at the morning profile of Hill 229. Beneath the hill, in the ditches and on the trails between barracks, there were no mama-sans filling sandbags. There were no Vietnamese nationals on base, anywhere. The morning was quiet without all their chatter. He turned from the window, reading cursorily through the enemy activity summary from the officer of the day. No ground contact or in-coming for 1st Cav Division HQ, and only one potential cease-fire violation. 23Dec71 had passed into morning report history without casualties. He scanned the III-Corps summaries from MAC-V, and the story was the same at Long Binh and Saigon. With a final hard look at Hill 229 he joined his staff and sat down.

"Everybody get a little sleep?" he asked curtly. "Is it reassuring or foreboding that there was no Victor Charlie activity last night?"

"Reassuring, sir," Borg said without hesitation. "Everybody's S-2 is negative."

Webb read aloud from the OD report. The only potential Viet Cong cease-fire violation within the entire area III-Corps area, twenty-five percent of Vietnam, was thirty miles east of Tay Ninh City. Before 2000 hours, a returning patrol from the 1st of the 9th bumped into what was reported as a fair-sized unit of VC, judging from the semi-automatic rifle fire that covered their retreat. Technically, the firefight wasn't a violation by either side, merely a "troop movement". The 9th Brigade platoon commander was sure his "fair-sized unit" was not NVA.

"A long way from here, sir," Borg pointed out.

"Half a day's walk," he answered. He glanced down at his wristwatch and appeared to lose his train of thought. "Colonel Shipp, I am not up to speed on the early warning system on this base. If we take in-coming, the siren goes and we hit the perimeter... take me through the SOP from there to the all-clear."

"Sir, if we take in-coming we sound the siren, which trips all the sirens on base. All branch commanders call in to this HQ. Every unit commander has emergency troops and a full-alert assignment. Non-roster officers and men report to the bunkers and wait for the all-clear. Sir, Sergeant Major Bierra has it down to an art, he and Colonel Borg. The alert teams go to their objectives, such as guarding this building with you in it, and when the all-clear sounds we decide how much longer to maintain alert status."

"We usually suit-up every swingin' dick for at least twenty-four hours," Borg added. "Front and rear barracks guards in every building, quadruple walking posts, and all lights out."

Shipp twirled his mustache and grinned. "That's when the admin boys all remember what C-rations taste like. That is, them that ain't got refrigerators in their rooms."

Webb wasn't amused. He tapped the pile of old 9th Infantry and early 1st Cav S-2 debriefings. "These tell me not once, in eight years of B-40s and 60 mike-mikes launched at this base from the villages around it, did S-2 get a heads-up. We don't have any friendly farmers in those villages?"

Borg blushed. "We've bitched at MAC-V about that for going on two years."

"And when was the last time an infantry brigade cleared the villages around Bien Hoa?"

Borg sought help around the table but all eyes were on Webb.

"I've been at Bien Hoa sixteen months... so at least that long. That's another area where Colonel Fish and I complained to MAC-V..."

"We're through begging from MAC-V, colonel," Webb replied tersely. "We're going to pull Kit Carsons from Catapult for those villages. That's an S-2 job, Colonel Wilcox."

The owl-face registered un-wise. "Beg pardon, sir?"

Webb looked from one officer to the next, as in an inspection. "Events... and individuals... over the last twenty-four hours have reminded me of what I remind others, that the Vietnam war is not over. It's not over until we get our troops home. And, while I objected strongly to my transfer to Bien Hoa, now I must accept it. I have to learn how to command the 1st Cavalry from this building, and I will."

"A fair strategic summary of the situation at Bien Hoa is that we have no S-2 from the villages around us, we have no infantry other than a few R&R and DEROS troops and we rely on a few M-60 machine guns, artillery, and air-strikes to control our perimeter. And, we probably don't control the biggest hill within our own wire. As I said yesterday, that changes now."

"Lieutenant Colonel Wilcox, after the cease-fire you will assume Colonel Borg's S-2 duties and your first job is to pull Kit Carsons from Firebase Catapult and install them in the villages around this base. I want advance in-coming warnings from an intelligence network second to none in this theatre. Do you read?"

"Yes, sir!"

"Colonel Geary, you're doing a fine job as the OIC at S-4 and I need you to remain there. Colonel Shipp, you are 1st Cav Executive Officer, effective now. Your first job is to find an S-1 to replace Colonel Wilcox. After the cease-fire," he continued in a softer tone, "I'm pulling the 8th Brigade back from Firebase Catapult to Bien Hoa, and Colonel Borg will command."

"Yes, sir." Disappointed, Borg lowered his head and wrote in his planner.

"Colonel, you will command your troops from this building, but your brigade will not be billeted in condominiums with refrigerators; they will sleep where they work, in the field. Between now and 1Jan72 you get with division artillery and set up an infantry air-mobile perimeter with offensive capability."

Webb stood and again checked his watch. "I'm overdue on the horn with General Garlett." The stunned support staff scrambled to its feet, eyes front.

"I want to leave you with this thought: today is 24December, day seven for me at Bien Hoa, which I find wide open. But it is understood... I do not hold this staff responsible for security oversights by previous base commanders. That's the past. But from today forward I do hold this staff responsible for security at Bien Hoa. Am I clear?"

"Yes, sir!"

"Argue all you want about Vietnamization, the peace talks, the NVA sitting on its can in Cambodia, troop reductions, ad infinitum. But nobody controls Charles. As you were."

The new support staff sat down and the door closed behind Webb.

"Hardcore," Shipp repeated.

"You were wrong, Ray," Geary said, "yesterday wasn't the worst day ever, but it's coming."

"Want to bet the news from LZ Judith was ugly?" Borg whispered. "Isn't Judith part of the 8th Brigade AO?"

Shipp nodded. "Guess if I'm XO I should call Catapult."

0550Hours 24Dec71
1st Cav Div HQ
Transoceanic Cable Service, Bien Hoa

In the gathering light of Christmas Eve morning, Pomeroy looked up and re-read the sign: "AT&T Transoceanic Cable, Restricted Access." He was fourth in line behind a squad of R&R grunts from 3rd of the 9th.

"What time is it in the world? Shit, what day is it?"

"I think around dinnertime yesterday," the corporal in front of him said.

On a farm, the evening meal was supper and the noon meal was dinner. Pomeroy clutched his orders and ID card tight enough to cut off circulation in his fingers.

"What if they're not home, over?" he asked aloud.

"Then the goddamn phone rings and nobody answers! Call somebody else, I don't know."

For five piasters or next to nothing, he thought, he'd turn and walk away. Big, fearless, indestructible Cleve Pomeroy, who could carry a Prick-25 or an M-60 machine gun on his shoulder all day long but needed somebody to hold his hand to call his mama on Christmas Eve. But he'd given his word to Deagle, on the sacred code of the radioman, so there was no chickening out now. The soldier in front of him moved one notch closer to the front door. Thinking what he'd say to his parents, his throat felt like it was packed with hot sand.

He tried thinking about Australia. Somewhere in this base, maybe the quartermaster AO, there was a locker where his few civilian possessions were kept, those non-military shirts and pants he'd had when he arrived in Vietnam. God, that was three hundred and three days ago. Clothes for warm weather or cold weather? He remembered it was cold when he shipped out of Fort Lewis in late February, 1970. He'd had a University of Iowa sweatshirt, a couple of wool lumberjack shirts, a pair of blue dress slacks and a hippy-looking wide leather belt. There should be a pair of new Levi's, some Chuck Purcell tennis shoes, some underwear and a t-shirt or two that weren't olive drab. In those clothes, he was sure, he'd look like a scarecrow; he'd lost thirty pounds in Vietnam, as much weight as Deagle had lost. It struck him as pretty dumb to have to buy an issue of civilian clothes to wear in Australia that would just go back in his locker until he DEROSed in February and be too small for him when he started eating three squares a day, back in the world.

Pomeroy stepped up on the porch, next man through the door. He got a quick peek of a reception desk and an older, round-eyed Red Cross lady. He looked behind him. Ten pairs of eyes stared at him. Nowhere to go now but inside. He remembered his boonyhat and snatched it off his head. Then the back door of the shack swung open; one very happy son-of-a bitch busted outside and loosed a rebel yell.

Facing the desk with the door closed behind him, Pomeroy watched the Red Cross lady take her next caller through the process of identification, a show of orders, filling out forms, and the censorship rules. He couldn't quite hear her voice. She was sixty maybe, the same age as his grandmother, with her same sweet, patient smile. She wore the red-and-white Red Cross uniform blouse, a strand of pearls around her sun-tanned wrinkled neck, and an AT&T operator's headset over graying hair. Behind her there was a small switchboard with red lights blinking, and Pomeroy wondered if she was going to listen in on his conversation. Too quickly, the soldier at her desk walked away and she was smiling sweetly, beckoning him to come forward. Knees rattling, face hot, unable to swallow the lump in his throat, Pomeroy wobbled to the desk while she wrote on a clipboard. She looked up at him with blue eyes. She was terrifying.

"Young man, have you chosen an R&R city?"

"Yes'm."

"Do you have a copy of your R&R orders?"

He dropped his ID Card and the folded sweat-stained paper on her desk, looking around. She read through it, glanced at his nametag and circled his name on the order, stamped it and initialed it.

"Did you know that your family was notified by postcard of your R&R? They should be looking very much forward to hear from you Cleveland."

"Yes'm"

"Are you going to call your parents?"

"Yes'm."

She passed him a blank, standard Cav form and asked him to fill out the top. Name, rank, SN, date, and time. State, city, street address, and telephone number. She said if he had lost or forgotten the number then an AT&T operator would call through her directory assistance but it would cost him a full minute of his allotted ten minutes.

"Thomasville, Iowa, Mr. And Mr. Edward S. Pomeroy. That's just fine. Now, before the operator places your call there are a few things we have to talk about, Cleveland. I know you're very excited but I want you to listen carefully to these instructions. Will you do that?"

"Yes'm."

"An army specialist in that office to your right will be listening to your conversation. That is a military requirement. When the phone is answered, you'll have ten minutes to talk to your family. You'll notice a three-second delay when you finish speaking before you hear an answer, that's just because you're 13,000 miles from home. There are certain subjects you can't mention, because if you do the army censor will break your connection for five seconds. You'll hear only a steady beep and you don't want that. You can't mention your location, your duty assignment, or the names of your superior officers. You can't mention any military weapons or operations. You may not describe any American or Vietnamese person as wounded, dead, or captured. Cleveland, do you understand those restrictions? That's just fine.

"What I tell all you young men when you call home is 'you ask the questions' and isn't that what you really want from this call? To know how your family is? Alright, now, you sit down in booth number two and pick up the receiver, and I'll have the operator place your call."

He sat on the small stool and picked up the receiver with a shaking right hand. He jammed it against his ear and heard nothing at first, then buzzing and a series of relay clicks. A male operator said "transferring", and then there was a long silence. He wondered why he had a male operator, some draft-dodging son-of-a-bitch. Can't say son-of-a-bitch, goddammit!

Swallowing was still no-go, his throat was swollen shut. He remembered to check the time, 0621. He reminded himself not to use RTO language. His mother did not know phonetics, she'd probably think he was speaking Vietnamese. And to say 6:30 a.m. instead of zero six-thirty hours. Nobody understands that shit in Iowa. Can't say shit... Pomeroy...

A woman's faint voice said, "Yes, this is the Pomeroy residence." There was electronic humming on the line. "Yes, this is the Pomeroy residence," his mother said in a voice was as strong and clear as if she was sitting beside him. "Hello? Cleve is that you, son?"

"Mom, it's me," somebody else's voice said.

"Oh, Cleve!" Then after another pause her voice trembled. "Oh son, it's good to hear you. Oh my lord. I'm going to get your father on the phone, we were just sitting down to supper."

"Mom I only got ten minutes. I'm on R&R calling you from Bien Hoa. I think I can say that."

He heard her call excitedly for his father. "You sound just the same. How are you dear?"

"I'm okay. I sure miss you and dad. But I've only got fifty-eight days left... I'm getting short."

"You're in my prayers every night."

"Well, it's working mom. Just keep praying. I've got some really great guys to cover my... to work with... where I work. I can't talk about that or the censor will pull the plug. I'm getting your letters, mom. They take about three weeks but I'm getting 'em. Are you getting my letters? Well, that's a dumb question because you write me back. I'm supposed to ask the questions. Did you hear from Jake or Junior or Joe for Christmas? Any of them back working the farm?"

"I'll let your father tell you about the farm. But I'll be listening in the bedroom. It's so wonderful that you're calling all the way from Viet Nam."

"Yeah, it's pretty wild," he agreed, as tears suddenly streamed down his face.

"Is this son-number-four?" said his father's voice. "How are you, Cleve?"

"I'm fine, sir."

"Your mother an' me watch the television news every night, since last February. Now she's got the kitchen timer set for ten minutes. How are you holding up?"

"Getting the job done, I guess. Fifty-eight days to go. Hey, what's the temperature there?"

"The temperature? Oh, we got... twenty-nine degrees... and flurries. Been awhile since you thought about snow, I'll bet."

"Right now its 6:30 am and feels like about eighty degrees already. This place gets pretty hot. It'll be over 100 by noon."

"Can you tell us at what kind of work you're doing?"

"Not really. If I say a no-no we'll get the hook. I'm still with the same outfit. But guess what: after R&R, the captain says he's gonna send me back to brigade where I can drive a truck my last six weeks in-country. Not bad, huh."

"Sounds like a good man. Son, do you know where you'll be assigned in the states?"

"Negative. I mean no, sir. I put in for Leavenworth, Kansas, but I'm hoping for a five month drop. Get out early. I mean, what are they gonna do with me. Feeding a guy my size is expensive. Dad, if I do get a drop... I mean... what's the situation on the farm? Have you got Jake or Junior or Joe working for you? And how come I'm your only son whose name doesn't start with a J?"

He heard his dad chuckle. "I wonder about that myself. I guess because we had your brothers and a 'James' and a 'John', your uncles. Ran out of J's when you come along..." then he heard his dad stifle a sob," ...maybe you were special. Anyway, no, the boys are all pretty busy. They got families. But they'll call on Christmas."

"Are you still milking seventy cows class-A?"

"We're milking forty cows class-A. But your mother an' me started a new business and it's working out fine. You old man's an official 'bull-inseminator' for Hatcher County. I drive all over the place with little blue sperm ampules in my trunk. We were even thinking of selling down the herd some more or maybe lease it out. Still talking about it."

"Sell the farm?"

After what seemed more like thirty seconds than three, he heard his father chuckle. "No, not the farm, Cleve. The farm's you boy's birthright. Just them darn cows, and that's only a maybe. Whoops, hope that one got by the censor. We'll talk more about it when you get back to Thomasville. You are coming back, aren't you son?"

"Thomasville, Iowa is looking real good." Something Deagle had said was still bothering him. "That is, sir, if you're not ashamed... I mean... it's a small town and you might not want me workin' for you..."

After the interminable delay, with his chest tight to exhale he heard his father saying, "...that I'm as proud of my son as a father can be. And I always figured my youngest boy would carry on."

"Dad, you can flat count on it! I'm going to be very, very, very careful these last fifty-eight days!"

"Son, someone here wants to talk to you. Ever since that army postcard come, about your R&R, she's been practically living in this house. Here she is."

"Hi, honey, are you okay?"

His heart stopped cold, "Fran?"

In full combat dress with his rifle on his shoulder, Deagle humped toward the new horizon looking for the 1st Cav chaplain's hooch. He glanced at his watch and grinned. By now Pomeroy should be on the horn with his folks.

Before 0500 he'd sneaked out of Vinny's hooch to shower and shave, then returned for his rifle and TO&E and wake up Pomeroy in time to get to the AT&T shack by 0600. Pomeroy had slept on his back, arms across his chest, straight as a corpse. "I'm gonna di di," he'd whispered, "Don't walk through any open gates."

"Roger. Same, same for you and Fuck-knuckle. Now off your ass and on your feet; you got a call to make. Word of honor, sacred code of the radioman. And if that little girl says yes, don't have too much fun in Hawaii. See you in a week."

Yesterday, somewhere east of the admin AO, he'd seen the division chaplain's hooch on his way to the PX. In 'Nam, a chaplain could always get a ride. He walked between the barracks beside drainage ditches with grass tall enough to hide a water buffalo. Strange, how empty the morning seemed without the mama-sans. No Vietnamese nationals on base during the cease-fire. They had other plans, he thought.

His trek was roughly parallel to the big plywood Cav patch on the top of Hill 229, and he stopped to look up at it. Negative. 'Victor Charlie', not 'Uniform Sierra'. He wondered about the unlucky bastards who had spent the night up there pulling ambush duty. Hooper probably. Right about now Hooper is trying to keep his eyes open a few more minutes. He turned away and humped until he saw the small building with the cross over the door.

He knocked and pushed the door open. It was Christmas Eve and the chaplain was in, a bespectacled young captain in jungle fatigues. Above his desk was a mahogany cross and a felt portrait of Jesus Christ. He asked the captain if he was going west for Christmas.

"Son, I'm afraid not. I'm spending it with my troops right here."

"Any ideas? Any convoys going west? Maybe a command jeep? I'll buy gas."

The chaplain laughed. He walked around his desk and stood in front of Deagle with his head bowed, eyes closed, and Deagle was a little slow catching on.

"Lord, we bow our heads in prayer this morning and beseech thee to watch over thy servant, Sergeant Beagle. Bless him and keep him safe against all harm, in the name of the Lord Jesus Christ, amen."

Deagle shook his hand. "Thanks."

"Talk to the CQ at admin, then Master Sergeant Trumpy at the motorpool," he said as Deagle left.

He angled west below the R&R detachment, through the courtyard and back between the rows of admin barracks. Christmas Eve, 1971, was a duty day; he smelled Cambodian Red and Lime Old Spice permeating the barracks screens. He reached the main road and walked north to the admin CP, where he stood at 1st Cav bulletin board reading Sergeant Trumpy's Vietnamese Christmas roster, still posted. He laughed out loud; now Trumpy had three volunteers for KP duty, all fictitious. Below the roster he saw a card offering a used Akai tapedeck in "good to excellent condition, $45, see Sp5 Hoag, thirty-two days" and he wondered how he'd plug it in at LZ Penny. Under Hoag's name was a peace sign.

He walked up the steps and pushed open the command post door, and pulled off his headgear. To his right, Major Andrews' office door was closed, and instead of 1st Sergeant Ree or Sergeant Hooper at the CQ desk a burly muscular E6 named Stevens sat there reading a Mad comic book. The guy was built like Cleve Pomeroy only shorter.

"Hooper around?" he asked.

Stevens looked up and saw the 11-Bravo standing by the door, M-16 on his shoulder. "For the 50th goddamn time, I ain't seen Hooper! But if he's AWOL, I know why."

"I doubt that, but thanks anyway."

Stevens shook his head and went back to his comic book.

Deagle heard boots on the wooden porch behind him and turned to face a portly, middle-aged master sergeant. By the look in his eye, and the fact that he didn't remove his headgear when he stepped inside, Deagle knew this E8 had a case of the ass. He directed his anger at E6 Stevens at the charge-of-quarters desk.

"Sarn't Stevens, you seen my roster! I'm truckin' outa here at 0730, so I'm goddamn short on time! You get off your dead ass and round me up some KP's. Otherwise, you're my KP."

Steven's grin was lewd. "Roster's workin'. Yesterday you had two volunteers, now you got three: Dick Hertz, Ben Dover, and Mike Hunt. Who else gives a shit about Vietnamese orphans. Not me. Besides, I pulled CQ since 1400 yesterday."

"You post me two clean rosters, one here and one at the mess hall, and I'll check back at 0700. Off your ass and on your feet."

With as much non-verbal disrespect as he could muster, Stevens slowly set down his comic book, closed the cover, and reached in the top desk drawer. He brought out another roster. He sauntered past Deagle outside to the bulletin board. Stevens wore spit-shined garrison boots and tailored fatigues with his shirtsleeves folded neatly on his massive biceps. Deagle wondered how he managed to lift weights in 'Nam.

"You a volunteer, son?" MSG Trumpy asked Deagle, looking him over boonyhat-to-boots. "Christmas chow for the Vietnamese orphan kids?"

"Sorry, sarge. I don't much like Vietnamese kids either. But I could use a ride to Firebase Catapult."

"Birds are grounded, trucks are parked," Trumpy told him curtly and walked outside. Deagle closed the CP door and followed, and he watched Stevens mash the last thumbtack into an 8x11 sheet of paper:

3rd Notice! Volunteers Needed
Vietnamese Orphan Christmas Dinner
0730Hrs 24Dec71 Admin Motorpool MSG Trumpy.

Trumpy looked behind him at the empty street, disgusted. "For all the goddamn good it'll do now."

"No sweat," Stevens yawned, "I'll send my runner down the mess hall."

"Sergeant Stevens, lemme tell you what; yesterday the commanding general of this division shook my hand and told me it was important what I was doing with them kids. I don't need no CQ runner, I need you to hand-carry my roster to the mess hall. Now get after it."

Stevens ignored the direct order and gave Deagle a quick inspection. "What're you gapin' at?"

"Who?"

"Who? You shit through feathers, buck sergeant?" He glanced at Deagle's nametag. "Beagle? What swamp did you crawl out of, mutt?"

But Deagle only chuckled. "Swamp called LZ Penny. I see you're having trouble finding KP's?"

"This detail ain't for grunts," Stevens told him, taking a longer look at Deagle's shabby jungle uniform., "just permanent party."

Trumpy said "It's for any swingin' dick that'll go, at this point. No thanks to you, Sarn't Stevens."

Stevens' tired red eyes focused on Deagle. "Mutt, top right drawer of my desk. Grab Sergeant Trumpy's other roster and double-time it down to the mess hall."

Deagle nodded. "Sure thing." But as he started toward the CP the question of Hooper's whereabouts still bothered him. "Sergeant Trumpy, maybe you know: have you seen either Major Andrews or Staff Sergeant Hooper since yesterday afternoon?"

"No, son, I ain't."

"Do you know if your S-2 followed up yesterday's sweep?"

"Talkin' about 'Andrews' last stand'?" Stevens butted in. "Commando games. You find that little piss-ant you tell him he's looking at a two-grade reduction. Borg wants his ass, Wilcox, everybody."

Trumpy checked his watch. "Sarn't Stevens I don't have time to listen to you flap your gums. Get on down to the mess hall. And Sarn't Deagle, you go about your business. Move out."

Deagle turned and looked high up on Hill 229. "I think I know where he is," he said. Hooper and Andrews both, he thought. He shot Trumpy a wristy salute and started humping down the air strip. Maybe the air force had a bird going west. "Good luck finding KP's."

"Hey, hey, hey, hey!" Stevens called after him, "I ain't finished with you, mutt. You got a little detail to do for me. And maybe I need to see some orders."

Deagle halted and turned, then he looked at MSG Trumpy. "Sarge, am I dismissed or pulling shit detail for him?"

"You got something to say to me, buck sergeant?" Stevens asked, smiling.

"I think talking to you would be a waste of breath. Here's my orders."

Master Sergeant Trumpy quickly stepped between Deagle and Stevens. He had seen Stevens in action before. Once or twice a month, it seemed, Stevens singled out some unsuspecting grunt for a ration of abuse and shit details. Stevens started a fight by throwing his rank around and finished it throwing his fists. Having barely avoided Long Binh Jail for fighting, Stevens' now preferred to squeeze an opponent unconscious while sneaking in belly punches. Stevens, Trumpy knew, would break this skinny grunt in half.

"Deagle, you go on to chow or wherever you're going. Sergeant Stevens, you gimme a military about-face and police up my roster. Move!"

By then Deagle had a copy of his orders in hand and Stevens came just close enough to snatch it out of his hand and read it quickly. Then he folded it and slipped it into his shirt pocket. He looked Deagle over from boots to boonyhat.

"You know what they say about rank, mutt, it's like ass: you're either kickin' it or lickin' it. In this case, I'll do the kickin.'"

"I'm kinda getting a case myself," replied Deagle.

"You look like a commando to me. You look like you sleep in a rice paddy. But the same don't go here. At Bien Hoa we're soldiers not animals. We get a haircut. We wear our fatigues sharp, and we shine footgear. We'll start with that. After you post Trumpy's notice, you report to my CP for a clean up."

But instead of backing up, Deagle took a step closer. "Sarge, listen up. I know you got a case of the ass. I got one too, and Sergeant Trumpy has one. We all got a case. Between you and me, let's leave it there."

Stevens rolled his shoulders. He looked down the empty street. There were no troops watching from the barracks or the mess hall. He took a step closer and braced his boots. His black eyes glistened and his neck swelled like a rutting bull.

"Un-sling that rifle, mutt, and drop it on the ground."

Deagle glanced at Master Sergeant Trumpy and left the rifle where it was, but he did slide his right hand from the sling to the stock.

"Sarn't Deagle, you walk away and that's an order!" Trumpy told him. "Comes to rank, I believe an eight is higher than a six, Sergeant Stevens. And unless you're looking to be a five again..."

"Stay outa this, fatso."

"Fatso? That's it. March your ass to the CP and I'm writing your Article 15!"

Stevens' face turned red and he all but blew smoke out his nostrils. He squared his shoulders and gave Trumpy a hard shove. The master sergeant stumbled but didn't go down, but as he staggered to regain his balance he was defenseless. Stevens quickly used his giant forearms to get Trumpy in a headlock. The old master sergeant choked for breath and his eyes rolled up in his head.

Deagle reached out with the muzzle of his rifle and jabbed Stevens hard in the temple. "Hey, shithead..."

Stevens let go of Trumpy and came like a charging lion, face first. He reached for Deagle's rifle with his left hand and threw his right fist at Deagle's chin, but the taller E5 sidestepped him. Stevens left-faced on a dime and attacked again, this time aiming a kick at Deagle's groin. Again the buck sergeant dodged aside and Stevens' momentum carried him on. A grinning Sergeant Stevens, after misjudging Deagle's moves as defensive, turned but was a split-second too slow to get his shoulders squared. Deagle had his boots planted, left leg pivoted, and the butt of his rifle already swinging in a tight, upward arc like a short right uppercut. The hollow stock of the M-16 caught the staff sergeant flush on his right cheekbone, a resounding, "thwack" that stunned him more than hurt him, and he dropped his heavy arms. Deagle shoved his rifle two-handed like a pugil stick, butt-first, into Steven's jaw, and his long-armed follow through gave the blow enough momentum to snap the E6's head and drop him to his knees.

Deagle waited while Stevens struggled to his feet. On his cheekbone was a golf-ball sized welt. Stevens' arms came up in a boxer's stance and Deagle drove the butt of his rifle between them into his teeth. Stevens rocked backward and lurched forward, face down on the street. He got his elbows under him and managed to roll on his back, but that was a far as he could go. His mashed lips began to bleed.

"Jesus Jumping Christ," said Sergeant Trumpy, staring down.

"You guys let this bozo walk around loose? If he was at LZ Penny somebody would throw a frag in his hooch."

Trumpy slipped an arm around Deagle and steered him toward the motorpool. "Thanks for what you done, Sarn't Deagle. Next, that maniac will be lookin' for you with a .45. Don't worry, I'll have Bud Bierra throw him in the brig. Tell you what... you wanna go to Firebase Catapult and I need KP's; you work for me this morning I'll get you a ride in a deuce-and-a-half anywhere you need to go."

A quarter mile down the street Deagle waited in front of the division motorpool while Trumpy sorted out his gate key from a ring of fifty keys. The front gate was chain-link, twelve feet high and twenty feet wide, suspended from heavy rollers. Trumpy saw the cut padlock lying in the sand.

"Now what the hell..."

He shoved the gate open and walked to the first office building on the left. A black metal sign on the door announced the offices of:

OIC - Lt. Colonel Douglas W. Geary

NCOIC - MSG Willard Trumpy

The door was wide open. Trumpy poked his head in and noted the colonel's office door was ajar. He snapped on the overhead fluorescent tubes and told Deagle to stand by the front door. The outer office was as he'd left it the night before and Colonel Geary's office was squared away as always, not a scrap of paperwork on the shiny desk, but the key cabinet behind the desk was open. Only one set of keys seemed to be missing, the admin battalion jeep.

From the doorway, Deagle read the cheerful Christmas poster on the opposite wall. It was signed with a flourish by Colonel Geary, wishing the officers and enlisted men assigned to the motorpool a Merry Christmas and Happy New Year.

"Hey, sarge," Trumpy called, "go back an' see if my PFC Pine is by the truck, but don't say nothin' about that gate lock if he is. Stash your rifle and TO&E there behind my desk, pick it up when we get back." When the door closed Trumpy sat down and called Sergeant Major Bierra.

"1st Cavalry Headquarters Division, Sergeant Major Bierra."

"Bud, this is Trumpy. What the hell is going on? A few minutes ago Sergeant Stevens practically choked me to death and now I got me a cut gate and a missing jeep." He got no immediate response and wasn't sure the division sergeant major heard him.

"Bud, you hear what I said?"

"I heard. Keep it to yourself for now, Trump. We have a dilemma. You want Stevens charged?"

"Damn right I want him charged!"

"I'll take care of it."

"What's a dilemma?"

"Problem. Major Andrews is AWOL. Colonel Borg put him under house arrest but it looks like he policed up your jeep and went over the wall."

"Holy cow... what for?"

"It's all S-2 stuff, Trump. When it goes to JAG, I'll brief all you command NCO's. Get on the horn when you get back from getting laid in Sin City."

"This is a Christmas dinner for orphan kids."

"Affirmative, Santa."

Deagle patrolled the open lots behind the garages, admiring the spanking new jeeps, deuce-and-a-half's, half-tracks, and armored personnel carriers. Vehicles still in crates piling up, he thought, another sign that 'Nam was about fini. He cruised back to alpha garage and listened to the sounds of a motorpool; engines revving, air tools hammering, hydraulics whining. It was Christmas Eve but the mechanics were already hard at it. He heard the sound of water shooting into a bucket and found a hatless t-shirt-clad troop cleaning the back wheels of a canvas-top truck. He walked around the truck and lifted the tarp to see what was inside. He saw a stainless steel field kitchen broken down in a dozen pieces. The soldier's fatigue shirt hung on a nail and the nametag on it was Pine.

"We're it, huh, sarge?" the kid said.

Pine was tall and lean with an overgrown butch haircut, a wide forehead, hollow cheeks, a tiny mouth and no chin. His triangle-shaped head reminded Deagle of a rattlesnake.

"I thought there might be one more, guess he slept in," Pine told him. He shut off the water and coiled the hose neatly. "You like gook kids? I don't. They're all hands. But we should have a full squad of MPs 'cause MPs don't get Christmas off either."

Sergeant Trumpy came hurrying up the street with the truck keys swinging in his left hand.

"Pine you about ready? We got to di di."

"Hell, yes."

Trumpy walked around the deuce-and-a-half giving it a final inspection.

"You volunteer or get drafted," Deagle asked the kid.

"Sarge, this is a shit detail and I'm on Trumpy's shit list. *Sin loi*, PFC Pine. For me to get Christmas off I got to feed his gang of brats."

They climbed into the truck, Pine behind the wheel, Trumpy on the passenger side, and skinny Deagle crammed in between. The PFC started the engine and rammed the clumsy truck into low gear through the open gate. Low man on the totem, Pine jumped down and closed the gate. Trumpy pointed to the admin road and Pine pulled up at the officer's entrance to the admin mess hall. He tapped the horn twice and Sergeant Arroyo stuck his head out and waved.

"You troops help Arroyo load my Christmas dinner," Trumpy told them.

Deagle dropped the gate and jumped up. Pine passed up folding chairs, portable gas burners, and footlockers stenciled with "POTS AND PANS". The food for the orphan kids was in big aluminum trays covered with tin foil, warm to the touch and delicious to the nose. Deagle caught the aromas of turkey and dressing, cranberry sauce and yams, and some kind of cake.

"Ho ho ho!" the master sergeant hollered. "Don't you troops worry, gonna be plenty of Christmas chow left over for you. Always is."

PFC Pine wheeled the heavy truck east toward the barren sand hills on the PX side of the base, the only vehicle on the road. Above the right front fender the morning sun was a blinding orange-slice; it's reflected fire through the windshield started Deagle's sweat rolling. Off to the south he watched steamy Hill 229 give up its morning humidity.

Beyond the 1st Cav AO the road flattened out and low jungle re-appeared. Deagle looked for the perimeter wire but didn't see it. Bien Hoa was a big place. The truck rolled past the air force's fuel depot, bunkered airstrips, and a complex of barracks and administration buildings. After ten minutes at thirty miles an hour, Pine turned south. The Christmas Eve sun burned Deagle's left cheek as the panoprimed highway degenerated into a pot-holed dirt road and everything green disappeared, replaced by bare reddish-brown defoliated ground. On the eastern skyline he saw a line of tall perimeter towers facing the open jungle between Bien Hoa and the South China Sea. The village of Sin City was inside the perimeter guns, "Uniform Sierra."

Pine downshifted as he approached a gate with an MP checkpoint. Deagle looked beyond the gate and saw four MP's holding back an army of black-haired, half-naked Vietnamese boys and girls. Beyond the kids he saw the usual ramshackle buildings at the outskirts of a Vietnamese village. Sergeant Trumpy jumped down to show his pass.

"Here we go," Pine said ominously.

The MP's shooed the kids clear and the truck shot ahead through the gate. Pine bumped the truck along in second gear another fifty meters to a festively decorated shelter building. The shelter had walls made of old army plywood nailed to 4x4s set in shallow hard-clay holes. The walls were painted green and trimmed with red ribbons and bits of bright tin foil, strung like garland. The children had written the words "Merry Christmas" and "Thankh You."

"This is where the medics give the whores their shots," Pine told him.

Deagle studied the village from his high vantage point. Straight ahead of him was a line of interconnecting door-less shacks where the elders lived, and squatting in front watching the goings-on were a few dozen sun-bronzed old papa-sans and mana-sans. A hunched, white-haired old man smoking a long-stem pipe caught Deagle's eye. He looked like he'd spent a hundred years in the direct sun. Deagle couldn't see past him into his shaded hooch but knew it was a single front room with a fabric-partitioned sleeping room, a dirt or canvas tarp floor. Overhead, his roof was scrap plywood fastened at an angle to direct the rain away from the street. Behind the old man's hooch was a barbed ten-foot fence and head-high jungle all the way to the tower guns.

Deagle searched among the faces in the street and did not see a fighting-age adult male in Sin City. Mostly boy-sans, girl-sans, baby-sans and very old mama-sans were home today. SOP.

He threw the truck door opened and jumped down. He looked back toward the gate and saw Trumpy and the MP's holding back two platoons of kids, all poised and watching the truck intently. Like the kids in the villages around Tay Ninh, they were barefoot, with dirty little arms and legs, and many wore shirts and shorts made from pieces of GI uniforms.

"Only the three of us today," Pine told him, "usually there's thirty or forty GI's with four-hour passes."

Deagle took off his hat and filled it with his watch, wallet, dogtags, pocketknife, belt, and compass. He had visited a few "sin cities," same, same Tiajuana; instead of Mexican kids begging for pesos there were Vietnamese kids pleading for Piasters. The kids in the fishing and farming villages had much better manners, and were even shy.

"Just stand still and keep sayin' 'no boy-san, no girl-san'," Pine said, grinning.

Released by the MP's, the fastest kids raced toward the truck and quickly had Deagle surrounded. They shouted "hey, Joe!" and told him where he could get his boots shined, where he could have his fatigues laundered, where he could buy a new GI hat. There was intensity in their upturned faces, urgency in their pigeon, GI English. Deagle shook his head and waved, "no boy-san, no girl-san," doing a Mexican hat dance to keep from stepping on small bare feet. As the crowd got deeper the bigger kids began to push their way to the center of attention. Deagle felt small fingers poking him and snatching at his cuff. The more vocal he got, the more physical the kids got: salesmen turned to outright begging, shouting for Piasters and MPC's to buy food. Poking turned to pushing. One boy-san tried climbing up his back. Another, ten years old and sixty pounds, laced his fingers on Deagle's bicep and tried to chin himself high enough to reach the brass ring, the contents of his hat. Little fingertips dug in like nails. Deagle turned, thinking of hiding in the truck; he saw PFC Pine on the hood of the deuce-and-a-half repelling all boarders with his boots.

Sergeant Trumpy's formation whistle ended the brawl. Dismissed, the boys and girls joined their grandmothers by the hooches. Deagle had a ripped shirt pocket, a missing button, and one bloody scratch on his forearm. There was an uneasy silence in the street. As Trumpy walked around and opened the back of the truck, Deagle noticed the eyes of all the Vietnamese on him. Old MSG Trumpy was head honcho in Sin City.

"Free enterprise," he told Deagle. "They gotta get it out of their system."

Pine jumped down off the hood and stuffed his hat on. "Yeah, the kids think everything's free."

"They're not all orphans, are they, sarge?" Deagle said. "That's every kid in the village."

"Aw, what's the difference."

Deagle and Pine unloaded the footlockers and carried them behind the shelter as Trumpy assembled his field kitchen. He lined up the big diesel-burning stoves and fired them up. Deagle carried four gas-cans filled with water and poured them into 30-gallon stainless pots. In one, Pine dumped in a whole box of Lipton teabags. Then, out came the bacon trays with the foil-covered Christmas turkeys nicely browned and basted by Sergeant Arroyo. Trumpy arranged the birds on his stovetop at dress-right-dress. Next, two five-gallon pots of bread stuffing, two pots of mashed potatoes, one pan filled with turkey gravy, and one small pan of cranberry jelly on cracked ice. There were green peas, yellow beans, and yams. When it was all set up and steaming, Deagle noted there was not a single kernel of rice in this Christmas dinner. It was all American chow.

The Omega reached 1000 hours. Deagle set up the chairs and tables inside the plywood shelter, enough to seat about fifty kids at a time. There was no roof, but he figured the kids would be okay unless the rain came early in Sin City. He walked back to the truck and opened a cold beer with the churchkey, and lit a smoke. There were two last items still in the truck, a big cardboard drum marked X-MAS and US ARMY and a stack of a half-dozen brand-new plastic garbage cans.

He blew smoke-rings in the dead, humid air, taking in the unbelievable scene around him. Sin City at Christmas. He thought about all the stuff he'd seen Vietnamese people eat. Like when a whole village turned out to butcher a bloated rotting water buffalo that caught 105 shrapnel. The old mama-sans sharpened their knives on rocks and had at it, cutting away the maggots and the blood-shot strings of soggy muscle, slicing what brown meat that was left into finer and finer chunks to flavor a pot of white rice. Then there were the dead monkeys and mangy-looking cats he'd seen hanging like laundry on a clothes line. The boy-sans said they'd snared them, having no rifles or ammunition in the village. But he'd seen the gaping exit holes made by fast small-caliber bullets. He watched an old woman make careful circumferential cuts in the dry tough monkeys hide just behind the ribs and over the spine. Then she took the front half and pulled toward the head, another old woman pulled toward the tail, and they ripped and tugged that hide like peeling the pajamas off a cartoon animal. The skin-less *cong khi* still had its tail, and was about the ugliest thing he'd ever seen. The women filleted every bit of meat except that tail. And just before he got malaria the 1st platoon captured one of the hundreds of one-shot Charlie's in their AO, a skinny old geezer, forty years old. He had a chi-com bolt action rifle and six rounds of ammo caked with green verdigris fungus, one glass jug of water, and three rice snacks prepared for him in his village. His rations were the foulest food Deagle had ever smelled. And that's how he'd been caught, a dead fish odor coming from a dry riverbed. The treats consisted of rice balls mixed with fish-heads wrapped in dry leaves. Since this spider-hole sniper couldn't remember how long he'd been sitting in his hole waiting to shoot somebody, only God himself knew how old those rice balls were.

Now, Christmas turkey, brown gravy, and yellow mashed potatoes.

He watched Sergeant Trumpy pay his respects to the village elders, sitting like a king in a lawn chair shooting the breeze in his excellent Vietnamese. They listened and smiled, and when one understood what he said well enough to tell the others they all coo'd and nodded and sometimes laughed. It was understood, Deagle realized, that it was time to eat all that good-smelling chow when Trumpy said it was time, and he seemed in no hurry. At 1030 Trumpy got up and took a big brown paper bag out of the truck and walked to a hooch.

Deagle's breathing was shallow in the morning heat and humidity. Looking beyond the hooches he saw more kids coming on the road. From where they came the road bent out of sight, at the bend was another MP checkpoint. Bet those guys had good duty, he thought, almost as good as the MPs at the PX. Get laid every day, get rich, go home. Around the corner from the checkpoint there would be more refugee shacks, then the original village, then the business district. The business district was where he planned to go when Trumpy released him. God it was hot. He pulled the boonyhat off his head and mopped his face with his sleeve.

When he looked up he saw the Master Sergeant Trumpy decked out in a full-length, red and white-trimmed Santa Claus suit complete with hat and beard. Santa in combat boots.

"Gimme a hand with the drum," Pine told him.

"What's in it?"

"Hell if I know. Trumpy wants it right in the center of the street."

The two of them rolled the heavy 50-gallon drum to the edge of the truck and heaved it down. It weighed a couple hundred pounds. They rolled it past the shelter to the middle of the street and set it upright. The lid was a secured to the drum by a thick tin ring that had to be cut. Deagle dug out his pocketknife.

"Jesus Jumpin' Christ, don't open that now!" Trumpy warned.

"What's in it?"

"Hard candy. Open it now an' we'll have a riot and lots of turkey to haul back. I got us some volunteers to help with KP and DRO duty, so Pine you take the sweet potatoes and stuffing, Sergeant Deagle you slice the turkey and plop them mashed potatoes. I'll do gravy. Kids eat everything dry, mostly with their hands. Only the older ones get gravy and just on the turkey. You'll see. Hell's bells, you'd never know the kids were starving. Well, sir, set out them garbage cans behind the kitchen and we'll get goin'..."

At 1100 hours the feast was hot, the tables were set with napkins, forks and spoons, and the KPs were on the serving line. Trumpy gave the okay, and Deagle could not believe the change in the kids as they filed in. From the frantic, greedy, rude little beggars a few hours ago, they came into the shelter shy, wide-eyed, arms straight down at their sides. Prodded by their grandmothers and great grandmothers, they formed an orderly line and took trays and stood uncertainly in front of each station taking whatever was given to them. They each got a spoon of green peas and yellow beans and red cranberry jelly, scoops of stuffing and potatoes, half a yam, and then Deagle topped off the tray with a nice slice of white breast-meat. Santa Claus Trumpy tried to get a smile when he spooned on the brown gravy. Then the kids sat down with their hands in their laps.

"Lookin' at 'em," Pine said, "you'd think we were gonna shoot 'em after we feed 'em."

Four mama-sans acted as dining room orderlies. In their marvelous sing-song gibberish, smiling through black teeth, they seated the kids and tried to get them to eat. Forget forks and spoons; they picked up golf-ball sized lumps of potatoes with their fingers. They liked the peas but not the yellow beans. Cranberry jelly that jiggled and reflected the sunlight stayed on the plate. Dry stuffing and yams got eaten but slices of hot white meat turkey disappeared into dirty pants and shirt pockets for later. As the kids finished, the DROs carried their trays behind the field kitchen to the squad of tray-scrapers.

Deagle watched the full mess hall tray come back from the tables. All that food wasted, he thought. He served the next wave of orphans and looked down into one after another pair of joyless, dark eyes. Maybe the kids were just doing their jobs, he thought. He chanced to look back outside the shelter where the tray-scrapers were at work, and there, finally, he saw Christmas happiness. It was in the faces of the mama-sans blithely stealing everything that wasn't eaten or nailed down. They had quietly procured every bag, jug, pan, and can in the village. As fast as the full trays of chow came back to be washed and re-cycled these beaming old broads scraped it all with a steady plop... plop... plop... into the receptacles. Gravy, potatoes, beans, dressing, all into homogenous piles. Other mama-sans were relay runners and carried the booty back to the hooches and returned for more.

Trumpy told Deagle to turn off the burners and begin breaking down the kitchen.

"You do this every year?" Deagle asked.

Trumpy nodded. "Third year. Well, it ain't their custom, it's ours. First time I put this suit on they all screamed and run off. What are you gonna do, it's Christmas."

Deagle shook his head. "It'll never be the same for me."

"You men pack up my kitchen and take chow in the truck." He glanced at his watch. "After I pass out the candy, you'll have some free time. Go get a steam bath or a blow job, suit yourself. Meet me at the truck at 1700 sharp and we'll di di back to the base."

Deagle took his plate of warm turkey, potatoes and gravy and sat on the hood of the truck to watch Santa Claus pass out candy. Now the kids were happy again, all smiles and nervous anticipation, like Christmas should be. The food had been for the adults, but the candy the kids got to keep. In front of the drum Trumpy had a column fifty meters long.

Sitting in his lawn chair, Santa Claus called each kid to the drum for a handshake or a quick kiss in return for a fistful... two fistfuls... and sometimes a pocketful! ...of the wrapped hard candy. Children who didn't quite accept the red uniform and long white beard were won over by Trumpy's warmth and gentle voice. Many of them smiled. With the really small kids Trumpy went down on one knee, and it was one of these tiny baby-sans, just a few years old and twenty inches tall, who wrecked Sergeant Trumpy's Christmas.

She came forward at the urging of the others, confused. She had no pockets, but she cupped her hands and Trumpy carefully placed a half dozen candies. He lifted her to his lap and wished her a merry Christmas but she started to cry. He laughed and she cried louder, and she dropped her candy in the street. The boys in line behind her made a grab for it.

"You boy-sans wait your turn," he told them in very un-Santa-like sternness. "*Di di mau.*"

Hearing the GI command to "go away", the boys came ahead instead. One made a dive for the spilled candy and another dived on top of him, kicking up a cloud of dust. Trumpy put the little girl down and hollered in Vietnamese for the boys to stop fighting. As he stepped away from the drum to break up the melee other boys snuck around him and began stealing handfuls of candy. He spun and charged back to the drum, shooing the thieves, but the brawl behind him escalated and the little girl who started it screamed. She was being trampled. Trumpy scooped her up and stood defending his drum, surrounded like Custer on the knoll by dark-haired children and a growing dust storm. One-handed, he pulled children from the piles and scolded them to get back in line, but there were too many of them. Finally, Santa Claus lost his temper; with a mighty kick he toppled the drum. A rainbow of hard candy swooshed onto the street and the kids swarmed.

Trumpy carried the little girl to her grandmother and ripped the white beard off his face. Without looking back he stomped off in his red suit and combat boots.

"Trumpy got a full-time mama-san here?" Deagle asked Pine, thinking he had to have a better reason that those kids to come to Sin City.

"He messes with the whores. Got a full-time girl-san. From what I hear she's plenty mean. She won't let him be no butterfly..."

He left Pine and cruised the street through the shantytown into the flea-market district. It was strange being the only GI in the quasi-Vietnamese village. But the mama-sans just watched him and the kids left him alone. They'd had their turn. On the right side of the street the compound fence slid away into heavy foliage behind wooden hooches that had porches, front doors, glass windows, and chipped tile roofs. There were older stucco homes on concrete foundations, a few still had white paint on them. Behind the houses were backyards with green grass and or fences to hold chickens and scabby-looking goats. On the left side of the street was the flea-market, small fabric hooches with rug floors and tin roofs. In front of these were tables with stacks of GI goodies and a friendly mama-san waited to bargain for the best price.

Brand new air force and army combat fatigues, camo fatigues, LRRP fatigues and field jackets. Baseball caps, wide-brimmed boonyhats with chinstraps, Aussie diggers, green and maroon and blue berets. Custom tailoring, free. There were tables of silver Zippo cigarette lighters with spot-welded 1st Cav insignias, others engraved with the names of army divisions and famous battles. About a third of the cigarette lights were some form of the ever-popular "Screaming Eagles" and "Yea though I walk through the valley of death I will fear no evil, for I am the most evil son-of-a-bitch in the valley". He stopped in front of the mama-san at the Zippo display. She pointed at the long-armature engraving machine in the hooch behind her: custom engraving too. But the papa-san engraver had Christmas Eve off. He smiled "no thanks" and moved on.

Maybe papa-san was out playing eighteen holes, too.

He strolled past displays of coffee mugs, t-shirts, divers watches, wide leather watchbands, and the inevitable assortment of cats-eye rings, bracelets, necklaces, and pins. All the souvenirs were new and cheaper than at the PX. He paid $1MPC for a Cav monogrammed handkerchief and wiped the sweat from his face and neck. Must be 110 degrees, he decided. He reached the MP checkpoint and offered a fake salute to the MP inside, reading a James Bond paperback.

Sin City's business district was a collection of larger stucco homes that had been turned into bars and ersatz hotels. The "Hotel San Francisco" looked like the Alamo, it's white front pocked with bullet holes. Next to it was the "Hotel Paris East." There was "Thu An's Annex", a hardware store that looked like a two car garage without the doors. "Laundry Thwaing Chu" and "Best Bar Bien Hoa City".

So easy, he thought, to forget where you are. Standing in the middle of the road he turned a slow circle. Half a football field behind the hotels and bars usually crowded with GI's there was a barbed wire fence and thick no-man's land jungle. Victor Charlie, fence or no fence. Between the "Hotel San Francisco" and a hooch offering felt, black-and-silver portraits of tigers, was an alley cluttered with old rusty bicycle parts leading to the perimeter fence. He walked the alley to the barbed-wire fence. The ground on both sides was trampled like a cattle trail. There were holes in the wire big enough for little people to slip through. He dropped to one knee to look at the small footprints.

"At night Uncle Khee comes calling," he said aloud, standing to his full 6' 4" and hands on hips. "And it ain't to buy a watch."

He turned his head and saw a dark-haired prostitute watching him from the street. She had long shiny black hair, wore a tight-fitting emerald satin dress and black high heels. She was not smiling. He dusted off his hands and started toward her, then she smiled.

She was fifteen or sixteen years old and 4-1/2 feet tall, but she looked older and taller. The optical illusion was created with make-up, four-inch spike-heel shoes, supple calves, and round hips. Her dress was standard-issue prostitute molded satin; bare shoulders, a top cut low over her small breasts, and a split bottom that showed lots of smooth right thigh.

"What you talk about?" she demanded

"Uncle Khee? You know Uncle Khee, and his brother Charles."

As he got closer she shielded her eyes from the sun with her hand. She looked him up and down and made a big deal of his height. "You too tau," she said, with a teenager's high voice. Clowning, she crossed her eyes and pretended to be dizzy. "You too tau, GI. You come inside, you buy me Saigon Tea." With the assuredness of a teacher leading a child she reached for his hand and walked him into the "French Riviera Hotel." In the doorways and windows of the other hotels they passed, he saw more green dresses, more long dark hair and oval eyes watching.

There were two concrete steps up from the dirt street to the railed veranda of the "French Riviera," then two steps down into the large single room that was the bar and restaurant and dance floor. The front door was off its hinges, propped against the inside wall. The door and everything beyond it used to be white, but apart from a few frescoed porch pillars and an arched stucco ceiling not much was French. The old papa-san bartender had white hair and rumpled white dinner jacket. The only color in the room was the black and silver felt animal artwork and the bright satin dresses of the half dozen other working girls. It was a slow day, and they sat at a table playing a dice game with bamboo sticks. As he was led into the room Deagle noticed a set of small stereo speakers on the walls but no jukebox.

They took a window table and Deagle looked out at the street pretending not to notice the girl staring at his face. Still avoiding her, he looked the other way and counted two red dresses, one pink, one aqua, and one more emerald green duty dress, all low cut and slit high. The other girls, since he was taken, played cards and ignored the GI. The barman shuffled over and smiled through broken teeth. Deagle couldn't see eyes inside his eyelids.

He asked for a cold beer and the old papa-san nodded enthusiastically. "Bommie Bom beer. Good beer."

"Schlitz? Black Label?"

"Bommie Bom," he repeated.

Trying to lessen the sting of the insult he spoke carefully. "Papa-san, bring me Bommie Bom, thank you. And one bottle opener and one glass, you bic?"

The old man nodded gracefully.

"How much Saigon Tea?" he asked.

"Two dollah, MPC."

He pretended to think it over. "You have one-dollar Saigon Tea?"

The girl's almond eyes went wide and then she laughed. She crossed her eyes again and made a face. "Nnnnnnaaaaoooowwww! You cheap Charlie! You buy me two-dollar Saigon Tea!" She looked at his nametag and tried to pronounce it. "Deagoooo."

It was all part of the game and he said okay to the papa-san, knowing he got most of the money anyway. He held up one finger. "I buy you one Saigon Tea, only one."

"You cheap Charlie," she answered. She tossed her long hair and reached down with both slender hands to his left wrist. "You hab officah watch! You buy me three Saigon Tea, cheap charley Deago." Her laugh was full and musical.

"I'm no officer, I work for a living."

He cocked his head back and glanced at her face. She was pretty, not yet coarsened by her profession. Even without the heavy liner and shadow makeup, her eyes were wide, dark, bottomless ovals. When she laughed he saw that she had even white teeth. Her button nose reminded him that this pretty face was still evolving and she was probably not old enough to get a California driver's license. Though she looked voluptuous in a whore's dress that rounded the tops of her breasts and emphasized the smooth roundness of her hips, she probably weighed ninety pounds. When she tried to hold his eyes he pretended to look across the room to consider his other choices.

His beer came in a long-neck brown bottle with the number "33" on the label, reasonably cold and with the metal cap still on tight. Her Saigon Tea was a shotglass of weak room-temperature tea, nothing more than a bar cover charge for which she got a small commission. He used the opener and popped the top, poured and inspected the amber beer for "additives", glass or bamboo slivers, and took a long drink.

"What's your name," he asked.

"My name Hoa. Like Bien Hoa." She sipped her tea and crossed her eyes again, now pretending the tea was strong whiskey.

A boy-san walking in the street caught Hoa's eye, and as she looked out the window Deagle got a better look at her. There were light brown highlights in the dark almond-shaped eyes. Her eyebrows were plucked but not too well, still full and dark as her hair. She had a narrow forehead and high cheeks, an attractive wide mouth under the heavy lipstick. She had a clean jaw, a rounded chin with a tiny dimple, a straight sleek neck. She kept her hands crossed in front of her on the table but Deagle could see the chipped nails under the red polish and rough skin on her fingertips.

"Why you look my hand not me?" she asked. "You not like Hoa?"

Deagle had made up his mind. He hadn't seen the others but Hoa was fine. "Hoa is nice," he told her, "Hoa is... numbah five... numbah four, maybe..."

Her dark brows knitted and she glared, "you boshit GI! You numbah ten!"

"How much short-time?"

"Short-time you gib me $25 MPC."

He shook his head. "Too much. I give you $10 MPC or you di di."

"You bo-shit Deago!"

He smiled as Hoa stood and showed him a haughty shoulder. He laughed at her expression of comic contempt as she pranced across the bar to join the other prostitutes. The instant Hoa's nicely-rounded rear hit the chair her expression changed, and she was full of animation as she described him. He knew most of what she was telling the others; he had long hands, skinny legs, that he talked to himself and wore an officer's watch, and he wore his manhood on the left side of his zipper, maybe.

The atmosphere in the bar had changed. Now Deagle was fair game again, but the girls had to decide who would get first crack. They chattered and giggled and took turns looking at his crotch, but as he looked them over he figured next would be the older one in the red dress.

He saw her coming and watched the roll of her hips in the red satin dress. The girls watched too, clucking and laughing in a decidedly vulgar tone. This girl was older, mid twenties, taller at 5' 6" in her matching red high heels. Her shiny hair was combed carefully down to the middle of her back and her bangs were cut straight above plucked brows. Her face was strong-featured, not soft like Hoa. Her eyes were more round than oval, dark and piercing, cheekbones high under dark rouge. She was bigger all over, a woman of experience. Her breasts were full, hips wider, with more thigh and bigger shoulders.

Playing to her audience, it took her all of thirty seconds to walk across the dance floor, which included a sensual side-trip to the bar where she leaned over and showed the flawless roundness of her ass. Then she tossed her hair dramatically and pretended to notice Deagle watching her. Like a model on a runway, she took a half dozen long strides and plopped down on the chair across from him. The other girls giggled out loud with anticipation. This one was pretty, but he had his mind made up on Hoa.

"Kinda slow today," he said. "Christmas Eve."

"I not see you before," she told him. "My name Mimi."

"I just got in-country," he lied.

"Nnnnaaaooooow! You lie, GI!. You buy me Saigon Tea," and she signaled the barman over. When he allowed her to order a $2 Saigon Tea the other girls cackled again.

"Been here six months," he said, paying for the drink.

She smiled triumphantly and put the shotglass to her red lips but didn't drink. She put the glass down and reached for his left wrist, turned it over to have a look at the officer's watch for herself. She held his hand and began a slow massage of his wrist with the ball of her thumb while appraising his face with her steady eyes. He enjoyed her touch, the sweet heaviness of her perfume. It was Mimi who first stirred heaviness below his belly.

"You go back soon. Want Mimi short-time?" She asked quietly.

"How much short-time."

"You give me $25 MPC short time. Stay all night, $50 MPC."

"How much time?"

"You give me $25 MPC I give you one hour short-time."

He shook his head. "I like to make love four or five times... need maybe three hours short-time."

She slapped his wrist lightly to protest his lying again. "Nnnaaaooowww. You not soul brothah... short-time one hour, I make you happy. Two hour same, same. All night you give me... $40 MPC I make you very happy."

He sat back sipping his Bommie Bom and pretended to think it over.

"Actually, I make love so good I should charge you $25 short time $50 all night."

She laughed and yanked on his wrist. "No boshit GI. We go make love now all night you pay me $50 MPC."

Deagle called the barman over and ordered Mimi a Saigon Tea, but her smile evaporated when he told her to take it back to the table and let him think about her offer. She gave him a shoulder shimmy as she stood, breasts close to his face, then she carried her shoulders high with indifference as she marched back to her table. The girls went into conference again and Mimi called the barman to the table.

He stared out the window at the jungle beyond the fence. The alcohol in his second Bommie Bom felt relaxing coursing in his malaria-thinned blood. Some GI's thought when the wrong mosquito bit you can never drink alcohol again, which was right up there with "Syphilis Island" in the Quang Tri Province. All that low-rent ignorance, he thought. Girls and beer are both good for you, the only possible way in Vietnam to take your mind off your job. Beyond the fence his eyes zoomed in as a bird landed in the top of a bush. A bird as black as Mimi's eyes. He watched the bird jump from limb to limb it until it dived for something on the ground. He felt his shrunken belly roll and rumble full of Christmas turkey and cold beer.

Lots of ways to die unexpectedly in the "Hotel French Riviera", he thought. And not just at night. The MP's in Sin City are assigned to keep an eye on the GI's, not the fence with the holes in it. The MP's probably had full-time girls, maybe Hoa was one of them. Maybe they told her how many GI's were coming every day and what was going on at Bien Hoa. Maybe one of those baby-sans who hadn't been able to steal his wallet, with nothing else to do today, would come running in here and end his life with a bullet or a quick blast from a satchel charge. Maybe some sniper out in that green morass was watching him through the window and sharpening the image on his jungle-rusted front sight... maybe.

"Where are... all the papa-sans today," he asked out loud.

The answer was music, the rolling electric-organ opening of the Door's "Light My Fire" carried to the big room by the small wall speakers. It was magic, Jim Morrison's voice but Hoa singing. In her emerald satin dress holding a bamboo stub for a microphone, she popped out from behind the bar and glided across the room toward him. She mouthed the words to the song and the girls at the table jumped up, paired off, and began to dance. Looking straight into Deagle's eyes she sang, "The time to hesitate is through... no time to wallow in the miyahhhh..."

She stood by his table and sang to him, hips rocking and shoulders rolling, eyes locked on him like a target. At first he was embarrassed and tried to look out the window or watch the other girls dancing but Hoa was irresistible. Gently she reached out and turned his chin to face her. "Come on baby light my fyahhh... time to set the night on... fyahh..."

The hypnotic organ played and Hoa closed her eyes and danced for him, black hair scissoring over her bare shoulders as she turned her body. Barely moving her high-heeled shoes, she kept the beat perfectly in her hips and shoulders. With a gossamer touch on his right hand, she coaxed him to his feet, looking almost straight up into his eyes. The song she'd chosen was not for waltzing and not for the twist but just right for a slow hip-to-hip seduction. When Morrison sang again, Hoa put her hands on his hips and pulled him closer. She sang the words with both arms around his waist, eyes closed and head bobbing and dark hair flying, and Deagle didn't care if she'd sung it a hundred times.

When the music stopped they both laughed. There was no question in Hoa's mind that she was invited back to his table and that he would buy her another Saigon Tea. Tiny beads of sweat glistening on her upper lip. The old barman was right on cue with a fresh full shotglass and a capped Bommie Bom.

"You numbah one dancer, Deago," she told him.

"*Choo Hoi*," he said. "I surrender. Papa-san bring one cola," he added to the stoic old bartender, and reached again for his wallet. Hoa nodded enthusiastically and glanced at the girls across the room. "Hoa numbah one," he told her.

"You not be buttahfly... like Hoa now, Deago?"

"Affirmative... Yes."

She laughed, mocking his serious expression, "Appermaaatib" and gave him a salute.

"Okay, no more bullshit phonetics."

"Boshit poneppics..."she parroted

"Close enough. Let's get the money out of the way. I say, I give Hoa $25 for three hours short-time."

"And two Saigon Tea."

"And one Saigon Tea..."

"I tell papa-san three hour and two Saigon tea... I make Deago happy happy..."

"Shit... okay."

"Shit... OK."

With that out of the way, she fanned her face and dipped her lips into the weak tea. "I not live Sin City," she told him forthrightly. "You not see me before, I live Saigon."

"Nobody lives in Sin City, I know."

"Same, same," she said, sipping now from her glass of coke. "Te te cold," she told him.

Most of the whores Deagle knew drank Coke warm. He called the barman over and asked for *nookdau*, which very much impressed Hoa. Waiting for ice cubes, he pushed his half-full glass of beer across to her and she tried to drink a little. She ended up laughing and coughing most of it up through her button nose. The barman brought ice and two napkins. Across the room, with the issue of who got the GI settled, the girls were back playing serious dice.

"You tau, you live Texas?" Hoa asked him.

"California."

"Cowafomya. Hot same same Vietnam."

"Yeah, down by Indio. When I was a kid my dad took me down there dove shooting and it was a hundred damn degrees in September."

Like all the working girls in Saigon and Long Binh, Hoa was really a secretary and her father and brother had been killed by the VC. She lived with her uncle in a suburb of the capitol city and was just visiting Sin City. Someday she wanted to live in America, maybe in a place like Texas or California. When she called the barman to the table to consummate the exchange of three hours time for $25 MPC, Deagle listened and wondered if the old man was her great grandfather. They disagreed about something, maybe the time. Hoa spoke to him with firmness, voice up and down the scale while she looked at the floor. The old man listened with his jaw ajar, a slice of dark eyes showing in unblinking lids. His answer was a shake of his head.

During the bargaining Deagle watched Hoa's face and learned more about his teenage prostitute. There was a tan line on her forehead from wearing a conical hat and working in the sun, maybe filling sandbags? The skin over her cheeks was absolutely smooth, not a blemish or freckle unlike his own imperfect skin. Her upper lip was as full as her lower. And she used her chin a lot when she talked so the little dimple there disappeared and reappeared. Finally she said something that made the old man glance at Deagle and nod his head. OK.

With business settled, Hoa was not in a hurry to leave the bar and Deagle understood why. It was not every day that a GI chose Hoa over Mimi, who was the number one horse in this stable. So Hoa showed off and he let her burn up some of his time telling stories of the people she knew in Saigon. Remembering all the bullet holes in the front of the "Hotel San Francisco" he asked Hoa when was the last time there was fighting in Sin City.

She shook her head. "Long time. But I live Saigon for sure. We go." Knowing Mimi was watching, she pulled Deagle to his feet and leaned against him. With her cheek against his chest she nuzzled her round left knee between his legs, and as they walked out she looked at Mimi and barked a single word that made her laugh.

He was 6' 4" and she was 4' 6". Hoa held onto his forearm as they strolled down the sunny street to her sleeping room. A gang of kids spotted them and walked parallel, shouting at Hoa in Vietnamese. They asked her if they could shine Deagle's nasty boots and starch his rumpled fatigues. Hoa was in charge. She waved them away and steered him into the residential hooches behind the flea market tables. A cackling group of mama-sans squatted in the shaded alley, and Deagle smelled turkey. Beyond the alley they entered another hooch and passed through canvas partitions to a small 8x8 room that was almost up against the security fence.

Without windows or a door, the sleeping room was dark and surprisingly cool, just four walls and a ceiling of black fabric stretched to wooden posts buried in the hard ground. Deagle wondered if the afternoon rain came through the roof. The back wall was left unattached to the floor, the stripe of sunlight peeking under it the room's only light source. The floor was green canvas with black and gold tiger throw rugs. Entering, Hoa took off her high heels and Deagle unlaced his boots. She walked across the room, a shimmer of green satin and shiny black hair. As his eyes adjusted, he saw a narrow neatly-made bed with white sheets and a small white pillow. Opposite the bed was a three-legged table, and on the table some white towels and a steel-pot sized bowl of water. In the table's only drawer was Hoa's mirror, a 12"x12" mirror tile. He undressed down to his dogtags and wristwatch and sat on the bed to enjoy Hoa's ceremony.

Smiling, she handed him her mirror to hold. She unzipped her green work dress and pulled it over her head, folded it neatly. She wore black bikini panties and a black, half bra. She folded his fatigues and stowed them under the bed with his boots. Facing him, she sat down on the floor, crossed her legs, and began removing her facial makeup with a moist towel. Close to the mirror, she daubed away the purple shadow from her eyelids and the red lipstick from her wide mouth. That done, she reached back and unhooked the black bra. Her breasts were small and upturned with a woman's large nipples. Still using her mirror, she brushed her hair to a blue-black sheen, wanting him to watch, until he put down the mirror and reached for her. His long right hand covered both her breasts, and she closed her eyes and breathed out through her child's nostrils. He tugged the black panties down and she lay beside him on the narrow bed.

The top of her head almost reached his chin. She kept her face hidden against his chest, small left hand warm on his hip. He heard rain spatter on the roof over his head. A tin roof, he thought idly. He rolled his long body over her short one, shining black hair on her breasts. He moved his weight to his knees and elbows to enter her but she smiled and reached down for him, saying "*te te* water." She was not yet lubricated. Her fingers were a teasing vice. He wanted to move down and kiss her nipples but she laughed softly and refused to let go. Finally she squirmed from under him and reversed their positions, ready, sitting on him. Eyes closed, dark hair falling forward, she joined them and began rocking very slowly. He felt the rough skin on the bottoms of her feet against his thighs. Hoa's small hips controlled the world, and down came the afternoon rain.

When he was finished she left the bed and came back wearing one of the white towels. She lay on top of him and he measured time by the sound of her breathing, the peppering rain on the roof, and the light slapping of the tent walls as the afternoon breeze picked up. She told him he had skinny long legs. He agreed. She had strong little hands and liked to use them to tickle. He let her. She rolled on her back and whispered there were things he must do. Not right now. Yes, right now. He used his hand to do some tickling himself, then his lips and teeth to make her nipples stand straight out. He propped his head on his elbow and looked into oval, mysterious eyes. She crossed her eyes and laughed. Then he held her eyes until she looked away. She tried tickling his ass but he stifled his smile. Finally the mischief left her eyes and she urged his hand to her breast. Now she didn't want to be tickled. Her acceptance was the quick flutter of eyelids, her quickened heart under his hand and her palms on the small of his back. He made love to her a second time without ever seeing her face, grinding her into the bed until she gave one sharp huff and went slack. Deago, there were things we must do.

She wrapped the towel around herself and pulled him to a sitting position on the bed. He climbed all the way to his feet and she scolded him again for being too tall for her small hooch. She insisted that he wobble on his skinny legs to the back wall, open the flap and walk to the fence. It was raining so hard he couldn't see the fence. Naked, he urinated a quart on a patch of weeds and dashed back inside, sopping, and Hoa waited with a towel. He sat on the bed and watched her squat above the helmet-sized bowl and clean herself with handfuls of water. Then with a sponge, clean water, and the most tender hands imaginable, she bathed him marine-style. He lay back down and lit a cigarette and sipped the warm bottom half of his Bommie Bom.

"Officah watch," Hoa said, stretching out beside him still in her white towel. She reached for his left wrist and rolled it over. She stared at the green and black face. "What time."

Nearly 3:00.

She took one of Deagle's dogtags and looked at the name and numbers. "You come back Sin City you be buttahfly?"

He blew a smoke-ring above her head and watched it break up against the black cloth wall. "Well... that Mimi is kind of pretty..."

She smacked him on the upper arm with the flat of her hand. "You boshit!"

"That's right, I boshit. Only like Hoa. Mimi is numbah eight... Hoa is... numbah one..."

Satisfied with his answer, she helped herself to a sip of his beer and made a face. "How old Mimi?" she asked. She held out five little fingers and flashed them eight times.

"Mimi is forty? Hoa you boshit... Mimi is old enough to be my mother?"

It took a second for that thought to sink in, but when it did she tossed her head and shrieked. Quickly she clapped a hand over her mouth and laughed with her eyes squeezed shut.

"Deago, no boshit, Mimi old..." She flashed five fingers five times. "And Hoa is.." and she opened and closed her hand four times.

"Hoa is twenty?"

225

"Twenny."

"No, Hoa is fifteen" and he flashed three times.

"Nnnnaaaoooowww. Hoa is…" three hands plus two fingers.

And Deagle is four hands plus two fingers.

She clinked his dogtags together. "You stay Sin City, $50 MPC all night, give full-time girl special present?"

She had his dogtags in her hand but she was looking at his Omega.

"I wish. Sergeant Trumpy's getting me a ride back to where I work."

"Sergeant Trumpy is big fat Santa Claus."

"Pretty good guy."

Her back was against his chest. With his left hand he reached into her towel and cupped her left breast. "I like Hoa."

"Nnnaaaooowwww. We talk now make lub later. You get pass."

"Can't."

Pouting, she wouldn't let him see her face but she allowed his hand on her breast. That was her Achilles heel, he decided. She liked her breasts touched.

"But I'll come back. Or we can meet in Saigon."

Suddenly she jumped off the bed and pulled the towel tight around her. She tossed her hair and pranced back and forth with an exaggerated thrust of hips and roll of shoulders. She was being Mimi, and she even had the voice pretty close. "…you lie GI, you buy me Saigon Tea gib Mimi $25 short-time… I go Saigon Mimi be your full-time girl!"

When he finished laughing, he said "I'm not butterfly. Hoa is much prettier than Mimi. I only want Hoa."

She stopped pacing but folded her arms. "Mimi get special present. Hoa get cheap Charlie."

"Okay. Come over here."

She sat on the bed with her arms, a brat.

"You to go back to Saigon and live with your uncle. Leave Sin City for good. How much MPC's to get you to Saigon."

Unimpressed, she stared at the wall and he studied the curvature of her right ear. "How much Hoa? I'm serious if you're serious."

Finally she said, "you come Saigon see me?"

"Affirmative… yes."

"OK, I go."

She went to his stack of clothes and dragged his wallet out of the back pocket and counted the MPC's but didn't take them. He had sixty-five MPC.

He plucked a twenty and a five and put the bills on the dressing table. He knew he was being conned but he didn't care. He didn't need any money on LZ Penny where cigarettes were free and beer was in oversupply.

She dropped the wallet and came back to the bed smiling. She crossed her eyes but he didn't laugh. Thinking that he'd made love to her twice and not yet kissed her, he pulled her down beside him and put his mouth on hers.

When he opened his eyes hers were crossed, and she laughed. When he still didn't laugh she took his hand and placed it on her breast. He leaned down to kiss her lips but she turned her face into his neck. Finally he got her face-to-face, eyes open, and placed a kiss on the corner of her mouth, another on her lower lip while she watched big-eyed. He covered her mouth with his and tried to show her, and for a few sweet seconds her eyes closed and her lips parted, but then she bit him and laughed again.

He rolled on his back and looked up. The rain on Hoa's roof was a consonant metallic rush. He closed his eyes.

1515Hours 24Dec71
1st Cav Div HQ
Hill 229

Wearing one satchel each, Tran and Nguyen force-marched down the trail and the rain drowned out all sound. Loc followed carrying the rifle. Through the elephant grass Nguyen held tightly to Tran's belt as they pushed down closer and closer to the bunkers and wire. Finally, Tran peeked through the grass and saw a blurred R&R barracks 2013. There were no soldiers outside. Tran sneaked close enough to the MP checkpoint to hear the rain pounding its metal roof. He watched it for a full minute. There was a guard inside.

Tran knew that he and Nguyen could sneak past the guard on the way down to deliver their bombs, but after the explosions the guard in the checkpoint would be the first to see them running away. Water dripped from Tran's dark hair as he eased his satchel off his shoulder. He looked at the road below the shack and saw no vehicles coming. He told Nguyen and Loc to wait for him.

He walked inside the tall brush as long as he could and then dashed to the south side of the shack and flattened himself. The guard's sliding window faced west, his door faced north. Drawing his knife, Tran dried its wooden handle and held it with the point forward. He put his ear to the side of the shack to listen for music, or, if his luck was very bad, conversation; perhaps there were two guards. But all he heard was rain smashing the tin roof. With a last glance at the barracks below he ducked under the west window, slipped under the gate, and put his left hand on the door-handle in case the guard should choose that exact moment to step outside. Again he listened and wiped the rain from his eyes. Did he dare try to peek through the window to see which way the guard was facing? No. Indecision yesterday had almost cost him his life, it was best to attack quickly. The door handle turned silently in his hand.

Tran flung the door open and threw himself in knife-point first. The guard sat in a chair with a book in his lap and barely had time to stand before Tran's knife drove into his stomach. The guard fell backward over his chair

227

and lost his helmet, but he scrambled to his feet. He saw Tran's knife coming at him and tried to block it with his hands. Too late. Tran thrust the knife up under the outstretched arms into the guard's chest. The guard shook violently and leaned against the wall. Looking up in his enemy's face, Tran cocked his elbow and shoved the knife hilt-deep into the guard's chest below the ribcage, into his beating heart. He jerked the blade free, ready to slash the soldier's throat to keep him from crying out, but it was finished. The guard's eyes bulged as he looked down at himself. His twitching right hand came up to cover all three wounds at once. Then life left his eyes and he fell soundlessly on the floor. Tran backed out and ran for the elephant grass. He found Nguyen and Loc where he'd left them and they stared at his bloody knife.

Tran led the way to the edge of the tall grass above R&R barracks 2013. Facing the two boys he pointed to his good ear: listen. Nguyen heard music. Tran looked at the sky, calculating how long the rain would last. No time to waste. There were no soldiers outside the barracks, none on the road or to the east. To Nguyen he pointed at the tall grass in the ditch between the first and second barracks. To Loc, he pointed at the rifle: stay here, watch, and cover. Now was the hardest part.

Tran and Nguyen crouched and ran between the checkpoint and the bunker to the outside wall of barracks 2013. They dropped and crawled to the drainage ditch, hidden by the tall weeds. Kneeling there, Nguyen listened to the rain splashing on the metal roofs and the music inside, and for the first time he felt fear along with his excitement. He watched Tran check his satchel charge and he did the same. The white tops of his C-4 explosive blocks were visible. Tran embedded the detonators and carefully placed the fuse wires, just those two inches sticking out. Nguyen wondered if they would burn wet.

Tran crawled away to his target, leaving Nguyen alone to wait. Just twenty feet from the barracks door, Nguyen was close enough to hear the soldiers talking inside. He was anxious to light his fuse and throw his bomb but Tran was not in position. Interminably, he waited, glowering dark eyes going back and forth between the two barracks. He watched for soldiers coming between the barracks, and he double-checked the road below the checkpoint. He looked again at the number of the barracks, 2013. Was it good luck or bad luck that the door was partially open. Good luck, he decided. Number 2014 further down the ditch was Tran's, and that door was closed. Rain rolled off his bare head and sheeted in his eyes, as he waited for Tran to show himself.

Suddenly he saw Tran's head above the grass, saw him jump up and make his dash to the corner of the barracks and flatten himself. Making eye contact, Tran waved for Nguyen to do the same. Nguyen ducked and ran until he felt the wood against his back. He pulled the satchel off his shoulder, light as a feather. Once around the corner he and Tran would not see each other again until after the charges were thrown, so now the timing had to be exactly as they had agreed. Tran pointed at his watch, now, and moved toward his target, out of sight. It was time for Nguyen to move and he looked down at the second hand on his watch. He had thirty seconds.

He slid along the wall and with just his left eye he peeked into the open door. Ten feet away he a soldier's green legs and black boots hanging over the end of a bed. There was a magazine on the floor. Down the hall there was another sleeping soldier, and past them a large group of five or six in a row sleeping. He had to throw his satchel at least that far. Remembering Tran's instruction to "do exactly as I do" he brought out his waterproof Zippo lighter and flicked it once, twice. Fifteen seconds.

The second hand on his watch ticked down to five seconds. Reminding himself not to hurry, he held the flame to the fuse until it hissed. He hip-hopped into the open doorway and hurled the satchel down the middle of the aisle. He saw it land on its side and spin once on the concrete before he turned and ran the wrong way.

To get clear of the blasts, the plan was to run toward the wire and then right to the checkpoint. In a panic, Nguyen ran toward the next row of barracks before he caught himself and reversed. Half blind from the rain, arms pumping and knees churning, he made it past barracks 2013 and saw Tran already at the wire and coming toward him. The rain stung his eyes and a voice behind him shouted "Hey!" A shirtless GI stepped out of a barracks below and watched them run, an astonished look on his face. Then Tran's satchel charge blew up barracks 2014.

It came as a flat, deafening "BAM" and a simultaneous whoosh of warm wind. Pieces of wooden siding blew out behind Tran, striking his back and legs. But he kept running for the checkpoint. An instant later came the second explosion, behind Nguyen. The deafening roar and rush was so close it knocked Nguyen forward off his feet. Dazed, he lay on his belly unable to move until suddenly Tran was there freeing his legs and arms from the sharp wire. They ran together for the safety of the elephant grass above the checkpoint. When they reached the tall grass Tran allowed the boy ten seconds to look back and see what they had done.

Barracks 2013 had a truck-sized smoking hole in the south wall. Pieces of beds and barracks siding were scattered to the bunker. Two crumpled green bodies lay on the ground. Further away, barracks 2014 had an even bigger hole in its side, and part of its roof had blown out. There were green-clad shapes on the ground inside and outside the barracks. One tried to crawl away.

As he stared at the destruction, Nguyen's face was a defiant snarl.

"You did well," Tran told him. "Now we go up and wait for the others."

"Let the soldiers try to find us!" he spat.

But Tran turned and started up the hill, leaving the chaos in the R&R detachment behind him. Nguyen heard the soldiers shouting and the siren that began with a low growl and climbed to shrill, repeating bleats. He looked up. The rain had stopped.

Deagle's eyelids rolled open. Seeing the darkened hooch and low canvas ceiling, for two heartbeats he didn't remember where he was. But Hoa's scented dark hair and steady breathing told him. She was neatly folded in a fetal ball with her head on his chest, left arm flung across his belly. He thought she was asleep but when he looked down he saw that her eyes were wide open. The rain tapped the corrugated tin with a spastic rap-tap... tap rap... almost over. It was getting close to departure time from Sin City. After the tapping on the roof stopped completely he heard something else, a faint ringing in his ears.

After playing grab-ass and wrestling to get her out of her white towel he had made love to Hoa for the last time. There had been no urgency, no ceremony, only the passing of time and bringing pleasure. He still had no idea if this sixteen year old enjoyed him or if her sudden shivers and huffs were part of the service. He wondered if she knew herself, and how many times she had practiced it. But it didn't matter.

There was that sound again in his ears. A very thin, very far off, intermittent horn. In his head? No. Outside. He rolled his wrist over and glanced down at the Omega, almost 4:30. For some reason he thought about Pomeroy and Grossnickel in the R&R detachment. He wondered if Cleve made that call to his folks or chickened out again.

Hoa hitched a little closer, eyes wide open as if she knew his thoughts by his heartbeat.

"Time to go," he whispered. "Papa-san will have the ass."

She was sluggish, petulant. "You stay," she told him. "Get pass."

He ran his fingertips down her lean, smooth spine, touching each spinal bump, then down to her round little globes, which he could almost span with one long-fingered hand. Her butt felt papery dry, a few goosebumps popped up as his hand settled between her warm thighs. 4:29. Then that sound again. He closed his eyes and listened hard. Not a hum. More like a stuck automobile horn traveling on the wind.

He threw his long legs off the bed and sat up, listening. Hoa's expression was blank.

"Am I freaking out? What the hell is that?"

Avoiding his eyes, she crawled out of bed and walked to her dressing table. She quickly got into her black bra and panties and began putting on her work face.

"You not get pass, Hoa go back to work."

Naked, he opened the flap and let sunlight into the hooch. Standing outside by the fence he urinated again and listened but the sound had disappeared. Back in the hooch Hoa squatted and sullenly applied her eye makeup in the little square mirror tile. She glanced at him in her mirror as he dragged on his shorts and fatigue pants, and he felt the weight of his wallet in his back pocket.

Then he heard them again. Horn blatts, but not a horn either, more a like a siren. The perimeter siren. He buttoned his fatigue shirt quickly, laced up his jungle boots. He eyed Hoa suspiciously as she mechanically applied lipstick. He had heard no in-coming. Sappers.

"You know what that sound means?" he asked her.

She didn't answer. Instead she pulled herself into her tight green dress.

"Sure you do. That's where the papa-sans went. Goddamn it."

Her faced clouded up and she stomped her feet. "No!"

He glanced at his watch again. "I gotta get back."

"No!"

Angry, he checked his belongings; watch, dogtags, pocket knife, compass. He stuffed his boonyhat on his head. "I hate your fucking country," he told her. "I hate it."

"You go GI! You boshit!" She snatched up her $25 MPC.

"Guess I won't see you in Saigon... that was all bullshit too."

He ducked under the flap and left her, walking quickly into the junk-littered alley to get as far away from the fence and the jungle as he could. Wary now, he headed for the main street looking for GI activity. Ahead of him the MP shack was empty. The women selling watches and cat-eye rings were gone. But Sin City wasn't totally deserted, the gang of kids that had been watching Hoa's hooch emerged on his right and started running to catch up with his long strides. He followed the bend of the road and saw the nose of Trumpy's deuce-and-a half. Relieved Trumpy hadn't left him he turned to face the hoard of beggars gaining behind him.

"No, boy-san. You di di!" They stopped and stared.

He turned and walked again and the kids followed. They shouted for MPC's. Some of them ran around in front to block him, faces intent and hands out stretched. Ahead, Deagle saw PFC Pine standing by the truck, laughing at him.

"You hear that siren?" Deagle hollered at him over the din of the children.

"What siren?"

The swarm of children blocked his way to the truck. He'd have to go through them or over them. At the point of putting all his stuff back in his boonyhat again he heard a woman's voice behind him, a single sharp command. He turned around and saw Hoa coming up the street.

In her tall heels, black hair flying, Hoa charged into the crowd and delivered a solid slap to the butt of one of the older boy-sans. Open-mouthed, he turned and stared at her, then he dodged away as she tried to grab his arm. Telling the other boys to di di, she caught one by the ear and twisted until he cried out. Another got a sharp-toed kick on his little rear and whined at her, but he backed off. In a few seconds she had the street cleared.

She looked up at Deagle and handed him his $5 MPC. Across the face the bill he saw a child's big handwriting.

"You come Saigon find Hoa. Deago."

Backing, he smiled and whipped one of his wristy salutes. She raised a hand to her painted eyebrow. He walked to the truck and asked Pine where Trumpy was.

"I seen it but I don't believe it," he said, watching Hoa. "That whore chased them kids away for you."

"You can't hear that perimeter siren?"

"Good-looking bitch. I think I had her once. What?"

Deagle dropped the tailgate of the truck and looked in, everything was packed and ready to go. But there were no M-16's in the truck. He slammed the gate closed and looked around for Trumpy. He found the motorpool NCOIC sitting bare-chested in a lounge chair, in the humid shade of his young mama-san's hooch.

"Hey, sarge! Listen up!"

Master Sergeant Trumpy cocked an ear and then quickly threw on his fatigue shirt. Deagle looked at his watch again. 1637.

"Hurry, sarge," he told Trumpy, and all he could think about was Pomeroy and Grossnickel in the R&R detachment.

"Pine, move your ass!" Trumpy commanded. "I'm drivin'!"

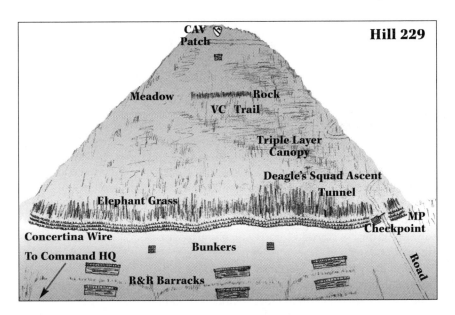

CHAPTER TEN

1620Hours 24Dec 71
1st Cav Div HQ
Reception Desk, Div Sgt Major Bierra

The first explosion slapped the south wall of division HQ and Sergeant Major Bierra lifted his head, thinking in-coming. He heard a window rattle as the second jolt of the double-concussions left the metal roof thrumming. He stood, watching the ceiling. In the hall behind him there were shouts and footsteps running in the corridor. After remembering to trip the base siren, his next clear thought was to double-time to the basement bunker; *sounded like mortars, probably more coming.* Then he thought about his application for a direct commission: better check on his commanding general before hauling ass.

He double-timed instead to the staff door and yanked it open. He saw the support clerks crowded in the hall, looking up, faces stiffened by panic. He ran past them and turned for the east briefing room and spotted General Webb standing in a huddle with Colonel's Borg and Wilcox. Webb carried a steel pot and wore a pistol belt with a .45 semi-auto hanging from it. Sp6 Meredith came running toward them wearing an ANPRC-25 radio on his back. Bierra straightened and reported to Borg as the in-coming siren built from low growls to shrill, full-throated shrieks.

"Could be the in-transit area, sergeant major," Borg said tightly. "Set up your desk in the reception room as command center, nobody and I mean

233

nobody gets past you! Colonel Shipp will be in the east briefing room and will co-ordinate communication. Stand by for my voice until we have a call-sign."

"Is everybody alright, sir? Do you need me to..."

"I need you doing your job at that command desk, ASAP!"

"Roger, sir."

In a steel helmet with a single star on it, Webb looked different to Sergeant Major Bierra, younger somehow, and he realized he and Webb were about the same age. He'd never seen a CG in combat gear, except in the movies. Webb charged past him to the outer door and threw it open, leaving Colonel Borg and RTO Meredith to catch up.

Webb sprinted south to Hill 229 and then west parallel with the concertina wire. He saw the smoke cloud in the R&R detachment from two hundred meters and was the first officer to reach barracks 2014. He raced toward a crowd of startled troops who glimpsed the star on his helmet and threw up salutes.

"Get away from that barracks!" he shouted at them. "You men spread out! Move! Spread out!" It would not be the first time Charles threw a satchel charge into a small crowd in order to draw a bigger crowd.

Then he saw the big gap in the sandbag flakwall, like a burst dam, and behind it the monstrous hole in the south flank of 2014. Inside the broken wall, a GI with both legs blown off screamed as two others tried to move him. Behind them a naked, headless torso, legs still twitching, lay in a pool of blood on the concrete floor. A third soldier lay on his back where the aisle had been; he was alive and writhing, arms mangled and his upper body and face bloody. Webb ran to him and leaned down in time to watch him shiver once, and die. He looked up the steep face of Hill 229. Whoever did this was only a few meters away, maybe still watching. He reached down and drew out his pistol.

"Son of a bitch!"

Webb turned and saw Borg's horrified expression, looking west. He sprang to his feet and dashed through a second crowd of on-lookers to the center of R&R 2013, another washed-out flakwall and torpedo-holed barracks. He peered inside the splintered wall and winced; more of his troops down. A group of a half-dozen wild-eyed survivors stood near the west door. Right and left of the ragged hole, where the barracks wall had withstood the blast, pieces of siding, bunk-frames lockers and uniform debris were piled like a beaver dam. He ducked outside and looked up at Hill 229 where the sappers had to have gone. His eyes panned east-to-west across the elephant grass. Fifty meters away he saw the open door of the checkpoint shack.

"Listen up!" Webb yelled. "You men double-time to the arms room, draw M-16s, and get back here! Move out!" Two full squads of soldiers snapped out of it and sprinted down the road.

Webb stepped back from R&R 2013 to take in the horrific totality of the attack. Two barracks hit, six of his men down, at least three KIA.

"Sir, perhaps you should be on the other side of the barracks," Borg told him, glancing at the hill.

Webb tasted the cold bitterness of command failure. Motion drew his eyes back through the hole in the barracks wall. A soldier crawled toward him with one arm dragging behind him leaving a blood trail on the concrete. Too much blood. Webb saw that his right leg was gone from the knee down. He walked quickly to him and knelt beside him.

"Take it easy, son. Try not to move."

The boy looked up at him, and the single star on his collar. "Get to my rifle, sir..."

The soldier's shattered right arm was trapped under him. Webb gently rolled him and freed the arm, and it was like handling a sock packed with rocks. The boy's face was ghost white and his eyes were glazed. He was shivering and going into shock fast.

"Medic!" He stood and snatched the nearest troop by his fatigue shirt. "Soldier, you stay with this man until the medic arrives. Elevate that leg to stop the bleeding, understand? This is your post, soldier! Don't you leave it!"

"Yes, sir!"

He sensed his own dry mouth and numbing sluggishness. Shock, the great disabler. He forced his eyes to look at what was left of Barracks 2013. Pieces of bunks and wall lockers tossed, a scorched shallow hole in the concrete floor that had been ground zero, and a chunk of roof hanging down. He heard the siren in the background, feeling more anger than sorrow. Borg handed him the radio.

"Webb!" he barked.

"Sergeant Major Bierra, sir. Standing by for your orders."

"Any other contact?"

"Negative, sir."

"We need medics ASAP. Call Big Ben and tell them we have two barracks hit, at least a dozen WIA's. Then call the air force wing commanders. Tell them we had sappers. Tell them they are on Hill 229 and to bring up as many men as it takes to control the base. I want that hill cordoned, you read?"

"Roger, sir. Anything else?"

He looked away from the jagged hole in 2013 to the middle of Hill 229. "Sergeant major, I want you to locate one-each special forces officer and have him report to me at the R&R detachment. I recall that we couldn't even police up a certain 7th Brigade buck sergeant yesterday... so you bust ass and get it done! I want a green beret standing tall in front of me in three zero minutes! No excuses!"

"No, sir! I mean yes, sir!"

Webb handed the receiver back to Meredith as a pasty-faced Colonel Borg approached. "Got two medics so far, sir. The air force is also sending medical specialists. Their side wasn't hit."

From Webb's left a pair of GI's came running toward him shouting and pointing behind them. "Sir! They got the MP!"

Still holding his blood-flecked .45 pistol, Webb ran toward the checkpoint. He reached the end of barracks 2013 and glanced down the admin street, and saw his platoon of reinforcements coming at the dead run with rifle-slings clacking and magazines rattling. He waved for them to take cover behind the barracks. The checkpoint door was wide open. He studied the jungle above the shack, thick enough to hide a whole squad of sappers. A young buck sergeant crouched and ran forward. With one .45 pistol and one M-16 rifle between them, he and the sergeant advanced on the shack. Angling up, Webb saw blood and rainwater dripping over the threshold. He saw the helmet-less MP slumped against the back wall. The wooden floor of the shack was still wet with the killer's small footprints.

Webb closed the door and looked up. Visualizing Major Andrews' map, he knew there was a garbage dump near the bottom of Hill 229 on its west side, somewhere behind this checkpoint. He waved for his platoon to follow and led the way across the road as he studied the jungle on his left. A crowd of GIs behind the finance branch stood gawking: those sappers hadn't gone in that direction, west. Past finance, south of the hospital detachment, was the road into to the dump. According to the map the road was routinely defoliated and mine-swept but the dump itself it was as wild as Hill 229. The road going into the dump was tactically part of the hill's west slope.

"Sergeant, call those men into a squad formation."

When it was done he looked into the young faces in front of him. They were R&R troops, experienced infantrymen but perhaps seeing rear-area terrorism for the first time. Some were plainly scared and others looked eager for a fight.

"You men listen up. The Viet Cong who blew our barracks and killed our MP are still on the hill. It's important that they stay on the hill. We can't allow them to sneak past us at the garbage dump." Checking collar pins, Webb saw that he had two buck sergeants and the rest were Sp4s and PFCs. "You, sergeant, lead these men to the dump access road. Run, and I mean double-time, to the dump. Pick three men and block that road going in and out. Get as high up as you can. Take the rest of the men and set up a blockade where the hill drops down to the dump. Look for trails. Keep at least a five-meter spacing with yourself in the center. You stay there until we call you in. As soon as I can I'll send radios and call signs to both of you. Go! go! go!"

The troops moved out with a metallic rush as more combat-ready riflemen struggled up the road from the arms room. A jeep-load of medics from Big Ben hospital threaded its way between them, turning left at barracks 2013. Webb strode quickly back across the road to direct the medics, and Colonel Borg approached wearing an apology on his face.

"Sir, I'm sorry. We moved the boy to the GR Point."

Webb looked around for a lieutenant, any lieutenant, and spotted MP Branch 2nd Lieutenant Fredrick.

"Lieutenant, get over here!"

"Yes, sir!" Fredrick stood at inspection distance holding up a salute until Webb snapped one off.

Webb pointed at the troops running up the road. "I want you to deploy those men, ASAP! Two in every bunker between here and the dump. I want two troops at each end of R&R 2013 and 2014 until the MPs get here, nobody but medics allowed in. Round up some senior NCOs and empty all R&R and DEROS barracks by 1800 hours; then cordon the area with walking posts. Move the in-transits into whatever barracks you have to. After the medics move out with our WIA's, deploy your MP's with orders to maintain R&R and DEROS as a secure area until further notice: no officers below the rank of captain, no enlisted, and no curious civilians. And I want a GI sandbag detail to begin repairing those flakwalls. How do you read, Lieutenant?"

"5x5, sir."

"Then move out!"

Watching Hill 229 all the way, Webb walked beside R&R 2013 and turned the corner, where Specialist Meredith had set up a hasty command post with the Prick-25. There, a dozen admin captains and lieutenants stood woodenly by until one of them screamed "ten HUT!" as Webb approached. He ignored them and grabbed the radio. After a short briefing from his division sergeant major he banged the radio down and walked to the make-shift GR point alongside a weedy ditch. There were five green body bags, so far.

"How in the hell did we let this happen," he said softly.

"Poor S-2," Borg told him bitterly. "After yesterday's sweep… I didn't think this could happen. I have no explanation, sir."

"Well, we better figure it out goddamn quick, colonel! Charles hits once, he hits twice."

The words stung. As did Borg's realization that he'd learned less about Hill 229 in sixteen months than Jeff Webb had guessed in a week. And there was going to be hell to pay now. He ordered Sp6 Meredith to get hold of Colonel Geary at the motorpool for an update on Major Andrews, and waited for his answer. Geary, in shock himself, told Meredith that Andrews and the admin jeep were still AWOL.

"Excuse me, sir," Borg heard behind him.

He looked around and found a short, fire-plug shaped young green beret major looking up at him.

"Sir, Major Allen Eiler. Sergeant Major Bierra asked me to report to you. Sir, should we move the commanding general back out of sniper range from Cav mountain?"

Cav mountain. Borg cursed the name. Not anymore it wasn't.

The young major wore his classic slanted green headgear over his whitewall haircut. He wore camo jungle fatigues and brightly polished garrison boots. Major Allen Eiler inspired immediate confidence. Meredith handed him the phone again. "The sergeant major again, sir."

"What now!"

Bierra's voice sounded strange. He said he had Staff Sergeant Hooper standing in front of his desk. Hooper had Hill 229 intelligence that Borg had to hear for himself. He added that the six west-coast reporters on base had learned of the sapper attack and were on their way to the reception room. Borg told him to keep them there.

Still too numb to think clearly, Borg walked the special forces officer to where Webb looked down at his fallen cavalrymen. Eiler snapped one up and held it, but Webb's return salute was merely formal.

"Major, please stand by," Webb said. "You're not going to get much sleep tonight."

"Yes, sir. Whatever the commanding general needs... will be done. There are about a dozen of us on base at this time, sir."

"Just enough," Webb answered.

Borg whispered into Webb's ear that one of their AWOL's had surrendered himself, Hooper.

"I think that horse has left the barn, colonel."

"And the press will be in the reception room soon. We'll need a statement for them."

Webb continued to stare at the green hill.

Borg followed his eyes to the elephant grass, looking for the glint of a gunbarrel from the evening sun. "Sir, you can manage this situation better from the east briefing room. Why don't we see what Hooper has to say?"

Webb turned and led the way. "Now we're on offense, colonel."

1650Hours 24Dec71
1st Cav Div HQ
Headquarters Motorpool

Sergeant Trumpy drove the two-and-half-ton truck with the accelerator mashed to the floorboard, thankful the rain had stopped. Leaving Sin City there was no traffic but at forty-five miles per hour the dirt road was treacherous, greasy and polk-a-dotted with water-filled chuckholes. He heard his field kitchen rolling around on the truck bed. Once on the panoprimed highway and approaching the air force AO he ran into a convoy of vehicles that clogged both lanes. On his left squads of airmen raced to guard posts around the fuel farms and runways. Armored personnel carriers formed a menacing perimeter around the diesel depots, with their .50 caliber machines pointed west and north.

"Looks like the invasion of Bien Hoa has finally come," he said.

From his side of the truck, Deagle watched the division artillery batteries being manned and rotated toward the perimeter. Just a precaution, he thought. Infantry units like his own 2nd of 7th needed those batteries for support fire. A convoy of deuce-and-a-halfs headed for the perimeter roared past, right behind it a pair of command jeeps crammed with looies. Trumpy dropped down from second gear to first as the motorpool fence came into view on his right.

Down to five miles an hour behind the convoy, Trumpy suddenly braked hard and slipped the gearshift into neutral. "Pine, take the wheel! Sarn't Deagle, you come with me!"

They jumped down from the truck and quick-stepped toward the open gate where an admin Sp6 directed truck traffic in and out. In front of Geary's office a group of officers in flakjackets smoked cigarettes, waiting for their vehicles. Trumpy looked around for Colonel Geary and found him on the top step.

"What was it, sir, 60 mike-mike's?"

"Sappers. They hit R&R. We have casualties." Standing a full head taller than Sergeant Trumpy, Deagle was conspicuous and Colonel Geary read his nametag.

Deagle stuck out his hand to Trumpy.

"Sarge, thanks for the offer of a ride but I got to get up to the GR point."

"GR point?"

"Graves Registration," Colonel Geary answered, watching Deagle. "Sergeant Deagle, my congratulations on earning a second Silver Star."

Deagle spotted the oak leaves on Geary's collar and saluted. "Thank you, sir. Okay if I hustle up to R&R? I've got buddies there, sir."

"I'll run you up in my vehicle."

Geary pulled Trumpy into the relative calm of his office.

"I assume you know about Major Andrews?"

"Yes, sir. Pretty damn strange."

"You assume command here. If Andrews shows his face with my jeep... you stick a .45 against that skin graft of his and put him under arrest. If he resists, you have the authority to shoot him. How do you read?"

"5x5, sir. What the hell did he do?"

"According to Bud Bierra, he had proof there were sappers on 229-er and kept it to himself. God only knows why."

Geary watched Deagle throw on his rucksack and pistol belt. "Sergeant Trumpy, tell me about Staff Sergeant Stevens. What happened to his face?"

"Stevens, sir?"

"Don't give me that look. Until an hour ago Stevens was chained up in the admin arms room with a deserter."

"Stevens is a head case, he belongs in chains."

"Well, he knows something about the other head case, Major Andrews. So he's up at HQ talking about yourself and a buck sergeant named Deagle?"

Trumpy grinned. "There was a disagreement, sir. Sergeant Stevens assaulted a senior NCO, namely myself, and Sarn't Deagle there had to adjust his attitude a couple times with the butt of an M-16. Deagle looks skinny but he's wiry."

"In an hour the whole base will know what happened to Stevens' face but keep it to yourself for now. And Andrews."

"Can do, sir."

Geary's personal jeep rolled up to the gate and he jumped behind the wheel, Deagle on the passenger side. As they spun up the admin street Deagle saw more combat troops on the road. He scanned the squads for one-each size small uniform and one-each size double extra-large, no Grossnickel or Pomeroy. Geary gunned the jeep past the admin CP up to the checkpoint shack, stomped the brake, and swung hard behind R&R barracks 2013. He parked between the gaping hole in the barracks wall and the first roll of concertina wire. Deagle stared. It was the first time he'd seen a satchel charge used on barracks. Two hundred feet east, barracks 2014 looked even worse. Sappers.

A military policeman with an M-16 informed Colonel Geary that Sergeant Deagle was not authorized inside the cordon. "Unless he's stacking sandbags, sir."

"What names," Geary asked him, stuffing on his helmet.

"Pomeroy Cleveland, Corporal E4, and Grossnickel James, PFC. Thank you, sir."

"Wait right here."

He leaned his butt against the hood of the jeep and lit a smoke. There were a dozen barracks designated as 1st Cav R&R Detachment and he didn't know which one Pomeroy and Grossnickel were assigned to. The odds were strongly against losing both his best friends to sappers, but he had a sick feeling in his stomach and a metallic taste in his mouth. Such a rotten way to get hit, sleeping in a bunk in a rear area. Looking at shattered 2013 and 2014, he knew somebody got hit. But if there was a God in heaven it wasn't Pomeroy or Grossnickel.

If there was a God in heaven. How many times had he and Pomeroy talked about God? For sure, every time somebody got hit. They talked about God after Sergeant Harvey got hit. Deagle was an FNG back then and blamed Harvey's death on the math, the odds not the gods, too many bullets streaming through their patrol position and one had to find somebody. But Pomeroy insisted God was watching because he was twice as big a target as Harvey and he'd been standing right behind the platoon sergeant with the Prick-25 on his back. Pomeroy heard the bullet hit Harvey. A month later, the 2nd Battalion's newest buck sergeant, proudly wearing his new chevrons on his collar, became more inclined to Pomeroy's way of thinking when a one-shot Charley put a bullet through 2nd Lieutenant Strauss' neck, just above the black bar on his collar. Deagle heard that bullet hit Strauss. He was a head taller than Strauss and fifteen feet in front of him when the rifle cracked. The sniper who got the 2nd looey had passed on the buck sergeant. Maybe God was involved, but just the same Deagle never again wore his chevrons on patrol.

Deagle field-stripped the burnt stub of his cigarette, then the filter, letting the fine white strands slip through his long fingers. He thought about never seeing Cleve Pomeroy or Jimmy Fuck-knuckle alive again, and who he would blame for that. How could any divine plan include those two guys getting blown away... short, on R&R, in a safe area, taking a nap... God's presence seemed doubtful, God's existence seemed doubtful. Deagle closed his eyes and said a short prayer to Jesus Christ instead, but there was no satisfaction in it and no resonance that anybody was listening. When he looked at 2013 again he felt anger and the urge to avenge. An eye for an eye.

Geary came striding back, eyes on the ground ahead of him and his expression troubled. "Negative," he said, climbing in behind the wheel. "But one KIA doesn't have dog tags." He stared at Deagle. "Yesterday during the sweep, did you happen to meet admin sergeant named Hooper?"

"Yes, sir. Good NCO. I guess Major Andrews dropped the ball."

Geary drove east across a base in full alert status. Headquarters 1st Cavalry Division resembled a motorpool, there were so many vehicles parked around it. Geary yanked the door open and marched into a reception room full of army and air force officers, Red Cross and medical personnel, and the American news media. Geary pushed through the crowd to the reception desk and a cameraman caught him with a bar of bright lights. SFC Grasso jumped out of his chair.

Deagle stood beside Geary. The desk plaque read "Division Sergeant Major Albert Bierra", a name he'd had seen on 1st Cav paperwork.

Geary leaned over the desk and whispered for Grasso to call Colonel Borg, tell him he had Sergeant William Deagle with him. Seconds later Geary and Deagle passed through the door behind Bierra's desk into a long corridor, and Deagle recognized the pot-bellied officer with the big ears, Borg, at the far end. Escorted by the two colonels, Deagle entered the small briefing room.

It was a war room with topo maps, blanketed windows, and a whole squad of Prick-25's and telephones. A sergeant with a dark pompadour haircut and a big black diamond in his chevrons sat watching him; Division Sergeant Major Bierra, the highest non-com in the Cav. Behind Bierra sat red-nosed Staff Sergeant Hooper, looking glad to see him, and fat-lipped Sergeant Stevens, sneering. On the opposite side of the room were three officers, an owl-faced light colonel, a full bird colonel with a handlebar mustache, and a tall brigadier general wearing a steel pot and .45 sidearm. Division Commander Webb, the highest ranking officer in the Cav.

Deagle came to the position of attention with his rifle still at sling arms, eyes straight ahead, as Webb approached. The general was exactly as tall as himself.

"Thank you, Colonel Geary," he said. He looked Deagle over. "Stand at ease, sergeant. My congratulations on your second SSM. Sometime I would like to hear about them."

Deagle brought his rifle down off his shoulder and spread his boots apart. He glanced at the ashen-faced Hooper. On the desk behind the commanding general he noticed a full-color map of Hill 229.

"Sergeant Major Bierra," Webb said, "grab yourself some chow and assume your command desk. Then stand by because tonight you're going to be my RTO. Sergeant Stevens, you are confined to quarters, move out."

"Yes, sir."

After the two enlisted men left the room Webb fixed his eyes on Deagle. "Sergeant, tell me about a VC you saw yesterday afternoon and a souvenir you gave to Sergeant Hooper."

1730Hours 24Dec71
1st Cav Div HQ
Admin Branch Enlisted Barracks

Telling the others the suspense was killing him, Vinny grabbed his steel pot and M-16 and stepped into the darkening hallway. Every door was locked and there were guards at both ends of his barracks. The guard at the west end heard him coming and turned around, it was morning report Sp4 Teal in steel pot and flak vest.

"Who goes there?" he whispered.

"Who goes there? Jesus Teal, Ho Chi Minh goes there."

"Vinny. I thought Ho was dead. You on one of the alert rosters?"

"Nah. Too short. I just want to see what's happening."

They stood together on the top step looking across the admin AO. The guard in the barracks across the ditch waved at them.

Vinny said. "Wow. Not a creature was stirring not even a mouse."

"Yeah, some Merry Christmas huh? I hear there's R&R guys laying around dead everywhere. We got a bunch of MR entries 'Change from R&R to KIA'. Can you imagine the Christmas cards from Uncle Sam: 'Merry Christmas, we are so sorry to inform you your son is dead...'"

Vinny looked at Teal, realizing the kid was actually scared. It was probably his first turn as a barracks guard in a real alert. "What's the password and counter-sign?"

Teal glanced at him. "We don't do that stateside bullshit... do we?"

"Nah. Who's the sergeant-of-the-guard?"

"Grasso."

"An E-7? Come off it..."

"It's Grasso. He's up at HQ."

"Grasso's sitting at Bierra's desk? Well, I'm gonna go talk to that p'aisson."

"You ain't supposed to be walking around. You're gonna get shot…"

"Nah. I'm too short to get shot."

He walked straight south up the slope toward the next barracks and recognized the EOB Sp5 standing in the doorway with his M-16 at port arms.

"Hey, Smitty, what's the password?"

Smith grinned. "Password is Kelo India Alpha, troop. KIA. Which is what you're gonna be if you don't get your ass back in the barracks."

Vinny passed in front of him and kept walking. In the next barracks he saw one of Brennan's smoking buddies on the barracks porch in a steel pot and flak vest. He gave him a wave with his rifle and joined him on the porch. "Spooky, huh."

Sp4 Fernandez shrugged. "Don't know why I'm guardin' this fuckin' barracks, man. It's empty. They're all at the perimeter. Lifer games."

Fernandez' dark eyes were wide and alert, for a change he wasn't stoned. Vinny looked past him at the dark profile of Hill 229 a dozen barracks further up. "First time we've had sappers since I been here," he said. "Almost two years. We had lots of in-coming but no sappers."

"So how come everybody's at the perimeter?" Fernandez pointed out.

"SOP," Vinny answered. "Like when we take in-coming we head for the bunkers."

Ten minutes later Vinny reached the R&R detachment, cordoned off and guarded by a squad of MP's, all floodlights on. Barracks 2013 was empty, and Vinny had not prepared himself for the reason why it was empty. Through the open west door, he saw greenish bright light pouring through an oval-shaped hole in south wall, and pieces of screening hanging down that threw a jailhouse shadow across the concrete floor. There was a four-foot wide crater in the floor. Broken bunks were piled like kindling. The MP told him it was the same story at 2014, big damage, all R&R troops moved out and gone. Looking right, he saw the third target the sappers had hit, the checkpoint shack. The door was closed and there was a light on. How'd you like to be that MP tonight, he thought.

With strange spring in his legs Vinny walked east and then north to 1st Cav HQ. The parking lot was full of jeeps but the sidewalk was empty. He opened the door and peeked inside and saw SFC Grasso in the center of a group of brass and civilians. Thinking fast, he opened his wallet and brought out his souvenir copy of his 2nd set of R&R orders to Australia. He slung his M-16 and closed the door behind him, and walked through the crowd to the NCOIC's desk.

"'Scuze me. At ease there, ma'am, message for Sergeant Grasso. 'Scuze me."

"Vincent what are you doing here," the slender Italian NCO demanded.

He waved his orders. "Roster for you sarge. Personal delivery from Sergeant Trumpy."

Grasso edged away from the division sergeant major's desk. When he unfolded the R&R order and read it he glared down at Vincent. "You little guinea fuck. What are you doin' to me."

"So what's going on?"

He threw a glance behind him, listening for the phone. "I'm CQ at the division sergeant major's desk in a red alert; you want to get me busted? Get the hell outa here!"

Vinny grinned. "You know, I remember being head honcho at senior enlisted records for a couple days. I proofed this one senior NCO 201 file, and I see where there's an old order missing from 1963 and where somebody tried to erase an old secondary MOS. This senior NCO didn't want to go to the field, imagine that? Sergeant Grasso, can you guess a) whose 201 that was and b) what was his secondary MOS?"

Grasso took Vinny by the shoulders and moved him further away from the desk crowded with visitors. "You pick now to hit me with this?"

"Timing is everything. Relax. Just tell me what's going on"

He glanced back at the closed support staff door. "All I can tell you is... our new CG has a case of the ass. He's got the green berets back there and some buck sergeant who saw those gooks yesterday. What's goin on is called... 'night ambush' and I'm glad it ain't me."

"Buck sergeant?"

"Goofy name, Beagle or something. Three squads are going up, two of 'em are green berets."

"Holy shit."

"You keep that to yourself. You and me are even so get the hell outa here."

"They're sending Deagle up there again because he knows where Charles is."

"He's used to it. He's a grunt."

Vinny walked back to his barracks too preoccupied with his thoughts to notice the guards eyeballing him. He knew the route from walking it a thousand times, past the ERB building, across the empty football courtyard, along the beaten trail back to the enlisted records branch barracks. His mind was a jumble. He had nineteen days left in Vietnam but suddenly there was no exhilaration in being short. He'd written his parents to expect him home this time, hopefully reassigned to Fort Dix, New Jersey, where he would have ten months of stateside duty before getting out of the army. Ten months of hell. Inspections, police calls, formations, confinement on base, ignorant NCOs, stiff-assed officers. Plus bivouac, forced marches, rifle practice, PT, and all the other pretend war games. After two tours of Vietnam. He might cop an attitude like Brennan: what are you guys gonna do if I don't pick up cigarette butts... send me to Vietman? No Vinny, we'll put you in the brig.

On the other hand, he thought, what if I extend again? Skelton would offer me E6 again and maybe I'll take it. Save some more combat pay in accrual, get another R&R in Australia, maybe an out-of-country leave to Hawaii... Which was worse, a third tour in Vietnam or ten months in hell? He walked past the barracks guard down the dark hall to his room and tapped on the door.

Brennan opened it a crack and stepped back. The room was dark, not enough light to read faces. Brennan flicked on a flashlight and quickly covered the lens with a green t-shirt, showing Vinny where to sit in the crowded room. He saw Pomeroy's great hulk on the floor along the west wall. Grossnickel sat next to the stereo, back against the wall, legs straight out. Brennan was in the center of the room rolling a joint.

"You were gone a long time, troop," he whispered. "We thought you maybe you ended up in a truck headed for the towers."

Vinny nodded. "I saw those R&R barracks. Now I know why Deagle wanted you guys to sleep here." He thought about telling them where their buddy was.

"No shit, so did I," Jim said. "Me and Pomeroy were in 2020. We could have been assigned 2013 or 2014, same, same."

"You think it's safe to smoke? Maybe we should wait 'til the all clear. Pomeroy what do you think?"

The big man shook his head. "I don't need a joint. I'm high on life. In two days I'm going to Hawaii, over."

Grossnickel wagged his head. "I don't even want to talk about R&R. Where the hell is Deagle, anyway."

Vinny looked from one to the other. "If six of my buddies got blown away... I don't know if I could think about R&R."

"Deagle went back to Penny," Pomeroy said, "where it's safe. He's gone, over."

Brennan held the unlit match away from the joint. "Vin, anybody else smoking weed when you walked through?"

"Nope, no dope."

"Damn. What's going on buddy? Is it safe to go out and take a piss?"

Brennan turned off the flashlight and the four of them sat in the dark. After a few seconds Vinny was able to make out the shapes of the other three facing him.

"Half the guards," he said, "are ready to blast you. The other half are asleep. Typical Bien Hoa bullshit, same, same except for..."

"Except what?"

"Last time we took in-coming, everyone was totally freaked out," Brennan whispered. "NCO's running around in their underwear, Officers pounding on barracks doors. It was escape-and-evasion, every man for himself. Vinny and I didn't even go to the bunker, we got stoned right here."

Pomeroy nodded and looked over at Grossnickel. "Hey, Jim, half and half. Remember that shit? Might as well tell the story. Nothing else to do."

After a moment, Jim grinned. "Affirm. That was the funniest thing I've ever seen in my life."

"Groovy," Brennan whispered. "A war story."

Jim folded his legs and leaned forward, holding his voice above a whisper.

"It was September, I think. The whole battalion was up against this huge rice paddy. It was at least a mile wide and a mile long to the tree-line on the other side. Shit, we just sat there, for two days eating C's and digging holes and doing guard duty. Waiting to cross that paddy. Nobody knew what we were waiting for. Finally this Arvin battalion pulls up on our left flank and they fuckin' dig in, eat C's and do guard duty for another two days. The captain said we were waiting for the Arvins to get rested.

"So finally one morning we get on line to cross the paddy, 2nd Battalion on the right flank and the Arvins on the left flank. Of course the officers won't let us walk the dikes so we have to drop into mud and water up to our assholes. That was some terrible humpin', lemme tell you." Jim paused to wag his head again and have a private chuckle. "So we get half way across and reach this dike where we rest and get a smoke break. It's still a half a mile to the tree-line. We're on the radio, talking back and forth to the captain and the Arvins... anybody see any gooks?... I mean, VC?... no nothing... So we crawl over the dike and into the water on the other side and move out. Hey, Gary, you think I could have a beer?"

Brennan opened the refrigerator door and passed out four cold beers. "You're in this rice paddy and..."

"And this one-shot Charlie opens up from the tree-line. One shot, one rifle. Bang. 2nd Battalion goes tearing-ass to the tree-line. We're splashing and crashing and falling and getting back up soaking wet and we're hollering at each other 'where is the fucker!' and 'get the '60 set up!' and the guys in Alpha Company are hollering the VC is in front of them so they lay down some fire and cover the rest of us. And finally we make the tree-line and hit it, down on our bellies." He paused to laugh again. "So I'm laying there and Pomeroy taps me on the shoulder. The asshole is laughing. I look back. Here's the whole Arvin left flank, four-hundred fuckin' guys, splashing and crashing back the other way. They did this battalion about-face and retreated, man. Because of one shot. It was the funniest thing I ever saw."

Brennan grabbed his belly and laughed until he coughed, but Vinny shook his head. "Did they ever cross it?" he asked, "the Arvins?"

"I don't know. We never op-conned with those guys again, did we Pomeroy?"

He shook his head. "Once was enough. Is finance open on Christmas Day? I need more money for R&R."

"Per SOP," Vinny told him.

"What do you guys know about Manila?" Grossnickel asked.

"We know guys who went there and liked it," Vinny said. "It's like any R&R city, same same, except maybe Hawaii where you're with your wife. They put you in a hotel for Americans. You get a private room. When I went to Sydney the first time I was still in my fatigues when I registered in my hotel. There was this old broad and her husband, Americans, in the lobby at the

246

same time. She sees me starts crying 'oh no, Henry!'... or whatever the fuck his name was... 'we mustn't stay here with the riff-raff GIs!' The bitch was ashamed to be in the same hotel with me, an American fighting man. She thought the place was a flophouse full of whores. Anyway, about the time you get unpacked there's a knock on your door. It's your driver. Did you ask for a driver? Negative, you get one anyway. He says he's your driver and he's going to show you Sydney. He doesn't say his real job is to keep you out of trouble. Some of Sydney is off-limits to GIs. So he takes you to the various houses of prostitution until you pick one out, the three of you go to dinner, back to the hotel, the driver says he'll pick you up in the morning. That's how it goes for five days and five nights and then you go home."

Vincent took a last pull at his beer. "Right. Okay troops, we gotta go bail out Deagle."

Pomeroy looked up sharply, bemused gray eyes suddenly wary. "Say again? Did you say, 'bail out Deagle?'"

"They got him pulling night ambush on the hill. I got nineteen days left in 'Nam and this is my last chance. So drop-your-cocks-and-grab-your-socks, lets move out!"

1805Hours 24Dec71
1st Cav Div HQ
Reception Room, Sgt Major Bierra

Sergeant Major Bierra returned to his desk and found the 1st Cav HQ reception room filled beyond its capacity, standing room only. The field radio Sergeant Grasso had left behind crackled, unattended. He switched it off. His desk was a mess, books scattered, crumpled notes and garbage in the ashtray, and an empty brown C-ration box. Also on the desk, Grasso had left a crude appointment schedule, first-in-first-out like a restaurant reservation list. Bierra glanced at the names. An air force colonel, majors and captains from admin, an assortment of JAG, engineer, and artillery officers from units all over the base. A bright light him in the eyes and he looked up. The lady reporter from CBS News had spotted him and directed her cameraman to get a shot. The phone rang and he snatched it up, looking to one side of the camera lens.

"1st Cav Div Headquarters, Division Sergeant Major Bierra."

"Bud this is Trumpy. Where's Grasso?"

He sat down and idly jotted Trumpy's name. "I'm at the desk again. I told you don't call me Bud."

"Oh. That's right, Sir Alfred Lord Tennyson."

"Might as well get used to just plain, sir."

"Not yet, asshole. Anyway, the answers are 'negative' on Major Andrews, no sign of him in my AO, and 'affirmative' on that command vehicle jeep situation. Bud... sergeant major, sir, you'll have three jeeps in zero five, and they'll drop the keys at your desk."

"Thanks... Mr Kringle.."

"Until today, I never knew what a GR Point was. Now I'm on my way to R&R to move it to Big Ben hospital. That's a job I'd prefer to delegate. I'll get back on the horn when it's done."

"Roger that."

"How are things up there?"

Bierra looked around. The CBS cameraman's lights lit up the twin portraits of General's Custer and MacArthur and all the 1st Cav campaign citations and decorations from one hundred years. "Somewhat officious."

He hung up the phone as Darcy Devlin approached his desk, a dozen pairs of eyes following her. Humidity had straightened her hair and her make-up-less expression was grave. She wore one of Webb's long fatigue shirts, without a nametag, and her yellow legal pad had pages of notes.

She picked up his copy of Roget's Thesaurus. "Sergeant major, do you know when a press conference is scheduled?"

"Ma'am, I'm sure Colonel Wilcox will open up a briefing room soon."

"Do you know if we can film the R&R detachment yet?"

"Negative. That area is secure."

"Can I see General Webb?"

"Negative ma'am. But I'll advise him you're here."

The phone rang and he grabbed it, "1stCavDivisionHeadquarters, Division Sgt MajorBierra!"

It was a lieutenant from div-arty, asking for his CO, Lieutenant Colonel Sutcliff. Bierra craned his neck around the room and spotted him and held the phone high. Sutcliff shouldered his way through the press, nodded at Miss Devlin, and carried the phone as far from the desk as the cord reached.

"Sutcliff." He listened with his back to the room, facing the portrait of General Mac Arthur. He saw the CBS cameraman in his right peripheral vision and felt the shock of floodlights. Aware of how bad it looked when a uniformed officer ducked away from a television camera, a common occurrence these days, Colonel Sutcliff stood his ground and tried not to blink. "Affirmative, lieutenant."

Sutcliff smiled as J.L. Gottlieb moved in close with her hand microphone.

"I'm sure MAC-V will go with close air strikes," he said, "instead of artillery, there are a hell of a lot of buildings around that hill." He hung up and handed the phone to Bierra.

"Colonel Sutcliff," Gottlieb asked, "is the 1st Cavalry making plans to strike Hill 229 during the cease-fire?"

He nodded. "Ma'am it's an option. General Webb and MAC-V will make that decision."

She pushed a microphone closer to him. "Are you saying, sir, that MAC-V has to approve any response to the Viet Cong attack this afternoon? Is that because we're in a cease-fire?"

"I'm saying the division commander and MAC-V will decide on a response to this communist attack, a clear cease-fire violation."

"Colonel, was 1st Cav Headquarter's S-2 aware there were Viet Cong on Hill 229?"

"You'll have to ask Colonel Borg." He shot a glance at Bierra and walked away from her. As Jan shifted her gaze to the division sergeant major the phone rang again and Bierra got it before the second ring.

"This is Lieutenant Epton, sergeant major. I'm at Big Ben and I have one-each buck-sergeant Gonzales with me. He's getting some pieces of bed frame cut out of his back but he's okay. He saw the two VC who blew the R&R detachment. Is it safe to bring him over to see Borg when he's patched up?"

Bierra glanced up at Gottlieb, watching him with her microphone at the ready. "Negative, lieutenant. I'll advise the colonel and we'll send a jeep. He'll be glad to hear that, sir. Good job."

He tapped the disconnect and dialed the east briefing room, wondering if the situation back there was still chaos. He carried the phone away from the desk and Colonel Wilcox answered.

"Sir, has Colonel Borg got a minute?"

"He's debriefing Sergeant Deagle. Give him zero five."

When he hung up Ms. Devlin stood in front of him, green eyes imploring. "Sergeant major, write my name at the top of your list. I need to speak with General Webb and it has nothing to do with the news. Please."

He started to tell her flat no then thought better of it. She'd spent one night with Webb at Bien Hoa, and if she decided to stay longer there was the possibility she might pass along a favorable impression of him to the commanding general. What he needed to show her was coolness under pressure, control of the situation, and above all discretion. In a quiet voice he replied, "I am fully apprised of all personnel, and personal, matters in this division, ma'am. At my first opportunity, when the general has a private moment, I'll hand-carry you back to his quarters."

"Thank you."

Darcy backed away. Bierra was pretty slick, she thought. Jeff's "first private moment" could be hours from now. All eyes followed as she drifted the room checking out military insignias and nametags. She spotted Peter Keating and Steve Grozik working the room, interviewing the officers of the 1st Cavalry. But on her yellow notepad, she already had most of the story of the Christmas bombing of the R&R detachment, and it hadn't taken long.

She finally had a story. After all the bland, canned press conferences, the tours, the staged artillery and air combat shows, and the quaint and carefully orchestrated interviews with GI-Joe, the bombing of the R&R barracks at Bien

Hoa was news. It was a story that reminded her what had drawn her to Vietnam in the first place. It was about death that defied understanding: American soldiers killed sleeping in their bunks while waiting for R&R flights, during a Christmas cease-fire.

The first air force officer she ambushed gave her 'in-coming alpha-to-zulu,' and why the two barracks had to have been hit by hand-delivered demolitions, such as a satchel charge. In rapid succession thereafter Darcy learned that two Viet Cong had carried out the attack, that they attacked from the hill directly behind the R&R detachment, in the afternoon when there were no guards in the bunkers, and during the monsoon-like rain that covered their approach. Not only was the attack a complete surprise, the two Viet Cong escaped back up the hill without a shot being fired. And they were probably still up there.

A surprise attack, that is, to everyone but Jeff Webb. She had unique knowledge of his concerns about Hill 229, off the record, and that the 1971 Christmas cease-fire would be unilateral. Now he was in his little briefing room and it was eating him alive. He'd guessed right about the Viet Cong but had been too late arriving at Bien Hoa to stop their attack. She scribbled two sentences on the bottom of blank page, ripped it off, folded it and stuck it in her pocket. Somehow she'd get a note to him. She looked at the rest of her notes and saw some loose ends. She had written the word "cyclonite", underlined and followed by two question marks. She had "VC or Friendly Farmer" underlined with three question marks. And she had written "Webb on offense?" double underlined followed by half a dozen question marks. The first two shouldn't be too difficult.

She scanned the faces of the officers in the reception room, avoiding the eyes groping her. Despite her shapeless jeans and a snug new bra under her oversize fatigue shirt, despite a half a dozen men dead and two barracks destroyed, it was "business as usual'" for Jeff Webb's officers in green and the air force boys in blue. An air force major in a flight-suit flashed her a smarmy smile. She smiled back but cruised past him. A group of army colonels took turns leering at her, no doubt speculating where she would spend Christmas Eve night. She walked to the colonels hugging her legal pad to her chest, and they all but came to the position of attention. Compared to Jeff Webb, they were little boys.

"Cyclerite," she said. "It sounds more like a tooth-paste additive than an explosive, doesn't it?"

The colonels looked at one another. "Cyclonite, ma'am. C-4 plastic explosive. But its military designation is M-5. I didn't know Colonel Wilcox had released that yet..." he added, voice trailing off. The colonels eyed her suspiciously.

Not too subtle Darce, she said to herself. Out of practice.

"I'm confused," she said. "I thought all the Vietnamese nationals were confined off base during the cease-fire. Don't you guys keep track of them?"

"It only took two, ma'am, and they were probably living up there for weeks."

The mood in the reception room struck her as strange. It was not somber, not consoling, and if these officers felt collective shock it had worn off. The atmosphere was more like a high school gymnasium in a sudden death overtime game, a point behind with five seconds on the clock. The room bristled with nervous anticipation. The anticipation, she figured, was in the fact that MAC-V was the coach and instead of calling a play General Garlett had called time-out. Which would also make Jeff Webb crazy. She needed a place to sit down and write her impressions. Along the wall behind her all the chairs were taken. An army officer in a dress green uniform sat watching her. She walked to him and smiled, made a show of writing his name from his printed name-badge; Castle, lieutenant colonel, Judge Advocate General Branch. She used her legal pad to draft some air across her face.

"Close in here."

He stood and offered his chair.

"Thank you, colonel. Does General Webb need an attorney?"

He smiled. "No ma'am. I'm here on a separate matter."

"What separate matter?"

He shrugged. "An AWOL offic... soldier, just routine."

"AWOL at Christmas? Doesn't sound routine."

He laughed.

Darcy watched tireless Jan Gottlieb, across the room, confer with Frank Stolle on their next interview. Jan didn't smoke but she kept an unlit cigarette in her fingers, and it was just a few seconds before the major in the flight-suit sauntered over to offer a light. While Jan puffed on the cigarette he checked out her chunky figure. He said something and Jan smiled up at him, not quite embarrassed but pleased. Colonel Castle offered her one of his Marlboro's.

"Thanks. I imagine the line to MAC-V is burning up right now," she said.

Castle nodded. "No doubt. And I imagine some rear area asses are burning right now. By reputation General Webb has a temper."

"What will he do?"

"Off the record? Webb doesn't run this division ma'am, Lieutenant General Ben Garlett runs it from MAC-V. Webb only accepted Bien Hoa to avoid a court martial."

"You know that?"

"Got it from my CO, who works in G-2, MAC-V."

She wanted to laugh in his face, inform him of a mini-war called the Parrot's Beak Offensive. But Castle's remark about Garlett running the 1st Cav from MAC-V had the ring of truth and she'd heard it before. Had Jeff signed the 'Bail Out' letter after all? Or was the control MAC-V exerted over the 1st Cavalry directed from even higher up? Now she needed Colonel Castle to go away so she could think. She glanced across the room at Jan Gottlieb just as Frank's lightbar flooded the west wall, bringing the twin portraits of Generals MacArthur and Custer into sharp black-and white relief. She flipped pages to a fresh yellow sheet and wrote in shorthand. After a few lines Castle drifted away. She wrote five pages.

A voice whispered in her ear. "When do you see the man again?"

She looked up and saw Jan. "Don't know. Trying."

"This could work out, " Jan whispered. "Your timely little indiscretion."

The officer next to Darcy smiled at Jan and gave up his chair, and she sat down. Darcy put her legal pad in her lap, face down.

"What have you got so far?" Jan asked.

"Not very damn much," Darcy lied.

Jan nodded. "Bastards are playing it pretty close to the vest. One thing for sure, the officers of the 1st Cav ran the cease-fire banner up their flagpole and expected the enemy to honor it, but instead the enemy shot it down. Nobody was expecting two R&R barracks to get blown up."

Darcy stared at her lap.

"I hear the east briefing room looks like a bunker. Do you know what Webb doing about the attack?" Jan asked her.

Darcy shook her head. "Blaming himself."

"It goes with the job, honey." Jan leaned closer. "I forgot to ask. Last night, while you were... getting to know him better... did he cop to the 'Bail Out' letter and become a hero?"

She shook her head. "He copped to knowing names. But if he signed that letter he's the biggest hypocrite I've ever met. You were at the press conference, you met the man."

"What's this? You falling for the guy?"

"We're oil and water. Irish and English."

"I'll tell you one thing Webb's not doing, he's not opening his R&R to the press. I have to tell you, Darce, we've got a story at Bien Hoa. If Webb won't let CBS News photograph those barracks I know a press-hound at MAC-V who will."

"Garlett?"

"Affirmative, girl. So if you get the chance, convince the man." She stood up and melted away into the crowd.

Darcy stood up and walked to Sergeant Major Bierra's desk. "Any news?"

"No ma'am I haven't had a chance to get back there." The phone rang. "1st Cav Division Headquarter Sergeant Major Bierra."

A voice asked, "Is this Captain Bierra?"

He recognized the voice as Major Carl Falk, S-1 MACV, Long Binh. "Someday soon, I hope, sir."

"Well Merry Christmas, sergeant major, someday is now. Your commission has come through channels approved. It's up to your commanding general to decide whether you begin your new career as an 01, 02, or 03. Congratulations."

"Thank you very much, sir. Can you tell me when it's official?"

"The approval will be in General's Webb's MAC-V package tomorrow,

December 25. Then it's up to him."

"Outstanding, sir." Bierra hung up the phone and raised his eyes to the ceiling, a prayer answered. "Encomium, sergeant major. Encomium."

"Congratulations for what," Darcy asked him.

Beaming, he shook his head. "Personal matter, ma'am."

She held out her note to him. "So is this. Would you please give it to General Webb, as soon as possible?"

He nodded. "Right now, Ms. Devlin. And you can count on my discretion."

1850Hours 24Dec71
1st Cav Div HQ,
Casual Hospital Barracks 2717

Except for the squads of combat-ready troops moving to the bunkers, the dust literally had settled in the R&R Detachment. Though 7X field glasses Major Andrews studied the holes in 2013 and 2014. He lowered the glasses and spat. Now they all knew who was right about Hill 686. Behind him the sun was down; by now, Webb's ambush teams were getting saddled up. Webb would need a leader.

He walked to the jeep and pushed the starter. Clipping along at thirty miles an hour in a steel pot, sunglasses, and a heavy field jacket, he was not recognizable on the busy street between the hospital detachment and the admin AO. Across from the hill checkpoint he pulled the jeep to the shoulder and studied the motorpool. Poor Colonel Geary had his hands full. Everybody needed transportation. Through the main gate troops ran in and out of the motorpool with rifles on their shoulders, trucks loaded with troops pulled out and headed for guard posts, officers from all over the base milled around waiting for jeeps and command instructions from Borg. He wondered if Geary was even aware of the missing admin jeep. Probably. He wondered if Geary knew about Lieutenant St. John's imported body-count. He swung his glasses up the street and watched the long line of enlisted men standing outside the arms room drawing rifles from Sp6 Karuda. He recognized the faces of some of his own troops plus a mix of enlisted in-transits. Outstanding.

He moved the binoculars up the slope to the admin barracks area, the dozen odd rows of barracks along the main street leading to his command post. In the gathering darkness a few barracks still showed combat preparation, stragglers racing home from their duty stations to get into helmets and flack vests, draw rifles, and report to alert locations. He felt the pride of command, seeing his admin troops showing a sense of urgency. Soon it would be lights out and all quiet, and they would be ready for whatever Charles threw at them. He lowered the binoculars and fired up the jeep.

He could not use the admin road to get to his quarters, too many enemy

253

eyes and ears. Instead, he drove around the NCO Club and back up between the motorpool and the admin mess hall, where he parked the jeep and walked. He unlocked his BOQ door and slipped inside. Quickly he changed from fatigues to camo tiger stripes with black collar pins and bloused canvas combat boots. He strapped on a black leather gunbelt with black flapped military holster for his loaded .45 auto. For headgear, he chose a tight-fitting helmet liner instead of his cavalry campaign hat, for now. The campaign hat would go with him along with his paperwork, debriefings, and his note to General Webb.

When it was too dark outside to read faces and collar pins, he locked his BOQ and walked toward the admin CP.

1900Hours 23Dec71
1st Cav Div HQ
East Briefing Room

Sergeant Major Bierra rapped on the briefing room door and poked his head inside. He saw General Webb and Sergeant Deagle standing in front of Major Andrews' map, Colonel's Wilcox and Shipp seated at the map table. Colonel Borg stood with his back to the room talking on the crypto line. Sergeant Hooper, a virtual prisoner, still sat alone on the other side of the room.

"Sir, the rest of your special forces teams are in your office."

"Be a few more minutes," Webb said

"Yes, sir. Also, Master Sergeant Trumpy has moved the GR Point to Big Ben Hospital, per your request, and Lieutenant Epton called saying he has a buck sergeant who saw the two VC who blew the barracks; a Sergeant Gonzales from 8th Brigade, sir. I told Epton my AO was too crowded at the moment."

Hearing that news Webb lifted a corner of the blanket covering the south window to peek outside. The sun was down and the hill was under the earth's shadow, all but the summit and the heart shape of the 1st Cav Insignia.

"What about Andrews?"

"Nothing yet, sir."

He glanced at his watch. "Call Epton back, tell him to hold Gonzales at Big Ben and Colonel Borg will debrief there. I don't want those reporters getting hold of him. Thank you, Sergeant Major. How is the reception room?"

"Sir, my AO is full of smoke and civilians and bright lights. A moment of your time, sir? Aside?" Webb looked down and saw the folded legal paper note in the sergeant major's hand. They walked to the hall door where Bierra palmed him the note.

"Some would argue, sir, that Ms. Devlin's affection is specious; she is, after all, a reporter. But my observation is that her concern seems genuine."

"Thank you, sergeant major."

He waited for Bierra to close the door before unfolding the note. Darcy had written "Too many eyes, think it best if I wait with the others. Call, let me help." He had no doubt that Bierra had read it too. He slipped it into his pocket and returned to the briefing room, all eyes on him.

"Specious?" he repeated aloud.

"The sergeant major applied for a direct commission, sir," Colonel Shipp advised him. "He's working on his vocabulary and now nobody can understand him."

Webb's expression said he knew nothing about a direct commission.

Wilcox dropped the phone on its cradle. "Beg pardon, sir. General Garlett will call us back."

Webb grunted and turned to Deagle, still studying the map "Go ahead, sergeant."

Standing alongside the 1st Cav commanding general, Deagle was self-conscious about the sad appearance of his uniform and rucksack. He aimed an index finger at the bottom of Major Andrews' map, just above the green-black band of elephant grass one hundred meters east of the MP checkpoint.

"Pomeroy and I met Sergeant Hooper here, sir. We humped over to the road and then down to the staging area where we told him about the VC and turned over the detonator. He said he was going to write his debriefing and pass it on to Major Andrews."

Webb filled his lungs let air out through his nostrils. "And you did that, sergeant?"

"Sir! I 'rit my r'port and surrendered the detonator to my commander. Sir."

Borg nodded agreement. "I saw Sergeant Hooper as I was leaving the admin CP."

The rest Webb already knew. Major Andrews instructed Hooper to keep his mouth shut and remain on the air force side of the base. Andrews then broke into the motorpool and stole the admin jeep. Where he'd gone and why he did that was a mystery.

"I'm sorry about my major, sir," Hooper added.

"We're all sorry. The families of six dead soldiers will be sorry."

Webb faced Deagle, "Sergeant, I have a dozen special forces troops in my office and I'm going to have them climb up that hill tonight and kill those VC, if they can. But I have a secondary ambush site." He pointed at the narrow white stripe on Andrews' map two-thirds the way up. "You were here once. Do you think you could find this meadow again?"

Deagle's eyes narrowed as he studied the map. "Pretty tough at night, sir."

Webb saw where Deagle was looking and shook his head. "Forget the road. Too noisy and too open and I've got squads of nervous rifleman at the garbage dump who'll see you on that road. You'll have to climb it."

"I could retrace my steps from east of the checkpoint, go straight up and find that cliff, then go east to the meadow... I can find it, sir."

"Good. Is it possible to block this trail that crosses the meadow with a half dozen men?"

Deagle pointed out the jungle above the meadow. "Up here is some really thick shit, sir. If Charles shows his face he'll be right on top of me. There won't be much time."

Colonel Wilcox leaned close beside him. "Sir, a word in private?"

"Just speak up, colonel. Quickly."

"My thought, sir; are night ambush missions appropriate right now?"

"Go on."

"MAC-V, and the cease-fire."

Webb squared his shoulders to the lieutenant colonel. "Make your point, colonel."

"Sir, General Garlett was very specific. He said there were to be no seek-and-destroy operations during the cease-fire without his approval. Perhaps we should wait to talk to him. We could send up the gunships..."

"Negative on waiting, negative on gunships, this is a job for men. I operate this division, not Ben Garlett, and I take responsibility for it. If you'd served with me in a forward area you would know that."

Wilcox blinked rapidly. "Sir, it's not a question of my serving in a forward area, it's a question of, perhaps, you're serving in one too long..."

Webb took a step forward, nose to nose with Wilcox, and spoke softly but firmly. "Come to attention, Colonel Wilcox."

"Sir, I meant..."

"I said come to attention! That means lock those jaws!"

The stunned S-1 pulled himself to a military position of attention, eyes wide and chin tight.

"I will ask you one question, colonel, and you will answer with affirmative or negative! Do you need to be relieved from this command center?"

Wilcox stared, mute.

"In six hours, colonel, I will intercept, engage, and kill the VC on hill 229-er! I do not seek or require your approval to do so! Now do you wish to be excused from this command center!"

"Negative, sir!."

"Then as you were." He turned to face Deagle and rapped a finger at the map. "That's your position, sergeant. You've pulled night ambush duty before?"

"Affirmative, sir." General Webb, Deagle thought, was a lot like himself. He would take a ration of crap just so long.

"Sir?" said Sergeant Hooper. "It'd be a honor to serve on Sarn't Deagle's squad. I know that hill pretty good, too."

Deagle nodded yes. "Hooper's a good NCO, sir, but I prefer to command."

Webb liked his brashness. "You hear that, Sergeant Hooper?"

"Roger, sir!"

"Sergeant Deagle, you command. You go by the book like you would at LZ

Penny. You maintain absolute silence. You use your frags first if Charles shows himself. Carry claymores if you wish, but your flanks will be close together and your field of fire is short. If you have to use M-16s you give them a mad-goddamn-minute and break it off. And don't you fall asleep, young man. Am I clear?"

"Yes, sir. I'll take a couple claymores. I should be able to cross-fire 'em."

Webb was struck by the tall buck sergeant's matter-of-fact acceptance. He was a stranger in a strange land, like himself. "Comment, Sergeant Deagle."

Deagle studied the map. "Sir, I agree Charles is back in his hole now and if we blow this ambush it'll be after midnight, like oh three hundred. But I'd say me and Hooper have the hot corner. Charles will hit the in-transit AO again."

After five seconds Webb shook his head. "Negative. This time he'll hit the air strip where all that Cav hardware's stockpiled. Lots of satchel charges."

"He can hit the air strip with 60 mike-mikes."

"Satchel charges are surer and it was easy the first time."

Deagle aimed a finger at the meadow. "Then he'll be slick and take the long way, drop into this meadow and go around. He won't mess with those APC's and .50 guns on the air force side."

"I hope so," Webb nodded, and pointed down at two points on another map of Hill 229. This one was a contour map from an aerial photo, taken straight overhead. "Because he'll walk into the guys in the green hats. Don't forget, stay off the road on the way up."

Deagle focused down at the contour map and saw the two green pushpins on the air force side. He calculated that if his squad's position at the meadow was designated as six o'clock they'd have special forces teams around the hill from them at nine o'clock and one o'clock. Webb was running the ambush right.

While Colonel Wilcox spoke on the MAC-V line the Cav phone rang, and Colonel Borg snatched it up. Bierra again. It had not been a great day for the S-1 or S-2 and when Borg hung up ten years had been added to his face. "Two things, sir. The Sergeant Major reports that Deagle's squad is here, combat ready. He says the press was eating them alive so he's moved them to quartermaster barracks 2939 to saddle up."

Webb looked at Deagle. "Your R&R buddies?"

Deagle tried not to grin. "Could be, sir."

"Does every swingin' dick on base knows about this ambush? Jesus Christ!"

"Two are 74-Hotels, Vincent and Brennan from ERB. They say they both have 11-Bravo secondaries..."

"That's them, sir," Deagle confirmed.

Webb threw up his arms. "Fine! Call Geary. Tell him I want a Prick-25 set to my frequency and a telephone in 2939 so Sergeant Deagle can police up what he needs, frags, claymores, smoke etc. Read that?"

"Good as done."

"What's else?" he snapped at Borg.

"Major Andrews is back. They found the admin jeep parked behind the mess hall"

Webb turned to Deagle. "Time your break-out for 2000 hours, radio check first then push plus-two for your primary frequency. That gives you three or four hours to reach your objective. Take it slow and quiet. Block that VC trail until either Colonel Borg or Sergeant Major Bierra calls you down."

"Will do, sir."

In a stiff, small voice Colonel Wilcox said. "Lieutenant General Garlett to speak to Brigadier General Webb", and handed him the phone.

"What have you got, Webb?"

Holding his hand over the speaker Webb looked at Deagle and then Hooper. "That will be all, men. Good hunting."

When the hall door closed Webb spoke in a calm voice to his immediate superior, the III-Corps commanding officer: "We have a cease-fire violation, sir. I have five dead R&R troops and one dead MP. Fourteen WIA's."

"How."

"Satchel charges."

"That's six more to go with the eleven dead infantrymen you reported this morning. Stand by, general."

Colonel Borg listened with eyes tightly shut. Wilcox stood up and helped himself to a cup of coffee, poured one for Shipp. While Webb waited, the very un-mechanical Wilcox examined all the tangled electrical connections of plugs and multi-plugs and extension chords that Chuck Shipp had Meredith setup in order to handle all the lights and electric typewriters in "The Bunker". Idly, he wondered if all that juice was a fire hazard.

"You still have American press on base?" Garlett finally asked.

"Affirmative. They were present when it happened, several hours ago. They're in my reception area now. Sir, let me put you on the speaker phone so my staff can hear you." He reached down and punched the button. "Go ahead, sir."

"Gentlemen, your first task is obvious. You have an enemy cease-fire violation. If you have not already done so you issue a statement making it damn clear to those reporters that the Viet Cong violated the truce. Any response we make is provoked, measured, and justified. Is that understood?"

"Already written, sir."

"What do I mean by measured and justified? At this point, that means air combat or artillery strikes after the cease-fire, and no ground activity."

"Sir, the Viet Cong used Hill 229 to stage their attack. You saw it from a helicopter. Air combat and artillery are not optional. We think we responded in time and have the VC trapped."

"What do you mean responded, general?"

"We have three night ambush teams on the hill."

Borg and Shipp watched the telephone while Wilcox nervously played with the cords.

"Bad decision, Webb," Garlett said. Then, in a voice steadily rising to the point of shouting, he added, "I'm assuming the reporters will know every detail of your ambush, shortly. This is not the sort of positive topic I had in mind when I sent them to Cav HQ. Far as I know, in III-Corps tonight and maybe in-theatre, this is a unique situation. There are no ambush teams operating on Christmas Eve 1971! We have a three-day cease-fire! Do you know the meaning of the word, 'cease-fire'?"

"The enemy struck first, sir."

"That's not the point! Webb, call your teams down."

"Sir, I can not do that. Those men are the only option I have. In the future..."

"You had the option to secure that hill instead!" Garlett snapped. "Well," he said, calming down, "I have a vivid recollection of night ambush duty; good men wasting half a duty-day. I will inform the Secretary of your cease-fire violation but you keep the lid on your ambush teams."

"And as to mission security, sir, only the officers in this room, my division sergeant major, and the participants are briefed on Hill 229."

"You goddamn well keep it that way. And since I'm not sure who's doing the thinking at Bien Hoa, I want all you gentlemen to keep this question in mind tonight: what are your career consequences if I have to inform the Secretary of Defense that his Christmas cease-fire was undermined by some loose-cannon cowboys called the 1st Cavalry Division! Keep me informed, no matter what time."

When the line became a busy signal Webb reached and disconnected it.

"Got a way with words, don't he," Shipp breathed.

Webb nodded. "Politics comes first with Ben Garlett."

Borg said, "I'll offer my resignation now, sir, and save you some embarrassment."

Webb looked at him. "I made it clear in this morning's briefing, colonel, I'm not interested in scapegoats. When you get punched in the face you don't back away, you start throwing punches. I have confidence that Major Eiler will score a Cav knock-out. There—on occasion I have a way with words myself."

Colonel Wilcox caught the next call on the first ring. It was Sergeant Major Bierra. He thanked him and hung up.

"Anybody expecting a call from Special Forces MAC-V? No?" He picked up the receiver. "Lieutenant Colonel Raymond Wilcox."

"Colonel Wilcox? And you are..."

"In 48 hours, I'm the division S-2."

"Colonel Wilcox, this is Colonel Cohen, special forces medical field director, MAC-V. I thought I should notify you personally about a TWIX from Walter Reed."

"That would be Major Warren Andrews?"

"Lieutenant Colonel Andrews until 1968, when his career was cut short by a bullet to the head. During rehabilitation in 1969 Colonel Andrews resigned his commission, but he was returned to duty as a major 04 after a fourteen-month stay at San Pedro Army/Navy."

"I guess the TWIX wasn't marked personal and confidential," Wilcox said, disappointed.

"I'm not stepping on anybody's prerogatives here. Your TWIX was re-directed to this office because of its content. Does Major Andrews serve in a sensitive command position at Bien Hoa?"

"Major Andrews is AWOL, colonel. I wonder if you could read me the TWIX"

In December 1968, Lieutenant Colonel Warren Andrews was the XO, 7th Brigade 1st Cav Division, operating outside the city of Vinh Din. His brigade was temporarily dug in at the base of Hill 686. The hill, having been fought for and cleared of Viet Cong earlier in September, was classified Uniform Sierra. Regardless, executive officer Andrews was ordered by his brigade commander to lead two full companies on a sweep of Hill 686 and clear it again. On December 23, 1968, while Andrews remained in his hooch, a perfunctory sweep was done with negative results and Andrews wrote a debriefing report stating Hill 686 was clear.

On the afternoon of December 24, a squad of VC sappers used the hill as cover to blow up half the battalion's Huey helicopters, killing a dozen enlisted. The afternoon and evening of the December 25, the 7th Brigade found itself in a see-saw Christmas firefight for control of Hill 686 and in thirty-six continuous hours of fighting suffered twenty percent casualties. Lieutenant Colonel Andrews was shot in the head and returned to Walter Reed hospital in Washington DC. Andrews recovered from his physical injury and was shipped to San Pedro for therapy and rehab, while there he resigned his commission from the army.

Wilcox listened to the rest of it and hung up. He took the news to Webb's desk and waited while the commanding general digested it all.

"Now I remember Andrews," he said quietly.

"Sir, San Pedro Army/Navy is a mental hospital."

"I know."

"If Andrews hadn't come up a WIA, JAG was going to bring dereliction-of-duty charges against him following the Hill 686 incident. If he hadn't resigned he'd have been court-martialed, sir."

Colonel Borg wearily folded his mis-shapen body into a chair. "I knew it."

"He was a very sick man," Wilcox told the Staff. "Depressed, suicidal. But he wangled a commission re-instatement."

Shipp slapped his palm with his fist. "He had Hooper's debriefing about Sergeant Deagle. He had the detonator. He knew there were VC on the hill and he walked away from it."

Colonel Wilcox nodded. "He let six men die to make a point."

Carrying his attaché and battle diary in his left hand, Major Andrew edged away from the BOQ and walked west between the buildings. For the first time since October, when they'd taken in-coming, the base was totally dark, totally quiet. His new canvas combat boots crushed the drying sand lightly. On his left the blackened profile of Hill 686 poked into the cloudy sky. Soon a three-quarter moon would turn its foliage from ebony to silver-tinged green.

He approached the first enlisted barracks in the admin AO and saw the shadowy form of a barracks guard standing outside the closed door. He looked down between the barracks rows and envisioned dozens of barracks guards standing vigil. Now this is more like it, he thought. Like freedom, the price of an operating base in enemy territory is eternal vigilance. A street guard walking his square-shaped post turned the corner and came toward him, sending a tingle up his spine. He waited until the soldier was almost in front of him before he stepped out of the shadow into this face.

"Password," he whispered.

The guard saw the major in his full tiger stripes and snapped to attention, bringing his M-16 to port arms. The guard had his night vision, even in the dim light he saw the major's frightening right eye. The burst vessel had grown from the size of a small bug to an angry, red spider with legs.

"Password," he repeated.

"Don't have one, sir."

Andrews looked down at the bridge of the soldier's nose. "Soldier I am standing inside your post during lights-out after an enemy attack. You read me? You challenge with the password 'Crazy Horse.' and my counter-sign is 'Major Reno' The whole base will be using it tonight."

"Sir the sergeant-of-the-guard didn't..."

"I just gave you the goddamn counter-sign, soldier!" He grabbed the muzzle of the soldier's M-16 and held it against his own heart. "You see somebody walking in your post you say 'Crazy Horse' and if you don't get 'Major Reno' in three seconds you better shoot that somebody, soldier. Now you challenge me."

"Crazy Horse, sir."

"No, not 'Crazy Horse, sir'. Just 'Crazy Horse.' Rank doesn't mean shit to a guard walking his post until the countersign is given."

"Crazy Horse."

"Major Reno. There, you see how it works son? Now you know I'm friendly."

"Yes, sir."

With the guard's heels still locked in front of him, Andrews looked around them. "Are you scared son?" he asked.

"A little bit, sir. But the grunts are on the hill, sir."

Andrews' eyes opened wide. "How would you know that?"

"Sir, everybody knows that."

"Lots of loose lips on this base. Do you know the name 'Crazy Horse', soldier?"

"Indian chief, sir."

"Big Victor Charlie chief. Ogallala Sioux chief credited with killing General Custer. Didn't happen. Crazy Horse didn't carry a weapon in battle. Know who Major Reno was? Brave man. Got bad-rapped, like myself, when he survived the battle of the Little Bighorn while his commanding officer got massacred."

The young troop stared straight ahead.

"Stay at your post, soldier. The firefight will be later tonight. I'm afraid... the cost will be heavy this time. Heavier than '68, heavier than '69, heavier even than '75. So as you were, soldier. You keep that M-16 on single-fire and you challenge anyone in your post. Good luck."

"Thank you, sir. Same to you."

He walked carefully in the direction from where the guard had come, between the barracks toward the admin street. Hidden between the flak wall and the barracks, he looked up and down the street. Nothing moved. His AO, including the CP, the barracks, the mess hall, the arms room, and the NCO club was lights-out. Knowing the barracks guards would see him, he walked in a straight line down the middle of the street to the CP. He saw the shadowy steel pots in the doorways following him but none of the guards challenged him. He heard the light click of an M-16 sling swivel against the plastic stock as he reached the CQ door. He opened the door and closed it quickly.

He set his briefcase down on Hooper's desk. In the top desk drawer he found a sterno can and Hooper's chrome Zippo lighter, and got some light going. He exchanged the plastic helmet liner for his blue cavalry campaign hat, then used the shiny Zippo as a mirror to apply shades of camo black and green to his face and neck. Satisfied, he snuffed the flickering sterno can, slipped back into the dark street, and walked a big loop around the enlisted barracks to get to division headquarters. There were a dozen jeeps lined up at the reception room door. Thinking of Sergeant Major Bierra, he ran the ball of his thumb over the cocked hammer of his .45 pistol. If Bierra refused the request to show General Webb the contents of his attaché case, he would be shot.

And then Major Andrews would personally lead the ambush teams up Hill 686.

The barracks was semi-dark, a single overhead bulb burning and army blankets tacked to the screening. Hooper entered first and Deagle followed, pulling the door closed quietly behind him. The buck sergeant gave his boonyhat a fling and wiped his sweaty face. He looked at his combat ready squad: M-16s, loaded bandoliers, steel pots, a couple of canteens each, and four smiling faces.

"What the fuck are you guys doing," he demanded, glad to see them. Pomeroy and Grossnickel stood peeking through the screen and Vincent and Brennan sat in metal folding chairs. "You two are going on R&R, you two are too short for this shit."

Pomeroy shrugged, glassy-eyed like he'd been smoking red.

Sp5 Vincent's swarthy Italian face shone. "Hey, Deagle, did you see all that brass at headquarters? Civilians, too. The whole world is watching us tonight. What a trip!"

Deagle pulled his M-16 off his shoulder and shouldered out of his rucksack. The barracks Webb had provided for him was an army furniture warehouse, with piles of mattresses, bunk frames, footlockers, and broken-down old chairs. But it had a nice open center aisle and plenty of room to sort out gear. There was a folding table set up with a brand new Prick-25 and two telephones. On the slab floor below were two ammo cans of .223 GI ammo, a third can marked '.50 caliber', and a pair of ellipse-shaped claymore ground mines still in their bandoliers. He inventoried one bandolier: mine, wire, and "clacker" squeeze-trigger.

"You gonna test 'em?' Pomeroy asked, observing.

Deagle shrugged.

Suddenly the east door opened and an admin barracks guard stuck his head in.

"Hey, when do you guys go up?" he whispered. His expression in the presence of the grunts was awe-inspired until he saw Sp5 Vincent sitting there. "Vinny! What the fuck are you doing?"

"Folding parachutes, douche bag. What's it look like?"

Deagle walked over to him and gently closed the door in his face. "Troop, we need to saddle up. Give us some time, you bic?"

The soldier read Deagle's nametag and looked up. "You're him, ain't ya."

"That's a Rog." He shut the door.

A muffled whisper came through the door. "I'll make sure nobody bugs you guys."

Deagle walked to a stack of GI mattresses. He yanked one of the flimsy pads off the stack. He held out his hand for Vinny's M-16 and the Sp5 handed it over. The squad watched as he dropped the magazine from the rifle and thumbed the first half dozen rounds out onto the mattress. Three of the six were tracers.

Pomeroy gasped, "They trying to get us blown away?"

"Tracers numbah ten, GI. So before we do anything else, we strip clips and dump the tracers. Brennan, you and Vinny re-load eighteen rounds per magazine, all GI ball. Not twenty rounds, not nineteen, eighteen rounds. You bic? Use the mattresses to keep the noise down."

"What's wrong with tracers?" Vinny wanted to know.

"Give away your position at night," Jim told him.

Jim looked over his rifle more carefully. It had been one day in the admin arms room and gleamed with fresh oil. He dropped the magazine and racked the action a couple times, and wiped the oil off the barrel on his fatigue pants. He jammed the same magazine back in rifle and let the bolt slide home on a live round. The rifle worked okay.

"Deagle, do I have to wear a stupid steel pot tonight?" he griped.

"Everybody wears a stupid steel pot, no exceptions." Looking over at Pomeroy he said. "I see that dumb grin on your face. You called your folks?"

Pomeroy's smile went ear to ear. "Dad wants me to run the farm, Fran's flying to Hawaii tomorrow morning. And life is 5x5, perfect!"

"And your buddy, Jim," Grossnickel added, "gets the shaft and has to go to Manila alone."

"Not Australia?"

"Levied up. Flights are full. All the fucking rear-area guys got Sydney staked out. What does the lousy grunt get? Manila. Where the fuck is Manila"

"Philippines." Brennan told him. "Nice and quiet. You won't see another GI the whole time, buddy, and that's something."

Jim was unimpressed.

Deagle clapped him on the back. "Well, the Spanish make great guitars, I hear."

"Yeah, nylon strings..."

"Hey, Deagle," Brennan called, "Ah, what's with eighteen rounds? Gooks can't count to twenty or what?"

"Full clips double-feed the first round, sometimes. Pomeroy will show you how to tape your first two mags together."

Pomeroy sat on a folding chair with the contents of his rucksack strewn out on a mattress. Matches, empty sandbags, a set of tripflares, one hundred rounds of M-60 machine gun ammo, spare fatigue shirt, small box of candles, compass, bug juice, and twenty empty M-16 magazines in a cloth bandolier. He called Deagle over.

"Notice anything missing? That armorer stole my smoke."

Deagle went to the table with the field radio and telephones. A voice on the other end identified himself as "Quartermaster, Specialist Brewer."

"Hey, specialist. This is Deagle. I need some smoke canisters, two whites and two yellows ASAP. And three entrenching tools."

"They're on their way."

"Watch out for the barracks guard."

Deagle tried on the steel pot the quartermaster had left for him and adjusted the liner. Watching Pomeroy re-roll his poncho he told him to bring some candles but dump the M-60 belt and empty sandbags. He turned and watched Grossnickel take an M-16 magazine out of the ammo can and drop the rounds onto the mattress, separating the red-tipped rounds in a pile.

Fascinated, Vinny watched Deagle dump his rucksack and re-pack it. He spread out his poncho and piled gear on it that he'd carry but didn't need for an ambush: .45 and holster, whistle, extra compass, GI wound packs, and his cav wallet. He folded the poncho three times lengthwise, rolled it like a sleeping bag , and tied it in a bundle with the arms of his spare fatigue shirt. The whole package, tight and quiet, went into the rucksack. He stashed his folding knife, compass, electrical tape, and a small coil of rope in his pockets and clipped his two double-grenade pouches on his pistolbelt. Before closing the rucksack he stuffed in Pomeroy's bundle.

Vinny found a little knot in his throat hard to swallow. "Godzilla doesn't carry his own stuff?"

Deagle shrugged. "His load's a twenty-six pound radio. After you pack it up, then shake it down. Make sure nothing rattles. Canteens full to the top."

"What's the rope for?" Vinny asked, trying again to swallow.

Deagle grinned. "So you can find your way out when I send you into a VC tunnel."

Vinny stared.

With the black tape, Deagle wrapped the sling swivels of the three rear-area M-16 rifles issued to Hooper, Vincent, and Brennan so they wouldn't rattle against the stocks. He taped two eighteen-round magazines together, one up and one down, and clicked one into the port of his own rifle, showing the trick to Vinny. With a quick flick he had thirty-six rounds available. The bolt eased home and he tapped the assist. Locked and loaded. The rifle seemed to have survived Hill 229, the first time, in working order.

Brennan held up a tightly rolled poncho liner before dropping it into a rucksack. "I got munchies."

"Nothing in paper, troop."

"Ah, ten-four and affirm. Licorice and Juicy Fruits, no bag."

Deagle strapped on his pistol belt, canteens, and empty frag bags. He walked to the .50 caliber can and opened the lid. He took two M-67 fragmentation grenades for each pouch and two more for the side-pockets of his rucksack. He passed Pomeroy six grenades to snap inside his three double belt pouches. In Pomeroy's giant hands they looked like green Easter eggs.

Then on second thought he passed him four more for a total of ten. Pomeroy raised his eyebrows but didn't ask.

"Anybody else get frags?" Hooper asked him, ready to move out. The NCO wore the tail of his fatigue shirt out over his round stomach and his M-16 slung up-side-down on his right shoulder. His red nose and shiny face were covered with dull camo paint.

"Tell you what, Hoop," Deagle told him. Carry a spare in your rucksack, plus the claymores. No offense, but if we need frags me and Pomeroy will throw 'em. Pomeroy can throw a grenade fifty meters."

"That's impossible," Vinny said. "Nobody can throw a frag that far."

"Seen him do it lots a times," Jim told him. "A frag is a grunt's best friend, ain't that right, Deagle?"

Deagle nodded. "Better than a rifle at night. We'll talk more about frags when we go to briefing."

Vinny was ready, having copied every move Deagle made. "...'Go to briefing'... 'Ambush'... 'sappers'... 'frags'... God, I love the army!"

"So, Deagle, lemme guess," said Brennan. "We hump up about a hundred meters just to make it look good; then we spread out, take a little chow, Pomeroy calls in we're ready to rock and roll. Then we smoke a little dope, fall asleep, then hump back down in the morning. That about it buddy?"

Deagle laughed. He liked Gary Brennan, and if he seemed a wise-cracking buffoon it was because he was smart and probably scared more than he showed. He was sure he could count on Brennan when the chips were down. He was equally sure of Hooper and that left only Sp5 Vincent as a question mark.

"Listen up. Everybody check your gear one last time. This may look like a half-assed ambush but nobody goes up half-assed in my squad. No tracers, no chin-straps or slings rattling, no lose stuff in your rucksacks. Put some bug juice on a handkerchief or a towel and keep it in your pocket so you're not slapping and scratching all night long. Everybody got an extra fatigue shirt? It gets cold after sweating two quarts and then sitting dead still all night. I'm gonna use the phone, Brennan you and Hooper help Pomeroy into the Prick-25 before we break out. Hold your questions for now."

There was a light knock on the east door. Their smoke and shovels had arrived.

"We gonna be digging?" Vinny asked.

Deagle shrugged. "Depends on the cover up there. But if we do dig in, you make sure it's deep enough you're not digging your own grave, you bic?" He handed one entrenching tool to Hooper, one to Grossnickel, and carried the third himself.

"We are gonna kick their asses," Vinny said. He looked at Hooper and grinned. "Hey, Deagle is face paint authorized for everybody or just Hooper the red-nosed reindeer here?"

Brennan smirked. "Yeah, Hooper can walk point so we can see the trail…"

"At ease, you guys," Deagle grumbled. "The only trail you'll see tonight is after we get there." He walked to the communications table and picked up the phone. Sergeant Major Bierra answered and connected him to Colonel Borg. Borg sounded subdued.

"What is it, sergeant?"

Deagle glanced down at the Omega. "Sir we're breaking out in zero five, exactly 2000 hours. Before we do we'll call in with a radio check."

"That sounds fine. Your RTO will be Sergeant Major Bierra. Good hunting."

From the west door of the barracks, five pairs of eyes followed Deagle as he hung up the phone and headed toward them. He snapped out the light and waited in the darkness until he recognized the faces under the steel pots. He spoke quietly, slowly.

"Listen up. This is a fire-mission briefing. At the hill, Jim you take point, Vinny you're slack man, right behind him. I'm behind Vinny, then Pomeroy, Brennan, and Hooper's drag. Got it? We're gonna do this by the numbers. We go through the elephant grass, then about three hundred meters straight up, then we'll feel around in the dark for the objective, which is a piece of flat ground about thirty-five meters deep with a trail running through it. Our job is to block that trail. Questions so far."

"That colonel with the elephant ears said we're the secondary ambush and the green beret's got the red zone," Jim whispered. "That means we sack out, right?"

Deagle's steel pot wagged side to side. "That colonel with the elephant ears is the S-2. It was his fuckin' outfit that didn't know there were VC on the hill. Webb says it's all red zone up there and that's good enough for me. My guess is those green berets are gonna sit on their hands all night and the gooks will come through us. The trail we're blocking looks like the Ho Chi Minh highway."

"Jesus Christ."

"Ah, this is sounding more and more like a bad idea, buddy," Brennan whispered. "And why would the gooks try to hit again when the whole base is expecting them?"

"Good question. Answer, I don't fucking know. That's why we're going by the book. We caught a break with the clouds, at least for a couple hours. Gonna be pretty dark for awhile. On the way up we don't talk, we whisper. We don't smoke, we don't light matches to see, and we don't make noise except the kinds animals make." He detached Pomeroy's mike and handed it to him. "Give 'em a radio check. We're all bugs tonight. The guys in the green hats are 'Spider' and 'Scorpion' and we're 'Firefly'. Base is 'Hornet's Nest'."

In a low, clear voice Pomeroy keyed the mike and said "Hornet's Nest this is Firefly, Hornet's Nest this is Firefly requesting radio check on 68.553. How do you read, over."

When the call came back too loud Pomeroy turned down the volume. "Firefly, this is Hornets Nest, read you 5x5 on 68.533, over."

"Hornet's Nest this is Firefly. Roger, 5x5, switching to primary, and Firefly out."

Vinny said. "Hey, Pomeroy, you really know your shit,"

Deagle's voice rose slightly above a whisper. "Everybody listen up. This is an ambush: see Charles - kill Charles. If it happens it'll be goddamn dark and from close range. I want this clearly understood: *nobody* fires a weapon unless I fire first. If we make contact, we throw frags. Pomeroy and Fuck-knuckle know the drill... so sound off with an affirmative... Sergeant Hooper you read?"

"Frags only, fire when you fire, affirm."

"Vinny?"

"Frags first. Got it."

"Brennan?"

"Do not shoot, do not pass go, do not collect... I got it I got I got it. Ten-four and affirmative."

"Okay last item. If we hit 'em with rifles, selectors on single-fire. Full auto is for hotdogs."

The base outside was as dark as the barracks inside, 'lights out' under a solid black sky. The only bright spot was low and to the left, the flare-bright glow of the floodlights at the base of Hill 229. Deagle took the lead and they trooped up the grade past the deserted enlisted records branch then angled right toward the R&R detachment. To maintain night vision, Deagle steered a course below the wire through the admin barracks, then up the road to the left side of the checkpoint. Passing R&R 2030 a voice in the dark whispered, 'good luck you guys.'

From the shadow of R&R 2013 Deagle looked up at the checkpoint, side-lighted by the R&R floodlights. He saw the shape of the MP inside the open door but wasn't sure if the MP saw him. He stepped out to the road and pulled his M-16 off his shoulder, raised it high. The MP threw up his right hand in a returning salute, okay to come ahead. He signaled his squad to quickly cross the last of the open ground to the brush east of the shack, thinking that the VC who killed the day-duty MP might have used this brush to hide himself.

He whispered for Jim to move into the elephant grass. Rifle hanging in his right hand, Jim stepped up, crunched loudly, and disappeared with Vinny holding onto his belt. Vinny stepped up. Deagle listened to the two of them struggling for balance and breaking off stems. Going to be a noisy climb, he thought.

Third man into the elephant grass, Deagle was immediately, totally blind. He could not see Vinny in front of him or the M-16 in his left hand. There was no air, only humidity. His first steps were awkward as Jim and Vinny took turns slipping back but he was hardly aware of Pomeroy's grip on his belt. The sharp grass caught under his helmet and dragged across his neck, forcing him to use his rifle as a shield. After just a few meters he followed Vinny to the left, realizing Jim had given up a straight vertical ascent in favor of a gradual angle to the east, longer but easier walking. Like circus elephants, tail to trunk, the squad bashed uphill until Jim sent word down he had to take five, a standing break. Deagle's uniform was soaked through as sweat rolled from every pore, and the tight liner inside his steel pot made his forehead sting like fire. He couldn't see the sky and was worried about the cloud cover holding. He gave Vinny an impatient little shove to get Jim moving again.

Brennan was glad to be moving again. Standing still he'd begun to shiver and he was sure Pomeroy ahead of him could feel it. Just twelve inches away, Brennan could not see Pomeroy, only imagine him, even though his right hand held the big man's belt. Staying close behind those huge shoulders and back, most of the sharp grass that tried to separate him from his helmet and his M-16 was either trampled or deflected. He wondered how bad it was up ahead for Vinny behind Grossnickel. And he was damn glad to feel Hooper behind him. What if Hooper let go suddenly? Everybody would have to halt while Hooper flailed around blind trying to find them again. Moving up, he tightened his grip on Pomeroy's belt. He would not want to be the drag, no way.

Pomeroy concentrated on keeping their life-line, the Prick-25 on his back and maintaining his balance, knowing if he went backward he'd take the whole squad with him. In front of him Deagle was a sure, long-legged climber and never a burden, but behind him Brennan and Hooper were a load. When Pomeroy stood still, Brennan used him for a tree limb to pull himself up, and when Pomeroy took a step up he felt harnessed to a plough. So it was Pomeroy who called for the first serious break after half an hour in the elephant grass.

They sat down in place and shared a single canteen, one of Grossnickel's, because half-full canteens gurgle. They passed the canteen down the line each taking half a dozen swallows and when it was empty Hooper flipped it into the jungle–garbage. Deagle okayed whisper communication to the man in front or behind.

"Freaks me out being blind," Vinny whispered. "How do I shoot when I can't see shit?"

Deagle leaned forward. "You don't shoot. A few more minutes... you'll be able to see."

"Hope so."

"Doing good. Maybe ten more minutes. Pass it up."

Vinny reached up to find Grossnickel and located a wet knee. "Deagle says we're doin' good. Ten more minutes."

Jim nodded and then realized Vinny couldn't see him either. "Affirm."

"I feel like a yo-yo," Vinny confided. "You're pulling me or Deagle's pushing me."

Brennan sat on his right hip, left leg trailing down the hill. He knew Hooper was below him because the E6 still had a hand clamped on his belt. He realized he actually liked the little lifer. He leaned down and whispered, "Okay, sarge?"

"Fine as froghair," came the reply.

"You believe this shit?"

"Makes you wonder if your eyes will ever work again, don't it?"

"Ah, not until you just mentioned it, sarge, no."

On the move again, Jim soon sent word down he was up against bamboo. Deagle advised steering around to the east, and as they rattled along the bamboo he kept a running score of his squad's whispered curses, loud canvas rustling, and crunching of combat boots. On top of too much noise, the bamboo added another ten minutes of blindness, and Deagle hoped when they got out of it he'd find the evening air currents going downhill. He had grass stuck in his steel pot, grass between his rifle and sling and trapped in his pistolbelt. His right boot was unlaced. A few meters after Jim began working up the hill again, Deagle thought he saw something. No, more accurately he saw less nothing, a lighter shade of black above. The sky? Remembering the new Omega, he checked the time and got the shock of his life. The watch-face was a green phosphorous monster, every numeral and hash-mark in stark relief against the black background. The glowing hands told him it was 8:43. So he knew the exact time when the squad went down like dominos.

He was leaning with most of his weight on his right boot when it happened, waiting for Pomeroy to climb up. His legs were tired. Staring ahead, he had convinced himself there was a break in the black void. Above him, Vinny took one more step and without warning Deagle was yanked forward and slammed face down on the ground. He felt Pomeroy's crushing 280 pounds on his legs and for a terrible split second he felt the fear of being trapped, unable to use the legs that had never let him down. He heard a cry of surprise below him, Brennan or Hooper, as they came down on Pomeroy. Fighting to keep his helmet on his head and his rifle in his hand he pulled his legs free and wriggled up alongside Vinny, whose right arm was stretched tight like a piece of wood.

"Jim's down a hole," he whispered, "I got him by the belt."

Deagle scrambled up blindly. He found Grossnickel's M-16 lying outside the tunnel entrance.

2045Hours 24Dec71
1st Cav Division HQ
Reception Room, Division Sgt Major Bierra's Desk

The reception room had cleared, some. The division artillery and air force officers had given up, the press was in their quarters, even the chaplain had gone back to his hooch. Only a few dozen 1st Cav JAG and admin officers remained to bother Sergeant Major Bierra. Taking a breather from the telephone he looked around the room at his competition. Who among these admin officers would the commanding general choose to run the admin battalion? He decided he liked his chances.

The phone rang and it was Trumpy back at the motorpool. "I ain't got a jeep left. There's more 2nd lieutenants cruising this AO in vehicles than guards walking posts. How is it up there?"

"Now I know exactly how Custer felt. Want to be my replacement? Hey, gotta go."

The other phone rang, this time a chain call originating at MAC-V Long Binh. A six-story building there had been damaged by an RPG hit. There was an unknown number of casualties. III-Corps command was advising all rear-area commanders to reinforce tower positions and maintain a high-alert status until 1800 26Dec. Bierra wrote down the info and slammed the phone down; all commanders should be prepared for "limited, harassing and disrupting VC activity throughout the truce," but no full offensive.

"No shit," he said to himself.

The phone rang again, this time a scratchy patched-in connection from the south perimeter. It was one of the young officers that Bierra found half-bright and respectful, and funny, Lieutenant Keely from the Corps of Engineers. Too bad Keely was leaving the army when his hitch was up.

"How's bedlam," Keely asked.

Bierra grinned. "Sir, when I hear that expression I always wonder what bedlam means. And I'll bet you're the guy who can tell me."

"Why of course, sergeant major. Bedlam is, or was, a well-known English sanitarium. A nut house."

"Thank you, sir. And that is exactly what my AO looks like right now. A nut house."

"Well I won't add to your misery. I'll buy you a good smoky scotch when this night's over. How do you read this transmission?"

"You're breaking up a little, but not too bad."

"Good. I'd hate to have to use phonetics to get through. I'm not very goddamn good at phonetic spelling. So here's the deal: tell Borg.. or is it Wilcox now... the perimeter is secure and quiet. I got enough 105 batteries aimed at the jungle to dig him a moat around Bien Hoa."

"I'll tell him, them, sir. Very good job."

The next call was from Colonel Wilcox, reminding him that soon he would move the command post to the briefing room. All the visitors and the press would have to clear the room.

"Sir, I still have about fifty briefing requests for yourself and Colonel Borg."

"You're doing yeoman service, Top."

"Sir, since you're the S-2... in reverse order, here are the most recent reports; Lieutenant Keely reports the perimeter is secure, MAC-V has been hit by one RPG with casualties, and Master Sergeant Trumpy has run out of jeeps."

He heard Wilcox mumble to someone nearby, then, "thank you. Find your replacement and get in here."

Bierra hung up and was startled to find Major Warren Andrews standing in front of his desk. His blood ran cold. Andrews wore the tiger-stripe fatigues of the long-range reconnaissance patrol, jungle boots, and full camo grease paint. He had the attention of every officer in the reception room, and he knew it, standing tall and straight as if he'd come to receive a Silver Star. The holster flap securing his .45 was open, right hand close to the butt, and under his left arm were books, maps, and a briefcase. Bierra's eyes traveled from the pistol to the livid scar on his forehead to his bulged, blood-streaked right eye.

"Major Warren Andrews to see General Webb."

Bierra picked up the phone. Thirty seconds later Colonel Borg opened the staff door.

Andrews marched down the hall and turned left to the east briefing room, Borg following. A pair of MP's got in cadence behind Borg. Inside the briefing room Andrews paused to admire the conversion to a command bunker, and his eyes sparkled with pride. The whole staff was there to receive him, including MPs in khakis. Standing beside his personal map of Hill 229 was Brigadier General Jeffrey Webb. Andrews nodded proudly.

"Major Warren Andrews reporting for duty, SIR!"

Webb walked up to inspection distance. The major's right eye glowed bright red.

"You found my S-2 right on the money, didn't you, sir."

"Where have you been, major."

"Saigon, sir. I felt that it was very important to put some time between the sapper attack and our ambush missions. Now I have a clear picture of where those ambush teams should be and I'm ready to lead them up Hill 686, sir."

Webb glanced at Wilcox. It was the first time Webb had seen his new S-2 wearing a sidearm. Behind Andrews, Borg had strapped one on as well. They had the major surrounded.

"Where would you put those teams, major? Show me."

Andrews advanced stiff-legged to the map and pointed. "Sir, I'll cover the dump but not as a main objective. Then I'll put a fire-team here at the meadow, blocking that trail. Then I'll put another fire-team here, covering the trail down to the air strip. Those are long climbs, sir. We can't use the road so we better get started. And the key to an ambush is good people. I need good, disciplined people."

Webb nodded. "We have good people up there, major. Now, you need some rest."

Andrew's jaw dropped open. "Rest, sir? That hill is Victor Charlie. There are hundreds of them up there, enough to engage a whole brigade."

Webb lowered his eyes. "We know about Hill 686, major. It was three

years ago. Look at the numbers on your map. This is Hill 229 and it's 1971.
You took critical S-2 to Saigon with you and caused the deaths of six more
fine young men."

Andrews stared. "Sir, I couldn't tell Colonel Borg. He'd have reported me
to Senator Symington! Those men had to die in order to save the brigade!
Charles hits once, then he hits twice!"

Webb signaled the MP staff sergeants forward. One of them whisked
Andrews' .45 from his open holster and the other pinched his arms together
behind him and kicked his feet apart. The MPs searched the major for other
weapons and then let him stand up straight. Registering only surprise at his
treatment he allowed the MPs to escort him back into the open hallways.

"I'm going to grab a bite to eat in my quarters," Webb said, and walked
out through his office.

At his desk, Sergeant Major Bierra watched the MPs take Andrews out
into the quiet night, then rubbed his hands together. He liked the sound of it:
Captain Bierra, Admin Battalion Commander, 1st Cavalry Division Air Mobile.

2045Hours 23Dec71
1st Cav Div HQ
Hill 229

Instinctively, as he dropped off the face of the earth, Jim threw out his
arms out wide to catch an edge. His rifle flew out of his left hand and the
fingers of his right hand dug into hard dirt. He hung by one hand with his legs
dangled and realized Vinny still had him by the belt. The toe of his right boot
scratched the bottom of the tunnel. He was about to scream when two strong
hands grabbed him under the armpits. He heard Deagle whisper close to his
ear "Jim, I got you!"

"Get me the fuck outa here!" he whispered back.

"Can you touch bottom?"

"Yeah, barely. You smell what I smell? Get me the fuck out!"

Holding on, Deagle turned his head to where he thought Pomeroy was on
the ground below. "Cleve! Crawl up here and give us a hand."

Pomeroy scrambled up feeling with his hands, getting close enough to
Deagle that their steel pots clunked lightly. The night was black but the hole
Grossnickel was in was blacker, and Pomeroy thought he could see the shape
of it, a man-hole sized opening with just Jim's steel pot and shoulders sticking
out. He got hold of Jim's left arm and braced himself on his knees.

"You smell what I smell?"

"Pull."

"I can almost see him."

"Me, too. We must be almost out of this shit."

They pulled Jim out of the hole and slid back down the hill in an unmilitary pile of legs and arms. Jim was okay, nothing broken, but Deagle heard him shivering with fright. He put Vinny on point and told him to lead away parallel to the hill and count fifty steps as best he could. From there it was a two-minute climb out of the elephant grass where they were able to see again. They huddled in an area of waist-tall brush and springy ferns. The sky was still black but breaking up to the east with enough silvery moonlight to make out the shape of the clouds. Deagle sat facing his squad holding up one hand for quiet and the other tight on his M-16. Quiet. Wait. Don't even breathe hard. He closed his eyes and listened to the night. There were no footfalls following them.

"New ballgame," he whispered.

"What was it," Vinny asked

"Tunnel," Deagle told him.

"God, how I hate tunnels," Jim shivered, "especially with gooks in 'em. Am I right, Deagle?"

Deagle was thinking what to do next.

"Affirm," Pomeroy told everybody. "I smelled 'em too. Now what do we do? If we move up, that might put gooks above us and below us."

Brennan's eyes bounced from Deagle to Grossnickel to Pomeroy, a ping pong match. "Ah, you guys are shittin' right? We don't really have gooks sitting right under us..."

"What'd they smell like?" Vinny whispered.

"Fish and tiger balm."

"What's tiger balm?"

"Oily shit that keeps evil spirits away," Jim explained.

Pomeroy nodded and raised a finger to his lips.

Deagle had made up his mind. "Listen up. Cleve, you and Vinny sneak over another thirty meters from here and call it in to Borg. From there you can whisper loud enough to be heard anyway. We'll sit tight here. Walk exactly parallel to the hill. You bic?"

"What do I tell him?"

"Tell him we found a tunnel below our objective and get permission to frag it."

"How are you gonna find it again?"

"Follow our back-trail. Go ahead. We'll wait here."

Pomeroy crouched low with his rifle at port arms and disappeared into the jungle, with Vinny right behind. After they were gone Brennan reached up and patted Grossnickel on the arm

"You got my respect little buddy," he whispered. "I'd have shit my pants."

Jim grinned. "Maybe I did shit my drawers. I better check... nope."

Deagle motioned for them to pipe down.

Hooper crawled up beside Deagle. "I'll go back with you, cover you."

"That's a rog."

Pomeroy reached rocky ground and carefully set down his rifle. He took the radio and keyed the mike. His voice was low and slow.

"Hornet's Nest, this is Firefly, Hornet's Nest, this is Firefly, over."

The voice that came back was strange but correct RTO technique.

"Holy shit, that's Sergeant Major Bierra," Vinny whispered.

"Hornet's Nest, this is Firefly. We have a tunnel approximately three-zero-zero meters below our objective. I say again, we have a tunnel below our objective, tunnel is confirmed Victor Charlie. Request permission to frag, over."

Bierra's right hand froze, finger above the transmit key. An active cave was a new wrinkle. Webb was taking chow in his BOQ and Borg was debriefing Sergeant Gonzales about the two sappers, which left new S-2 OIC Wilcox and new XO Shipp in the room, neither officer with recent combat experience. Knowing his commission depended on his performance in this situation, he walked to map tables. Wilcox and Shipp stood alongside him and the three of them looked down. Neither Major Andrews' map nor the newest topographical photos of Hill 229 showed caves or tunnels that far down. Shipp glanced at his watch.

"We need Webb, ASAP," Bierra told the officers.

Colonel Shipp peered at him over his glasses. "Young man, you ain't an officer yet. In this AO we refer to the division commander as General Webb."

"Sir, I apologize."

"I think Colonel Shipp and I can make this call," Wilcox told him. "Sergeant Deagle can't be much more than a hundred meters above the R&R detachment."

"New tunnel?" Shipp asked.

"Or he's playing games, and wants to quit early," Bierra replied. "Damn draftees, you don't know which ones to trust." He walked back to Prick-25. "Firefly, this is Hornets Nest. Say again, over"

"Hornet's Nest, this is Firefly. I say again, we have a confirmed Victor Charlie tunnel below our objective, request permission to frag, over."

"Confirmed, meaning what?" Wilcox whispered.

"They seen one or smelled one," Shipp told him.

"Even so, blowing that tunnel is not a great idea this early, sir," Bierra pointed out.

Shipp leaned closer, one hand adjusting his reading glasses the other nervously twirling his mustache. "If he drops a frag down that hole every freakin' VC b'tween here and Sin City will know he's up there. Order him to move out."

"Firefly," Bierra said loud and clear into the radio, "this is Hornet's Nest. Negative, I say again negative on your frag request. Proceed to your objective. Firefly, give me an affirmative on that, over."

Pomeroy stared at his transmit key.

"That's bullshit!" Vinny whispered. "We'll be surrounded. Cuss Bierra out."

Pomeroy shook his head. "Never cuss on the radio, never use names on the radio. Only call-signs. Sacred code of the RTO. But I could give him some squelch... better yet, I'll let Deagle give him some squelch." He held down the key and spoke softly. "Hornet's Nest, this is Firefly. Negative, your last transmission, will advise squad leader. Firefly out."

Listening hard, Wilcox shook his head, confused. His glasses sagged from his beaked nose. "Did I just hear radio double-talk?"

"I don't know who the hell he thinks he is," Bierra boomed, "but I can be pretty slick, too."

"Hold on, sergeant major." Shipp crossed the room to the south window and peeked under the corner of the shade. "Shit, if I was Deagle I'd disregard that order, disable the radio, and blow that tunnel so I ain't flanked. Let's wait an' see if he's smarter."

Pomeroy and Vincent duck-walked back to the squad, and Vinny broke the news to the four faces waiting in the dark.

"Bierra wants us to move out. Can you believe that son-of-a-bitch?"

Deagle looked to his old friend for an explanation.

"I told him you'd confirm."

The buck sergeant grinned. "So it's up to me? Well, I was a corporal once before, guess I can be again. How'd you feel about goin' on R&R as a PFC?"

He glanced at Grossnickel, who said. "Let's blow the bastard."

Deagle nodded. "Bierra's right, tactically. We should move out. But I'm just a dumb buck sergeant and we're not getting flanked tonight. So give him some squelch and I'll take the heat."

Pomeroy cranked up the knob. He tapped the mike like sending morse code while talking mush, mouth full of marbles, and the only clear word was "Deagle." Chuckling to himself, Pomeroy forgot to shut the radio off.

"Here's how it works so listen up. Hooper and I are going back; we can see good enough now. Cleve, you take the squad fifty meters straight up and wait for us."

"Roger. You heard the man, move out troops".

But before they could move, Jim Grossnickel held up his hand for quiet. At first it sounded like wind moving through the brush. But there was no wind. Jim turned to face the sound, below and to the right in the elephant grass. Looking at Deagle he pointed northeast. A branch swished lightly and this time Deagle heard it. He watched the secondhand on his Omega tick two full revolutions, listening. Then Pomeroy held up his big palms. Footfalls paralleling, going up.

Pomeroy mouthed the words, "our guys?"

Deagle listened intently and pointed a finger at the sky. "Definitely up."

"Now what?" Jim whispered.

Vinny watched Deagle, unable to see his deep-set eyes. Sp4 Brennan poked Deagle's shoulder and pointed toward the road. Deagle shook his head no.

"Wait right here," he whispered. "And make like a rug."

In Deagle's mind the route back to the tunnel had three legs: down a couple dozen meters, parallel twenty meters, then a body length up to the entrance. He crabbed down the trail of trampled grass to where it turned left, leaving Hooper there with both rifles. He pulled out one fragmentation grenade and held it tight, handle against his palm. The elephant grass was not quite as thick as the stuff down below, he was able to distinguish shades of black under a clearing sky. He low-crawled a light-shaded line that was his squad's back-trail to the tunnel, and suddenly it occurred to him that there might be other entrances to Jim's tunnel. Maybe the hillside was a maze of tunnels. Too late now, he was committed. He reached the corner and started up, feeling ahead with his hands for the tunnel entrance. He reached out with his right hand to grab another foot of real estate, pushing with his right knee and foot. His hand went into the tunnel and he yanked it back as if from the mouth of a shark.

He pulled himself to a sitting position, skin tingling and all his senses keyed. The night seemed brighter and his nose caught the updraft putridity the troops called "old gook", a foul mingling of cigarettes and stale sweat, a faint fish stink, and excrement. Maybe they were still in there or maybe they'd just heard them leaving. Maybe a frag dropped in their living room would make them stay put all night. But it wasn't good enough to just pull the pin and let the frag go.

He felt around the cave's edge until he found a small pebble. If 5' 6" Jim Grossnickel could touch the bottom with his toes, Deagle could stand in it. Every hair on his long arms bristling, he took a last deep breath and held it, then lowered himself down until his boots hit bottom.

Quickly, he felt for the tunnel walls and found that the opening went back toward the road. That was a break. Underhanded, he flipped his pebble and heard it skip once along the wall and again further away with a slight echo, at least fifteen feet. Flattened tight against the wall where he couldn't be shot, he listened to the crash of his heartbeat for five seconds. He heard a sound a few meters away, like water trickling. He yanked the grenade pin and let the handle fall. He chucked the grenade like a bowling ball and then performed an Olympic standing-jump out of the cave. Four.

His eyes found the trail and he crawled on hands and knees. Three. In order to make it to Hooper he'd have to get up and run. Two. He crouched and ran, slipping, legs churning, grass holding him back. Can't make it back to Hooper. One. He dived onto his belly and covered his head. Zero. The grenade let go with a cushioned roar and shock wave that shook the ground under him. It reverberated and rumbled as hunks of rock under the ground broke loose and settled.

Above, Pomeroy reacted to the grenade by ducking his head, and seconds later he heard Bierra's insistent call sign.

"Shit, I forgot the radio!" He gave Bierra some class-A radio squelch, then snapped it off.

277

He strained his eyes in the darkness below. He knew Hooper and Deagle would be coming hard, possibly disoriented, so he whispered for the troops to fan out the squad five meters apart to intercept them. He heard them before he saw them. They came tearing up through the elephant grass, sounding more like the Iowa State offensive line than a secret night ambush. He raised his rifle high. Over here! They were almost home when one of the bunkers behind R&R opened fire.

GI rifles at the bottom of the Hill spat .223 bullets into the sky below them and tracers winged overhead. Pomeroy hit it, face down, not sure what the hell was going on. A magazine fired full-auto strafed the elephant grass, hacking and cutting. Another M-16 joined the firefight with staccato double-taps. Bap bap... bap bap. Then over the M-16s there was the unmistakable, slower-spaced booming of an M-60 machine gun and .30 cal bullets wrecking the hill..." voom vooom vooom vooom voom vooom..." With a final long string into the treetops to Pomeroy's right, the thirty-second barrage ended and the night was quiet. A GI's shout echoed across the DMZ and up the hill "I got him! I got him!"

Deagle lifted his head. He'd landed in thick brush under a tree and his legs were caught in its hanging vines. He heard the echo of boots running hard between barracks, a squad or more.

"Don't shoot!" one of them hollered. "Our guys are up there!"

When the night quieted Deagle found Hooper huffing and blowing and motioned for him to follow. The rest of the squad was just ten meters up the hill.

"Those guys down there are spooked, "he said.

"Hell, I'm spooked," said Hooper.

"Hey, Deagle, how about I wish those jerks a Merry Christmas with a few rounds," Jim offered.

"We heard the frag," Pomeroy said, "how'd it go?"

"Right in Charlie's living room. We'll take five, then move out."

"To the road?" Brennan said hopefully.

Deagle pointed. "Up."

The squad shared another full canteen and Brennan passed out a few stalks of red licorice. Overhead, the sky was clear along the western horizon and low clouds drifted toward the strengthening glow of the moon. The night was bright enough for Deagle to see faces again, to read their eyes. Without words he set them up in line order and signaled Grossnickel to steer them around to the right, west. Walking side-hill, Deagle picked the grassy crud out of his rifle sling and belt. Pomeroy whispered in his ear that the radio was dead. Good. With all that shooting below Sergeant Major Bierra had his hands full, anyway.

Webb read Darcy's note again. He shoved his dinner tray to the side of his desk and reached for the phone. The muffled roar of Deagle's grenade brought his head up. Now what the hell!

He took long strides through the outer door, down the long empty corridor to the east briefing room where two startled officers and a division sergeant major huddled around the Prick-25. Then, from the bunkers in front of the R&R barracks, they all heard the staccato of full-auto M-16 fire, followed by the sluggish burst of an M-60 machine gun.

"Is that what I think it was?" he asked his staff.

Bierra stood. "Ten hut! Sir, the colonels and I advised Sergeant Deagle NOT to blow that cave but he did it anyway. He disobeyed a lawful order."

Webb went to the window, pulled the corner of the blanket, and looked up at the sky, then at the hill. At its base, Hill 229 was a color between green and black, a flat depth-less mural in the harsh floodlights. Higher up was a cone-shaped silhouette against the brightening sky.

"How about that guy," Wilcox said, still amazed. "He just blithely ignored a division XO and compromised a mission given to him by a brigadier general!"

"See if you can reach him," Webb commanded.

Bierra tried but the answer was soft static.

"Turn it off, sir?"

"Negative. The other squads are due to call in their positions. Any contact from them yet?"

"Sir, spider and scorpion are moving up on course."

"And, sir, you might be a pretty good target in that window with light behind you," Bierra pointed out.

Webb took a step back. "Colonel Wilcox, take a walk up to R&R and see what that firing is all about. Probably guards reacting to the grenade but try to calm them down."

Borg jammed his helmet on. "I'll go with you, Ray."

"Sergeant major, would you call Specialist Meredith and have him bring the rest of my dinner here?"

"I'll get it for you myself, sir."

Alone with Webb in the command bunker, Shipp stroked his mustache and said: "all that racket might work our favor. Deagle's still low enough that old Charles might think the grenade was thrown from the bunkers."

"Let's hope so. But our money's on Major Eiler." Webb sat down and rubbed his eyes.

"Very sorry to hear about those men on LZ Judith, sir" Shipp said. "I ain't told the staff yet. Do we know how the hell it happened?"

Webb threw a glance. "Affirm. Malloy found a PFC still alive. The LP's fell asleep."

Unable to speak, Shipp put a hand over his eyes.

"VC outfit just walked in on them. An officer and ten men, KIA."

Webb pushed out his chair and strolled to tables where his maps were laid out. With a pencil he traced Deagle's squad from the MP checkpoint where he'd entered the elephant grass to a point above and slightly east, and wrote the words, "Firefly tunnel."

"Charles just left them there," he said. "I suppose he figured victory was complete. When I informed our III-Corps commander about LZ Judith his first reaction was positive: he said at least I hadn't ordered a night ambush mission inside Cambodia. Then he ordered me to pull the whole 8th Brigade back from Tay Ninh."

Shipp's voice came out raspy. "As you said, we can use the infantry at Bien Hoa."

"What do you think, colonel," he asked. "Is a night ambush on Hill 229 the right mission? Or should we have just say the hell with it, like Garlett."

"It's the right thing, sir."

"I'm not sure I can take another 1st Cav massacre."


```
2150Hours 24Dec71
1st Cav Div HQ
Hill 229
```

Resting again under the triple canopy, Deagle huddled the squad and washed down a salt tab with luke-warm water. The steady uphill forced march had popped the sweat again. Knowing his feet would get cold the minute he settled into his ambush position, he unlaced his boots and pulled off his wet socks.

"Everybody listen up," he whispered. "We're almost there. We're below and maybe a little west of where we spend the night. The place looks like what ploughboy Pomeroy calls a hayfield, knee-deep grass, flat, about thirty-five meters between the elephant grass and the thick shit where the hill gets steep again. Got the picture?"

He saw five steel helmets bob.

He thought the squad looked pretty heads-up now. The physical demand of the climb, so steep at times they'd had to relay each-other with gunbarrels for rope, helped overcome the mental tension of being in Victor Charlie country.

"When we get there, we find the main trail and we set up on both sides."

"What do we hide behind." Vinny asked.

Deagle looked up at the sky. "We'll see what's there. We should have the moon behind us, which would be fuckin' perfect. If there's no cover we'll dig in under the shadow thrown by the elephant grass. We'll be invisible from anywhere on the hill."

"Okay, but what do we hide behind."

"Nothing."

The twenty-eight year-old Brennan popped a handful of candy in his mouth and said to the twenty-two year-old sergeant. "Deagle buddy, have you thought this out?"

"You got any ideas let's hear 'em."

"Cool. I'm no grunt, but here's how I see it. We blew our cover when we blew that tunnel, but we had to. Those yo-yo's shooting down below probably told Charles we're ready and waiting for him. Then we made all that racket with the radio and crashing through the jungle. We got a bright moon and nothing but fuckin' grass to hide behind... plus the mosquitoes... ah, that all adds up to one thing: the road. It's been a blast, so to speak, but I think we're busted."

Vinny waved that idea off. "Ignore him. That's what I've done for a year. This is just getting interesting."

Deagle got to his feet. "Move out, Jim."

Brennan grunted.

Grossnickel on point, Vinny five meters back covering him, Deagle and Pomeroy within eyesight of both, then Brennan and Hooper watching the rear. Walking under the canopy was easy, uphill at a gradual angle to the east with enough skylight filtering through the vines to see twenty-five meters in every direction. The humidity was bad, the temperature warm, and the bugs were out in force in the dead air. After half an hour of steady progress Jim found a tall rock shard to use for a look-out. He signaled for a halt and the squad dropped in place. Deagle mopped the sweat from his face with the damp sleeve of his shirt, watching for Jim's signal to move up. But Jim jumped down he wagged his steel pot, no, still couldn't see the meadow. They moved up another fifty meters, until Jim stopped, crouched, and dropped on his belly. Vinny whirled and waved down! everybody down! Deagle low-crawled to the point. A dozen meters away the canopy played out and the night sky was marbled with white and platinum. It was an opening. After a good hard look at it, Deagle signaled the squad to come forward.

"Un-fucking-real," Vinny whispered crawling alongside.

On Vinny's left was black wall of elephant grass twenty feet tall, on his right was a slanting black morass of jungle all the way to the top of the hill. Between the elephant grass and the jungle, under a sky of thinning silver clouds, was a level-ground pasture of dew-glazed grass stalks that reflected moonlight like a billion Christmas-tree icicles.

"Psychedelic," said Brennan.

Pomeroy looked down. "Can they see it from the base?"

Deagle shook his head. "Elephant grass is too high."

They had reached the west end of the meadow. The VC trail was further ahead but it was all Victor Charlie from here, north and south. Tight, Deagle thought, only thirty-five or forty meters between them and us. For the rest of the night this squad had to maintain a near perfect silence. He studied the drooped tips of the elephant grass on the windless night, and the direction of the moon sliding across the sky at a low angle. The shadow of the elephant grass was as long as the grass was tall, a natural hiding place.

He told Jim to lead out, tight against the elephant grass, dead slow, eyes right. He was already thinking the tall grass was a break-away option if they got into the shit with Charles: just jump into it and roll down the hill, away from counter-attack. The big thing, though, was the moon. For a Uniform Sierra ambush to work, the moon had to stay behind them, to the north. He was looking at the sky when Vinny jabbed him; up ahead, Jim had raised his rifle for another halt. Deagle slid past Vinny to investigate and saw Jim had found another rock.

This rock was a boulder, smooth and waist high, and right at the edge of the elephant grass. It was big enough for the whole squad to hide behind. He looked ahead, no sign of the trail yet. He studied the wall of jungle on his right. Glancing behind him, he was startled to see moonlight gleaming off bare vertical rock. The cliff where he'd fallen, he'd almost walked by it. Not far to the trail from here. With the squad covering the cliff, Jim ducked low and moved out alone to find it. Ten meters from the rock Jim vanished in the shadow of the tall grass, gone. Deagle kept an eye on his watch: in less than one revolution of the phosphorous second-hand Jim came running back, eyes huge. Got it, he whispered. Only about thirty meters straight ahead.

"You didn't tell me the trail was a fuckin' interstate!" he whispered.

"This rock is a fall-back," he told the squad. "Remember where it is and how far away it is if I start hollering three o'clock."

He moved the squad to the trail. There, he saw no cover for an ambush. Visibility was a uniform thirty-five meters from nine o'clock on the left to three o'clock on the right, field-of-fire in front unobstructed. The ambush plan taking shape in Deagle's mind was to dig the squad in under the shadow of the elephant grass where it would be invisible and any VC showing himself along the tree-line would be caught in the moonlight. Close enough to look in his eyes before sending him to meet his ancestors.

"I want to make sure of a couple things," Deagle whispered to Pomeroy. "I'll take another pair of eyes. Brennan, follow me."

Pomeroy gave him thumbs up. Sp4 Brennan rolled his eyes.

Staying to the side of the trail, he and Brennan low-crawled through the light grass toward the tree-line. Over the first dozen meters they were in shadow, beyond that their uniforms were a soft light sheen of motion, easy to see. He reached the dark jungle and stuck out his hand to touch a four-inch forked tree that seemed to grow out of a rock. Beyond the tree the direction was up at a 45-degree angle, visibility two meters. He confirmed one thing he needed to learn, that the trail was a straight shot from this tree-line to the elephant grass, no turns or secondary trails. From Victor Charlie straight down to Uniform Sierra. He turned Brennan around and whispered in his ear to try to find the other four guys. They were thirty-five meters away sitting or kneeling at the base of the tall grass.

At first Brennan saw only moonlit sky above a jagged black line, the tops of the elephant grass. The moon was too bright in his eyes, like standing inside a lighted house looking out at a dark night. After twenty seconds his eyes were able to separate the elephant grass from its shadow as two shades of black. After thirty seconds he began to pick out vague shapes, possibly round steel pots and square shoulders. After a full minute he identified Pomeroy on the east side of the trail. Another steel pot out on Pomeroy's left, Hooper? He nudged Deagle and they low-crawled back across.

"Wouldn't believe it if I hadn't seen it," Brennan whispered. "The moon blinds you."

"We could sure enough see you," Hooper told him.

"Gunfighter's moon," Deagle said. "Let's hope it holds. You guys start digging, quietly."

"But I'd still rather be behind that nice rock," Brennan said.

"Make the ground look natural, spread your dirt."

While they dug, Deagle put out the claymores. Set up, the book-sized anti-personnel ground mines always reminded him of the banks of lights in Dodger Stadium. He aimed them to cross-fire so their back-blasts wouldn't hit the squad, one on the right and one on the left, ten meters from the tree-line, angled slightly up to spray the trail area. He pulled the shipping pins, fed the wire through, and seated the blasting caps. He duck-walked backwards to his position, hiding the wire deep in the grass. He slipped the trigger bails to the FIRE positions.

He stood in the shadow of the elephant grass looking over his set-up, thinking Sergeant Harvey would approve. Left to right he had Grossnickel on the flank, seven meters from the trail, then Vinny and Pomeroy in a two-man trench, himself and Brennan in another double-wide hole smack on the trail, and Hooper seven yards away on the right flank. Everybody was tight against the towering grass and snug in holes deep enough to sit in and duck his head. All six men had a clear field-of-fire from nine to three o'clock. The most important ambush position, for two reasons, was Pomeroy's: big Cleve was just an arms length away on his left.

For one, Deagle needed his RTO within whispering distance. There was almost no chance Pomeroy would be talking on the horn once the squad was set for the night, but there might come a time when he'd have to sneak off a safe distance away to listen in or call in, then brief the squad leader. As if one of the special forces teams blew their ambush. And the second reason,

Pomeroy was right-handed. Positioning Vinny on his left gave him plenty of throwing room. With a grenade in his right hand Cleve Pomeroy was a night-time secret weapon. Almost casually he could throw a frag fifty meters, further if he had to.

Deagle looked up, wondering if Charles was looking down. You fuckers try to cross this meadow here tonight, you're body counts. Me and Pomeroy will sit tight and chuck frags and you won't know where the hell they are coming from.

"Prick-25 shut down?" he whispered, settling in beside Brennan.

Pomeroy's steel pot nodded. Deagle looked past him at Grossnickel, then 180 degrees around to Hooper. He saw their steel pots but couldn't see their faces or read their eyes. He looked down at the Omega, startled to see its bright green dial.

It was almost Christmas morning.

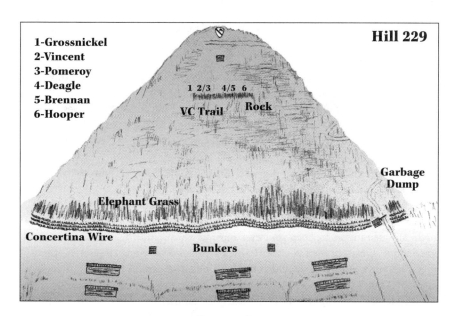

Hill 229

1-Grossnickel
2-Vincent
3-Pomeroy
4-Deagle
5-Brennan
6-Hooper

1 2/3 4/5 6
VC Trail   Rock

Garbage
Dump

Elephant Grass

Concertina Wire

Bunkers

CHAPTER ELEVEN

2225Hours 24Dec71
1st Cav Div HQ
Hill 229

A mosquito whined by Deagle's ear and landed on his cheek. He squashed it with the ball of his thumb and rubbed it out of existence. First blood, he thought. He checked the Omega and held himself perfectly still, listening for Jim. Gone five minutes now, Jim volunteered to run a recon to the bottom of the elephant grass, to see what was down below. Deagle low-crawled across the trail and huddled with Pomeroy.

"Radio off?" he whispered.

"Third time you asked. Affirmative, over."

"We don't need that sergeant major blabbing about me disobeying orders."

"Vinny says Bierra applied for a direct commission."

"No shit? Who would want to be an officer in this fuckin' army."

He crawled back in his hole and got face-to-face with Brennan. "Get comfortable but keep your rucksack on in case we have to make a break." He pointed right–west–toward the road. "That way's three o'clock, Behind us is six o'clock. When you hear it, you move out and don't look back."

It was all-quiet until Grossnickel's helmet popped out of the tall grass.

"Nothin'," he whispered.

"What kind of nothin'?"

"No tunnels kinda nothin'. This tall shit behind us is about ten meters deep," Jim told him. "Then there's lighter stuff below where we can see. The trail goes off that way," and he pointed toward the road.

"Good work. If we make contact it's going to be quick and dirty, with frags." He pulled out a couple strings of licorice and handed Jim one. "On your way back remind Vinny that if Charles shows up to make like a rug and keep his eyes on me."

"Rog, but what are the odds?" Jim asked. "This is all fucked up. Fragging that tunnel, all those guys down there yelling and shooting at trees? Us digging. You'd think the gooks would hear every move."

Deagle shrugged in his unique way, lifting his shoulders with no change of expression. "Could be they'll sleep in Christmas morning."

"Well, Merry Christmas troop," he said and crawled away to his position.

Deagle scanned the tree line and recalled the first advice he was given about night ambush missions: keep your eyes moving, always moving. If you stare too long at one spot your eyes will play tricks on you and see things that aren't there. If you see something that shouldn't be there look away, count to three and look again. If it's still there… keep a tight asshole.

He looked to his left. It took five seconds to find Grossnickel's helmet hidden in the shadow ten meters from Pomeroy. He studied Cleve's helmet, imagining he could read the pewter-colored eyes and see his powerful jaw rolling as he shucked sunflower seeds and spat the hulls, slick as a squirrel. He looked right and checked out Hooper. All five of his troops were sitting up and alert.

He surveyed the tree line from the far right to far left and back again. It looked tall because of the steep angle. Knowing how his eyes deceived in the shallow shadows and shades of black, he played a game Sergeant Harvey had taught him. After identifying what appeared to be a real image he decided on a name for it and looked away ten seconds, then tried to find it again. Twenty meters right of the trail he found a clump of four heavy bushes with vines crossing from side to side that created a chair. No, more like a kid's chair with a tall back. So, highchair. He looked away, and when he looked back the highchair was still there. His eyes moved on down the line and back again. The highchair vanished, never to be seen again. Shadows? The moon sliding slowly along?

He rested his eyes in wide-angle, tired but not ready to relax. He tried closing his eyes and listening to the tree line. Then he moved his head slowly right to left letting his eyes penetrate any holes, but there were few. Not a sound, not even a mosquito, nothing moving. The tree line was a homogenous fence. He kept his eyes moving and made three more scans back and forth before he identified that v-shaped notch just to the left of the trail where it disappeared into the tree line. He knew that was real, he'd touched one limb. The "V" was a half-shade lighter than the thick jungle behind it. He looked away, counted to ten, and found the notch. V for victory. That was one image that would not vanish with daybreak. He pointed it out to Brennan, who finally nodded yes.

A brass .223 cartridge dropped silently in the grass from his right. He turned and found Hooper sitting up, arm pointing straight ahead. He glanced quickly around at the squad. Whatever it was, only Hooper had heard it. His watch said it was 0103 hours Christmas morning. In silhouette, Hooper sat at the position of attention, listening, the muzzle of his M-16 in front of his paint-blackened bulbed nose. Then Deagle heard something far off to his right... between Hooper and the road? Between Hooper and the rock that was their fall-back? No, farther away. The faintest of fabric sounds, like the scratch of a finger over a bedsheet. Then again, farther up. Charles working around toward the garbage dump? The green beret's way off course? Too far away to tell. Then there was no sound at all but his heart thumping.

At 0135 hours they heard a light popping sound, a flare not a rifle, followed by a volley of shots on the opposite side of the hill. The sky over Hill 229 became two shades lighter, and the jungle in front of Deagle loomed taller and closer. Alarmed, he waved everybody down in his hole. Down! Under the edge of the steel pot he waited and watched the trail at the tree line. Carefully, he pulled the flaps on one fragbag and set two smooth hand grenades by his right knee. Thirty seconds ticked by. Then they heard one more furious, far-away M-16 assault by half dozen rifles in sustained semi-automatic bursts that echoed around the hill. When the bursts ended the flares burned on for five more minutes before it was black again. The moon was still low behind them.

He found Pomeroy's helmet turned toward him, a question. He nodded, go ahead.

Pomeroy grabbed the radio and his rifle. He crawled out of his hole and eased down into the tall grass, a great, green African rhino vanishing in the bush. He slid down on his butt out of the tall grass and found a clump of brush with a stout tree to rest his back against and very carefully turned on the radio. He had no intention of transmitting, only listening. The Prick-25 made a thin static rush. Hunkering over it with his body to deaden sound he heard the green beret major calling in.

"Hornet's Nest, this is Scorpion, Hornet's Nest, this is Scorpion, over."

"Scorpion, this is Hornet's Nest, over." General Webb's RTO was still Division Sergeant Major Bierra.

"Hornet's Nest, this Scorpion, we have made contact and request recon, over."

"Scorpion, this is Hornet's Nest, roger your recon. Do you need support, over."

"Hornet's Nest, this is Scorpion. Negative on support. Stand by Hornet's Nest, Scorpion out."

The guy's pretty good, Pomeroy thought. Here's hoping the guys in the green hats got one and this long night is over.

He popped a handful of sunflower seeds in his mouth and spit the hulls. Technically, he thought, those guys are supposed to recon first and advise later. Too much air-time. Charles is listening. You don't need permission to recon. Green berets are high profile operators, he supposed. When scorpion finally called in Pomeroy had a nice pile of hulls by his elbow.

"Hornet's Nest, this is Scorpion, over."

"Scorpion, this is Hornet's Nest, over." Pomeroy quit chewing and held his breath.

"Hornet's Nest, this is Scorpion, recon is negative. I say again, recon is negative. Will change position and advise, over."

"Scorpion, this is Hornet's Nest, roger that and stand by, over."

"Scorpion standing by."

Pomeroy glanced at his watch. Ten minutes after two in the morning. He allowed himself to wonder if Fran was on the airplane yet, if so maybe somewhere out over the Pacific Ocean. Bad luck, Cleve, he whispered, shutting off that thought, considering where I am right now. Guys who get killed short are guys who think they got it made in the shade. He waited long enough for one last transmission from hornet's nest, to see if Webb was pulling his ambush teams off the hill.

"Scorpion, this is Hornet's Nest, roger your change of position. Call in with distance and direction, over."

He waited another five minutes listening to the soft static before he gave up and shut it off. He crawled back up through the elephant grass and told Deagle the recon was negative. They had to stay put. Merry Christmas troop.

Deagle unlimbered his long legs and stretched. The night seemed even quieter to him now and it took him a minute to figure out why. It was the base down below, those 5,000 guys all watching and waiting, some of them watching this hill. Some of them knew there were Uniform Sierra's on the hill. For the first time there were no troops moving or slings clicking or canteen cups clinking, not even any coughing. The night was dead, morbid quiet. He rolled onto his left hip and the ground where he put his hand gave back warmth. A shiver passed through him but he wasn't yet cold enough for a spare fatigue shirt.

How many times had he and Pomeroy and Grossnickel waited in the dark for a clean chance at Charles? Not that many, a dozen or so. He looked left to check on his buddies. Pomeroy had the same thought, watching Grossnickel. In a steel pot Cleve did look different, not quite a monster. Beyond him old Fuck-knuckle was still wide awake, and Deagle imagined his slack-jawed straight-ahead concentration, eyelids about half mast and blinking every two minutes. He wondered why the hell they had volunteered for this harassment but the answer was obvious. They figured since their buddy got drafted, they got drafted. You don't find friends like that back in the world, he thought. Jim lived in Virginia, Cleve's folks were in Iowa, and he planned to return to California. All the same, back in the world the three of them would somehow stay friends for life.

Deagle was daydreaming about California beaches when Grossnickel was suddenly beside him with a hand on his shoulder. It startled him. Pomeroy's helmet was turned toward him. He glanced at the Omega, almost 0230. What? Jim pointed off to the east along the meadow where the curvature of the hill carried it out of sight. Deagle sat up and strained his ears. Nothing. Eyes anxious, Jim showed him two fingers up for the number two, then two fingers down wiggled back and forth, for two walking. Deagle pointed to Jim's eyes and he nodded. Yes, saw them. Crossing the meadow on the far left flank. Which way? Up.

Deagle's right hand came up with a claymore clacker in it, and for the first time he felt the gut-tightening certainty of contact. He sent Jim back to his hole in the ground with the stern admonishment to "stay down". He looked right and found Brennan watching him, mouth the shape of an O. He showed him two fingers and then the palm of his hand lowering. Stay down. From a foot away Brennan's eyes gave away his thought: this can't be happening.

The hour between 0230 and 0330 was the longest time in recorded history. Deagle watched the tree line in front of him knowing his ears would tell him if Charles was coming down. But there was no sound from behind the black wall. He reminded himself that the hill was steep and to listen higher up. Then he wondered if Charles had another trail, if this was the wrong trail, and their break out was somewhere around the hill. Maybe the air force side where the green berets had opened fire. Another ten minutes crawled by, and he caught himself sitting so tense he'd stopped breathing. He took in a slow, deep breath and let it out it little huffs. Something was happening up there, invisible and barely audible. Movement.

Then, high on the hill in front of him, there was a scuffing, rubbing noise. He heard it; the whole squad heard it. Seconds later a branch sprang back with a rush of leaves. Not the wind, there was no wind. Deagle glared so hard at the top of the trail he saw purple and blue blotches in the black void. He shook his head and looked up into the clear night sky full of faint stars. One more time he rolled his wrist and checked the Omega, 0345. Then he heard two men start a mumbled conversation in Vietnamese.

In slow-motion Deagle turned his head to the right, saw Hooper scrunch lower, only his steel pot showing. Brennan stared back at him and began to shake audibly. Deagle put a hand on his shoulder; stay down. Around to the left Grossnickel's helmet was tilted up, Vinny and Pomeroy were tucked down watching the trail where the voices came from. Pomeroy had maneuvered himself into a sitting, right-handed throwing position. He flipped a small rock in front of Pomeroy and showed him the claymore triggers, and Cleve showed the frag in his hand.

The conspirators behind the tree line carried on a casual dialog as if they were the only men on earth. They were so close Deagle could tell their voices apart. He heard a third voice, maybe even a fourth. There was a laugh, the breathy low chuckle of a joke, followed by a grunted command. Searching for targets, he was not yet able to pinpoint the voices behind the wall of trees. At first he thought they were in a tight formation above the trail but then they sounded scattered back up the hill. More than four?

Beside Deagle, Gary Brennan whispered "Oh my god..."

"Stay down. Eyes on me."

Brennan hunkered lower, shaking.

Deagle closed his eyes and listened. He wanted to be certain. He waited another ten seconds and then he was sure; realization was an electric jolt to every nerve in his body. He slowly turned his head left to find Pomeroy's gray eyes under the lip of his steel helmet, watching him. Cleve realized it, too. He nodded.

Charles didn't know they were there!

He arranged himself in kneeling throwing position, his first grenade sitting on the ground in front of him.

Exactly in the apex of the V-notch tree at the top of the trail he watched a pair fat black worms materialize through the jungle wall. In the moonlight they were lighter than black, more shiny than dead flat. First one, then the other, curling and un-curling over the limbs of V-notch the tree. Side-by-side, they became legs in black pajamas, the man's upper body still invisible behind the trees. A second pair of legs stepped over the notch and joined the first and they continued their conversation in low whispers. The second man was misshapen, a square lump growing from his right hip. A satchel charge. Then there was a third voice behind them.

The right-flank claymore trigger smoldered in his hand but he told himself to wait. Wait, sergeant. Let 'em form up in the open. The third VC stepped through the notch and stood beside the first two. He walked two steps into the meadow and stood out so clearly Deagle saw his baseball cap. Above his right shoulder was the straight black line of a rifle barrel. The rifleman gazed across the clearing above Hooper's head and casually produced a cigarette and lit it. He smoked quickly and the coal of his cigarette glowed red with each pull. Then he turned the other way and looked straight out over Grossnickel's head. He spoke to the others and they lit cigarettes. That's fine, Deagle thought, enjoy those cigarettes that fuck up your night vision.

One more VC squeezed between the first three and stood looking across at the elephant grass, another baseball cap. The four of them were crowded into a tight group at an easy throwing distance, thirty-five meters away. VC number four was a non-smoker who carried his rifle in front of him in both hands, and the bill of his cap flicked nervously right and left. Standing under the direct moonlight he was tall, not small. They were all tall, oriental giants with guns and bombs. Deagle watched the nervous VC rifleman, now concentrating, baseball cap steady. He seemed to stare right at Pomeroy, and Deagle knew if he stared long enough he'd see the round shape of his helmet above the grass. Deagle held his arms wide and slowly lowered them. Down. Everybody down. His fingers crushed the right clacker.

The flat, abrupt WHAAAAM! of the claymore mine in front of Sergeant Hooper shattered the night silence, and in the flash of its pyrotechnic strobe the claymore in front of Grossnickel cross-fired: WHAAAAM! Deagle sat up, aware of motion on his left. Under their chins, he and Pomeroy pulled pins and two grenade handles dropped soundlessly. They threw together, but not in perfect synch. Pomeroy's grenade toss was effortless, with same arm speed going back and forward, launching his M-67 grenade in a high arching parabola. Deagle's motion was more like winding up and throwing a fastball at a forty-five degree angle, as hard and high as he could to land on those baseball caps. The two grenades chunked down softly and close together, thump-thump, like rocks landing on sod, and before going face-down in his hole Deagle saw that two VC were down and two had disappeared.

Not much more than a basketball court's length away, the grenades made a single ear-splitting blast followed in a nano-second by the slicing zzzzzzz of flying metal casing and core wire. As the shockwave died away, Deagle was up again and Pomeroy right with him. Yanking the pin from his second grenade, he saw a blur of black silk pajama legs and threw for the center of it. He watched his grenade arch out of sight with Pomeroy's higher and farther right behind. Before he hunkered down again in his trench he had a flashing vision of Vietnamese crawling for the cover of the trees behind them. This time the twin explosions were half a second apart but right on the same spot, a jungle-tearing "ba-boooom!" that preceded a human shriek.

Pieces of jungle filtered down and Deagle lifted his head. Incredibly, there were no VC bodies lying on the trail. He fumbled into his second fragbag for a grenade, and he was still staring at the spot to throw it when a rifle opened fire at him. He saw the orange muzzle wink and heard the crack and felt the bullet snap overhead. Before he dug his steel pot into the dirt a half dozen more rifles opened fire.

Bullets cracked triple super-sonic across the meadow, a spastic uncoordinated counter-attack. Deagle heard bullets whipping into the elephant grass backdrop headed for 1st Cav HQ below. Fighting the instinct to keep his face buried, he raised his eyes high enough to see a dozen muzzles flashing up the hill. Another bullet cracked above his helmet. The VC riflemen were lined up at different elevations on the hill like a squad caught in mid-descent, but shooting high. Their grenades landed short! A phosphorous-red streak crossed the clearing six feet over Deagle's head and left him momentarily stunned. Impossible. Another red line scorched the air far left of Grossnickel. Tracers. Charles had tracers. But with the squad in their holes tucked in the shadow of the elephant grass, Charles still had no idea where to shoot his tracers.

The return fire died away. Deagle watched the muzzleflashes on the hill extinguish. At least a dozen rifles, he thought. He was outnumbered but he still had the upper hand. An eternity of ten seconds passed before a sniper fired a single shot. Quitting? Covering their retreat? Then a second single shot three seconds after the first. He watched a tracer burn into the tall grass over Grossnickel. Then he knew what they were doing, the oldest trick in the book. With a rage building inside him, Deagle got his knees under him and sat up. Pomeroy caught his signal. High and far this time.

Waiting for Pomeroy, Deagle held his grenade with handle tight against his palm and his left index finger in the ring. Another VC riflemen probed fire, hoping to goad his squad into firing back and giving away their hiding places. Not this time you son of a bitch! A rifle cracked sending a red laser ten feet over Hooper's head, but the E6 hunkered low and waited for Deagle. Another bullet snapped overhead and Deagle flinched. There were four or five VC riflemen willing to draw fire to themselves so that the others could locate the enemy. He marked their locations in his mind. Ready.

Pomeroy arched his third grenade effortlessly for a spot five meters back in the trees. To hit the same target, almost fifty meters way Deagle had to arch his back and really put the mustard on it, and he threw too low. His grenade crash-landed in the canopy long before Pomeroy's dropped straight down. He jerked the pin from frag number four and stood up to his full 6 feet 4 to let it go, a better throw arching almost as high as Pomeroy's that landed smack on one of those rifles. Then he hit the hole.

The first two grenades were an almost simultaneous, rolling concussion that shook the earth. "Chhhhaaaaangggg" as the metal cases broke up and sent shrapnel flying. The second pair was separate blasts, and when those echoes rolled down the hill and died away Deagle lifted his head. Five seconds passed as five hours and he checked his squad. Hooper was still down and Brennan was curled up like a caterpillar against him. Grossnickel sat up tall with his rifle out in front of him, Vincent and Pomeroy peeked up over the edge of their hole. High behind the tree line there was a scurrying sound... Charles changing position?... withdrawing? Looking and listening hard, Deagle heard a whimper of complaint. Scratch one VC. But at the V-notch where the trail disappeared into the jungle he saw scattered foliage and no body counts. Good enough, he thought. Time to take what we got and break it off. He showed Pomeroy three fingers and jerked his thumb to his right. Break it off at three o'clock! Pomeroy gave thumbs up and turned to catch Grossnickel's eyes. But a single VC rifleman opened fire, a shot that snapped between Deagle and Pomeroy and sent them face down again.

Deagle hadn't seen where the shot had come from but felt safe sitting up and digging out his last frag from the side pocket of his rucksack. Want to play some more! We'll play some more! Another probing shot. With his ears super-tuned he heard the low far-off moan of the in-coming siren through the giant speakers, a background noise gaining in intensity. A VC rifle cracked and another tracer crossed the meadow not far from Grossnickel but still eight feet high. Crack! Another sniper tried to sucker Hooper. Deagle put his left index finger into the pin ring watching for the next orange flame in throwing range. But he didn't throw that grenade because the unthinkable happened. Jim Grossnickel sat up and fired back.

Hearing the shot Deagle's head whipped left and he saw Grossnickel in a frozen frame, rifle to his shoulder and finger pulling the trigger just as he'd been taught, in single-spaced aimed shots, bap...bap... and with each one an orange flame blew out the muzzle. Frantic, Deagle waved his arms for Jim to CEASE

FIRE! No time now for a three o'clock break, he changed it to six o'clock, back into the elephant grass! He signaled Pomeroy and Vincent and Hooper but Grossnickel couldn't hear or see him. Jim sat with his elbows braced in perfect position squeezing off his rounds. Deagle saw the sudden, sickening sight of Jim's fourth shot, a bright red laser that smashed the jungle wall and broke up into fluorescent chips. Seeing it, Jim lowered the rifle and stared at it.

Deagle watched the first answering tracer streak past Jim's helmet. His scream of protest suffocated in his chest. Instead, his command was a hoarse snarl "...down down down down...down...!" Pomeroy was already down. Vinny heard the command in time to bury his helmet before a spray of bullets ripped the ground in front him and Pomeroy. Then the whole hill became an assault line against them, a spontaneous barrage of automatic and semi-automatic gunfire spewing a wall of bullets that sizzled through the short grass and whined off the dirt. The VC that he and Pomeroy had hit with two claymores and eight grenades had multiplied, and now the squad was caught in the killing zone of their counter-ambush.

A volley of slugs tore up all four sides of Deagle's hole. Cowering, with his last frag still in his right hand, he felt himself being buried alive as dirt and bullet metal showered his steel helmet. The broadside kicked earth over to Hooper's hole and back across to Grossnickel before slowing. During the short lull Deagle thought he heard Jim's M-16 again, a single dissenting shot that renewed the counter-attack and brought another hail of fire on his left. The VC counter-strike ended with a one-second "brrrrrrrp" of a full clip fired full-auto on Grossnickel's position.

They killed Jim, he thought, and then made Swiss-cheese of his body.

He heard a shout from high on the hill. Charles.

An answering shout from the trail. Uncle Khee.

Then the meadow, and the night, was silent except for the in-coming siren, a million miles below.

Deagle's whole body shook. No, it was Brennan shuddering against him, but still alive. He turned his head and saw Cleve's helmet sticking out of his hole.

"How many frags you got", he whispered across to his RTO.

"Got six," Pomeroy whispered back.

They searched the black holes in the tree line. Pomeroy saw a dozen dark shapes emerge. "Bill, I think they're coming..."

"I see the fuckers," Deagle said. "Put three frags in the air and then fire on me." On his knees Deagle straightened his back and arched his last grenade at a black ghost at the top of the trail. He got a glimpse of Pomeroy's first frag sailing high, a sliding spot of green paint swallowed by the dark hill. Pomeroy quickly yanked the pin of frag number two and fire-balled it, and as soon as it left his hand, pulled and launched number three. They dropped and waited for the quadruple explosions.

"Ba-boooommmm... Boooooommmm! Boooooooommmmmm!"

Deagle brought his rifle to his shoulder. "Let 'em have it."

Unable to see his sights or his targets, Deagle pointed his rifle with both eyes open and yanked the trigger eighteen times. He fired at memories, orange flashes from murky holes. Pomeroy and Vincent opened fire as one rifle. Deagle reversed his double clip and fired eighteen more spaced shots, and he heard the admin right flank, Hooper, join the fight. He jammed in another clip as Brennan's rifle came alive, inches from his right ear, a jackhammer that deafened him. He yanked his trigger three times before he realized his action was locked open again, empty. He slammed the clip down and shoved in a full one, risking a quick glance to his left; Jim's rifle was silent now. He saw only Jim's helmet lying inverted on the grass. Looking up the trail again he held his rifle with dead arms, sending bullets in a reckless spray back and forth. He fired another clip and reloaded, and most of another clip before he felt a heavy hand on his right shoulder.

Brennan, with a pile of empty clips in front of him, flashed five fingers plus one: six o'clock. Deagle nodded.

"Six o'clock! six o'clock!... six o'clock!... go go go go go go go...!"

Pomeroy stood and lay down covering fire as Vinny dropped back into the high grass. On the right Hooper finished his clip, lunged sideways and disappeared. Brennan's rifle splatted a dozen more times before he turned and broke away. Deagle climbed out of his hole and fired spaced shots at the left flank as Pomeroy's magazine went dry. The big man turned and heaved himself chest-first. Deagle lowered his empty rifle and glanced at Jim. Standing, he could just see the top of his head.

The last man in the meadow, Deagle forced his rigid fingers to push the magazine release, pry one more clip from his bandolier, and click it home. He raised his gun-barrel level with his hip and a clock ticked in his brain, one-thousand one, one-thousand two... From the black void above the trail a muzzle sparked orange and crimson, a final north-bound tracer cut off by the jungle wall. Holding on the spot Deagle slipped the selector over to full-auto and burned eighteen rounds in one-and-a-half-seconds. Then he took one long step and jumped into the tall grass.

Blind, he struggled to his feet but misjudged the steep slope and fell sideways, rolling the whole ten meters as the sharp grass sliced his face and hands. He piled up on the forty-five degree slope in light jungle, alone, minus his helmet, listening to the pounding of his heart and the high-note screams of the base siren, but able to see again. He heard his name whispered and flinched hard. The grass on his left rushed and he heard a loud clattering sound, like marbles in a glass jar, as Vinny low-crawled up beside him. Vinny's rucksack was shot to pieces and had come apart, but he couldn't hear it. Finger to his lips, Deagle reached up and helped him out of it. He sat up in the grass, turning his head slowly. A dozen steps away were the poised, crouched shapes of Pomeroy and Hooper and Brennan. Pomeroy showed him thumbs up. Five had made the break.

A full minute crawled by with no fire from above. Two minutes. Deagle listened to his heart and the in-coming siren. He wished they'd shut the damn thing down. Then at the bottom of the hill the base woke up with shouts with doors slamming, but no shooting. Deagle re-set his M-16 for single-fire and shoved it deep in the grass to muffle the click of his next full magazine locking home. He ran his hands down his ribs and thighs, no clammy spots but he was soaked through with sweat. With hand-signals he re-deployed the squad into a circle to cover anything moving on the hill. Listening and waiting, it was Brennan who heard Charles first. He pointed a finger up.

"Moving again," he whispered. "Up, I think."

Brennan's voice was muffled. Deagle realized he was deaf from a hundred M-16 rounds fired a foot from his ear. Brennan had showed him something up there.

Vinny pointed down. "Base siren quit."

Rifles at the ready, the squad waited and listened. Pomeroy thought he heard the smallest of sounds up the hill. A light whisk of canvas on rock. A faint hollow "tonk" of a rifle-butt against a tree. Silk scratched bark. With each sound he glanced at Hooper, who nodded. Deagle found his steel pot. Before pulling it on he wiped the sweat from his forehead and upper lip. His legs were rubber and his right ear felt stuffed with cotton but his heartbeat had slowed and he was able to think again. Vinny cupped a hand beside his ear and then pointed up. The VC were leaving. Deagle couldn't hear him.

"Had enough," Pomeroy whispered.

"We kicked their asses!" Vinny rasped back.

"Think we got some?" Brennan asked in Deagle's left ear.

He gave one of his noncommittal shrugs and looked in the grass for his helmet. "We got some. First time I ever saw Charles stand and fight."

Hooper whispered back. "There was a whole p'toon of 'em up there! Twenty or thirty, maybe. They coulda overrun us!"

"Twenty hell," Brennan answered. "More like fifty!"

Deagle shouldered out of his rucksack and stuffed his steel pot on his head. "You three guys hold this position," he whispered. "If me and Pomeroy aren't back in fifteen minutes move out straight down and stay the hell off the road."

The question was in Vinny's raised eyebrows, but there was no answer from either Deagle or Pomeroy as they low-crawled away in the dark.

"They're goin' back for their buddy," Hooper whispered.

0355Hours 25Dec71
1st Cav Div HQ
East Briefing Room

Webb listened to the numbing silence in the darkened briefing room. He was the first man to leave the safety of the outer flackwall and jump to his feet. At eye level, a bullet had punched through the wall beside the window and dozens more had ripped through the metal roof. His hands shook as he strapped on his .45. Those last four grenades told him some of Deagle's squad were still alive but the furious 500-round barrage that ended the firefight left him in doubt. The base siren had just begun its stop-and-go climb to full alert. He turned on one of Colonel Shipp's emergency lanterns.

Colonel Shipp was on his feet. "Listen," he whispered. "Quiet. Our boys in the bunkers are holding fire."

"It's over," Webb said. "Colonel Wilcox I want that base siren shut down now. Sergeant Major, try to raise Deagle on the horn. Quietly."

Wilcox scrambled to his feet, eyes wide. "They're only forty yards apart up there...

A dazed Colonel Borg sat up.

Wilcox duck-walked to the hall door, pulled it open and disappeared.

Colonel Shipp ripped the Cav phone from its cradle. "This is Colonel Shipp! Get Big Ben on the horn and have them warm up a medevac chopper! ASAP! Call Colonel Pugh at army-air and tell him I want Puff in the air in zero five minutes with mini-guns and flares. You tell him to light up that damn hill! But mini-guns on my voice command only. Read me? Mini-guns on my command only!"

Webb caught his eye and nodded.

"Then you call Geary at the motorpool. Tell him to put together a convoy of Cav troops and stand by on the road below the checkpoint by 0500!"

The siren flattened out and started winding down.

Webb walked to the map and stared at Deagle's position at the meadow. "We'll truck the troops as far as look-out and walk in from there."

Shipp glanced down at the map and then turned to Sergeant Major Bierra. "Sergeant major, call the squad leader at the garbage dump. Tell him to stand his ground but don't fire toward the convoy that will be on the road after first light. You read?"

"Yes, sir."

Webb looked down at his boots. "When Colonel Wilcox returns... have him get General Garlett on the horn, much as I hate to wake him up. Colonel Borg I need you to..."

But the full colonel was still crouched on the floor, eyes wide open and hands over the top of his bald head. The color was gone from his face. Colonel Shipp walked to him and shook him "Phil, it's over. Phil you okay?"

Borg sat quaking.

Sergeant Major Bierra finished his transmission and helped the colonel to his feet. "Take it easy, sir. A half a dozen automatic rifles can sound like a hundred. Especially when they're shooting at you."

Borg looked helplessly at his commanding officer. "Major Andrews..."

"Get hold of yourself, colonel!" Webb barked. "Sergeant major, you stay on that radio until you get Deagle."

"Yes, sir."

Colonel Shipp walked to the window and peeled the army blanket up from the bottom. He leveled his binoculars two-thirds the way up on the hill.

"See anything?"

"Not yet."

Bierra softly repeated Deagle's call-sign but there was no answer from Pomeroy. The hall door opened and Colonel Wilcox returned, still ducking incoming bullets.

"Sir, when I get Deagle, do I instruct him to recon?" Bierra asked.

"Affirmative. Tell him to recon and stay in the area. Have Sergeant Hooper move the squad and any WIA's west to a med-evac point. If there are body counts up there our support troops can bring them down... before Charles buries them."

Shipp turned from the window. "Deagle's a cocky son of a bitch but he can fight. He was outnumbered, but, sir, I think he got the last word."

Webb's teeth clenched. "I hope so, colonel.

Shipp walked to footlocker under his make-shift desk, and brought out a new bottle of Johnny Walker Red. He dumped an inch of it into a canteen cup and handed it to Colonel Borg. "Drink that, Phil. Damn VC had the good grace not to shoot my scotch."

"We move out when the hill's lit up. Colonel Shipp, you and Colonel Wilcox hold the fort here." He looked at his dazed S-2 sipping scotch from the canteen cup. "Colonel Borg, you will accompany me. Sergeant Major Bierra, you're my RTO and I hope your legs are in shape."

"Yes, sir!"

"Did you get General Garlett?"

"Working on it, sir."

0355Hours 25Dec71
1st Cav Div HQ
Hill 229

Deagle low-crawled, pushing his rifle in front of him, stone blind. His right ear was working again but ringing, his overall hearing cluttered by the base-drum pounding of his heart in his chest. One meter at a time he and Pomeroy climbed back through the elephant grass. Fifty meters above them he heard muted Vietnamese that stopped him in his tracks.

He watched the phosphorous second-hand of his Omega tick a full revolution and let his breath out. Talking stopped. He waited another minute then crawled a body-length. He figured Jim was somewhere to his left and there was no sound from that direction. He warned Pomeroy that Charles might try to sneak down to finish Jim off. He eased up another body-length and saw brass-colored light. He pulled off his helmet and carefully parted the last stalks of elephant grass.

The battleground was empty, no live VC and no body counts at the tree line.

Strange, he remembered the meadow as stark silver but now it appeared dull gold. The meadow was as he'd first seen it yesterday, deserted but threatening, and almost as bright. The pale gold moon had climbed a little, and two-thirds of the elephant grass shadow was gone. He was too low to see their four shallow trenches, and the only signs of a firefight were the broken vines and branches at the top of the trail. The knee-high grass in front of him had absorbed a thousand bullets and the jungle on the far side had blotted up a dozen grenades. No sign of Charles. With Pomeroy behind him he crawled to the motionless dark shape of Jim Grossnickel.

Jim sat in his hole Indian-style, slumped to the left, rifle still in his right hand. Deagle put a hand on his shoulder and Jim opened his right eye.

"Knew you'd come," he whispered. "Fucked up again, didn't I?"

Deagle put his finger to his lips and let out a ragged breath. He whispered for Jim to sit still while he and Pomeroy checked his back and legs for holes. Deagle found sticky dampness under his right armpit. Pomeroy whispered there was a leg wound, the muscle above his right knee, but no broken bones protruding.

"Yeah, you fucked up," Deagle chided in his ear, "can you feel where're you're hit?"

"Arm."

Jim's left arm was under him and he moaned when Deagle touched it. Carefully, Deagle hugged him while Pomeroy straightened his legs and pulled him out of his hole. A bullet had passed through Jim's left forearm and at least one of those bones was broken. Jim's eyelids hung half-way, he was conscious, but how alert he was Deagle couldn't tell since Jim's eyes were always half open.

"Jim, we can't stay here, you bic?"

"You guys kick their ass?"

"Most affirm. We have to move you down where a medevac chopper can pull you out. Lay on Cleve's back and hold on with your good arm, and I got your legs."

"Hey Pomeroy; when I fucked up I figured I better keep shooting so you guys could make your break. You hear my sixteen?"

Deagle tried to smile as tears welled in his eyes. "We heard you. You did great. You want me to recommend you for E4 or a medal?"

Pomeroy let out a gasp, and Deagle looked down to where his right hand found blood above Jim's belt buckle. The expression in Cleve's eyes stopped Deagle's heart.

"Vinny okay? Brennan?" Jim asked

"Everybody okay." Pomeroy rasped, starting to cry. He handed Deagle his M-16. "Hold on little friend."

"Goddamn that was a lot of shooting. Don't forget my sixteen,"

"Deagle's got your sixteen so just hold on. We got you." Pomeroy started to slide straight down but Deagle reminded him they had to grab the Prick-25 to call for medevac.

Pomeroy low-crawled the edge of the elephant grass with Jim on his back.

Deagle crouched behind them, one long hand on Jim's ankles and his eyes on the tree line. Up there, nothing moved. Deagle snatched the fallen radio by its harness and dragged it behind him, as Cleve, like a human sled, gently backed Jim down through the grass.

Hooper had found a place to regroup under the canopy in light brush with decent visibility. The little NCO had canteens, ponchos, GI wound packs, and a candle ready to light. He saw Pomeroy sliding toward him like a big crocodile with a baby on his back and stood tall, chest heaving and dripping with sweat, smiling relief until he saw the dark faces. He helped ease Jim over onto his back. In the moonlight, Jim's blood glistened black on Pomeroy's fatigue shirt.

Vinny scrambled over and pulled off his helmet, and it left a red ring around his head. His black hair was matted flat with sweat. "How you doin', buddy?" he whispered

They all crowded around Jim. "Sorry guys," he said. "We were pinned and I got so fucking mad..."

Brennan offered a canteen but Deagle shook his head. Belly wound. Brennan saw tears in Deagle's eyes. He saw blood leaking from Jim's left forearm and thought stupidly, he'll never play a guitar again. Of all the places for the VC to shoot this GI. A dark blood stain on Jim's belly looked like sweat. Brennan ripped open his rucksack and spread out his spare fatigue shirt on Jim's lower chest.

"We need some more blankets for his legs."

Deagle spoke in a tight whisper. "Listen up, you guys. Jim covered us while we made our break." He pulled off his rucksack and dug for his spare shirt. "Don't you hate a damn hero?"

Vinny glanced up at Deagle, understanding. "Yeah. Nice work troopie. Look ma, no holes."

Pomeroy had the radio operational and was ready to transmit when they heard Sergeant Major Bierra's call sign.

"Go ahead and answer him. Quiet as you can."

"Hornet's Nest, this is Firefly, over," Pomeroy whispered.

"Firefly, this is Hornet's Nest, over!"

"Hey, Jim," Brennan whispered, "now I WILL practice the, ah, official four GI life-saving steps. 1) restore breathing... are you breathing? You WILL keep doing it. Ahhhh... 2) stop the bleeding... you bleeding?... Negative, don't do that. And don't worry, I'll fix that buddy. 3) protect the wound... we need more wound packs here guys... 4) treat for shock. Unfortunately the official four life-saving steps don't tell me how to treat for shock but I think that means pile on the blankets and keep the patient warm. You warm enough? Deagle, I have to have light. I need some fucking light!"

"I am feeling kinda cold... "

Deagle ripped the liner out of his steel pot. He mashed the ground flat with his elbow and set up the candle under his propped helmet, throwing a cone of light down the hill.

"More shirts guys, whatever you got."

"Firefly, this is Hornet's Nest! Come in, over!"

Pomeroy ignored Bierra and stripped his rucksack of clothing, his spare fatigue shirt and poncho.

Brennan pulled Deagle aside. "He's in shock so he doesn't hurt."

Deagle nodded, swallowing. "Save as much blood as you can."

In the candlelight, Brennan cut away Jim's sleeve and daubed the area around the forearm entrance and exit holes with a clean GI handkerchief and then gently wrapped the arm with woundpacks. Using Deagle's pocketknife, he cut more of Jim's shirt to expose the nasty-looking graze wound on his upper right chest. The wound was a couple inches long and exposed two ribs. He mopped it as dry as he could and placed a woundpack there for Jim to hold in place with his elbow. Seeing the spreading stain above Jim's belt he tenderly freed the bloody fatigue shirt and felt with his fingertips. He looked up and saw Deagle watching him, tears streaming from his eyes. The bullet had torn a baseball-sized hole. Brennan covered it with two wound-packs.

Watching Jim's eyes, Pomeroy keyed the mike and spoke slowly and carefully, the consummate professional RTO.

"Hornet's Nest, this is Firefly. Zulu report follows: We have one WIA up here. I spell Whiskey India Alpha, with multiple tango-tango wounds, require medevac ASAP! I say again, we have one WIA and need medevac ASAP, over!"

"Firefly, this is Hornet's Nest. Roger your medevac request, we will put a bird up ASAP. Advise squad leader to recon immediately. I say again, advise squad leader we need recon, ASAP, over."

Pomeroy looked up at Deagle, shaking his head. "That desk commando wants a recon right now"

"After we get Jim loaded."

"Cuss Bierra's ass out," Hooper whispered.

"No cussing and no names on the radio," he said. "Hornet's Nest, this is Firefly, roger your request for recon. Will carry out when medevac has left the area, over."

After five seconds Sergeant Major Bierra came back. "Firefly, this is Hornet's Nest. Negative, advise recon ASAP, do not give ground. Move your WIA due west with white smoke, over."

Pomeroy relayed the command and Deagle looked to the sky. In the flickering light of the candle, Hill 229 had closed in, he had lost his night vision. No stars, no moon. But there was plenty of light for Charles. He wiped the tears from his cheeks.

"Hill's crawling with VC," he whispered. "We just traded a couple thousand rounds with 'em. When we move, it'll be down not up. Cleve, tell him to send that chopper and I'll start recon, whatever he needs to hear, but get that chopper in the air NOW."

"I'll tell the son-of-a-bitch," Pomeroy said bitterly. "Then I'm shuttin' him down."

Jim Grossnickel stirred, eyes still open at half-mast. "Getting' sleepy..."

Pomeroy keyed the mike.

0405Hours 25Dec71
1st Cav Div HQ
East Briefing room.
Brig Gen Webb's Offices

Sergeant Major Bierra fought with his radio controls. Deagle confirmed the recon command but Pomeroy was messing with the squelch. He looked up at General Webb at the window watching the hill through field glasses.

"Playing radio games again, sir."

"He's moved down," Webb said quietly. "Got a light going."

A quarter mile away through binoculars, Deagle's light was a pale dancing splotch, but in Webb's mind it was as bright as a flare. His hands were steady and his heart thumped evenly in his chest. Deagle had reported only one casualty.

"Why don't I hear that medevac bird!"

"Very soon, sir. For my money, Deagle will ignore your recon order."

"Well Sergeant Deagle is consistent," Shipp said. "He disobeys everybody."

"Turn it up, sergeant major, so we can all hear. And keep sending. When you get Corporal Pomeroy again let me talk to him. I understand the kind of stress they're feeling up there."

"Sir, if he is moving down it's going to be next to impossible to recover body counts. You know how the VC operate."

"Colonel Wilcox, how's our posse shaping up?"

"Colonel Geary says it's coming, slowly. He and Trumpy are briefing volunteers as to mission security. They're saddling up at the motorpool and should be ready to roll on your order. Puff's in the air, but we're still waiting for the medivac bird. And, sir, I'd like to go with you..."

"Call again!"

But the black phone rang and Colonel Wilcox answered it. "MAC-V, sir."

"Good morning, sir, this is Webb. Sorry to wake you but I thought you'd want to hear the news."

"Go ahead with it, general."

The voice wasn't Lieutenant General Benton Garlett's, but Webb vaguely recognized it. "Who is this?"

"General, it's Lieutenant Colonel Joe Quigly. I'm Garlett's aide now."

"Congratulations on the promotion, where's Garlett?"

"In the rack. He and the other corps commanders were on the phone all night with Kissinger's people in Paris. He asked me not to disturb him until 0600. He's tired, sir."

"Maybe you better wake him up. One of my ambush teams has engaged an unknown number of VC, about ten minutes ago. Probably 2000 rounds were fired plus a dozen M-67's. We have at least one casualty, a WIA at this point. We're preparing to re-engage or recon, which ever it comes to."

"Re-engage? Above your R&R? Sir, that's not a great idea, Garlett wants to... that is... did you say 2000 rounds?"

"Affirmative. Colonel, you can wake the III-Corps commander or not, you have ten seconds to decide. I've got to get up that hill."

After a slow five-count Quigly said. "I'll let General Garlett sleep."

"Fine. But log in that I called." He hung up the phone.

The only sound in the briefing room was the soft rush of radio static. Sergeant Major Bierra glared at the Prick-25, feeling the eyes of four of his division's highest ranking officers on him. Out of character, Bierra's pompadour was mussed and the flip grin had turned upside down.

"Hornet's Nest, this is Firefly," Pomeroy called in quietly. "Hornet's Nest, recon is negative and request you send medevac chopper ASAP, over."

Bierra glanced at his watch. "That's crap! The recon that took all of two minutes! Add mendacity to the list of charges against Sergeant Deagle."

Pomeroy's voice came back again, a little less professional and a little more shrill. "Hornet's Nest, this Firefly! Where is that medevac bird, over!"

Wilcox looked at Major Andrews' map. "Sir, why don't we move spider and scorpion over from their positions for a recon?"

Webb shook his head. "I'm not calling them down just yet."

"Firefly, this is Hornet's Nest! Medevac is on the way. Advise squad leader of a direct order from the division sergeant major! Take two men, return to your position and carry out a recon! Over!"

Waiting for the reply, Bierra smacked his fist into his palm. "I am personally going to court-martial that punk!"

But after thirty seconds of purring static it was Corporal Pomeroy's voice again in the speaker, sounding stilted and unsteady. "Hornet's Nest, this is Firefly. Sergeant Major Bierra, this is RTO Corporal Cleveland R. Pomeroy, US 53986202, 2nd Squad, 3rd Platoon, Bravo Company, 2nd Battalion of the 7th Brigade. Cancel medevac, I... ss...say again, cancel medevac. Be advised... be advised you can re-classify our WIA as KIA. I say again... Kelo India Alpha! He's dead. Advise you can TAKE YOUR FUCKING RECON AND SHOVE IT UP YOUR FUCKING ASS! FIREFLY OUT!"

Webb's chin fell on his chest. Then he turned on his heel and stomped out the door.

"Well, that makes seven," said Borg, speaking for the first time. "Another 1st Cavalry massacre and I'm responsible."

"Phil, I strongly advise you get your shit together," Shipp told him. "Now, you and Sergeant Major Bierra go catch up with our commanding general. Go on."

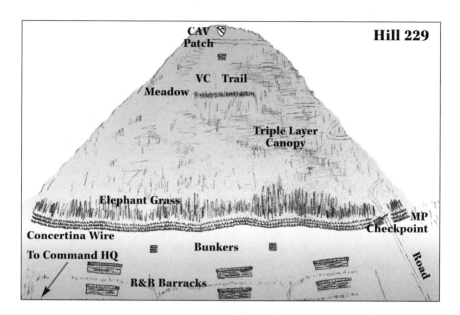

CAV
Patch
VC   Trail
Meadow
Triple Layer
Canopy
Elephant Grass
MP
Checkpoint
Concertina Wire
To Command HQ
Bunkers
Road
R&R Barracks

CHAPTER TWELVE

```
0410Hours 25Dec71
1st Cav Div HQ
Hill 229
```

Deagle shut off the radio. His breath came in gulps and he clenched his teeth to hold back a scream into the darkness. Below him, Jim's eyes gleamed and dimmed in the fluttering candlelight. He reached out and rolled them closed.

"Kill the goddamn candle," he grated.

Hooper pinched it out, thankful he couldn't see Jim's face anymore. For half a lifetime the only sound was Pomeroy's sobbing. Finally, Hooper stood and pulled off his steel pot, his voice was a cracking whisper.

"Lord, please bless this soldier who was our friend, and find a place for him in heaven with you, amen."

"Amen."

After an endless silence Hooper rasped, "Sarn't Deagle, you ain't to blame."

Vinny looked up into the night-bright sky, oily face streaked with tears. "I can't believe this shit. I can not believe this shit!"

"Listen up," Deagle whispered, "We hit, and now we run. We'll go down about a hundred meters and listen for awhile. Hooper, you take Jim..."

"I'll fuckin' do it!" Pomeroy snapped.

"Hoop, you grab the Prick-25, Vinny you got the point. South by west until you find some heavy stuff to hide in."

"South by west."

The break-away was noisy and hurried under the triple canopy. Vinny angled down toward the checkpoint not knowing if he was going west or east, only down. His legs felt strong enough to leap tall buildings but his brain was overloaded and dull. He dodged between dark trees where a thousand VC might be hiding in ambush until he saw open sky and stars, and some chest high brush as thick as a Jersey hedgerow. He pushed his way into it, lungs bursting for air, and the jungle closed around him. Brennan crashed in close beside him, panting, with a sullen Pomeroy right behind. He asked Cleve if he needed a break carrying Jim but the big man shook his head.

Deagle formed them in a tight little perimeter to wait and listen. At 0430 he heard the drone of a small engine, a lazy circle a half a mile overhead. A firecracker popped and a basketball-sized area flare on miniature parachute floated toward the South China Sea. More flares crackled until the sky took on the gray look of dusk. Deagle kneeled, eyes low, numbly watching their back-trail and listening up the hill. That high-altitude prop has to be puff the magic dragon, he thought. Mini-guns. As the sky brightened he became aware of Hooper's shallow breathing beside him. By 0445 on his Omega, Hill 229 was lit up enough for him to read all four of his squad's dumbstruck expressions, as the paralyzing reality set in that Jim Grossnickel was really dead in Pomeroy's arms.

Unable to stop himself, Deagle looked at Jim's serene face until tears rolled. He looked up and found Pomeroy watching him. Cleve's blood-crusted hands couldn't hide his own wretched expression.

"That's it," Deagle whispered, "but this hill's still Victor Charlie."

"What are we doing?" Vinny whispered, "what are they doing?"

Deagle shook his head. "Lemme think a minute."

Pomeroy choked out the answer. "Hiding their dead buddies... carrying them off, who gives a damn. Maybe taking chow."

"Chow?"

"Moldy white rice and fish-heads. Looks like an ice cream cone with chunks."

"Ralph. I'll never eat rice again."

"Or," Brennan offered, "if we didn't fuck up their plans bad enough, re-grouping to hit again?"

Hooper rubbed his knuckles over his eyes. "Some S-2 we got here. They were setting up a damn frontal attack and we walked into it!"

"What a damn screw-up start to finish," Pomeroy said.

"I'm sorry, Cleve," Vinny said.

"Shit, it's not your fault."

"What's screwed up," Brennan said, "they were coming down on Christmas day to hit the base, like that psycho Andrews said they would."

Hooper stared bitterly. "He's to blame..."

"We're in a lot of trouble, aren't we Deagle," Vinny said. "This time it wasn't lifer games. We walked away from Bierra's fucking body counts."

"Well, what's he gonna do," Brennan argued, "send us to Vietnam?"

"I broke the sacred code and he can bust me," Pomeroy said bitterly, "but he better not take away my R&R."

"That's enough, you guys," Deagle said. "Here's how all that shit works: I'm in command, I'm writing the debriefing, and if Bierra has a problem...," but the pop of a flare cut him off.

"Don't look directly at a flare if one floats by," Pomeroy said.

Vinny followed the sound of puff's engine. "What's Bierra doing?"

"Keeping the gooks in their holes. Reinforcements coming."

"Yeah, the cavalry."

Brennan crowded close to Deagle. "That plane has mini-guns, buddy. Should we be bailing out pretty soon?" Waiting for an answer Brennan looked at Deagle's face, gaunt and starkly pale under the flare-light. Deagle's wispy day-old mustache reminded him he was barely out of his teens.

He nodded. "Brennan's right. We're going down. But first I got something to say, so listen up. You three guys.. .Hooper... Vincent... Brennan... you showed me and Pomeroy something up there. If it wasn't for you guys jumping in with firepower when you did all six of us would laying dead up there. Those were M-16s shooting back at us, lots of 'em. So the fucking army isn't taking away shit, they're gonna give you something. Maybe a medal doesn't mean much, that's up to you. But you got my word.

"Okay next. Ambush is fini. You got two minutes to drink some water, take a salt tab, and pack it up. Then we move out toward the road... real quiet."

Hooper tugged off his steel pot and mopped his face. "Don't worry, Sarge. We'll get off this thick son-of-a-gun without walking into an ambush our own selves."

The DC-3 droned overhead. A dead flare floated down behind the R&R detachment but another one popped right behind it and lit up the sky to the west. Chewing licorice, Deagle heard the clang of tailgates closing and truck engines starting up at the motorpool. He felt the chill in his thinned blood as the morning thermal lifted moisture off the ground and pulled it up the slope. He knew if Sergeant Major Bierra was coming with a recon mission, it would be after first light and after a couple platoons had secured that meadow. He gave the nod for Vinny to lead the way down.

The area flares made trail-walking easy but turned Hill 229 into Halloween fright house. The overhead light shocked the foliage and threw black shadows into every void and crevice, places where monsters and snakes and Charles Cong hid. Vinny led a slow westerly patrol, communicating with Deagle by hand signal, with each man taking turns clearing the jungle where the enemy might be waiting to hit back. When Vinny finally saw the road he dropped to one knee. It was almost 0530 Christmas morning. He searched the tree-trunks and groundcover carefully. Pomeroy came alongside and stared up and down the road, nodding. Vinny looked down at Jim, the right side of his face against Pomeroy's chest. Under the greenish bright sky, Jim's skin was opaque, a black-and-white photo of dead soldier. So small, his blood leaked out, and his life over.

Deagle moved forward to check out the road. He whispered "Good job. Cleve, take Jim down the hill. Vinny, you and Brennan cover."

"Where are you going?"

"Me and Hooper are going back to the meadow."

"And do what?"

"Finish the job. Tell butthole Bierra we'll be on the west side by that rock. At ease, I'll tell him myself. Gimme the radio."

"Ah, Deagle, good buddy," said Brennan "I say again, that DC-3 circling up there is puff the magic dragon. Mini-guns? Bierra's dumb enough to spray the whole hill with us on it."

"Webb's got two other squads still on the hill. Hornet's Nest, this is Firefly. Hornet's Nest, this is Firefly, over."

Sergeant major Bierra's subdued voice came back "Firefly, this is Hornet's Nest, over."

"Hornet's Nest, three of my men are coming down. They'll be on the road above that checkpoint in zero five minutes. You think you guys can avoid shooting them? Over."

Pause. "Affirmative. We'll... discuss this again, buck sergeant."

Pomeroy switched the radio off and shook his head. "Now I got something to say: too many VC, GI. I don't want to lose another friend on this damn hill."

"Never happen. Get going you guys. C'mon, Hoop."

Fifty meters above the checkpoint, Vincent, Brennan and Pomeroy eased out of the jungle onto the road. Walking softly on the shoulder Pomeroy carried Jim around a steep right-hand curve and saw the glow of the floodlights behind R&R and the rows of aluminum roofs further north. He thought about the first time he and Grossnickel saw this base, all those buildings. Now it seemed like home, and he was almost off this son-of-a-bitch hill. The road swung left and then sharply down a final right-hand turn before he saw the checkpoint and the buildings below.

Then he had to squint against the glare of a dozen truck headlights aimed straight at him.

Pomeroy saw the long-legged soldier in a steel pot jump down from the lead jeep and walk toward him, but it wasn't until he was a few meters away that he recognized Brigadier General Webb. He figured he'd be shaking in his boots if he had to stand in front of either Webb or Bierra again, but he felt strangely calm.

Webb looked down at Jim Grossnickel's expression in death, a child sleeping in the arms of his big brother. He looked behind Pomeroy at Sp5 Vincent and Sp4 Brennan, both holding positions of attention at sling arms.

"Deagle and Hooper?"

Brennan came two steps closer and spoke quietly. "Still up there, sir. On the west side of the meadow waiting for you."

Webb nodded and let out his breath. He looked from one soldier to the other. He didn't recognize Pomeroy's face but he knew him. In forty-two months of leading a combat division in Vietnam he'd faced a thousand pairs of reproving, stone-cold eyes like Pomeroy's. The young corporal carried his dead buddy and the weight of world on his broad shoulders, and in his gray eyes was a flat statement: "look what you did, sir." Nor did he know the two admin clerk/typists, only that they had probably just faced death for the first time. The nearest nametag read "Brennan". In the aftermath of Brennan's first firefight his steady blue eyes showed an absolute absence of fear and a different message: Brennan's eyes said "go look what I did, sir." Specialist Vincent's dark eyes had the same look. Webb's chest swelled with morning air and his mind cleared.

He reached out with his arms and took Jim Grossnickel's body from Corporal Pomeroy. He carried his dead PFC through the illuminated exhaust-pipe fog and laid him in the back of his jeep. He pulled off his steel pot, closed his eyes, and lowered his head. He spoke to his driver briefly and walked back.

He scanned the sky for the DC-3 dropping area flares, then looked into Pomeroy's spit-colored eyes. "What am I going to find up there, corporal?"

Pomeroy's voice had an edge to it. "Sir, your hill was Victor Charlie."

Webb nodded. "You men go on down and get some chow, get some sleep if you can. Debriefing at 1500 in my office."

"Yes, sir." Pomeroy's heels came together and he held up a salute. Brennan and Vincent offered two more.

Webb snapped one off and looked at the three of them. "I know what you walked into up there. I am very... very... proud of you men."

Two platoons of admin reinforcements waited in trucks as Webb, Colonel Borg, and Sergeant Major Bierra started up the road at forced-march pace. Webb climbed a hundred meters without looking back and reached the garbage dump overlook. Daylight was minutes away. He waited impatiently for Colonel Borg to catch up, the stoop-shouldered officer struggling up the hill, bent over, arms churning, wheezing for breath. Right behind him in an ill-fitted steel pot was Bierra wearing the heavy Prick-25 on his back. Webb used his field glasses to scan the dump but it was still too dark down there to see anything but bare ground holes. After another hard climb up the twisting road Webb signaled a halt and consulted the map. He was near the middle of the hill, below and west of Deagle's ambush position. At least he was sure the road was clear.

He told his sergeant major to call for the troops. "Truck them as far as the first overlook, and from there a column of twos at port arms, absolute silence."

Fifteen minutes later Webb single-filed his troops into the jungle at a five-meter spacing. Thinking about the 9th Infantry Engineers in 1964, Webb walked behind his point-man and experienced the foliage on Hill 229 first hand. Much of it was above his head, everything leafy was wet with morning dew, visibility at dawn less than ten meters. He angled uphill for twenty hard minutes and called for a five-minute rest in place, no smoking. He signaled Colonel Borg forward.

"I need Sergeant Janco."

"I sent a jeep for him, sir," Borg panted. "I'm sure he's coming."

"We need him to identify our body counts."

"You think we'll find any now?"

Webb nodded. "Yes, I do colonel."

He moved the column higher and found an intersecting trail of freshly broken limbs and flattened brush. Deagle and Hooper, possibly. He followed the trail but it ended at the triple canopy. Under the cloud of vines and horizontal branches visibility was improved enough to deploy his men in squads of a dozen each, having them maintain eye contact and cover one or the other flank, uphill or downhill. There was not a breath of breeze under the canopy, not a sound. A hundred meters further east Webb saw dawn filtering through the trees ahead. He signaled for everybody to drop in place. Down! He brought out his field glasses to study the meadow for the first time.

Elephant grass on the left, steep hill terrain on the right, and a nice flat little strip of meadow in between, just like Major Andrews' map. Sweat dripped from his armpits and down his neck. He gave the signal to move out and five minutes later he crept up behind Sergeants Deagle and Hooper, observing the meadow from behind a bolder.

"Activity?" he whispered.

Deagle shook his head. "Nothing, sir. Nothing moving since we got here."

To Webb, young Deagle looked the same but Sergeant Hooper was a changed man. His head was up, chin was out, the comic quality of his small eyes and painful-looking round nose was merely irregular. Even with the remnants of camo paint on his face, Hooper looked like a soldier.

"They're gone, sir," Hooper told him "They done di di mau'd in the face of a superior force."

Sergeant Major Bierra and Colonel Borg sneaked forward and there was room for all five behind the rock. Bierra slipped in beside Deagle and shrugged out of the heavy radio. "I'm real disappointed in you," he said.

Deagle glanced at the Cav's highest ranking non-com. "Likewise, sergeant major."

"I'm looking forward to your court-martial, private Deagle."

"Better leave it alone, sarge," Deagle said calmly. "I still got the ass about that medevac bird."

"How far to the trail?" Webb asked.

"Maybe fifty meters, sir. Sergeant Hooper and I will take you there."

Webb looked behind at the column. "We'll wait here a few minutes for Master Sergeant Janco."

"I hope those troopies ain't got tracers," Hooper said.

Webb looked at the sky. "Almost daylight anyway."

Sergeant Major Bierra decided he was also obligated to get in Hooper's face in front of their commanding general. "Sergeant Hooper, how the hell could you allow a buck sergeant to disobey a brigadier general? What were you thinking?"

But Hooper didn't buckle and Deagle answered for him, keeping his voice low. "Field priority, sergeant major, and I was in command, not Hooper."

"In a combat emergency, sergeant, you disobeyed at least two lawful orders and then you jammed the radio. You can play that game at LZ Penny but not at Bien Hoa."

Deagle looked him in the eye. "Why don't you shut your damn hole."

Webb put a hand between them. "For now, both of you shut up. How many VC, Sergeant Deagle? Best guess."

"Best guess, sir, between twenty and forty."

"Target?"

"You called it: the air strip. We saw the satchel charges."

"General, I've served at Bien Hoa for seventeen months," Bierra said, "There aren't forty VC between here and the South China Sea."

Borg whispered. "Then who was doing all that shooting? Apes?"

"There aren't going to be any body counts up there," Bierra insisted. "There never are. Even if there were, whatever chance we had to recover them was lost when Deagle disobeyed my recon order."

It was another five restless minutes before Master Sergeant Janco came forward, and the reason for his delay became obvious. Instead of double-timing along the elephant grass Janco could only duck his head and shuffle because he was handcuffed to a Vietnamese prisoner in leg irons. The E8 saw the black star on Webb's helmet and threw up a hasty salute, and Webb snapped one back.

"Sorry I'm late, sir. We caught this one sneaking back into the compound. Name's Nguyen and he works on my water trucks."

He brought the boy closer, a surly teenager who appeared not the least bit intimidated to be displayed as a prisoner of war. Janco took him by the shoulder and turned him around, and pulled up his ratty khaki shirt. Nguyen's back was dotted with oozing shrapnel puncture wounds.

"He was with 'em, sir. Hell, he's one of 'em!"

Deagle thought he'd seen the boy-san before but said nothing.

"Bring him along, sergeant."

Webb looked back at the two columns flanking the meadow. "Colonel, I don't want my columns crossing that opening up ahead. Move the whole company up to the tree-line from here."

It was daybreak of Christmas morning. Webb mopped his forehead and listened, studying the battlefield in front of him. He'd sent Deagle's squad to block a jungle trail that crossed this narrow strip of flat open ground. There was no cover. Looking right, Webb imagined the VC rifleman up on the hill raining down fire, throwing bullets into the meadow and over the tops of the elephant grass into his HQ. He put a hand on Deagle's shoulder.

"Sergeant, did you take any fire from below?"

Deagle showed a wry grin. "Some, from our guys. From Charles, negative."

"Where's the tunnel you blew?" Borg asked.

"Against orders," Bierra reminded.

Deagle glared at him.

"How far to the tunnel?" Webb repeated.

"Couple hundred meters. You could post a squad below the elephant grass, sir."

Borg wiped sweat from his forehead. "My God, my backyard in Florida is deeper than this meadow. It's a wonder you're not all KIAs."

Webb nodded, "Listen up. Sergeant Major Bierra, pick a squad leader to take a dozen men and a Prick-25 and set up a blocking ambush below that elephant grass. Remind them their weapons will be pointed at my base and not to fire into the skyline. The rest of us will form an assault line in those trees. We're going up. We'll either re-engage the enemy or we'll dig him up. Whatever it takes, I want this hill."

Webb studied Deagle's intense profile: bony jaw and deep-set eyes and light, day-old beard. "Take the point, sergeant."

Deagle eased to a standing position, rifle in front of him. He looked up at the jungle and took a deep breath. His long muscle-weary legs were stiff from sitting behind the rock for an hour, and it felt good to move again. His belly growled for food and he had a burgeoning case of the ass, an urge to smack Bierra in the mouth. He pulled back the bolt of his M-16 far enough back to make sure a round was in the chamber. He lightly heeled the bolt-assist then dropped his clip in his hand. It felt full and he clicked it back in the rifle. With

Hooper a step behind him he walked to the tree-line that his squad had pounded with claymores, grenades, and .223's just a few hours ago.

The steep hill on his right was hushed, teeming with morning humidity; the flat meadow on his left empty. Leading eighty men, he still-hunted toward sunlight streaming through the trees ready to shoot the first thing that moved. His concentration was up high where Hill 229 was still dark. The double-layer ceiling of branches and leaves was thick, he thought, but not thick enough to stop a grenade falling out of the sky. At first, he saw no sign of last night's firefight. He didn't expect to see dead bodies lying everywhere, but there was no trampled jungle, no broken limps, no weapons or brass casings left behind, not even a tree with a nick in it. Malaria nightmare? This jungle had absorbed two claymores, five hundred rounds, and a dozen grenades. But then Hooper grabbed his canteen belt from behind and pointed at a fresh gash in a tree. Further ahead, a broken vine caught on Deagle's boot. He picked it up and looked at the sheared branches. He moved soundlessly toward the light and stopped again, realizing he was standing on the VC trail. Below him was the V-shaped tree where the jungle gave way to the grass, and where he'd aimed a pair of hand grenades. Ground zero.

General Webb stopped beside Deagle and Hooper pointed, "Up there, sir."

Pistol in hand, Webb checked his watch. 0620. His command was a traffic cop's wave, every other man move forward, maintain silence. Forty men filed quietly past Deagle and Hooper, chin straps clinking softly, pistol belts creaking, half-full canteens jiggling. The admin soldiers stared at the tall unapproachable Sergeant Deagle but they celebrated beaming Staff Sergeant Hooper. Sergeants Dornhaus and Timmerman showed him thumbs up, others shook his hand. By 0630 hours Commanding General Webb had an assault belt that stretched two hundred meters around the north side of Hill 229.

"Not much cover," Borg whispered, looking down at the meadow. He spotted the four deep trenches flanking the trail. He saw Grossnickel's steel pot lying in the grass and gritted his teeth.

Deagle pointed down. "We were dug in with the moon behind us, sir."

"Sergeant, the S-2 at Bien Hoa is poor at best, and I'm responsible."

Responsible. Deagle thought about Harvey and Emerson and Strauss and Rinaldi... and Fuck-knuckle.

Webb signaled to move up on-line. The jungle in front of him was chest-high brush and heavy tree trunks that grew ten feet before leafing out in the lower canopy layer. Visibility was ten-to-fifteen meters. With every step he expected to put his boot down on a VC gravesite. He watched the assault line begin to lose its discipline on the steep slope and held his arms out wide to encourage the troops to climb on line. Twenty paces to his right, Webb saw an admin soldier stop, bend down, and then gouge at the ground with the butt of his rifle. Webb sent word up and down the line to stop and drop.

Webb double-timed behind the assault line and signaled Sergeant Janco

311

to follow with his prisoner. The admin Sp4 had found a monsoon run-off filled with green foliage. On hands and knees he dug down into the shallow hole, and under the pile of vines, and branches and leaves was a Vietnamese curled on his side. A male, eyes shut, mouth open and full of dirt, knees folded to his chest, his arms crossed. His black pajama shirt was splotched with stains like the plum-colored pool of blood under him.

Sergeant Janco looked down and shook his head.

"Score one, sir. But he didn't work for me." Something caught the master sergeant's eye and he dropped to one knee. Reaching into the hole he moved the pajama clad legs. The pool of blood under the Vietnamese was another bloody shirt, a second VC buried below the first. Janco located the torso, then the shoulders and head by cleaning away the dirt and vines. He shook his head.

"Make it two. Don't know him either."

He stood up and dusted his hands, then pulled Nguyen close enough to the hole to look into it. Nguyen refused to look down or speak. Janco fired rapid-fire Vietnamese at the boy but he continued to shake his head.

"Yeah, he knows one or both. Bet your paycheck he knows 'em."

"Colonel Borg, sir?" a voice called. "Would you come over here, sir?"

The Colonel hiked across the hill with Webb behind him where three GI's stood surrounding a boulder three-quarters submerged like an iceberg. At the downhill end of the boulder was a crack that deepened into a fissure covered with collected leaves and branches. But the branches were all green. Crammed into the bottom of the fissure was a Vietnamese, but Borg couldn't tell if was boy or man, a bullet through the back of his head had torn off most of his face above the nose. Borg grabbed the rock to keep from falling. He quickly looked away and sucked in deep breaths.

Janco looked down and winced. "I ain't sure, but number three here could be Cham. Born in Cambodia and worked at admin mess."

Bierra looked away. "I talked to that boy-san a few times."

At left-flank center, a group of soldiers followed a foot trail. Colonel Borg walked behind them taking deep breaths and using a walking stick to keep his balance. He watched them knock down brush and surround a patch of ground the size of a bathtub where fresh dirt had been packed. He drove the toe of his boot down into it and it felt loose. The troops gouged the soft ground with rifle butts and a few inches below the surface they found three Vietnamese lying in the bottom. Thankfully they were all on their stomachs. Borg stepped back and called Janco over.

The three VC had sustained so many wounds and there was so much blood in their grave it was hard to tell which body belonged to which head. One had lost his shirt and his torso was covered with bloating jagged wounds, as if a 155mm round had landed beside him. Janco unearthed his face and saw that death had been agonizing and slow for this Vietnamese fighter of fifteen years.

"Four, five, and six. Meet Dai. One of my sandbag honchos. Don't know the other two." He stood up and grabbed Nguyen by the neck. "Look at him! He done that to his self!"

Webb moved away. He sipped cool water from his canteen as he turned and looked down though the jungle to the edge of the meadow, not quite as far away as from home plate to the pitcher's mound. He saw that every tree and every limb thicker than a half an inch had bullet and grenade scars in it. A few hours ago there had been an army of Viet Cong in these trees shooting down at the meadow while taking heavy return fire. Thinking like a terrorist, he looked for a tree to hide behind and found one a few steps away. He dropped to one knee behind it, looking down. Deagle had said the VC carried M-16s. He searched the ground to the right of the tree. A pair of admin soldiers watching him got the message and joined the hunt, running their hands in the damp grass. One found a shiny 5.56 NATO hull, then another, then a handful. One soldier separated his steel helmet from his helmet liner to use as a catch bin. Sergeant Major Bierra descended the hill and stood beside the commanding general, and he watched in disbelief as the empty brass cases clinked into the steel pot until it was half full.

Webb searched the jungle for his former S-2's tall shape but didn't see him. Then he heard Borg calling for Sergeant Janco up above. He saw Hooper and Deagle amid a squad of GI's, staring down. He climbed and pushed through the stunned crowd.

"Lord almighty," Hooper said.

They were packed head to toe like sardines, four of them. Three were face up and the fourth was face down. The closest lay staring straight up, arms folded on his bloating stomach. He had thick black hair. In the center of his chest was an exit hole the size of a fist with still-glistening gore and bone hanging from it. Beside him was a middle-aged Vietnamese killed by a single bullet through his forehead, face partially covered in blood and dirt and his wide bulging eyes fearsome even in death. He wore a black silk shirt and Arvin fatigue pants. Sergeant Janco had stopped counting.

"Look there," Hooper said, pointing. "His one ear's shot off."

"Just a minute, colonel," Janco said, as Borg started to walk away. "This one in the middle is special."

He pointed at the VC with thick black hair lying face down. There was a bald spot above the base of his neck about the size of a US quarter. Borg had seen soldiers with similar bald spots caused by impetigo or jungle fever. But this was different; hair had been hastily cut with a knife. Janco tugged on the black shirt with both hands, partially unearthing the VC. Below him was another layer of leaves and brush. Under the leaves was a cache of M-16s bundled like kindling, and a pair of canvas satchels filled with the blocks of C-4.

"That shaved spot shows the location of the rifles, sir. Seen it lots a times with the Americal Division in '69. These VC are from up north. Hardcore."

Sergeant Major Bierra turned away but Colonel Borg took another deep breath.

"I want all these body counts moved to the clearing," he said. All their weapons, satchel charges, all their brass, all of it policed up and trucked down to my office. And handle those explosives carefully. Sergeant Janco, I need to know what the hell went wrong on this hill, so I also want you to photograph and catalogue these Vietnamese before you notify Arvin Commander Penh. How do you read? "

"5x5, sir. Wilco."

Deagle climbed back down. He faced the bright orange ball that had become the Christmas morning sun, and its heat felt good. He walked to the trench where Jim Grossnickel fired the last round from his M-16 and tried to light a smoke with shaky hands.

"Debriefing at 1500, sergeant," said a voice behind him. It was General Webb.

He turned and faced his commanding general at arms length. For the first time he noticed the dark stains on the general's fatigue shirt. Blood. Jim Grossnickel's blood, very likely. His voice quavered when he spoke. "Right here, a best buddy got shot four times, sir. I just wish I could tell him..."

"Me, too, sergeant. We'll tell his family."

"I'd tell Jim... the six of us against six times that many of them... it was a fair fight."

Hands on hips, Webb looked up toward the top of Hill 229. "There were fifty Viet Cong on this hill last night. The rest are still up here but we'll dig them out." Then he walked to where Bierra had set up the Prick-25 and Deagle heard him call for his chopper.

There was an excited shout from farther up on the hill where another grave had been found. Deagle smoked his cigarette watching the tree-line as Hooper stepped out of the jungle and yanked off his helmet. With a big grin Hooper showed Deagle four fingers. Then Sergeant Janco appeared in the meadow pushing Nguyen ahead of him. He tried to force the boy to sit down but he was too wiry and dodged away, hands 'cuffed in front of him and leg chains dragging. Hobbled, Nguyen looked across the meadow to the elephant grass for an escape route, but if he thought of making a run for it he changed his mind. He kicked at his leg chains and stood defiantly.

"Dung lai! And stand still or I'll shoot you myself," Janco warned.

At close range the fourteen-year old Viet Cong fighter raised the hair on the back of Deagle's neck. He took three lazy strides and stood over him, half again as tall. Nguyen refused to look up.

"Tell him it was me," Deagle told Janco. "Tell him in Vietnamese so he understands."

Janco spoke softly in Vietnamese and the boy lifted his head. The hatred in Nguyen's eyes turned him uglier than the ugliest old mama-san. "You were only lucky," he barked in clear English, "*du mi ami!*"

Colonel Borg came striding down and called the senior NCO's together. A cave had been discovered. The hill, he said, should still be considered Victor Charlie. He took sixty men and set up a broad perimeter while the NCO's supervised recovery teams who relayed up and down the hill carrying enemy dead, captured weapons, and satchel charges. The dead were aligned in the sunshine and covered with ponchos. By 0730 the troops climbed down empty-handed. They stood in small groups drinking from canteens and smoking cigarettes and throwing glances at Deagle, who sat on his helmet lost in thought. The tension melted in the morning heat and the sense of finality was everywhere.

"Sir, the boys in air force blue," Bierra informed Webb, "just picked up two Choo Hoi's on their side, both wounded. Also, Colonel Wilcox called again. General Garlett would like you to return his call, ASAP."

Webb nodded. "My chopper's coming. Stay with Colonel Borg. I want this hill, sergeant major."

"Yes, sir."

Borg squinted the length of the meadow. "Might be good, sir, if we finish what the French started. Put a company of infantry right here."

Webb shook his head. "Good idea, but I've got other plans." He turned to face his 7th Brigade buck sergeant "Sergeant Deagle, I'll see you at 1500."

Deagle answered with a crisp military salute.

At 0745 hours the commanding general's bubble-glass, light-observation army helicopter swept above the trees and made a graceful turn parallel with the meadow. The LOACH hovered in the center of the clearing and whipped the grass flat as it settled down on its skids. Deagle watched the tall one-star run for the open door. The door closed, the chopper's tail lifted, blunt-nose glass front went spinning toward the west. The lithe machine gained altitude and banked steeply to the north and disappeared behind the tops of the elephant grass.

One hour later, finally alone in his office, Webb poured three fingers of scotch. He leaned back in his chair and made the call to III-Corps Commander Lieutenant General Benton Garlett. Told by one of Garlett's aides to stand by, it was only a few seconds before he heard the polished voice.

"This is Garlett."

"Webb. Colonel Quigly advised you of my call this morning?"

"Yes, he did. But I wish he'd woken me."

"At oh four hundred this morning, sir, one of my ambush team engaged the Viet Cong on Hill 229, twelve hours after the sapper attack that killed six of my men. I moved troops up on the hill to support and secure and I now have the full results from the 24th and 25th to report to MAC-V."

"Webb, I don't care about the results on the 25th . Only the 24th. Have you briefed the press?"

"Of course not, sir. But say again about the 25th?"

"Twenty-four December at Bien Hoa goes into the MR book as an unprovoked communist cease-fire violation, reported as such to the Secretaries of State and Defense. Twenty-five December will go in the book as a theatre-wide cease-fire day of non-action."

"Non-action? Sir, I'm reporting a second cease-fire violation and an overwhelming 1st Cav victory. More important, it's the tip of the iceberg. Bien Hoa is wide open, the whole AO is Victor Charlie..."

"Webb, stop. I'm not listening. There's more at stake than Bien Hoa."

"If MAC-V has a bug up its ass about negative press coverage, be advised this mission was solid, justified, and by the book. General, you know how I feel about the press, if there was anything negative for them to write about... good God."

After a moment the III-Corps commander replied, "That is affirmative, Webb. Your R&R detachment."

Webb stared at the telephone in his hand.

"Through this office," General Garlett continued, "Ms. J.L Gottlieb has received clearance to film your R&R detachment for CBS News. She's probably standing in front of Sergeant Major Bierra's desk right now. Secretary Kissinger is expecting that this 'atrocity', an appropriate term, committed by the communists during the Christmas cease-fire will make the front page of every newspaper in the world."

Webb took a deep breath and let it out. "You son-of-a-bitch," he said quietly.

"One more word and I'll take your star, brigadier."

"One more? I've got two: listen up! Four hours ago six of my men engaged approximately fifty Viet Cong armed with stolen M-16s. So far I have nineteen confirmed enemy body counts, two Choo Hoi's, twenty-six captured rifles, and a dozen satchel charges. I lost one man. And you're telling me... you'd rather have a bargaining chip?"

"Inflated body count numbers impress nobody."

"I've got 'em stretched out on the goddamn ground! Come up here and count 'em yourself!"

"Six men did that?"

"That is affirmative."

"Then, I am sure, brigadier, you will quietly accord those brave men full honors. And, after you stop sniveling about your career, you will personally nail the lid on the 25th at Bien Hoa. If it makes you feel better, put a full de-briefing in your MAC-V bag marked for my eyes only. Those are your orders, and that is all. And now I need to hear a 'yes sir' on that, Webb."

"That is not all. You've been out of the field too long, general. You forget the goddamn North Vietnamese don't control these southern terrorists. You think Charles is going to follow your cease-fire rules of engagement because if he doesn't you'll report him to the New York Times! Bullshit! I caught the sonsabitches in a second violation!"

"None of which changes the decision."

"And another thing, you people at MAC-V have to stop telling the world this war is over. It is not over until the last American is out of this theatre. Be advised, sir, in my new assignment and as I interpret 'Vietnamization', I WILL aggressively secure not only this hill in my backyard but all of Bien Hoa. I remind the III-Corps commander that I AM NOT THE ONE WHO SIGNED THE GODDAMN BAIL OUT LETTER !!!"

In the silence that followed the outburst Webb picked up his scotch and tossed it down.

"We're not on the crypto line, Webb."

"I could give a damn!"

"If certain details of the 'Bail Out' letter were to be made public right now... I would be embarrassed, but I would survive."

"Sure you would! You'd be a folk hero and run for the senate! Of course, Chairman of the Joint Chiefs goes out the window..."

"All right, Webb," Garlett said quietly. "Our careers aside, you resolve what's more important: an unprovoked enemy atrocity that moves the peace process forward or a token 1st Cav victory. Call me back before oh nine hundred." He hung up.

Webb dropped the phone in the cradle and leaned back. He poured more scotch and threw his long legs on the desk. "Son of a bitch." He jumped out of his chair and paced from one side of the office to the other, and on the way past his desk he picked up his chair, cocked it back like a nine-iron, and hurled it legs-first against the block wall where it broke apart. "Son-of-a-BITCH!"

Specialist Meredith carefully opened the door and poked his head in. "Everything all right, sir?"

"Everything's great! I need another chair! Find Colonel Shipp and have him report to me ASAP."

"Yes, sir!"

With no place to sit, he paced until Shipp rapped on the door and entered. Seeing the chair in pieces against the wall, Shipp stood in front of Webb's desk at a rigid position of attention The bloodhound colonel looked tired, uniform rumpled and mustache limp. Webb poured two inches of scotch in two glasses and passed him one.

"At ease, colonel. Drink that. It'll help you sleep. Second time this morning I've had scotch."

"Sir, if I might ask, what'd Garlett say?"

"We had a pissing contest. He wants the 1st Cav to... take one for the team, so to speak. We were asleep and the VC hit us, we lost six troops Christmas Eve and that's a damn shame. But we honored the terms of the cease-fire. CBS... CBS News, colonel, is going to film our R&R detachment for the six-o'clock show! My god. The 1st Cav is up to its ass in honorable defeat. Custer at the Little Big Horn, MacArthur at the 38th Parallel, the Central

Highlands and the Ashau Valley... and Bien Hoa. Because Mr. Kissinger needs all the help he can get. Son-of-a-bitch."

Shipp sipped scotch and grimaced. "What Charles done to us gets on TV... What we done to Charles... gets a damn crypto clearance! That's the story of this war, sir."

Webb nodded. "Garlett thinks I overreacted sending Deagle up there."

"All he needs to see are the results, sir." Shipp put down his scotch and re-assumed a position of attention. "And if this old colonel is permitted to say so general, congratulations, and I'm proud to serve under you." He brought his right arm up and stared straight ahead.

Webb snapped one back. "Thank you, colonel."

"And I know Ray Wilcox feels the same and will do a fine job for you in S-2. But we both kinda feel bad for old Phil Borg. A couple days ago he was thinking he was in line for XO. Now... "

"Borg will get another chance, commanding 8th Brigade. He needs the experience."

Shipp grinned. "Just had a thought. Maybe some uninformed colonel close to retirement should call the *Washington Post* about Hill 229-er?"

"Negative. That's the hell of it: Garlett's right this time. Anyway, the reason I called you in: clear my schedule this afternoon. I've got debriefings to write and an awards ceremony. Then get yourself some sack-time because I'd like you to be there. 1500 hours. And you did a damn good job this morning."

"Thank you, sir."

"On your way out ask Specialist Meredith to send a jeep to pick up Ms. Devlin. Have him bring her to your Eisenhower Bunker."

Darcy came dressed as he'd first seen her, long-tailed olive army t-shirt, clean jeans, GI boots, a 1st Cav baseball cap, carrying her purse and briefcase. Dressed for the road. She piled her bags on a desk and joined him at the corner window where they looked out at Hill 229 in its early-morning soft satin green. Off to the right, a deuce-and-a half rolled up to the MP checkpoint and after an exchange of salutes the gate lifted. The truck chugged ahead out of sight but they heard it whine in low gear slowly up the hill.

"It was rude not to call you last night," he said.

"I'm sure you were busy," she answered, looking around at the command bunker.

"Moving on?"

"Saigon. Jan Gottlieb got a call from General Garlett so she's staying. But I'm sure you know that. CBS is running the R&R attack as the six-o'clock lead, but when I described it to my editor he said maybe 'page three' in San Francisco. Same old stuff. So I wrote a little piece about cyclonite."

Webb's eyes stared a hole through the Cav Patch on top of Hill 229. "I just read the draft of Colonel Shipp's briefing to CBS News; there's no mention of C-4 in it."

"We all work independently. Anyway, the rest of us are going to do Bob Hope." She reached out to formally shake his hand. "Bien Hoa was a surprise. You were a surprise."

He turned and took her hand. Then he took her shoulders and gently pulled her closer.

Darcy looked up, hands clamped sympathetically over his wrists. Tonight, Christmas Day 1971, at about the time she sat down to yuk it up with Martha Raye, the world would learn the commanding general of the 1st Cavalry Division was sending six more soldiers home in green bags. She searched his face, expecting to see dark eyes dulled by recrimination and lost sleep, a proud jaw gone slack. She hadn't slept much herself. But empathy turned quickly to inquiry. Under the day-old beard his jaw jutted. Between his dark eyebrows and deep circles his eyes smiled.

"I feel good, Darcy. First time in months. It's partly because of you. There's a question you've been asking me. Why don't you ask me again and I'll take my chances."

"Take your chances?"

"Some people think the officers who signed the 'Bail Out' letter are heroes."

Unable to read his face she said, "the 'Bail Out' letter isn't important, Jeff."

"You said it was an important story."

"Your answer might be on page one in San Francisco. Are you sure?"

"I'm sure."

Her fingers tightened on his wrists, green eyes narrowed. "All right. For the record, General Webb, did you sign the 'Bail Out Now' letter to the President of the United States?"

"No. After reading the letter, I declined."

In his flat statement there was a strange relief, then inspiration. "Did General Benton Garlett sign the 'Bail Out' letter?"

The question came as expected, because she was damn good at her job. "Quoting an anonymous army source?"

"No way. Quoting a high-ranking 1st Cav officer still in-theatre and who worked under Garlett at the time."

Webb nodded. "Bet your bippy he did. Signed it, authored it. Nixon decided Ben Garlett had one shot left to save his career: ramrod 'Vietnamization'. That's why he's third banana at MAC-V."

Darcy smiled.

"What, no short-hand notes on a legal pad?" he asked.

"Quid pro quo, general?"

"That is affirmative, I have given something to get something. Darcy, last night six of my men climbed Hill 229 and killed the terrorists that blew up my R&R. If it can be said, what those men did more than makes up for our loss. I have nineteen confirmed enemy body counts so far."

"Nineteen? ...killed by six men?"

"I lost one."

"When?"

"0400 this morning."

"What about MAC-V?"

"Nothing about MAC-V. I set up that ambush and I have no apology to offer. I am so proud of those men. But due to circumstances beyond my control to make the ambush public would be... "

"An affront to the peace process?"

"Yes. So tonight Ms. Gottlieb will be on TV talking about another 1st Cav massacre and for now I have to live with it. But in a year or two the peace accords will be signed, Nixon will have been re-elected, and you and I will be back in the world. Darcy, I need a keeper-of-the-truth for the 1st Cav; I want you stay at Bien Hoa and meet some real heroes. There were six in Sergeant Deagle's squad, now there are five."

Scowling, she walked to the desk where her bags were piled. She dug a new legal pad from her briefcase and turned. "Spell that name."

Webb nodded. "With a D, as in Delta."

At 1500 hours in the privacy of his office, Commanding General Webb presented three bronze star valor medals to 1st Cavalry Division admin battalion enlisted soldiers. Darcy Devlin from the *San Francisco Chronicle* sat at Webb's desk taking notes on a yellow legal pad. The battalion chaplain was permitted only one photograph: Staff Sergeant Hooper receiving E7 chevrons from Executive Officer Shipp. At 1530 hours Webb presented two more BSV's and one posthumous Silver Star medal to 1st Cavalry infantrymen from the 7th Brigade. Corporal Cleveland Pomeroy accepted sergeant's chevrons from Colonel Shipp. Afterward, with just the reporter and three soldiers present, Webb, Shipp, and Deagle, there remained one small black box on Webb's desk.

"You don't think much of officers, do you Sergeant Deagle," Webb said.

Confronted, Deagle was embarrassed. "Nothing personal, sir. Some officers I respect and some I don't."

"I just got off the horn with your CO, Captain Rule. And I talked to your battalion commander, Colonel Hutton. You don't think much of senior NCO's either."

"When they use rank like a hammer... it sometimes gives me a case of the ass."

"Did Sergeant Major Bierra give you the ass, young man?" Colonel Shipp asked him.

"Sir, the sergeant major and I are going take off our fatigue shirts, then I'm going to knock that grin off his chops. Sir."

"Negative," Webb said. "Bierra is no longer the division sergeant major, he's an officer. Direct Commission. Come to attention, sergeant."

Deagle's heels locked and he stared ahead.

"Captain Rule says you're the best young leader he's ever commanded."

Webb reached down and picked up the black box. He took out the silver bar and admired it in the palm of his hand.

"You know what this is?"

"Lieutenant's bar, sir."

"Negative, not just a 2nd lieutenant's bar, this is a 1st lieutenant's bar. I've been both and there's a big difference between 2nd and 1st ... as in all things I suppose." Webb reached up and pulled the chevron from Deagle's right collar and replaced it with a single silver bar. "It's gaudy for Vietnam service. Wear it around the base until the 27th when you catch your bird for LZ Penny. Have black bars stitched on your new uniforms. And personally, I think officers should wear as-issue fatigues in a combat zone, same as their troops. Congratulations, 1st Lieutenant Deagle."

Deagle stared straight ahead. "Thank you, sir!"

"You don't use rank, lieutenant, as a hammer unless it's for the good of the army. You question orders if you need to, but when confirmed you follow them."

"Yes, sir."

"As with tunnels," Shipp reminded, grinning.

"You don't realize it yet, but you like army life and you're good at what you do. This field commission will cost you two more years of army life. When you get back to LZ Penny, lieutenant, you pack your TO&E and say your goodbyes. Then you report back here by the new year where you'll be attached to Colonel Shipp, my XO."

"Bien Hoa, sir?"

"Most affirmative. Where you'll have one immediate assignment and six months to carry it out, although TET is coming around again February 17th. Lieutenant, I WILL NOT... ever again carry a dead soldier off Hill 229. Colonel Geary tells me, thanks to your squad, he still has enough munitions sitting on an air force runway to flatten the Pentagon. I want you to relocate the R&R and DEROS detachments, take what explosives you need and co-ordinate with div arty and the 4th Air Combat Wing, and then you flatten that hill; wipe it off the face of the Earth until it is no longer a topographical feature. Do you read me, lieutenant?"

"5x5, sir."

"Then that is all. Dismissed."

Deagle held up a straight salute and Webb snapped one back.

Lieutenant Deagle about-faced and walked back through the hallway, out through the 1st Cav reception room into the afternoon monsoon. Warm rain pummeled his boonyhat and shoulders as he stepped away from the door. The rain at Bien Hoa, he thought, sounded so different. He'd heard it crashing on the roof of Hoa's little sleeping room and he'd heard it pounding the triple canopy on Hill 229. Here on the panoprime street outside 1st Cav headquarters the heavy drops sounded like a rush of hailstones smashing on concrete.

321

A dozen soldiers stood nearby in small groups talking, smoking, holding cigarettes in cupped hands. One of them was size double-extra-large. Smiling under the cascading brim of his boonyhat, Sergeant Pomeroy walked up and offered Deagle his first salute and then a crushing bear hug. Behind Pomeroy, Deagle noticed former Sergeant Major Bierra standing with a group of NCOs. For just a moment he thought about giving him a little of the hammer but instead he and Pomeroy walked west toward the admin mess hall. They hadn't walked five meters when Deagle heard his last name called sharply. He turned and saw Bierra splashing toward him.

Bierra stood in front of Deagle and Pomeroy at inspection distance. Rain danced on his gleaming bright-brass 2nd Lieutenant's bars, one on his collar and another on his helmet liner. Lieutenant Bierra opened his mouth to speak but he saw the silver on Deagle's collar, and his eyes turned saurian, a lizard tracking a slow-moving fly.

Deagle stood tall, hands on hips. "Come to attention, lieutenant. Now I think I better see one."

Bierra's heels came together as they had a ten thousand times. His eyes locked ahead and his right arm came up, index finger at his eyebrow and wrist straight.

Deagle snapped a salute back at him. "As you were," he said. Then he and Pomeroy turned and disappeared into the gray curtain.

It rained at Bien Hoa until 1630, when the clouds headed for the South China Sea and the setting sun showed itself in the west. At 1700 hours Christmas day Webb's jeep arrived at his BOQ to pick up the commanding general and his civilian companion. Webb was shaved and refreshed in clean jungle fatigues, Darcy had changed to a bright blue golf shirt, jeans and white tennis shoes, and carried a yellow legal pad. The general's driver ran them first to the 1st Cav chaplain's hooch for a private Christmas service and then to the 1st Cav R&R detachment, where they left the jeep at barracks 2016 and walked west toward the checkpoint. R&R barracks 2014 and 2013 were condoned and guarded by a platoon of MP's. At the center of barracks 2013, pointing his camera away from the setting sun and toward the splintered twelve-foot hole in the barracks, the tall CBS cameraman took his final light-meter readings. In new green fatigues and polished black boots, J.L Gottlieb paced back and forth reading her note cards. North of barracks 2013, out of camera range, were television news crews from Japan and Australia. Darcy cradled her legal pad and recorded every detail.

"Any time, Frankie," said J.L. Gottlieb.

"Eat my shorts, Janice," Frank said.

Frank lined his eye behind the camera, Gottlieb licked her lips one last time and said "go", and Jeff Webb watched from the concertina wire as the CBS evening news was taped.

"As usually agreed to," Gottleib told the camera, "a military cease-fire

322

between two enemies is a specified time when the guns stop, the armies pull back from forward areas, and rear areas are safe places from in-coming rocket and mortar fire. Soldiers take time out to rest, to pray, to celebrate life. The 1971 Christmas cease-fire between U.S. forces and the Communist North Vietnamese began December 23rd at 1800 hours, 6 pm. 22 hours later the agreement was broken, by the North Vietnamese.

"For the American forces here at Bien Hoa, a supposedly safe rear area, there have other Christmas cease-fires marred by violations. Three years in a row during this most sacred of holidays, 1967 through 1969, Viet Cong rockets and mortars hit targets just north of here. But this Christmas promised to be different, as chief delegate Xuan Thuy and Secretary of State Henry Kissinger are locked in serious peace negotiations in Paris. 1st Cav Headquarters Bien Hoa was to be a haven for weary infantrymen going home or going on R&R. Yesterday afternoon, in what is fast becoming an international incident, the Viet Cong struck during the cease-fire, destroying these two R&R barracks and killing six soldiers including a military policeman at a checkpoint fifty yards from where I'm standing.

"The attack was bold and deadly successful, carried out in daylight from this hill known as Cav Mountain. With R&R flights suspended during the cease-fire, the barracks were full of soldiers who had earned a week of rest and relaxation, going to places like Hawaii, Australia, Taiwan, Kuala Lumpur, and Singapore. Tragically, six families will be notified their sons are coming home early, to the Unites States instead. The Viet Cong claim this attack is a response to a 1st Cavalry sweep the day before."

"If the Viet Cong intended this Christmas attack to be a morale breaker, you won't see it at Bien Hoa. The officers and men continue to carry on their mission, providing support for the infantry and artillery soldiers at the forward firebases. Around Cav Mountain the guard has been doubled, helicopters search with floodlights, and flares brighten the night sky. Another R&R attack, I'm told, isn't going to happen. And, while 1st Cav headquarters is literally an American island surrounded by suspected Viet Cong villages that could be hit in retaliation for this attack, that hasn't happened. A Christmas cease-fire, says the 1st Cavalry Division, is in effect until 6 pm the evening of the 26th and delegate Xuan Thuy must answer to the world for his side's violation."

"And the war in Vietnam goes on... This is J. L. Gottleib at 1st Cavalry Division Air-Mobile Headquarters, Bien Hoa."

Webb walked slowly along the rusty spirals of concertina wire toward the MP checkpoint. An admin troop in a wobbly steel pot and carrying an M-16 at port-arms came running at him. He offered a salute and Webb looked him over before snapping one back. The commanding general had walked into this private's guard post.

"Sir!" he said, "you might want to step back. That hill has more tunnels than an ant farm! It's Victor Charlie, sir."

323

Webb looked over the coiled wire at the clumped bamboo and elephant grass on the steep north slope. In the dying sunlight, Hill 229 had a two-tone look to it, dark and shadowy at the base and lime green up above, as soft as waving stalks of corn in August. His mind wandered, to lawful commands and VC tunnels. Just above that elephant grass there was one Victor Charlie tunnel with its insides collapsed, like a D-9 Caterpillar got after it.

"Not for long, soldier," he said smiling.

END

GLOSSARY OF MILITARY TERMS AND ACRONYMS

201 File: Personal history file.

5x5: Radio communication jargon meaning "loud and clear", the best.

Acting jack: A temporary unit commander or non-commissioned officer.

AK-47: Infantry assault rifle used by the NVA and some VC, most Chinese made.

Ammo: Ammunition.

ANPRC-25: The "prick 25" field radio with a short-antenna range of about five miles, depending on weather.

AO: Area of operation.

APC: Armored personnel carrier.

Article 15: A commander's punishment for a soldier, can be loss of pay, loss of rank, even imprisonment.

ARTY: Artillery.

ARVN: Army of the Republic of Vietnam, south.

ASAP: As soon as possible.

Ass, a case of: Irritation, anger.

AWOL: Absent without leave.

B-40: A shoulder-fired rocket, see RPG.

Battalion: An infantry organization of about 850 men, made up of companies and platoons. A field-ready Vietnam-era battalion, subtracting out AWOL's, KIA's, MIA's, R&R's and other in-transit-status troops was far smaller, sometimes half.

BIG RED ONE: 1st Infantry Division.

Bladder: A collapsible fuel tank.

Body count: Dead VC or NVA.

BOQ: Bachelor officer's quarters.

Brigade: An infantry organization of about 6,500 men, made up of battalions.

Cache: Hidden supply, as in a captured "cache" of VC weapons.

C-4: A pliable, stable explosive, also called "plastic."

CG: Commanding general.

Charlie: Nickname for Viet Cong (see VC); in phonetics, the language of radio field communication, the letter "c."

Cherry: A replacement troop.

Chevron: Uniform hashmark, one for PFC E-3, two for CPL-E4, three for SGT-E5, etc.

Chi-com: Slang for "Chinese-communist," referring to a certain cheaply manufactured bolt-action rifle made by the Chinese government.

Chinook: CH-47 double-rotor cargo helicopter, used for re-supply.

Chloroquine: Anti-malaria pill, or "Monday" pill, military designation M-11.

Chopper: Any helicopter.

CIB: The combat infantry badge.

Clacker: Electronic trigger used to fire a claymore mine.

Claymore: Ground-level mine used to defend a position or perimeter consisting of C-4 explosive and pellets.

CO: Commanding officer

Cobra: AH-1G attack helicopter, armed with mini-guns and 40mm cannon.

Company: An army unit of about 120 men, made up of platoons.

Conscientious objector: Usually, a draftee who objected to military service on moral or religious grounds, prior or subsequent to being drafted.

Contact: Meeting the enemy in the field, as planned or otherwise. Ambush, firefight, or just "in the shit" all describe contact.

Corps: A military region or area of responsibility. In Vietnam there were four, designated I, II, III, and IV, north to south.

CP: Command post. In practice, any tent, hooch, or outpost building a commanding officer called his "office."

CQ: Charge of quarters.

C-ration: Individual combat meals in brown cardboard boxes, portions wrapped in plastic or canned.

Crypto: A security clearance level above "top secret."

DEROS: Variously, date of expected return from overseas, date eligible for return from overseas, and date of established return from overseas. Every soldier knew his DEROS date, and how many days he had left in Vietnam.

Deuce-and-a-half: The army's two-and-a-half ton workhorse troop and cargo truck.

Division: Usually three or more brigades, total strength near 20,000 men.

DRO: Dining room orderly. A military waiter.

DMZ: Demilitarized zone. A heavily fortified buffer zone between enemies, sometimes called "no man's land."

Dog tags: Metal identification tags worn around the neck, containing name, service number (now SSN) blood type, and religion.

Drag: Variously, a "bummer" or bad experience, a hit from a cigarette or joint, also the last man or unit on a field maneuver "covering the rear."

Duffel: Large oblong canvas bag used by troops to store uniforms and gear.

E-1, E-2, E-3, etc: Enlisted grades, Private E-1 through Sergeant Major E-9.

ERB: Enlisted records branch.

ETS: End termination of service, the last day of a draftee or volunteer soldier's active duty. Besides his DEROS date, every soldier knew his ETS date.

Fatigues: Basic green combat shirt and pants. Jungle fatigues were lighter in weight than "stateside" fatigues.

Fire Base: Artillery support base secured or occupied by the infantry.

First Sergeant: Highest ranking non-commissioned officer in a company or larger unit.

FNG: Fucking new guy, replacement, "cherry."

Flack Jacket: Chest vest made up of ceramic plates to protect against shrapnel from mortars and rockets. In helicopters, troops sat on their flack jackets.

FOB: Forward operations base.

Frag: Usually the M-67 hand grenade.

Freq: Field radio frequency.

Gary Owens: Actually "Garryowen," circa 1875, marching song favored by G.A Custer.

Gook: Slang for Asian, used in Korean and Vietnam.

GR Point: Graves registration, in the field.

Green Berets: The army's elite fighting unit, see Special Forces.

Grunt: Infantryman, also "groundpounder."

HE: High explosive. HE artillery and air warheads were used to destroy property.

Horn: Radio or telephone.

HQ: Headquarters.

Huey: The UH-1 helicopter, utility helicopter.

Hump: Walk.

I-Corps: The northern-most military region, where II-Corps was the central highlands, III-Corps was the capitol city of Saigon north to the highlands, and IV-Corps was the southern region including the Mekong Delta.

Incoming: NVA or Viet Cong mortars and rockets, coming in.

In-country: In Vietnam.

In-transit: Temporary morning report status, en route.

JAG: Judge advocate general branch of the army.

KIA: Report designation for killed in action.

Kit Carson: American-trained Vietnamese scouts. Spies.

Klick: One kilometer, about six-tenths of a mile.

KP: Kitchen police.

LAW: Light anti-tank weapon, basically a one-shot, fiberglass-tube bazooka. After firing, the idea was to break it in half against a tree so the VC couldn't recycle it somehow.

LBJ: Long Binh jail, ironically the initials of the President of the United States through most of the Vietnam war.

LBSOL: Left behind and shit out of luck. A troops who stayed behind, dead or wounded or disoriented, after a firefight or ambush.

Lifer: Career soldier.

LP: A team of soldiers, most often, positioned outside a perimeter assigned to watch and listen for the enemy.

LZ: Helicopter landing zone and forward base for air-mobile units, with distinctive American names like "Buttons" and "Betty."

M-16: Standard-issue .223/5.56mm NATO military rifle used in Vietnam, replacing the M-14 .30 cal rifle in 1966-67.

M-60: .30 caliber lightweight machine gun.

M-67: Smooth-surface fragmentation hand-grenade that replaced the WWII "pineapple" grenade.

MAC-V: The Military Assistance Command, Vietnam.

Mad minute: Officially, maximum fire power for about sixty seconds. Unofficially, a practical field solution for ammo oversupply.

Mag: Magazine, clip.

Malaria: Blood disease sometimes called "jungle fever" caused by the bite of a female anopheles mosquito.

Medivac: Field helicopter medical evacuation.

MIA: Report designation for missing in action.

Mike: Phonetic name for the letter "m."

Mini-guns: Extremely rapid-fire turret machine guns mounted on Cobra helicopters and "Puff" assault aircraft. Able to blanket an area the size of a football field in seconds.

MOS: Military occupational specialty, or job. Enlisted troops carried primary and secondary MOSes.

Motor pool: Vehicle storage and maintenance.

MP: Military police, army.

MR: Morning report. Personnel strength report including all "present for duty" and all categories of "not present for duty."

MSG: Master sergeant, E-8

NCO: Non-commissioned officer.

NCOIC: Non-commissioned officer in charge.

NVA: North Vietnamese Army.

OIC: Officer in charge.

OD: Officer of the day, responsible for administering daily duty rosters.

Out-of-country: Vernacular for a trip outside Vietnam, to an R&R city or other city in Southeast Asia.

Panaprime: A watery asphalt-like coating sprayed on dirt roads to keep down dust.

PFC: Private first class, or E-3.

Phonetic alphabet: Standardized set of words or names for the letters of the alphabet, with the emphasis on easy recognition, used for field radio/telephone communication. A-alpha, B-bravo, C-charlie, M-mike, V-victor, W-whiskey, etc.

Platoon: Army unit of about 46 men, comprised of four squads.

Point, Point man: Front man in a patrol, the most dangerous position.

Poncho: Standard-issue plastic rain gear

POW: Prisoner of war.

PRC-25: See ANPRC-25

Puff: "Puff the Magic Dragon" AC-47 airplane. Earned its name from the sound and appearance of mini-gun fire at night; out of a dark sky comes a solid red line of bullets aimed at a point on the ground, followed by a belching "urrrrrp" noise.

Piaster: "P" for short. The currency of South Vietnam.

Push: Designated ANPRC-25 radio frequency, on a megahertz dial.

PX: Post exchange, military ID cards and passes only.

Quartermaster: Supply, S-4.

RPG: Rocket-propelled grenade, shoulder-launched, Russian made and used by NVA and VC.

R&R: A five-day rest and relaxation vacation earned during a tour of duty in Vietnam war. Eligibility for R&R came after six months, but many soldiers waited until their tenth and eleventh months. R&R destinations included Hawaii, Australia, Manila, Hong Kong, Singapore, Kuala Lumpur, Taipei, and others.

RTO: Radio telephone operator, who carried the "prick-25."

Rucksack: Standard issue backpack of the infantry.

SFC: Sergeant first class, E-7

SGT: Sergeant (buck sergeant) E-5

Short-timer: A soldier getting close to his DEROS date, soon to leave Vietnam. Under 100 days a short-timer was a "double-digit midget", under ten days a "single-digit" midget, and under two days was a "micro midget" with "one and a wake-up."

Slack man: The second man in a patrol, behind the point.

Slick: Going by helicopter, a helicopter.

SOP: Standard operating procedure.

Special Forces: Specially trained army infantry. In Vietnam they were often used in dangerous hit-and-run operations.

SSG: Staff sergeant, E-6

Tet: The Vietnamese lunar new-year and high holiday, culminating Feb 17th. The Tet offensive of 1968 was a Vietnam war turning point.

Top: Nickname for highest-ranking sergeant in a unit.

UCMJ: Uniform Code of Military Justice, military law.

VC: Viet Cong, the communists, the insurgents, guerrillas, terrorists, "Charles", "Charlie", and "Chuck."

VCM: Vietnam Campaign Medal.

VSM: Vietnam Service Medal.

Wake-up: The last morning in Vietnam.

WIA: Wounded in action.

WO: Warrant officer. Also CWO, or chief warrant officer. Most helicopter pilots were warrant officers.

World: The USA.

XO: Executive officer.

Zulu report: Casualty report. Zulu is the phonetic name for the letter "z."

VIETNAMESE TERMS, EXPRESSIONS, AND SLANG

Ao dai: Worn by Vietnamese women, a thin-fabric slit skirt worn over pants.

A Shau Valley: A series of valleys and mountains, key entry point of the Ho Chi Minh supply trail.

Bic: Understand, as in "you bic?"

Bommie bom: Correctly Ba Ma Ba, "33" Vietnamese beer.

Boom, boom: Make love.

Caca dau: Vietnamese for "I will kill you."

Choo hoi: (Chieu Hoi) Originally an amnesty program; leaflets dropped over Vietnamese villages, to promote VC defectors. As used by GI's, "I give up" or "he gave up;" also the person surrendering.

Choi oi: "Jesus Christ!"

Cong bo: Water buffalo.

Cong khi: Monkey.

Di di mau: "Move out!"

Dinky dau: Crazy.

Du mi ami: Vietnamese curse (from the French) meaning, "fuck you"; or in its more derogative form, "you mother-fucker."

Dung lai: Stop, halt.

Fini: Finished, over.

Khong biet: "I don't understand."

Lai dai: "Come here now!"

Nookdau: Ice.

Number one: The best, very good.

Number ten: Bad.

Number ten thousand: Very bad, the worst.

Sin loi: Too bad, tough shit.

Te te: Little, not enough.

Tu dai: Booby-trapped